"In Jalita's world, everyone is fair game, and she has a scheme for us all. Andrea Blackstone brings a new voice to the literary world."

—Richard Holland
Sepia, Sand, & Sable Books
Baltimore, MD

"Emotionally forced to grow up fast and learn how to survive by any means necessary, Jalita La Shay Harrison is a prime example of how keeping your pockets "laced" is irrelevant when it comes to life's most treasured blessings."

—Monique Baldwin
founder of A Nu Twista Flavah

"The book's main character Jalita has drama with a capital DRAMA. From the first page, the author sets you up for one of the quickest reads ever. The book is interesting and real life lessons linger well after your read is complete . . . Ms. Blackstone is sure to shake up the publishing game with her street fiction with a splash of morality debut novel. I give this book a ten!"

—Kalico Jones
Author of When Gucci Came First

"Two thumbs up for Schemin'. I enjoyed Schemin' from the beginning to the end. The characters are so magnetic they pull you into their lives to experience the drama with them . . . an absorbing page turner you won't put down until the last page is read."

—Regina Neequaye
Author of 360 Degrees . . . Life is a Full Circle

$CHEMIN'
CONFESSIONS OF A GOLD DIGGER

A novel by
Andrea Blackstone

DREAM WEAVER PRESS

This book is a work of fiction. Names, characters, places and incidents are the products of the author's imagination or are used fictitiously. Any resemblance of actual events, locales, or persons, living or dead, is entirely coincidental.

All rights reserved, including rights to reproduce this book or portions thereof in any form whatsoever.

Dream Weaver Press
P.O. Box 3402
Annapolis, MD 21403

www.dreamweaverpress.net

Copyright © 2004 by Andrea Blackstone

ISBN 0-9746847-0-8
Library of Congress Catalog Control Number: 2005923633

Cover art by Roger James
www.rjamesgallery.com

Distributed by Writersandpoets.com - Printed in the United States of America

Second Printing

DEDICATION

This novel is dedicated to young girls and women who grew up in adverse circumstances, anyone who has been seduced by the desire to live large at any cost, and anyone who is searching for the strength to become empowered and remain independent.

ACKNOWLEDGMENTS

Thanks be to the Creator of all things who inspires, guides, and strengthens me. Without Him, I wouldn't have the privilege of taking this journey.

To my family: To my deceased grandmother, Zeona Hatcher Haley, thanks for introducing me to books and correcting my letters with your red pen. I miss you every day, but I know you watch over me. To my mother who exposed me to the arts, supported, and encouraged me to live my dream, you are love. I could not ask for a better mother than you. To my father who sacrificed for me in my formative years, I hope to make you proud someday. To my brother Michael, thank you for encouraging me to write this story and giving a positive word when I was typing on the PC at odd hours. My brother Alfred, thanks for being a kind brother and someone of whom I can be proud. To my sister-in-law, Patricia, thank you for listening to tales about my characters when you stopped by. My sister, Lisa, you'll always be my big sister. I love you. Dana, words can't express how thankful I am for the trip to the computer show and helping me lay the busted PC to rest. (I still won't throw it away though.) Eric Hill, thanks for your willingness to share your lyrical beats on my website.

To my friends: Special thanks to those who prayed for me, encouraged me to follow my dream, and understood this project was a real job that consumed my time, energy, and thoughts. Thank you,

Lorraise Brooks, for taking the time to read my first story. You have no idea how important that was for me to progress to this phase.

To my mentors: Mr. George Trotter, my high school principal; and my English professors, Dr. Ruthe Sheffey and Dr. Milford Jeremiah. Cliff Sosin, Michael Holmes, and B.C. (you know who you are), thanks for encouraging me to keep writing. Words can go a long way. Special thanks to Michael Holmes for reading everything I ever asked him to—I know your eyeballs hurt, man—and telling me to take breaks when I didn't have sense enough to stop on my own. Richard Holland, thanks for reading the rough draft and keeping it real. I won't forget your kindness.

To authors: Scott Haskins, thanks for the tips and letting me talk your ear off every now and then. Winston Chapman, thanks for being honest, down to earth, encouraging, and sharing information that many wouldn't. You are a gem. Urb'n Anthony for offering to help. Special thanks to my deceased uncle Alex for encouraging me to write and giving me the courage to take this journey seriously.

To my editor, Chandra Sparks Taylor, for her encouragement and wonderful work; Roger James for his artistic skills and patience through my changes in scheduling; my typesetter, Tania Kac, for her professionalism; to the members of Black Writers United who responded to my questions online; anyone I've neglected to thank who believed in me; and to the readers who are willing to giving a burgeoning author a shot.

SETTING IT UP

My name is Jalita La Shay Harrison, and I'd like to officially welcome you in to my jacked-up world. Me and my big mouth have been on this earth for almost twenty years, and for twenty years I've endured living a chaotic, dysfunctional life. The madness started when my irresponsible parents made a choice not to use condoms or some other form of birth control back in '83. As a result, my childhood memories include covering my ears with both hands while hiding in the nearest closet when my parents began cussing, fussing, fighting, and fucking to make up, then forgetting all about taking care of what should have been their first priority: me. That cycle was a daily occurrence until they got sick of living with responsibilities they created. My Black dad went his way and my White mom eventually went hers. The next thing I knew I was unpacking in foster home after foster home where I found out that no one caters to little abandoned Black girls. They cater to abandoned White infants. Rent-a-fathers saw fit to try to molest me and rent-a-mothers saw fit to beat and belittle me just because they could get away with it.

After I figured out that I was bound to end up in an overcrowded group home, and my pocketknife I began hiding as protection couldn't always assist me in keeping my privates off limits, I ran away at fifteen. I rolled out of the last rental home with no plan but not to go back to foster care; not to get tangled up with a drug dealer pushing a Mercedes, ruthless thugs, or criminals; and not to wear the teenage public assistance momma crown. My mission in life was to escape from poverty, street politics, and noisy squad cars in Baltimore City, and live in the suburbs with pretty trees, a nice yard, and work the kind of job that required wearing stockings, heels, and toting a briefcase someday. I wanted to become the kind of grounded adult who would shake off the dead weight of my past, reaping the benefits of adequate planning, and behaving like I had good sense. In a perfect world that plan would've had merit but the world is anything but perfect.

A snafu at college over Christmas break of 2003 started an avalanche of new drama I needed like a hole in my head. After being double-crossed one time too many, experience taught me that I need to take my big head out of the clouds and accept that nice people are perceived as stupid pushovers—this ruthless world is no place for the honest, naive, passive, or financially deprived. I reevaluated how I approached life and decided to deal with the people in it as if no one could be trusted. In turn, I made a pact with myself that I would never play the fool again. I would always pink-slip someone who owns a penis first and also concluded that I couldn't trust anyone else with estrogen, which meant having zero home girls. It was all about me, my needs, and wants, only I expressed that to others in a sly way. Not one sucker would see I was the type of woman whom he should run from if I headed his way 'cause I hid my agenda behind my good looks, ability to use my silver tongue, and quit wit, all of which could keep a typical man easily distracted. I became my own business product and my own saleswoman to sell it—even to eccentric men with whom most women wouldn't consider spending time. I learned from observing drug dealers hustle that one should never discriminate against a paying customer: All money spends.

Using my best assets to raise petty cash was a temporary solution to get me through a rough spot—I was needy, not greedy—until I took one taste of schemin' and got hooked. Having easy access to dead presidents became an addiction since I'd been forced to go without basic necessities like food, shelter, clothes, and a decent health care plan at many turns in life. I started gold digging to survive without returning to the streets where I vowed I'd never end up again, if even for a short time. So when a once-in-a-lifetime kind of opportunity seemed to drop out of the sky when I was in dire in need of paper, this greedy woman surfaced from within me that I didn't know existed. I developed an insatiable appetite for snatching any handout that was being offered by a duped man. At this point, I had a choice between returning to a situation where I was barely getting by or one in which I could live large if I kept ego stroking a man with long paper, so I did what most people would do—you fill in the blank.

Now I know that you snooty, judgmental females out there are ready to cop a righteous attitude, but you can't fathom what you would do if you were nineteen years old and in my shoes with the background noise of growing up in a dysfunctional environment and along the way you met a handsome NBA player who said he'd take care of you if you kept the hook-up on the down low. You don't wear my shoes so don't lie about what you say you'd do until you know the whole story. And as for you men out there, too many of you pick the women who walk over you like sidewalks, not the ones who don't stress you out, legitimately treat you like you're someone special, and would still like your ass if you were broke. If you fit this description, zip your lips in the morality department. I just wanted to get all of that straight from jump.

Not too many groupies, actresses, and everyday women who messed with a basketball star or slept with a man for some ends are gonna put themselves on blast and tell their personal shit like I'm about to do. If they ran their mouths then you'd know what to do to get what they got, or men who care about their paper would know how to stay away from lady pimps who discretely flip the script. I'm qualified to testify that schemin' ain't all peaches and cream. What I thought was paradise turned out to be a big slice of hell that still leaves me shedding tears. After I take a deep breath, I'll be ready to explain why a few more folks and me took a trip to a separate corner of hell on Earth. Okay people, here it goes.

1
A ROUND OF MISBEHAVIN'

"Tony," I say spiritedly.
"*Jalita?*" he answers with surprise.
"Yeah, it's me all right."
"What the fuck? It's Christmas Eve."
"I think I noticed. So, are you going to invite me over?"
"Over where?"
"To your crib. Where else, fool?" I peevishly remark.
"You haven't called me, in what, a year?"
"And what about it?"
"So why are you dialing my digits now?"
"Why not holler at my boy now? You act like your phone number has an expiration date or something. Look, do you or don't you want to see me live and in living color?"

Tony chuckles the way a man with a confirmed agenda does. Then he adds, "I've got plans."

I challenge him by saying, "Undo them. I just rode seven hours and twenty minutes total on two crowded Greyhound buses, and I'm not feelin' like chatting over the damn phone in twenty-degree weather. I can't even feel my toes—they're completely numb." There's a gap of silence for about ten seconds.

Tony clears his throat, then asks, "You want to see me, just like that? It's not like I was expecting your call or any shit like that."

"You're the one who always told me to call you anytime. Plus, I've got something you've been wanting for years, so yes, just like that," I say to tempt him.

"Are you telling me you're down for a round of misbehavin'?" Tony's pitch changes. His voice loosens up.

To feel him out, I sit on the fence with my response, and reply, "Possibly. I'm legal now. I'm not a puny fifteen-year-old girl anymore."

"Well damn, what a Christmas present. Where you at, ma?"

"Me revealing information of that sort depends on your plans."

Tony loses no time responding, and asks, "What plans?"

I blurt out, "That's more like it. At the Popeyes over on West Fayette Street."

"Give me fifteen—no, better make that twenty," Tony says energetically, sounding like he took a swig of liquid ginseng and got an instant energy boost.

"Got some explaining to do, huh?"

"Uh, yeah. Something to that effect."

"Well hurry up. I'm cold and wet, and I'm not tryna have to knock somebody out on these streets tonight."

"Okay, okay."

"Don't take forever and carry me like a chump, Tony."

"Now that ain't gonna happen. Bye."

"It better not. Bye," I respond then hang up.

I let out a sigh of relief because I know Tony's word is as good as it gets. I don't care what he's gotta do, what plans he's gotta break, and who he's gotta lie to to get over here to rescue me from my personal hell because all I've got is $5.14 in my purse, my best friend ditched me, and I wanna forget that I had that nasty run-in with Ebony, my R.A., even if it means I've gotta pay a price to do it. After all I've been through, having sex with a man I secretly care about can't be that complicated or traumatic.

When I ran away from my foster parents, the Rodells, Tony surely wasn't obligated to put food in my mouth or let me spend the night at his place on occasion until I got myself together enough to get a gig on the Harbor while working on getting my GED. He could've left me in Druid Hill Park where he first laid eyes on me tryna rest on a park bench when I balled up my jacket and used it for a pillow. When I confided in him about the abuse I'd endured, he gave me my share of you-can-make-it-Jalita speeches. Anytime a music producer with his own company tells you that he built his shit at twenty starting with a five-thousand-dollar small business loan, and you can accomplish something, too, you start believing like he's a damn prophet who said it's so. He even let me sit on a recording sessions with a famous singer a few times. That's why I look up Tony C. Jones, my one and only mentor. He's got it goin' on.

I know it's kinda freaky for a nineteen-year-old to contemplate laying up with her thirty-five-year-old mentor, but it is what it is. I'm legal now, plus, I developed a crush on him over the years. I use to get these vibes that he liked me back but wanted to respect the fact that I was under age. After looking at all of the facts, Tony is worthy to be my first, so there's no use holding on to my virginity one more day. There's no real soul mate waiting for an abused, emotionally battered half-breed with bad luck. I might as well use what I've got to get the comfort of having what I need, at least this once. I hope Tony handles his business promptly and comes correct 'cause this ma has never been the patient type. If his ass is molasses slow, I just may change my mind about my booty-call plans.

$

Tony looks and smells good, real good. Good enough for me to pretend he's my man, and I'm his woman, and we are about to make love for the very first time. He's rocking these ultra-neat cornrows that look like he had them done by some creative top stylist in New York. They barely touch his shoulders. Not too long, but not too short either. The Negro reminds me of a chocolate-dipped, rough-neck Fabio. So when he says, "Dance with me. Come on, boo" in a velvety smooth voice, and pulls me into the center of his chest, enveloping me within his heated warmth, I know that Jalita can't leave his crib a virgin. But me feelin' like we're on the cover of a romance novel is for me to know and his butt to figure out.

"I'm still wet from the shower, and my hair's all curly and nappy," I complain as I look up at him.

"Girl, you look even better than I remember. You've gotten PHAT in all caps! Those curls are sexy. The natural thing is in. I know if anyone can work it, it will be you. Two years has done you good. They say most people gain weight in college but your pounds fell just right, everywhere important."

"I know I've gotten thick, and I'm use to having more of me now. I'm tired of dealing with this head of mess though. Maybe by the time my hair grows out, I'll have enough funds to get some of those stylish Alicia Keys braids," I say. I'm fresh out of mousse or hair oil to make it act right. I freed myself from being a perm addict a year ago due to my lack of funds, so I've got to face what Mother Nature gave me. Tony's compliment makes me nervous, but flatters me at the same time.

"It looks great. Stop worrying about your wig. Hold on tight and just groove with me to prove I didn't break out my new Brian McKnight CD for nothing," Tony says, grinning and grabbing my waist.

"I'm cold. I don't have any night clothes."

I maintain a stone face, but Tony keeps working on my ego by saying, "Women like you don't need no clothes, just heat to keep you warm in a nigga's crib."

"Well I'm use to clothes, and in case you haven't noticed, it's winter and I got caught in the soaking rain."

"Let me go find you something, if it's that critical to you, Jalita. While I'm at it, I'll throw your clothes in the dryer. Give me a few. I'm going down the hall to the laundry room." Tony disappears from view. I hear change clank while it sounds like its sliding out of some jar.

In less than five minutes he returns. I can tell he's slightly annoyed that I'm being difficult while he's tryna set the mood for romance.

"How's this?" he asks, holding up a red silky, short nightie that is at least worth forty bucks.

"Nice stuff. Who does this belong to?" I ask while inspecting the garment.

"Do you want it or not, girl?"

"Answer my question first," I insist.

"Damn, you're just bent on trying to fuck shit up. You know you women are always leaving shit behind at a nigga's crib. Some old girlfriend left it a long time ago. Satisfied?" Tony snaps.

"Fine. Give it here," I say and slide into it.

"What about thank you, Tony?"

"Thanks, but dag, it's not mine."

"Now can we dance?"

"I'm standing here, aren't I?" I put my arms around him like we're deep in love.

"Mmm. Girl, I can't believe this is happening. So you turn nineteen and finally come to your senses," he says, bending and pressing his right cheek against mine. We begin to sway from side to side.

"How'd you get such a nice crib? The rent's gotta be at least a grand for one bedroom and knowing you you've got two bedrooms."

"Stop trying to ruin the romance. Will you stop this bogus shit? Same old Jalita," he says, kissing me behind my ear, then using his tongue to massage my canal.

"That feels so good."

"It's supposed to."

"Your phone is ringing. Aren't you going to answer it?" I tell him slowly as I travel to some erotic zone where life only feels good and perfect.

"Fuck the phone. I'm not gonna let you go ever again. It's probably one of my boys checking in. I waited four years for this night, and I'm not trying to hear what he's got to say right now."

"Tony, I don't feel right. Make it stop ringing."

"Okay, okay," he says. He releases me, then goes over to touch a button on the side of the noisemaker.

"It's off. No more interruptions. Now where was I, for the tenth time?" Tony says sarcastically.

"I'm not sure," I say, laying my head on his shoulder.

"Well since you can't remember, go in the bedroom and let me give you something to jog that memory of yours."

"Maybe I will." I feel his eyes glued on my ass as I walk into the bedroom.

I slide between the satin sheets and close my eyes. It feels so good to be dry and warm, and I pretend Tony loves me. I could be content living in this moment for the rest of my life. Tony comes in, hits a dimmer switch on the wall, opens the blinds that cover two windows, and walks toward the bed with lust lighting up his dark brown eyes.

"Why'd you open the blinds?"

"Damn, Jalita, you act like you're still a virgin or something. It's romantic to make love under the moonlight, don't you think?" Tony asks.

"I guess so."

"Are you telling me you still haven't had any?" he questions. I don't answer and look away in silence.

Tony says, "Awwww, boo. I'm sorry. I just assumed that one of those horny college niggas tapped this juicy ass by now."

"Well a horny college woman tried to tap this ass earlier today," I mumble.

"What?"

"Yeah, that's why I'm here. I finally get accepted into a Historically Black College only to be officially disrespected when I begin making some headway. The only thing I may have now is what I was able to carry out of the dorm."

"Slow down. What happened?"

"Well in a nutshell, Ebony Tyler, a resident assistant at my dorm, told me this Mr. Moore guy in charge of housing didn't give her the green light for me to staying the dorm over the Christmas break. I knew that I didn't have anywhere to lay my head so I requested that I stay and visited his office at least three times to confirm things. Ebony told me that I should've put my belongings in storage and gone back to whomever birthed or put up with me before enrolling in Bentley. She had plans to roll out to Brooklyn in the morning. The next thing I know Ebony implied that Sharon Diggs, my only friend, ditched me to get freaky with this woman in Washington, D.C. I began to feel that she was telling the truth 'cause naked pictures of Sharon were pasted in an album with other woman posing in the buff. I held the photo album while Ebony started telling me dick ain't nothing but a headache on layaway and women need to get liberated from the brothas that think they have it made treating us wrong."

"So a gay woman was trying to pull you. So what, Jalita? If I were a gay woman I'd be interested in you, too," Tony says, laughing.

"Wait, there's more. Before I had a chance to blink, Ebony pulled out a strap-on and told me I could stay in the dorm if I bent my fat ass over and calmed down her throbbing pussy. Before it was all said and done I couldn't hold in my desire to retaliate when she squeezed my ass, stuck her tongue into my mouth, and started reaching for my punani. I punched her square in the jaw as hard as I could manage. She fell to the floor and slid across the room like her pants were lubed up with Crisco. She starting dialing up campus security. I ran up to my room, grabbed a few things that I stuffed into a duffel bag along with my book bag and got the hell out of dodge, so here I am." By the time I finish my story, Tony stops laughing.

He says, "Oh, damn. That was going too far. I've always heard gay women can be as aggressive as men. A strap-on, huh? Well I'm all man with real equipment who can make you forget all about the stunt Ebony tried to pull. I've got your back over the holiday. Now do you want the shades closed or the lights off?"

"No, I'm cool, but I have one more problem."

"What now?" Tony asks.

I blurt out, "My money is funny. I started out with eighty bucks. The cab from Bentley to the train station set me back eleven. The roundtrip Greyhound bus ticket set me back another fifty-nine. After the second transfer, I blew $4.86 on some grub from Popeyes. Now all I've got is a measly $5.14 in my purse."

"That's all, Jalita? I've got your back. Stop worrying and please stop busting the flow of what's happening between us now. I'm not Ebony, so leave that gay ma's drama back in Norfolk."

"Thanks, Tony. I knew I could count on you."

"It's no big thang, boo," he answers.

Tony lays down next to me, pushes the nightie up, and slides his fingers into my vagina. I feel it getting all slippery and wet as my nipples harden and rise toward the heavens. I feel like I'm in heaven, and maybe I've crossed over into the after-life.

Tony softly whispers in my ear, "You like that, don't you?"

"Maybe," I say as my heart begins to race. I know I do, but I try to play cool like I'm unfazed.

Tony climbs on top of me and rubs his penis close to my wet spot.

"Sweet love, you ready for me to love you?" he asks, looking so deeply into my eyes, I can barely think of a response.

Instead, I say, "Love me?"

"Yeah, love you."

"Tony, who's gonna love me?" I belt out with a sincere confidence that I have every right to know where he's coming from.

"I am," he assures me.

"No, Tony. I'm not talking about just tonight. Do you really love me? Are you gonna be there for me? Can we be partners in the end? If this doesn't have a future to it, this wouldn't be a good idea because—"

Tony interrupts me and says, "Shhhh, stop all of that bullshit. I don't have anyone special, and I'm not going anywhere. I hope we'll be a team for a very long time, if things go well. Trust me. I'm not out to hurt you one bit, and I'm not that kind of brother anyway, so just chill out. You know I've always liked you better than anyone else. Do you understand where I'm coming from, boo?" Tony kisses me gently on the forehead, then looks at me with tenderness in his eyes. The kind that every woman wants a man to show her when it counts the most.

"I think I hear what you're saying," I answer. Tony tears open the condom wrapper and covers his erect penis.

"Good. Just relax your muscles," he whispers softly as he strokes my face and hair.

"Oww, it hurts. This is what I waited to feel? I thought making love was supposed to be a good thing," I say as I flinch and close my eyes.

"Give it a little time. It'll go away. I'll push it in nice and easy."

"If you say so," I mutter, waiting for it to feel good.

In a few moments, it does. Before I know it, I'm moaning and making erotic sounds I've never released from my vocal cords. I can't believe my romance novel fantasy is coming true, but it is. Tony is rhythmically thrusting his powerful hips against me, and we're both drenched in hot, lusty sweat. Hours pass, and I've grown use to the shadows dancin' on the opposite wall. I've heard about one-minute men, but Tony surely isn't a member of that club. He's still lovin' me up, and I finally experience my first orgasm in life, drinking the feelin' of the intense physical release. I hear the front door lock click, then open. My body shuts down as quickly as the incredibly good feelin' rose up.

"Did you hear something?" I ask, flinching again.

"No," he says, still grinding on top of me.

"Shhh. I think somebody's in here," I say as I tense up.

"Look, this is my place, and I run this. Nobody's in here, and nobody's got a key to my crib. If you didn't notice, this is a controlled-access building. Now let's finished what we started, boo," Tony says in a cocky tone, still working his hips.

"It may be controlled access, nigga, but somebody's in here all right."

"Who's that, Tony?" I say, pulling the sheets on top of Tony's naked body. He hops up like a bolt of lightning. I pull down the nightie and sit up in the bed.

The woman hits the dimmer switch on the wall. With revenge in her eyes, she moves toward me, asking, "Who are you, bitch, is more like it, and why are you wearing my lingerie?"

"Your lingerie? Tony gave it on me to put on because I was cold. I hope I don't catch crabs or somethin' fatal," I say to taunt her.

"Now, Charlene, I can explain," Tony says, throwing himself between us.

She spits back, "Fast, nigga. It better be lightning fast!"

"Who are you?" I interject with much attitude.

"His damn fiancée who pays half the rent. His baby's momma, bitch. Now what you got to say about all of that?"

"What?" I scream as I inch into a corner of the room.

"So this is your sick aunt, nigga? I came to bring you some damn homemade sweet potato pie so you'd have something good to come home to, after worrying over your aunt who's supposed to be laying up in ICU after having a heart attack, and you're in here getting laid by some freak of the week? You had me thinking I needed to drive all the way to Capitol Heights to take our son to my momma's house tonight so I could console your ass, when you were supposed to come back tired and in need of a fucking good night's sleep? And where's the baby's picture and my picture? Oh, so you think your black ass is slick, I see," Charlene says.

"I don't know where the pictures are, baby. Maybe they fell over when I was cleaning or something," Tony lies, nervously scratching between his cornrows.

"You know good and well your ass don't clean. I'm sure they fell over all right while you were banging this barely legal bitch on my Downy fresh sheets. Aww naaaaw. Charlene Margaret Daniels don't play this shit!" she says, taking off her gold rings, bracelets, and large hoop earrings. "Where's my damn Vaseline? Niggas be tryin' to run game. No-good motherfucking players. I've got something for you. I can get down your way, if that's how you want to roll," she mumbles.

"Whhhahaaat you need Vaseline for, baby? I told you I can explain," Tony says.

"I'm 'bout to whip some ass and tear your shit up. The hell if I'm gettin' scars doin' it."

"Hey sista, I'm not even in this mess. I didn't know he was in a relationship," I tell her, running across the room, tryna put a bid in for my ass to be spared from whatever brutal act was running through her mind.

Charlene turns to me, and says, "But did you just ask?"

I look her dead in the eyes, and reply, "I asked several questions, and he said he didn't have anyone special, if you must know, Ms. Daniels." At this point we both have our hands on our hips like we're having a standoff at high noon in a Clint Eastwood western movie.

Charlene nods to the left and says, "Did you bother to push the damn bedroom closet door open or check under the bathroom cabinet for signs of another bitch? If you had, your ass would have seen everything from clothes to tampons and douche bottles."

I'm beginning to become hypnotized by her fake dancin' ponytail, and tell her, "Shut up your clucking, you chicken head. I had no reason to snoop in someone else's goods. I'm no ghetto bitch. How was I supposed to know Tony goes around sharing his pinky-sized dick? I took Tony's word for what he said, and what he said was that he had no one special. Don't blame me because you've got a weak-ass fake negro on your hands who you made a baby with and are stuck dealing with until your little Ray Ray or whatever the kid's name is grows up. And look, you took off all of your other jewelry, aren't you going to take off that $99.95 cubic zirconia engagement ring, girl? I know he's taken, now, so there's no need to cock block by flashing some fake ice," I fire back.

"Oh, so now you talkin' trash about me, my ring, my man, and makin' fun of my baby boo?"

"It appears he's not your man, just your part-time piece when you come home, announced. No, my fault, I take that back 'cause I'm supposed to be the dumb bitch, and your genius ass knows everything. Let the record speak for itself. He was kissing this body right here and sharing my sexual energy when you reminded him he forgot all about your ass. What you got to say about all of that, Charlene?"

"Stop. Stop. Both of you," Tony interjects, blocking Charlene from walking toward me. She acts like a woman scorned, and is operating with the attention span of a kid with attention deficit disorder. Charlene drops our conversation, looks Tony up and down, smacks him like he's a cheap trick who didn't bring a pimp enough cash, spits in his face, walks over to his stereo, then kicks it like she's determined to break it on her first attempt. She grabs an African wooden statue of a warrior and throws it at the dresser mirror. Glass falls and crashes, then she flings open a top drawer and starts grabbing jewelry.

"No, not my sound system and bedroom set. Please Charlene, stop. I'm sorry. I'll never do this again. Please baby, please," Tony pleads, ignoring the large glob of spit streaming down his nose and rubbing his cheek.

"Since you jumped in my way to protect the bitch, I'm gonna take this out on everything I can get my hands on that your selfish ass values. You better not hit me back neither 'cause I'd love to call the police on your unfaithful ass on Christmas Eve," she informs him.

"Come on now. We can work this out, and you know I don't hit on no women," Tony says as he follows Charlene out of the bedroom and into the bathroom. "Can't we have a civil conversation about this, Charlene?" Tony pleads, standing in the doorway of the bathroom. I hear her grabbing things, then returning to the bedroom with a bottle of Clorox. I scan the room for an exit, but I know I'm not tryna jump off nobody's balcony. I work as hard as I can to tie the strings of my pleather sneakers, in a bona fide hurry. I'm still wearing Charlene's nightie but my clothes are in some laundry room, so all I can do is throw on my coat. I begin to swear to myself.

"Oh, so now you want to talk and give a bitch conversation? Oh no, fuck the come-lately shit," Charlene says. She flings the metal closet doors open, throws Tony's clothes on the bed, and pours bleach all over the pile. Charlene lets the plastic jug fall to the floor, opens the balcony door, returns to the closet, grabs an assortment of shoes, then hurls enough over the balcony to cause Tony to have to work barefoot until he shoe shops. The drops of bleach have already begun to make these white craters on the tan carpet, and I'm thinking they can kiss their security deposit good-bye, but that was Charlene's doing, not mine.

"How could you do that to my work clothes and shoes? And look at this carpet. Shit, Charlene. Would you please calm down?" Tony says, holding his head with both hands like he's grown a migraine headache.

"Shut up. Your ass is gonna pay for gettin' with a Happy Meal kind of bitch when you've got a Big Mac kind of a woman right up in here. And the clothes bleaching was for Little Tony," she shrieks.

"I do love you and Little Tony. I do, baby. You and Little Man are my world. I just made a dumb mistake. She don't mean shit to me. I barely even know this ho," Tony responds, pointing at me.

Charlene storms into the kitchen and removes something flat from a paper bag. I peep around the corner. Then I hear a high-pitched, "See this, nigga?"

"See what, Charlene?"

"This is what I think of you, your lying, and your dick sharing," she shouts and whops Tony in the face with a large sweet potato pie. He's struggling to see, wiping two holes from his eyes to view what he's in for next. By this time, Charlene has reached into a plastic bag, grabbed a handful of walnuts, and begins throwing them in Tony's direction.

As Tony is ducking and shrinking back, I throw my book bag on my back, grab my duffel bag and take one look around the room. My eyes halt on Charlene's purse. While they're arguing at the top of their lungs and are engaged in a walnut chase, I find her wallet, grab all of her cash, which amounts to four one-hundred-dollar bills and five ones and snatch a small bag sitting next to her purse. I tiptoe out of the apartment door and decide to take the stairwell instead of the elevator. Once I'm around the corner, I spot Tony running after Charlene who's screaming about how much damage she's going to do to his Escalade.

"You better get back in the apartment, you naked dog," she screams at Tony. I notice her weapons have been upgraded to toting a snow shovel in her left hand and a canned good in the right.

"Baby, please, not my ride. Pleeease! I'll do anything. Don't hurt the truck!"

"Get your ass out of my way, Tony!" Charlene says, pushing him across the hallway.

"What are you gonna do with the shovel and the canned good?"

"There ain't no snow to shovel, so I must be getting ready to put them to good use, nigga! And expect trouble from child support as soon as the damn office reopens after the holiday! This is what I get for being too easy on your ass," she says. She heads for the elevator, mumbling to herself and still cussing up a storm.

I hear Tony change paths, so I ease into the laundry room where it's dark. I look out of the small window and see him covered in pie, wearing nothing but his birthday suit and a dead erection, tryin' his best to save his ride from Charlene's psychotic wrath.

For the first time in too long, I feel like cheesing and even giggling like I heard the funniest Bernie Mac joke of all times. I stroke my breasts, close my eyes, and figure out that I like misbehavin'. When I open them, I turn on the light long enough to find out what kind of clothes are drying in a dryer that's throwing heat. Not wanting to risk running in to Charlene while searching out my own, I let Charlene's garment hit the floor and slide into some woman's brown terry cloth jumpsuit.

I grab my stuff, haul ass outside, and quietly easing past the scene where Charlene is goin' to work on Tony's silver Escalade. I walk down the street, then a hack rolls up in one of those old unmarked police cars that anyone can own if they bid right at an auction. I'm glad too see the bootleg taxi driver come my way 'cause I know I can save a few bucks on my fare.

A man with a toothpick hanging out of the side of his mouth pulls up next to me and asks, "Need a ride?"

"Yeah, unless you're not a hack," I answer.

"Where to, miss?" he asks. I pause.

After I think things over I reply, "My momma's house." I give him the address. He nods and begins chewing on his toothpick, causing it to move up and down. I hop in the car, throwing my bags in at the same time.

We pull off and I'm about fifteen minutes away from ringing my momma's holiday doorbell. Last year I found out where she is. I think I let Kate off the hook long enough, so the bitch who abandoned me better get ready to serve Jalita some piping-hot turkey and jellied cranberries.

2

MY MOMMA'S THICK, THICK DRAMA

Just as I cram five dollars into the hack's hand, it starts raining again. I guess he doesn't have the courtesy to help me unload my stuff 'cause I felt I could only spare a dollar tip. He pulls off. I grab my bags, walk up to Kate's door and press the doorbell.

"Yes?" a White man with an enormous, nine-month-pregnant-looking belly covered by a T-shirt with a hole in it says to me.

"I want to talk to Kate," I say rudely, noticing the green-and-red tattooed dragon on the top of his right arm.

"About what?"

"You tell her Jalita's out here to see her, or I'm coming in. It's cold out here, mister, so don't play with me right now."

"I don't know what your problem is, but I don't have to tell her a damn thing."

"No you don't, but I suggest you do. Why don't you mind your own business and just go get her if she's in there, okay?"

"You can't come around my house telling me what to do. Who do you think you are? That's so typical of *you people*."

"And just who would *you people* be?"

"Niggers."

"I'll tell you one thing, Jethro. You better not say that too loud in this town. Someone's liable to rip your balls off, you racist piece of shit! You have no right to insult me this way," I say without taking a breath. I feel my heart quicken again.

"I'll say it three times, if I have to. Niggers, niggers, niggers," he says, throwing around the "n" word like there's nothing dangerous to it.

"I guess the Klan ran out of robes to fit your ass. Shouldn't you be keeping your face covered like the rest of the cowards with the conehead hats?"

"You're the one who knocked on my front door, giving orders, so I'll call you whatever I see fit. I'm sick of biting my tongue around you people. I make it known that I don't like your kind."

"Look, all I want you to do is go in your house, tap Kate on the shoulder, and send her out here. This has nothing to do with your racist butt," I insist.

"You people don't have any manners to save your lives. Didn't your mother teach you any better? I'm sure you don't know who you father is. All of them unwed mothers causing my taxes to go down the drain with all of them special benefits they get is ridiculous."

"My objective is to take all that up with Kate. In fact, I'm wondering if she ever collected the kind of benefits you're referring to."

"And why would that be?"

"I'm her daughter, that's why. Now go get her, and you can just kiss my biracial ass all up in my crack," I say.

"Look, you crazy nigger, get off of my step before I call the cops. Yeah, right. Her daughter. My wife wouldn't sleep with a nigger if her life depended on it, and she's been married to me and only me," he says, half chuckling between sips of beer. He reminds me of trailer park trash that gets arrested on *Cops*. The nerve of him.

"I don't know if her life depended on it, but I'm not moving until I see Kate's face. Call the cops if you want." Doors begin to fly open, and neighbors begin to stand on their steps to get a closer look at the action.

"I bet your welfare check ran out, and you're trying to pull a stunt before Christmas so you can buy your five kids some toys and a holiday meal. I know your type, always wanting a handout or coming around here trying to sell us stolen goods. Go get a damn job. Why don't you do that since you've got so much mouth?"

"For your information, I don't have any kids. I attend Bentley University in Virginia, and I'm just tryna have some words with my momma, you ignorant asshole!"

"College? Yeah right. You probably can't even read on a sixth-grade level. Go back to smoking your crack in the alley around the corner. It's a left turn that way," he says, bending and pointing.

"No you didn't go there. What's this look like?" I say, unzipping my book bag and throwing one of my thick books on his step. My seventy-dollar book makes a thump as loud as a firecracker.

"Well even if you are in college, you probably got there by affirmative action. You people expect special treatment for everything. After all the help you get, you still blame the White man. We're the real victims; White people catch all the hell. You people walk around here with that nappy hair standing all over your heads, talking about racial pride, Kwanzaa, and slavery, shoving the way you believe down our throats, and you expect us to like you? I wish every one of you would hop a ship and sail back to Africa," the man says. More lights turn on. I'm guessing that Jethro's neighbors mistook my falling book for a gunshot. The entire block is lit up like a heavily decorated Christmas tree. Before I know it, an audience has assembled.

"And I wish you would go back to your trailer park with the little wheels," I spit back with defiance.

"Kate. Get out here, *now*," he yells. I rub my hands together for warmth. I'm drenched in this soaking rain, my nose is running, and I can't stop sniffling. I feel like a five-foot-six ice sculpture that's about to be displayed in Time Square, and I don't appreciate Kate taking her time to greet me.

"What you want? I'm trying to get this turkey stuffed. Damn, can't I cook without someone bothering me every five minutes? I can't get anything done like that," she yells back.

"Shut up your back talk and just get over here, woman," he says. I hear heavy steps and a female voice cussing with each one. I feel the row house shake, and I'm confused. Last time I saw her, four years ago Kate had model-good looks, and was barely 110 pounds wringing wet after a heavy meal.

"What is so damn important?" she asks, looking at him with stuffing on her hands, facing the sea of confused faces. I watch her wipe them off on a red-and-white checkered towel, noticing that her features are a lot like mine, only her nose is sharper and longer. She looks worn by a troubled mind, joyless, has obviously let her figure go, but still she's my momma and I want her to love me just the same. Although she looks torn up from the floor up, I'll still take her as she is. I want my blond-hair, blue-eyed momma who's dressed just like I'd expect a 250-pound woman to be, to invite me in and beg me to put my two legs under her table for Christmas dinner. The man points, turns and looks at me, then yells, "*Her*, that's what!"

"Hi, Kate. I'm your daughter. Remember giving me up when I was ten years old? I'm Jalita," I say in a trembling voice.

"I don't know what she's talking about," she says, digging her nails into flesh inside of her loose top.

"Did you sleep with a nigger? I swear I'll kick your ass out of here right tonight if it's true," he says, rubbing the gray stubble of the right side of his face.

"How dare you insult me like that. You know better. I've never seen her before in my life. Where did she come from?" Kate asks. She turns to her husband. He shrugs.

Kate turns toward me and says, "Lady, you must be mistaken, and I don't appreciate you upsetting my husband and causing problems in our neighborhood. Maybe you have the wrong address." I see the truth in her eyes. She recognizes me as her daughter, but refuses to put reality into words. It's obvious that it would unmask too many secrets that will turn her new life upside down.

"No, I've got the right Kate all right. How about *this* then?" I say, holding up a small, rusting locket with her picture in it against the screen. Jethro and Kate are speechless, but I keep talking to let them know I've got cold, hard facts that will solidify my little evidentiary hearing.

I sniff loudly, then say, "Your mother's name was Betty, and her husband's name was Tom. Tom worked at a lumberyard. You were originally from Charleston, West Virginia, and came to Baltimore when you were seven. Is your amnesia cured yet, Mom?" I ask Kate. Her mouth seems to be glued shut. She struggles to find the next row of words.

Jethro breaks the silence, and says, "She knows an awful lot about you and your family. You better explain quick 'cause something funny's goin' on."

"She did it. Those White women love brothas, especially the big fat ones," a black face says, then turns to walk in the opposite direction.

Kate answers, "I don't know how she knows those things. I never had no Black kid. Why are you trying to ruin our Christmas? Is this some kind of sick game? We don't got no money, so try this shit somewhere else, and let me finish making our holiday dinner. I've got a family to feed and cleaning to do. I don't have time for this shit." I watch her nervously scratch her greasy-looking hair. I think that if I were after money, I definitely wouldn't be hitting them up for some. Kate could think of a better one than that.

I dig down deep within my soul and suddenly feel more empowered and less intimidated. In a crystal-clear, powerful voice, I say, "This is hardly about money, Mom. This is about the choice you made to abandon me and rob me of a normal childhood. The kind of mother that

MY MOMMA'S THICK, THICK DRAMA   27

abandons her child in a welfare office isn't a real mother, but you're what I was stuck with until you rolled out. I ended up becoming a ward of the state and packing and repacking a total of seven times in one year thanks to you. I've been fondled, abused, lived on the street with crack addicts, eaten out of pollution-coated trash cans, and have worn drawers I grabbed from church freebie tables. That was no way for me to have to live. Why didn't you use condoms to keep me from coming here if you didn't want me?" I ask.

"I said I don't know you!" Kate screams.

"Since it doesn't look like you'll be inviting me in for turkey, I just want to ask you, who's gonna love me? Who is going to make up this hard life of having no mother or father to me? I've waited all of these years to find out if you ever regretted the pain you've caused me, and I won't wait one second longer. Admit what you did to me. Just be a woman and admit it to my face."

"I told you I'm not your damn momma," she yells back. Out of nowhere, a loud boom of thunder cracks. Just like an omen that Kate is lying her ass off, the sky opens up, and it rains like it will never rain again. While lightning brightens the sky, a soaking rain chills me, and the crowd is sent running in a frenzy, but they're determined not to let go of their nosiness. Most of them stand in front of their windows and screened doors, still eager to eavesdrop.

"How old are you?" the man asks.

I lean forward and scream at him, "Nineteen, Jethro." I'm cold and wet, but I ignore the fact that I've become a soggy mess and continue to stand on the steps.

"Hmmm. Well, about nineteen years ago I was away in Germany for a year. Kate? Are you sure you've told me the whole story?"

"What? She's lyin'. I told you. That's it. Who you gonna believe? Her or your wife?" she asks.

"Looks like Kate shacked up with my dad on McCulloh Street until he cut out and left us while you were away, Mr. Stepdad," I instigate because I see Kate's not gonna admit a sliver of the truth.

"Leave, and don't you eva come back here again. The next time we'll call the police. Got that? Then you can call your Black momma to bail your hustling ass out!" Kate yells as she slams the door in my face. I stand alone and abandoned, just like old times. The observers turn off their lights and shut their doors. I want to cry, but I can't make the tears form and fall. I can hear Kate and Jethro arguing behind the door. A baby starts screaming, then I hear wrestling like two WWE opponents are goin' for the championship title. Kate screams and pleads for her husband to leave her alone about what this Black face standing on their steps just stirred up. I don't feel sorry for Kate. Really, I don't. She can lie her way out all she wants to. We share the same bloodlines, and that's how it is.

Now that I asked my question and see that she doesn't give half a damn about who's gonna love me, I stand directly in front of my mother's steps, bend my elbows, and hold my hands out to my sides while spreading my fingers. I tilt my head backward and look upward into the face of the sky, letting rain drench me all over my brown face, dulling my senses for at least two minutes. As I slowly turn around and around, breathing heavily and feelin' my heart pound, I promise myself that I'm gonna figure out who I am, what I need, and who's gonna love me and give me attention, all by damn self. When I snap out of my trance, I let my arms fall against my drenched coat, and my feet stop moving. I conclude that I don't need a momma or daddy because they don't need me either, and that's just stale, tough biscuits for me. Shit, no one ever said life was perfect or easy. The thing that I don't understand is why it's got to be so damn unmerciful when you try to live right.

I walk across the dirty sidewalk full of pink and white gum wads, glass, and smelly trash, then continue until I find a bus stop about a block up near a roller skating rink and bowling center called Shake and Bake. My back is hurting from carrying all of those heavy books and my duffel bag. My feet are too tired to keep doing their job, thanks to my buy-one, get-one-half-off Payless pleather shoes, which are rubbing my pretty feet the wrong way. I stand at the bus stop shifting my weight from foot to foot thinking that I just can't bear to sleep on the streets tonight.

The number 320 bus pulls up. I don't care where it's goin' 'cause I wanna get off my feet and get as far away from Kate as these bus wheels will roll. I step on it and ask the driver how much it's gonna set me back to go to the next destination.

When he replies, "That'll be $ 4.25 to get to Laurel," I twist up my face, wondering if he's tryna rip me off.

I ask, "You're not bullshitting me, are you? I just want a one-way fare."

He replies, "Miss, $4.25 is the commuter fare I must charge 'cause of the zone I'm going to. Look, this is the last bus running tonight and none will be on the road on Christmas Day, but you can take it or leave it…don't make me no difference, my check stays the same whether you get on or not."

I wish I could smack his smart ass, but instead I suck my teeth, drop four dollar bills and a quarter into the money collector and sit my ass down on the plastic blue bus seat.

3

A CHANCE ENCOUNTER

The bus driver and I roll out to Laurel solo. Apparently, it's not a jumping hot spot. That's okay though 'cause as I'm stepping off the bus with my belongings I spot a Motel 6. I ain't here for nothing exciting, more like sleeping in peace. Now I know where I'm gonna be for Christmas. Mystery solved. After I check in and get my room, I pop two extra-strength Tylenol, minus the water, and crawl between the itchy, cheap sheets that don't feel half as good as Tony and Charlene's. I know I'll be safe at this Motel 6 and look forward to sleeping the rest of the wee morning hours of Christmas away. I can feel the medicine moving down my throat too slowly, like I swallowed two peach pits whole, but the discomfort doesn't motivate me to locate and pour some chlorine-smelly water.

I'm thinking that I'm so numb with disgust over every direction I turn in my life leading to a damn negative experience, that I see no use in bothering to show back up for spring semester. Now that my head is out of the clouds, I can get real and face the funk. That Barbara Walters mixed with Oprah vibe I was tryna hone and craft won't get me anywhere in life but another fat disappointment. Girls like me will never have it goin' on. You can educate ones like me, but you can't take the nitty-gritty essence of what I'm made of out of me. I can never have pride 'cause my momma nor my daddy taught me how to own it. Who am I foolin'? I'm not college material. Jalita Harrison ain't shit, just busting her ass pretending. Fuck it. Time to face facts. The education game is over. A mind can't be a terrible thing to waste if it's all fucked up, and mine is definitely fucked up.

The curtains are so concealing, I can't see a sliver of daylight peeking through any corners from around the motel window. My internal clock tells me that it's time to budge, so I stumble out of bed, sleepily walk toward the bathroom and pee. I wash my hands, then wrap a towel around myself. I unlock both locks and open the door enough to see a sliver of light. My stomach is growling like a baby lion, so I search out the small cake of complimentary soap, lather up the abrasive washcloth, and listen to the hypnotizing flow of water hit my skin.

I finally feel clean, like my life isn't bad, and I'm here because I'm on some business trip or it's a pit stop for my family who's been pinned up in a motor home all summer. I drink these fantasies so long that my fingers begin to wrinkle like old prunes. I consider drumming up some anger over what Tony's trifling butt pulled to hit this, but it's not worth my time, nor does it put me in the mood to feel like singing no deck the halls or fa la la la la la la la la shit. Instead I step out of the shower, remembering to look in the small plastic bag I stole from Charlene and am pleased to find a Tweezerman Eye Care Kit, Crest Whitestrips, and Dr. Scholl's Pedicure Essentials Foot Bath Salts. I laugh to myself, deciding I'll try out these things when I feel like focusing on my looks. I know one thing, now is not the time.

I dry off quickly, slide on my jeans, throw on a T-shirt minus a bra, grab my purse, cover myself in my powder blue stadium coat, and sniff around for some food. I spot a Citgo across the street and head in that direction. I'm feelin' so worthless, I don't even look before I cross and risk getting hit, but all I hear are horns and one expletive fly in my direction. I shrug and open the glass door of the convenience shop. I discover a microwavable sausage biscuit and a half-rotten banana, and grab a tall carton of watered-down orange juice from the fridge. I nuke my micro meal while I'm wandering around the store looking for more processed grub to add to my breakfast stash. I spot a super size bag of Doritos and a large glazed doughnut, so I grab those, too.

All of the sudden, I hear, "Meeeerry Christmas!"

"What? Who said that?" I respond.

"Over here, ma," the man says as he emerges from a back room. His chocolate-colored dark skin makes his teeth seem gleaming white. He's about five-five with these strange eyes—his pupils are brown and the perimeter is grayish blue. Despite his height, his exotic attractiveness still stands out.

"Oh, whatever, merry freaking Christmas to you, too," I say, rolling my eyes.

"What's your problem? Not in the spirit, I see."

"Did I say I have a problem? Who are you to tell me all about what's on my mind?"

"Well, you seem like something's bothering you. Damn, you sure are uptight."

"I'm tired of people telling me I'm uptight. I'm not uptight. I just want to be left the hell alone, that's all. I just came in here to get some breakfast, and maybe some lunch and dinner, since I don't feel like bothering to find some fast food that's open and in walking distance in this town."

"That don't sound like no way to start off Christmas."

"Well maybe it's not, but that's how it's gonna be for me, myself, and I in my motel room."

"Damn. So what's your name, ma?"

"What's it to you? I guess you just want to hit it like all the rest. Well I've got news for you, I'm not interested in getting felt on the ass or poked, so there's no need to try to mack. Try it on another customer," I say, collecting my plastic-wrapped breakfast.

"Girl, you are *mean*. I was just trying to be nice. I don't have no motive up my sleeve, and I ain't trying to poke nothing, so there's no need to jump to no conclusions."

"Whatever. I didn't ask you to like me. Like I care what you think. Here, ring this stuff up so I can get out of here," I say, half irritated.

"Ma, how long you plan on stayin' in that motel room?"

"Did anyone ever tell you you ask too many questions? Can't you tell when you need to mind your own business? Damn!" I snap.

"Give me a break, shortie."

"First I'm ma, now I'm shortie. Make up your damn mind. I should be calling you shortie. Why should I give you a break? No one sure 'nuff gives my ass one," I complain.

"Look, I told you I was just trying to be nice, and I meant that. No more, no less."

"Be nice to someone else who gives a rat's butt. Now how much is it?"

"That'll be nine dollars and twelve cents, and you didn't have to cut me down about my height, either."

"If you're short, you're short. Don't stress about it. Here," I say, letting a hundred-dollar bill float onto the counter.

"Dag, you're cold. You don't even want to put the money in my hand?"

"I don't want to touch you, and I see no reason to pretend I do."

"Well I don't want to touch you either. I'm just doin' my job."

"Your job sucks, doesn't it, shortie?"

"I may pump gas and wait on people in here, but it keeps my probation officer happy. Look, please don't call me that, okay?"

"Whatever. You did time?" I say with a new interest.

"Just something stupid that I'll never do again. Now I'm paying the price."

"My name's Jalita."

"I'm Shawn."

"All right, Shawn. Now that I've got a name, I won't have to call you shortie." I hear an unfamiliar sound. Then I ask, "What's that noise?"

"My two-way pager."

"Your what?"

"Two-way. Where you been, girl? People type messages and send them. I can type them back."

"Like an electronic phone?"

"Sort of."

"That's tight."

"Yeah. Damn, I can't believe this shit," he says, looking at his pager.

"What's wrong with you?"

"I can't believe this shit! Motha—"

"What?" I say. Shawn walks from behind the counter and starts pacing, pumping the air, cursing so much that I'm reminded of being on the streets of Baltimore, on the worst side of town. Then he returns to his spot behind the counter and bangs his fist down so hard, I think he's gonna break every bone in his hand.

"What is it, Shawn?"

While Shawn shakes his stinging hand, he explains, "My fiancée typed me. I can't believe this. I talked to the woman just this morning, and everything was fine between us."

"So what's the problem?" I ask, nibbling on my nuked sausage biscuit.

"She says she's moved out, left town, and is gonna marry her ex. I been taking care of her ass…wining her and dining her for the last six months. She had *my* engagement ring on her damn finger, that I paid for at nineteen percent interest!"

"Damn," I say while steadily eating.

"If I weren't on probation, I'd *kill* that punk ass!"

"But you are on probation, baby boy," I remind him.

"I know. I know. She won't tell me where he lives, but I could find him if I really wanted to tell him I just spent six hundred dollars on her

Christmas shit and just paid off the last payment of her damn three-thousand-dollar ring last week. *Motha fuck*!" he says as he slams the lid of the pager shut then crams it into his jeans pocket.

"Oh well, life is a bitch, then you die," I say as I throw my tightly balled up sausage biscuit wrapper in the trash.

"You act like this is nothin'. Oh well, you say?" he screeches.

"I've been through worse. Get the freak over it already," I say.

"Shit, I can't just get over it. She went from telling me two weeks ago she's excited about the wedding to whispering on the phone with the bathroom fan on this week, and doing a disappearing act. Shawn turns to me and remarks, "How am I gonna go to dinner with my cousin and boys tonight like nothin's wrong?"

"Two-way them and tell them what issues you've got and show up anyway. They'll understand. They're your peoples."

"You're right. I like you, Jalita. You keep things real."

"Don't make the mistake of liking me too much."

"Not like that, aiight. I just got dumped. I'm not tryin' to holler, but you are a dime."

"Good, because if you were tryna holla, I'd have to school you on what I think of all men."

"You wanna come to dinner with me? I mean, Jackie fucked shit up, and it appears you're here ready to eat up everything. Tonight is gonna be crunk."

"I don't know," I say, throwing half of the rotten banana in the trash.

"Look at that shit, Jalita. That's no Christmas breakfast."

"Yeah, I know, but I'm over it."

"All I'm trying to do is help you out."

Shawn cracks a slight smile, then I face him and say, "You did remember my name. I'm staying at the Motel 6. My room number is 416. And you better not try to chop me up in little pieces or anything, 'cause I've got plenty of street in me, and I'll give you a run for your money," I inform him.

"I knew that a long time ago. I don't want nothing but some company."

"Hurry up, too. I'm not big on patience or waiting on negroes."

"I'll be off soon."

"If you want to get penciled in, you better tell me what soon is and give me my change. Are you tryna keep a commission or something?" I joke.

"My bad. Noon," Shawn says as I collect my change from him.

"Okay, well after 12:10, I don't unlock the door . . . I go deaf."

"You are trippin', Jalita."

"Maybe so, but I meant what I said, and when I speak, I make my words count."

Shawn smirks as a man walks up. He's a red negro, about three hundred pounds, six-two, refrigerator wide, and fit to be on someone's football roster.

"Hold up, let me ring this brother's things up." Shawn says.

"You better work fast," I tease.

"That will be three dollars and seventy-five cents, please," Shawn says.

"Three dollars and seventy-five cents, my ass," the NFL look-alike says to Shawn while holding him up by his shirt collar with one hand.

"What's your problem, man? I don't even know you. Would you put me down?"

"Don't be calling Jackie no more. She don't want your pint-sized punk ass, so let it go, my man."

"And what's it to you?" Shawn asks. I gulp hard.

"Don't you worry about all that. You just stop pressing the issue because she finally made up her mind, and she wants to be with Jerome," he says, releasing Shawn who coughs from halfway choking and massages his neck with his left hand.

"And thanks for the powdered doughnuts and super-size bottle of Sprite. If I didn't already have a full tank of gas, that would be on you, too. Consider this your first and last friendly warning. If you need me to translate, let me say it to you straight: Chill the fuck out," he reminds Shawn. He kicks the door open and pulls off in a black Lincoln Navigator. The mystery of who he is remains.

"You let him carry you like that, Shawn?" I ask.

"You saw the size of him? What was I supposed to do?"

"He was a big dude. That was a cross breed between that Brawny paper towel man and Mr. Clean. You don't see them built like that every day. He coulda crushed you like a fly."

"I can't believe this is happening to my ass. The ex-playa who wrote the book," Shawn says, reaching in his wallet and filling the register with three ones and seventy-five cents in change.

"Believe it, ex-playa playa."

"Her damn ex, I know he's behind this," Shawn says while gritting his teeth again.

"Shawn."

"What?"

"Don't go off tryna kill nobody. I'm not big on bloody hands."

"I'm cool. I'm just ventin'. I was dumb to think things would be fine since she'd been acting a fool this week. What could I expect?"

"It's called dealing with mixed emotions during a holiday. That's never easy, so don't be so hard on yourself. The thing is, you've gotta reach your limit with this woman at some point."

"Thanks for your words of wisdom. I agree with everything you just said. Later, Jalita."

"That's right. Say my name," I say as I wink.

"You are a mess."

"You tellin' me? Why are you looking at me like that?"

"I've got an idea."

"What?"

"Let's give you a makeover for tonight. I want you to give some stuck-up women a run for their money."

"What in the heck are you talking about?" I say as he disappears into the back room again. He returns with two large shopping bags.

"This is yours, if you want it. Look inside."

"For real? You don't even know me and are willing to give me all this fly gear?" I say, checking out the items.

"Obviously, Jackie ain't thinkin' about Christmas with me. Because of her, I almost got an ass whippin' I don't deserve. So could you use this stuff or what, Jalita?"

"You aiight, Shawn. Thanks. I'll put it to good use," I say, looking down into the bag. I glance up and smile.

"At least someone appreciates it," he announces like he's expecting a consolation prize.

"What's the hair color, blow dryer, and curling iron about?"

"Jackie asked me to pick that stuff from the Sally's Beauty Supply so she could throw some highlights up in her hair and style it some way she had in mind. She likes to keep up with fashion and is always watching music videos or that cable channel Style."

"That's slick. I do like this golden color. A whole lot of sisters have been rocking light hair lately. Maybe they think blondes have more fun, like the White sisters have always sworn."

"So find out and be one of them."

"I never did this before. I hope I don't burn it out of my head with these chemicals."

"I know you can read. Follow the directions, that's all."

"I think I will."

"Here, take these, too. I think these clothes and shoes will fit."

"Thanks," I tell Shawn while halfway smiling.

"Go have fun."

"Now you stop trippin' over Jackie. Enough about that moody chick. She isn't worth sweating and risking an ass whippin' from Big Boy. She lost a good man. Merry Christmas. By the way, you're a cutie, and it's not all about the height, but how you work what you got," I say, pushing the door open with my rear, happy that Santa Claus just gave me a reason to think that it just may turn out to be a Merry Christmas after all for little ol' forgotten, bad-luck-havin' me.

4
BIG TIMIN' IN MITCHELLVILLE

"Why are you stopping at this funny-looking gate?" I ask Shawn.
"I've got to give my name to homeboy."
"Why? What's that all about?"
"It's a gated community. You know, it weeds the unwanted, uninvited people out."
"I've never seen anything like this before."
"Well welcome to Mitchellville, Jalita."
"What?" I utter, wrinkling my forehead.
"The town we're in," Shawn tells me like I'm a simpleton.
"The people up in here must be rolling in piles of ends."
"Something like that. At least the ones who aren't perpetrating. You'd be surprised. Some are struggling to keep furniture in their cribs," he says as we pass mini-mansions and sprawling homes with perfectly manicured lawns.
"We're goin' in *there*?" I say as I look at Shawn. His car halts in a semicircular driveway at the largest home on the block. The crib has these columns in front as big as the White House.
"Yeah," he answers casually.
"How come the gate keeper didn't weed me out? I don't think I'll fit in," I say, watching a tall man dressed to the nines step out of a black Bentley.
"Oh, yes you will. Trust me on that," Shawn assures me.
"Whose mansion is this?"
"My cousin's."

"Shawn, I don't know about this. Your cousin must not be on the perpetrating list."

"He's not. You got your hair did, you have that fly gear on, and look like the price of this house. There's no reason why you shouldn't meet one of Prince George's County's most famous. Just relax 'cause you're going in."

"If you say so," I say as the door opens. A Japanese woman dressed in a multicolored kimono bows with her palms pressed together, asks for our shoes, then leads us up to a room to the left of the breezeway.

"Shawn, what's she doing?"

"Getting ready to wash our feet and give us robes."

"What kind of crib is this? You've got to be kidding me."

"Actually, I'm serious. My cousin is a clean freak. He can't stand smelly feet, and I should say he lends robes because he's got Persian rugs and all kinds of exclusive furniture he doesn't want dirty shoes and street clothes to touch. Everyone's got to do this to come in to a party or a dinner. I didn't tell you, but both are about to go down tonight."

"This is weird and almost too strange to be real. I don't think I'm going to like this."

"Come on, now, cooperate. It's all good. Don't you trust my judgment?"

"I don't know you enough to trust anything."

"Well you can," Shawn insists.

"I've never been in a mansion before. What does your cousin do?"

"Sports."

"What?"

"You'll recognize him, if you own a television set."

"Don't you mean if I *watch* television? I can't say I have much time in my life for sitcoms. Those people are paid. I still have mine to get," I say as the woman dries my feet and hands me a robe.

"Girl, you need to let the stress go. Go in that room and change. Hang your street clothes up on one of those hooks."

"Now wait a minute, Shawn. First you rant and rave about me needing a makeover and now you're telling me all this dressing up in new clothes and primping was unnecessary?"

"I never said it was unnecessary," Shawn answers.

"Apparently it was. I also didn't even have to bother to shower and wash my own stinking feet."

"Will you let it go? We're going to try to get you to loosen up tonight," Shawn tells me.

"Good luck tryin'," I answer, wondering how Jackie could leave this man if he had access to all of this legitimately good life. Most women would kill for an open invitation to hang around an athlete's private crib.

When I meet back up with Shawn, I feel like a complete idiot. I haven't even met his cousin yet and I'm leaving my new clothes on a hook. Part of me wants to notify the owner that I'll walk barefoot in his crib, but that's my limit. I consider it, but decide I won't embarrass Shawn since he's the one who gave me the clothes to hang on the hook in the first place.

I cut the brotha some slack and go along with the charade. I look at Shawn decked out in a rust-colored robe that stops around his calves and say, "Oh, you're dressed—or should I say undressed—already?"

"Yep," he answers.

"So let's go meet the mystery man."

"Let's," he says, motioning to me to follow.

We walk up a marble staircase, and my eyes grab and hold the sight of a crystal chandelier that's as elegant as the ones they have in those houses on *MTV Cribs*. When we reach the top of the steps, I hear smooth jazz spilling out of somewhere I can't see. An extremely tall, brown-faced famous man with a sparkling diamond in his left ear approaches Shawn. He's lean, leggy, chiseled, and the ideal piece of six-foot-plus chocolate eye candy.

"Give me some dap, boy. Give it up!" Mr. Mysterious says with the cutest dimpled smile.

"Wes, it's good to see ya," Shawn says, pulling his arm away, after their fingertips lock.

"Who is *this*?"

"A new friend."

Wes turns to me seductively, and asks, "And you are?"

"Jalita," I reply.

"Ahhh, Jalita, the pleasure is all mine, beautiful. Welcome to my home," he says. He grabs my hand and kisses it so sensually that it gives me goose bumps. I can tell he likes showing off by the way he announces it's his spot. Truthfully, I'm wondering if all of this living in the lap of luxury is paid for in full, or if he's in debt up to his neck. Around my way, you only hear about drug kingpins in Miami or somewhere doing the damn thing like this. I had no idea Black people live like this not far from pissy-smelling hallways in high-rise buildings in the projects and spots where people loiter and guzzle liquor on corners 'cause life ain't taking them any place better. Damn. This is a shock to see from the inside view.

"It's a pleasure to meet you, too."

Our eyes lock, then Wes replies, "I know." Then I realize that I do recognize him from television.

"Don't you, umm, play for the—"

"Blitzers? Yes, that would be me, the point guard who earned two All-Star MVP Awards. I'm everything the press says I am and more," Wes answers smugly.

I feel like feeding Wes's ego, and say, "It's such an honor to meet you."

"Thank you. It usually is." He kisses my other hand the same way. He adds, "Would you like a tour?"

"Sure, I'd love one," I answer, looking around.

"I'll give it to her then," a new voice says, interrupting quickly. A woman peeks from Wes's side, physically pushes her way between us, and breaks up our conversation.

"I'm Tomi, his woman. Welcome to *our* home."

"Nice to meet you, too," I say, sticking out my right hand to shake hers while noticing her perfectly clear skin, fresh french manicured nails, and the good size ice in her ears. I'd guess she's standing about five-nine, has a model-thin frame, and is about two shades darker than Mariah Carey.

"Mmm-hmm," Tomi grunts, giving me a bitchy grin, then hugs all up on her man. She never bothers to shake my hand, so I withdraw it, and gently let it hang next to my side.

Tomi puts me on the spot, telling me, "I noticed that you neglected to drop your business card into the crystal bowl near the front door. Why don't you remove a card from your wallet and run down to put yourself in my networking mix."

"Actually, I don't have a card to drop in the bowl. That's why I didn't do it," I tell Tomi. Wes looks cross-eyed at Shawn who returns the same look to Wes. The air is so tense, I could have cut it with my trusty knife . . . had I brought the blade with me.

Tomi adds, "I figured that whatever it is that you do doesn't require a card. Let's proceed with the tour then, so you won't tie up Wes. I don't mind taking over from here." Now I detect she's a stuck-up pain in the ass who's convinced her shit don't stink. I already don't like her, and if you ask me, she ain't all that with her B-cup titties and her miniature booty. She's got a gorgeous face, but if she turns sideways, she will disappear. She needs to go look in the mirror to discover that and also remember this Wes dude is the one with the real ends. I can't stand no perpetrators, and I'm looking at one.

"Well, I think it's time for me to tend to our other guests," Wes says just like his Tomi is listening for any indication to get on his hide for flirting. He is careful and escapes without having to defend himself for bumping gums with me. I'm thinking he's had a lot of practice making these kinds of sudden departures.

"I'll come with you, cuz. I'll see you in a bit, Jalita," Shawn says as Tomi quickly disappears to the right.

"This here is the living room. I decorated it myself, down to the family pictures. Notice the large ones of Wes and me sitting on the front side of each end table," Tomi tells me.

"Nice touch," I say to play along with her.

"Just a hair down this way is the den. I decorated that myself, too. My favorite thing in here is building a library that our children will inherit someday. Reading *is* fundamental. I tell the poor kids that all of the time."

"You two have kids?"

"Not just yet. Now come along, dear, and stop being such a chatterbox. You tend to walk slowly, don't you?"

"Not really," I say.

"This is my private lounge. A wife needs her own space, if she wants to keep a healthy marriage. Won't you come in and sit down for a moment?"

"Well, if you insist, but I did want to see the house. How long have you and Wes been married?" I ask, sitting across from her on a soft black leather sofa.

"We'll be newlyweds soon, and technically speaking this is a mansion. It's rude to ask so many personal questions, don't you think? And to you, he's Mr. Montgomery. Don't let it go to your head, just because he gave you a few one-liners!" Tomi snaps at me.

I wrinkle my forehead, and tell her, "I don't know how this conversation took this ugly turn, but can we not go wherever it is you're tryna take me because I'm not interested."

"No, we will take this turn and get all up into the curve because my man likes you. I see it. I've been through this damn shit before and I'm tired of sharing him. For once in this relationship, I'm making some noise this season. No more walking over Tomi. Those days are over!" Tomi announces, pointing to me like I've committed a crime.

"All he said was—"

"Shut up. I'm talking here," she yells. Tomi's got game, I see. Her pitch is sounding a bit like Tony's girl, Charlene.

"Umm, what's your problem, Tomi? I'm tryna respect your house—I mean mansion—but you're making it hard for me to keep biting my tongue."

"Well, let me tell you one damn thing. I'm going to hurry up and correct this little situation, *right now*. I put up with all kinds of you groupies, 24/7, 365 days of the year. I'm not having it from a big behinded one on Christmas Day. You all are like cockroaches—I get rid of one, and you still multiply and find your way to Wes. I hate to break it to you, but you've just met your most lethal can of Raid."

"I'm not a groupie. I don't even watch basketball. As a matter of fact, I find watching men fight over which way to run the ball boring. I just recognized his face, that's all. There's no need to get nasty, sister. I've told you several times that you are barking up the wrong tree," I explain. I really want to instruct the chick not to hate on Wes, just play the game and be thankful she's in the mix.

"Mmm-hmm. Let me tell you something. An athlete of Wes's caliber wants a woman he can show off, like me. They like White women, or ones close to it, like me. If I so much as catch you breathing in my man's direction while you're here, or at any point in time in life, you'll be sorry, *sister*. You just keep your distance, and stay in your place, which is five hundred feet behind me. He's going to church now and trying to do better by me so don't you dare get in the way of progress."

"Girl, you've got some issues dancin' around in that head. I'm not here on a dick hunt."

"It's still early. You'll see how the ballers roll, but when you do, remember what I said. I may have attended boarding school in London, then earned prestigious degrees from Duke and Yale, but I know all about nasty little hos from the wrong side of the tracks."

"Are you threatening me?" I ask her bluntly.

"Just making a pushy request," she says, making her fingers form the shape of a gun.

I've been exposed to a lot of wackos in my day, and something tells me to keep my tongue still when it comes to firing back my typical wisecracks at Ms. Tomi who ain't all there upstairs. "I see," I say calmly.

"Good. I'm the queen bee around here, and I will become Mrs. Montgomery. The whole world will know it thanks to this ring that makes the one Ben gave J.Lo look like something for a Little Leaguer. And to be sure Wes stays put, I'll seal the deal with a rugrat, and own half of what he's got in his bank account, pocket, and coming in the future. I worked hard to land him, and no one is going to get in my way of being able to travel around the world with all expenses paid. No one else's ass is ever going to sit on back of that BMW bike and put on my Furla helmet. No one else is going to ever sit in the driver's seat of my black Mercedes 320 SLK and have their buns warmed by my heated seat. And no one else is *ever* going to attend NBA All-Star Weekend events with Wes. He's mine, before and after taxes . . . basketball season or not. That's how it is, permanently."

"I don't want your man. As a matter of fact, I don't want *any* man," I say half irritated.

"Mmm-hmm. I've heard it all before," she mumbles like she doesn't believe one word I've said.

"Really, Tomi. That's the truth, straight up. Your agenda has nothing to do with me."

She has the feel like she's a detective interviewing me in one of those little rooms when criminals get picked up for questioning after a crime. Tomi blurts out, "You ever been around people with money?"

"Can't say that I have."

"They buy everything they want. Remember that. I was groomed, bred, and educated for a man like this. I wear suits that cost more than most people's first cars. It's a tradition that I intend to pass on to my daughter. She will grow up privileged. Wes will give daddy's girl the moon. I've already picked out her name. It's Isabella Alexis Montgomery. I don't want my princess having some Black sounding name, and if she takes after my genes, she can pass for something else someday."

"So what's that got to do with me?" I ask Tomi, thinking that name sounded like a drunk woman came up with it.

"Jachita?" she says as she smooths down the fabric on her lilac-colored silk robe, then stands.

"What?"

"I've already explained my position. Now this girl talk was a private conversation. Capeesh?"

"Of course. It's your house. You make the house rules, Ms. Queen Bee."

"Don't be funny, Jachita. I think we understand each other now. By the way, if you're thinking I stole the queen bee thing from Lil' Kim, I was saying that ten years ago. There are no carbon copies of who is gracing your presence, and don't you forget it. And speaking of stealing, if anything is missing, I know who to come looking for. I'll be watching you like a hawk."

"My name is Jalita, *not* Jachita, and I don't steal," I correct her promptly.

"Same thing. It doesn't change my impression of you. I haven't met one of you who isn't capable of having sticky fingers. Some of the last kleptomaniacs walked their scheming asses into the downstairs guest bathroom and stole anything they could get their hands on. Just because I have a lot doesn't mean I don't know what I have around here. My best towels, Origins Salt Butter, Molasses Hair Mask, and of all things, my used, cheap Victoria's Secret drawers that read PAMPERED CHIC in fake rhinestones were gone. I told you, I know what you are, so drop the act."

"And just what would that be?" I ask.

Tomi looks over her shoulder while smiling, then says, "Your name says it all. A trashy, low-class bitch." I hold back the same kind of words that were waiting for Ebony, the R.A., as Tomi turns back around and proceeds to give me the rest of the tour. I wonder how long I'm going to manage to stand and be the bigger person as Tomi's voice returns to one of a gracious hostess, switching back to Ms. Etiquette from refined baby girl from the hood. I wonder if Wes knows what a nutcase he's got on his hands, but it isn't my place to ask or care.

Tomi and I walk downstairs in silence. I draw my own conclusions about what I'm seeing as we pass various rooms with themes. In one room men are smoking what I assume are imported cigars while shooting craps with stacks on money riding on bets. Other men and women are playing cards and Twister in the buff. The next room that holds my attention is a spot decorated with candles, throw pillows, and Arabian costumed women delivering full-body massages to a few dudes on massage tables. I raise my eyebrows and keep walking. As we pass the last room I peep a well-known local newscaster being whipped by an Oriental woman dressed in leather fetish attire. By the time Tomi and I reach the spot where the tour began, my gracious host disappears and I'm thinking that this party, which is already off the damn hook, is just getting started.

The buffet-style dinner was the best meal I've ever had. Since I didn't even peep one person watching how much I piled on my dang plate, I stuffed myself like a holiday turkey and even managed to wrap up some cheese balls, garnishing, and bite size hors d'oeuvres. I don't know where my next meal is gonna come from so I don't see shit wrong with hiding my stash somewhere until I hit the road. These rich fucks will probably throw out the leftovers anyway. Half of these lushes are spending more time keeping the three bartenders busy than bothering to eat what's on their plates. I would've given my left arm to eat what they're throwing away when I was sleeping with hunger in my belly on cold nights in abandoned row homes. Having been here for four plus hours, getting my grub on, watching a movie in Wes's personal movie theater, munching on popcorn with a few other guests, playing some video games without having to put in quarters, and feeding his ducks in the back pond, I could suddenly understand why Tomi is a possessive, raging nutcase.

Most people in this world think they're living good when they're making a little something like my mentor Tony, have a slick ride, and the ability to pay their bills on time, but this right here is some Cinderella shit. Even the owner of the b-ball team swung by to rub elbows with Wes and drink apple cider. Like they say, money talks, and I'm beginning to sense how loudly it says what it's got to say. Life to me was never about having money, but now I want some dead presidents. Now the faces on the bills are what I call fine-ass men.

The guests dwindle to about a good thirty, although some may still be hidden in theme rooms. Everyone's chillin', looking half buzzed from expensive wine and liquor poured from elegant-looking bottles, listening to Walter Beasley. I'm halfway falling asleep, 'cause the turkey and smooth jazz is bringing on niggeritis, until I hear someone breathing in my ear. Without opening my eyes, I assume it's Shawn and tell him to stop goofing off.

"No, it's Wes," the voice says softly.

"Hi, Wes. Where's Tomi?" I inquire cautiously. I'm not tryna get smoked while my back is turned.

"I don't keep tabs on her. She's around here somewhere," Wes remarks nonchalantly.

"Oh. I'm not trying to be funny, but could you back up off me?" I request.

"If I were on you, you'd know it, and this isn't it, beautiful," Wes says.

"Why are you such a flirt? You need to check yourself."

"I like the feisty ones like you, baby. A challenge is a turn-on since it doesn't happen too often," he tells me.

"Yeah right, so where's Shawn?" I ask, rolling my eyes and pushing him away.

"Shawn is indisposed," Wes answers, moving backward.

"What do you mean indisposed?" I parrot back.

"Go in the bathroom down the hall and find out," he says, pulling my wrist toward him and kissing my hand again. I'm surprised that he knows how to use a large word like *indisposed,* but I don't have the energy to harp on that. My heart is pounding much too hard. The niggeritis leaves, and I make it my business to find out where my ride is and why he's busy. The bathroom door is shut, so I knock three times until I hear a response.

"What!"

"Shawn, is that you in there? It's me, Jalita."

"Yeah," he answers, sounding despondent.

"Are you okay?" I ask in a confused tone.

"I guess so. I'm still breathing."

"You're not in there crying over what's her name are you?" I ask sarcastically.

"Naw. She's history after I mourn tonight."

"How are you gonna mourn?"

"Open the door if you really want to know."

"You won't pull anything slick, will you?"

"I told you, I'm not trying to hit it."

"Okay," I say. I push the door open to find Shawn sitting on the toilet lid, sniffing a powder that is perfectly organized in a long line on a mirror-looking contraption. He sniffs, then smiles like a girl would, completely zoned out, holding his head back like he is looking up at the sun.

"What in the fuck?" I mutter.

"Want some, Jalita?" he asks slowly. I observe his dilated pupils.

"You use blow? I can't believe this. I thought you were on probation. What are you thinking, man?"

"You think I'm the first to do a line of coke in this bathroom or anywhere in this mansion? Please, girl. As far as the cops, they ain't bothering no one. You just ate with the damn chief of police. Welcome to this world, Jalita," he says, extending his legs.

"Man, this is not the way to deal with problems. Just say no to drugs before they grab you and kick your butt with big-time addiction. Come on now, you know all about the chaos written in fine print. The shit is trouble."

"Maybe I need an addiction. No one cares about Shawn. Shawn is there to support, not be supported. Shawn is there to do right, then get dissed. Shawn is just the favorite doormat. Shawn is just tired of being Shawn," he blurts out.

"I'm not exactly cared about my damn self, but there's no use in making a drug boy's boss rich."

"I know all about your life, Jalita. I'm good at reading eyes, and I see your sadness. How long you been hurtin', too? How long you been wantin' people to do you right? How long you been wantin' to erase your past?"

"You're way off base," I say to divert him from confirming the accuracy of his intuition.

"No, I'm not, I've been around the block. I just tried to explain that to you."

"Well unless you want to go back to the block, I suggest you use your head, Shawn."

"I slept on a few park benches after people turned their backs on me myself, Jalita. Ain't no one sympathetic to my goals. Ain't no one even give me a damn Christmas card who should be thanking me."

I gulp, then tell Shawn, "Well you and Wes seem like you're tight. He must care about your butt, even though he never said it with a Hallmark. Men aren't into that card-giving shit, so cut the brotha some slack."

"It's more than that. Wes got signed; I didn't get signed. He ain't the sharing type, if you don't wear a skirt," he says all dreamy eyed. I sigh. He reaches for my hand. He's been right about everything, and my walls of defense crumble. He knows some of my pain, and I suddenly want to bond with him 'cause I catch his drift that he's in a lot of pain, too.

"Do this line. Don't leave me. Just tell me you understand, Jalita."

"I do understand, but I can't do that," I announce, staring at it with wide eyes. I've seen cocaine, but I've never considered putting it inside of my body. I considered indulging nothing short of a death sentence.

"Yes, you can. We're in the same boat. No one cares about our feelings. Shit, no one cares about us, period. This is what cares about us," Shawn says, then reaches down to take a long sniff.

He raises his head and says, "I did one for my no-good ex. Who you gonna do one for?" His words stick and grow. Kate's face flashes before me. My hope that anyone is ever gonna love me is destroyed. I suddenly don't care about my body being a temple, and I accept his offer.

"My White momma who don't love me. I'll start with that heartless bitch," I blurt out as his arm wraps around me, like I'm being held together. I impulsively roll up my sleeves, bend down to the white powdered trail, then inhale deeply, until I'm higher than a kite in the park. I feel good. I feel loved. Everything wrong doesn't matter anymore.

I've escaped the hurt, the pain, the lies, and the years of rejection in one long snort. I sit on the floor, smiling just like Shawn, and I'm thankful that I've taken my first trip into the high life.

A while later, the door opens slowly. Shawn and I are still half high, but manage to turn our heads to find Wes standing in the doorway.

"Well, I see Ms. Jalita got with the program around here. Come on out, you two," he says, helping me up off the marble floor.

Wes doesn't let go of my hand, and this time I'm too high to know that I should be watching my back for Tomi. We walk into a pool room, halfway stumbling. The water is fuzzy looking, but I can make out that the pool is shaped like a huge C. There's lots of room around the water to chill out in lounge chairs or creep into a corner. Wes leads me to a reclining chair and tells me to rest for a while. Loud, thumping go-go music is being played by a D.C. band whose name I can't recall, although the leader hitting a cowbell while other band members drum should make it impossible for me to forget. I lay back, waiting to see where this is goin', looking out through eyes that feel heavy and in need of two toothpicks to hold them open.

"Hold up, wait a minute. Ain't no party like a Wes Montgomery party, and a Wes Montgomery party don't stop, so let's paaaaaarty!" Wes screams on beat. He throws off his robe like he's anything but a clean freak, then dives into the pool. He's swimming around like a fish, naked just like has momma birthed him. The crowd screams "paaaaarty" and mimics the host. Everyone is in the buff, splashing water, laughing, just plain acting wild and freaky. I want to keep watching, but my eyes completely shut. I can hear everything clear as a bell, so I listen intently.

After a few moments, I regain all of my faculties. My head is aching from the buzz I've had, but it's tolerable. I spot a naked Tomi sitting on top of Wes's shoulders, playing chicken in the water with another couple. I recognize the man's face, but I can't place it until a swimsuit model and video ho not doing a good job of whispering that he's the center for the Blitzers who just got his divorce papers help jog my memory that he's Travis Russell. I know the women's claim to fame 'cause they start talking about how a baby could ruin their figure, but not modeling for the magazine or shaking it in videos could be worth it if they could get ten thousand dollars a month to be a baby's momma to this legend who has no idea one of them is plotting to hook him into having an illegitimate rugrat. The shorter one claims she'll get him in bed before dawn and says she will demand twenty thousand dollars a month plus hush money.

This bit of gossip leads me to look around the rest of the room and observe White chicks, Black chicks, and a few foreigners pawning over dudes whose height tells me that they must take it to the hoop for a living. I finally spot Shawn as he pops up from under the water. He waves, then I wave in return. I decide to loosen up and stop judging this private freak festival, and give a sigh of relaxation.

"Come on in!" a lightly tanned woman screams at me.

"I don't swim," I scream back.

"You do now!" she says, chasing me into the water. I jump in the shallow end, and laugh. The water is warm. It feels as good as the line of coke I had. I'm a little self-conscious that everyone is nude, but decide to look at faces, not body parts.

I back up against the wall on the shallow end as I listen to what I recognize to be a Chuck Brown cut. I listen to the pulsating beat, beginning to bop my head and bounce my shoulders. I'm not alone—many other guests catch the vibe, too. The go-go funkster retires the cowbell then strips down to his sweaty undershirt and boxer shorts. He spits lyrics that make the crowd go wild, as the drumbeats kick in. I feel like I'm at some type of live summer concert at the Pier Six Concert Pavilion on the Inner Harbor.

The energy of the partygoers and hypnotic music arouses me, and I can feel my nipples harden the same way as when Tony gave me my first dose of lovin'. I continue to sway back and forth, until the song ends. I open my eyes and discover I'm being watched. Wes is looking over his shoulder and winking at me while sliding his tongue across his sexy, plump brown lips. Tomi holds on to the edge of the pool, thinking that everyone's laughing at the scenery of Wes fucking her doggy style, when they're really laughing at him flirting with me while Tomi is busy bouncing off his dick, unable to see a damn thing. The water makes these huge ripples as she moans with pleasure, sounding happy that she has an audience. The devil in me makes me lick my lips and grab my nipples, returning the same intense gaze to Wes. His hips begin to move faster as Tomi moans louder. Peer pressure gets to me, and I laugh heartily along with the crowd.

A few seconds later, I suddenly feel more ripples of gentle waves. The laughing turns into a sea of soft, sensual moans. It seems like everyone's fucking but me and Shawn. I know it's not that kind of party goin' on with us, so I tune Wes out. I close my eyes, pretend I'm being touched and loved, and concentrate on the next cut, until things get so heated that I feel completely out of place. Shawn follows my lead, and we are like two voyeurs, both just as aroused, watching a live porn flick at his cousin's house. By this time, a few guests make it out of the pool. I watch one woman openly suck a man's dick while kneeling. He lays back in a lounge chair with this shit-eating grin on his face.

Shawn says, "You wanna go to bed? I'm getting tired of just watching these freaks."

"Me, too," I reply.

"Who would've ever though that Wes spoke to a youth group yesterday about abstinence and morals. If you've seen it once, you've seen it fifty times, down to the president of basketball operations getting head on Christmas Day. Now what kind of example is he? I wish the owner hadn't left. He needs to see this shit. Come on, Jalita. I think we've both seen enough of Wes's party," he says, leading me out of the pool by the hand. Shawn and I dry ourselves off, shower around the corner, then walk into another wing of the house that Tomi didn't bother to show me. I'm sure she intentionally kept me away from seeing the bedrooms and private quarters.

"You wanna sleep in bed with me or by yourself? It's up to you," Shawn says, stretching and yawning.

"Excuse me?" I say.

"How many times do I have to tell you? I'm not trying to hit it. Why can't you realize you don't have to worry about that with me?" he snaps.

"Because a man will be a man. People are always tryna get in my pants."

"Well you won't have to worry about me trying to unzip them. I don't have an agenda."

"You're one of few. What planet are you from again?" I joke.

"Earth, and like I said I just think you're cool. I may even like you for you. So what's it gonna be?"

"I'm use to sleepin' alone," I reply.

"I'll put you in here and lock the door behind you. I'll be just across the hall. If you need anything, holla."

"Just as Shawn and I are about to part, six naked women I remember from the pool trail behind two extremely tall men who have to be Blitzers. We hear, "Y'all bitches got to be quiet until we get into the room. Our wives think we're watching a movie in the theater. They're around the corner playing cards."

"Shhh, Tammy. The man said quiet. Stop laughing, you drunk ass. I told you liquor goes straight to your big head," a woman says then giggles.

The tall White player asks, "You girls are over eighteen, right?" Before I hear the answers, the door shuts to a room. I hear faint giggling.

I turn to Shawn and say, "Don't worry. You don't have to tell me to lock the door with all these freaky-deaky people wandering around this joint."

"I hear that. Night."

"Night, Shawn," I say, locking the door, wondering what kind of bizarre dream I'd conjure up.

5

THE MORNING AFTER

It's 5:30 a.m. I walk over to the window 'cause I hear a rhythmic swooshing noise like someone's raking dry leaves, but I can't see from where my source of irritation is coming. This is a strange-ass neighborhood, that's for sure. Who in the world gets up 5:30 on a Sunday morning after Christmas to tend to yard work? I bet Wes and Tomi don't hear shit since the last straggling Blitzers stumbled out of here at about four o'clock. Well, actually three wives came looking for their husbands at 3:30. Wes lied and said they'd left for home already, when really they were passed out in bed with the women I heard giggling the night before. I heard movement, I woke up, looked at a clock in the room, and put my ear to the wall. I heard Wes next door waking them up, explaining that his crib ain't no hotel and throwing the groupies out around 3:45. Actually, the groupies were all but pushed out of the door with their eyes still halfway shut, but I know Wes wanted them out of his spot so the wives wouldn't come back and pin his ass down. I guess since Wes's teammates had their fun there was no need to be polite to their "fans." As for Shawn, he's in there sawing wood like he hasn't had sleep in a hundred years. I know he, too, will continue doing an impression of Rip Van Winkle and won't be getting from underneath of those covers any time soon.

Since that just leaves yours truly, I don't see why I shouldn't go visit the fish in the back pond and get some fresh air. While I'm out there I can see who in the fuck woke me up when this bed slept way better than I had when Kate had me sleeping on a mattress on the floor, until she gave me up. My own mother didn't see fit to buy me a real bed, so instead I slept on a piece of crap with no sheet that had a split down the middle, the stuffing falling out and metal broken springs scratching my legs if I slept wild enough to make them stick out. Enough of that though. I refuse to allow any more thoughts of Kate to ruin my day. I know these people have all kinds of alarms around here and I hope a motion detector isn't on 'cause I'm goin' downstairs to the room where my clothes are hanging on that hook so I can dress and slip outside. I can always redress and slip this robe back on like I was never missing. Sounds like a plan; that's exactly what I'll do 'cause I'm grown.

Damn. Look at him—he's fine. This brotha can wake my ass up anytime. So this is who disturbed my rest. On a scale of one to ten, I give him a ten on the body, a ten on the face, and a ten on the sex appeal. I can see he has a nice body although he's wearing sweat clothes that look like he saves them for chore-filled mornings like these. You've got to be a fine-ass motherfucker if you're wearing dirty work boots and garden gloves, have dirt on the knees of your pants and can still turn my head. I can tell this man is mixed with something but I have no idea what races are floating around in his gene pool. I'm not into men with really long hair or light skin, but this time I'm willing to make an exception for this honey the color of roasted cashews. Some people have all the nerve and others have none. Me, I have enough to put an end to talking to myself 'cause I'm about to get good and up close to get real personal with homeboy.

The man is still raking away, but I ask, "Excuse me, can you tell me where the grocery store is? I'm visiting my cousin and I'd like to surprise her before she gets up and make breakfast for her and her fiancé." He takes one last heavy breath, then pauses.

He looks up, then replies, "Yes. When you get to the main road coming in to the development, make a right, drive one mile, and you can't miss the Safeway sitting on the left hand side of the road."

"Thank you so much. I'm sorry to have interrupted you," I say. I can't see his hands but I know they're large enough to palm a basketball like Wes and his friends do from the way he wraps his big gloves around the top part of the rake and sets it in front of him.

"It's all right," he answers. I notice his yard and house is smaller than Wes's, but they're still nothing to sneeze at. I guess Wes's house is worth about four million, while his might have a market value of about one. I know my shit, including not to let this man off the hook since he isn't sporting a wedding ring and has no tan line on his finger either. His red, shiny Porsche sitting in the driveway with the vanity tag that reads LIVN-LARGE tells me he's materialistic—that make's him more interesting since meeting people who are very paid is brand new to me.

"On second thought, I don't think I'll go to the store. I'm not sure where my cousin keeps her keys, and I don't want to wake her. I just have a thing about being a helpful guest. I wait on her when she comes to my place so I guess I'll have to call this one even."

"Well it was nice of you to be thoughtful, just the same," he says. The man takes off his gloves and wipes his hands on a rag that's lying on top of a pile of something in bags, then walks closer to me.

"Where are my manners? I'm Seth," he says, extending his long arm for a handshake.

"I'm Jalita," I say, wanting to add, "and I wish I had your money. Speaking of money, how and where do you make it?" Instead, I say, "It looks like you're up early to put in a full day's work."

"That was a good guess. I've got to rake, bag leaves, put some mulch down, and take down these Christmas lights," he answers.

"A man who's not afraid to get his hands dirty is a good thing."

"I'm definitely not afraid to do that," he explains. I wonder why he won't hire someone else to get dirt under his nails. I'm figuring out that most people in this neighborhood wouldn't be caught dead buying a rake, let alone using one. Using their logic I'd say that's what landscapers are for. Then again, maybe this Seth is a little thrifty so getting sweat funky is no big deal to him. Then he adds, "I think my ancestors had it right to have been content with getting close to Mother Earth. It does something good for the spirit."

"May I ask you a personal question?" I ask.

"Ask away."

"What race are you?"

"My mom is Lumbi Indian, and my dad was Creole and Irish."

"Interesting. That mixture doesn't happen every day."

"I know. I was the brunt of many a joke growing up in Oklahoma. How about yourself?" he asks. I wonder why. It's like he has this sixth sense. Hardly anyone ever picks up on the fact that I'm mixed. Most just think I'm plain fine and phat butted! How does Seth see past my looks? He hasn't looked at me like he wanted to hit it yet. This never happens.

"I'm biracial. My mother is White, and my father is Black. Plain and simple."

"I thought so."

"How did you know? I'm far from high yellow or a redbone."

"I'm very intuitive. I just don't speak out loud right off," he says. He bends down to tear open one of the plastic bags. When he stands back up he lets his arms hang to his sides. It makes me notice his broad, square shoulders. All I can do is stare at him and all he seems to do is to be able to stare at me, too. In my case, I hope it's not 'cause I have something hanging out of my nose since I was dumb enough to skip looking in the mirror before hightailing it out here to be nosy. I guess that's not it 'cause Seth says, "I hope I'm not being too forward but I'd like to talk to you later."

"Not at all," I answer before realizing what I've said.

"Good. As you can see I don't have anything to write my number down but—"

I cut him off and finish his sentence, "If I have a good memory, will you tell me what it is?" We both smile. I feel a natural energy flowing between us. I find myself wishing he'd invite me inside.

"Yes. It's 443—" he pauses. My eyes follow his to a woman standing in the doorway wearing a robe, house shoes, a face full of green masque, and a head full of yellow magnetic rollers. She looks like her chain has been yanked too hard. I can tell she's eavesdropping, too. Seth looks startled, like he knows flapping his gums with me was off limits. I feel betrayed. His sex appeal dwindles and dries up.

"Jalita, I've got to go. It was a pleasure chatting with you though," Seth says. He runs to the doorway. I begin walking toward Wes's place but I hear low rumbling conversation and can tell the woman is chewing him out for some reason. I don't know if she's ugly or cute 'cause all that shit she has on makes it impossible to tell. If that is his woman, why did Seth allow me to be all up in his grill? If he had a live-in pussy like Wes, all he had to do was keep raking and give me the cold shoulder. If Seth had time to tell me it was a pleasure chatting with him, he just could've finished giving the kid the digits. See, this is why I can't catch any more feelings for men. I'll be better off sticking to hating on people with penises— especially the pretty boys 'cause their asses are always taken. Like Tony's baby's momma says, "No-good motherfucking players."

"Good morning!" Tomi says, bright eyed and a million times friendlier than I recall.

"Good morning," I repeat.

"How do you like your eggs?"

"Scrambled please."

"Scrambled it is. Mary is off on Sundays, so I'll be whippin' up breakfast. I hope it's up to par, and you can do more than stare at it, Jachita," Tomi says, giggling. I don't bother to correct her about my name because I know it's not worth the trouble of making me look stupid in front of people who had no idea of what was said during our previous conversation.

"That's fine with me," I say, waving at Shawn who emerges with a fresh robe. I return to watching the unexpected cook to ensure she doesn't poison my butt accidentally on purpose.

"Good morning," he says in a scratchy, bass voice.

"Good morning," I repeat again.

"Gooooood morning!" Tomi says, extra chipper. "I think the stereo's already tuned in to gospel on WHUR. Hit the power button on the silver remote, would you, Shawn? It's Sunday, and we've got to praise the Lord around here on His day," Tomi says. I wonder if she's sincere, after her triple X performance last night, but she doesn't flinch or make the corners of her mouth form a smile. Serious as a heart attack, yes she is. I can't hold in the irony of events and nearly choke on my pulp-filled orange juice. I begin to cough.

"You okay?" Shawn asks.

"Yeah, thanks," I tell him, just as Wes walks in decked out in lounge wear and a light-colored silk robe.

"Shawn."

"Yes, Tomi," he answers.

"I've got another box of things to be donated to those people."

"What people, Tomi?" Shawn asks.

"I mean the poor people you took the last boxes to for me. I know they're plenty who live on your side of town, so could you please take it with you? I need my space. You know Wes nor I can stand clutter. The Salvation Army takes too long to pick it up," Tomi explains.

"Sure thing," Shawn responds. I roll my eyes, but no one catches me.

"Gooood morning, people," Wes says, kissing Tomi on the back of the neck. We all answer. I'm wondering when last night will be the topic of discussion, but the moment never comes.

"Here's your *Washington Post*, honey," Tomi says to Wes.

"Thanks," he replies.

"Two scrambled eggs for you, Shawn, and three for you, honey, right?" Tomi asks. They both nod.

"Coffee's up," Tomi announces. I'm so nervous from these folks acting like they're full-time conservatives. I can't just sit around and pretend I'm at ease. I pitch in and won't allow Tomi to take no for an answer.

"You're so sweet to help, Jachita. Thanks," Tomi says. I grow goose bumps as I reminisce over her threat and ability to grip the side of a pool something fierce.

"No problem," I say, pouring some gourmet brew into three mugs. I'm not a caffeine addict, but I feel the need to pretend this morning. I watch Wes from of the corner of my eye. His legs are crossed, he's freshly shaven, and looks well rested. I feel like I imagined everything I'd seen and experienced but I know better than that. Tomi walks over to the table with hot eggs, a stack of bacon and toast on a serving tray. She and I sit down.

Let's say grace," Wes says sternly as we all join hands. I'm the first one to begin eating. Then Shawn and Tomi follow suit.

After about two or three gospel numbers, the radio host says, "We just heard selections by The Southern Hummingbirds and Mahalia Jackson. Now family, hearing those songs brings back some down-home memories for me, and I'm wondering if it does for you. Can anyone remember the day God became real to you and turned your life around?"

Tomi lets her fork fall and puts in her two cents' worth, hollering, "Yes, I do. Praise God. Hallelujah. Hallelujah." After I watch Tomi throw up her right hand in affirmation, I can't contain my laughter, and the bacon I'm chewing catapults from my mouth. Thankfully, no one sees it fly into the side of the counter, but Tomi does detect that I'm humored about something.

She asks, "Jachita, is something funny?"

Just as I begin to browse through my Rolodex of possible responses, Shawn takes me off the hook when he announces, "Hey people, Jackie paged me! She says she's sorry, and she's waiting for me at the crib. I knew she'd be back. Who's the man now? Yeah, booooy!" Shawn stares and grins at his two-way.

Wes rustles his paper, and says, "No, not again. Brother, you need to let it go. What is this, like the fifth time this month?"

"You can do much better, Shawn," Tomi agrees.

"I know, I know, but I really love that girl," Shawn admits. I want to remind him that he was lovin' coke the night before when he was reminded how little she loved him, but I keep my jaws locked tight.

"Man, you're on your own with that. I wash my hands," Wes says from behind the paper.

"Honey, put down that paper so that you can eat. We don't want to be late for church. I hate it when we can't get a seat in the front. I can never see around all of those heads and wide-brimmed hats the elders wear. What a nuisance. They really should have to sit in the back if they just have to wear those awful flying saucer–size things," Tomi tells Wes, rolling her eyes.

"I know, but age takes precedence over logic," he answers.

We all hear someone walking down the hall toward the kitchen. I can smell whoever it is before they turn the corner since they reek so bad it smells like they bathed in liquor. When a man appears he looks as if he has something personal against getting a fresh shave and haircut. His hat is turned backward, but some of his uncombed hair is peeking out of the sides and his quarter-length leather coat is buttoned crooked. Tomi scrunches up her nose. Shawn looks blank. Wes looks like he's ready to let the man who looks like his double have a dose of something that's gonna start some serious static.

Wes says, "What's wrong with you? You know better than to come up in my place stinking like a liquor distillery and not taking off your shoes and changing into a robe."

He stumbles over to Wes and says, "Come on now, bro. It's Malik—your peoples. Why you gotta be like that to blood?"

"Just because we're twins doesn't give you a right to disrespect my place. In case you need reminding, my name's on the title to this crib, not yours."

"Well good fucking morning to you, too, bro," Malik answers. The man unbuttons his coat, lets it drop on to the floor then picks up a slice of bacon off Wes's plate.

While the muscular man is standing in the floor chewing and spilling bacon crumbs, Wes asks, "What do you want, Malik? As you can see we're in the middle of breakfast. You're making a mess on my floor."

After he finishes chewing Malik says, "Pardon me. Hi, y'all. Bro, I need you to spot me some funds. You know I wouldn't be asking if I didn't really need it. So can you help a brother out, Wes?" Tomi and Shawn don't bother to reply to his greeting. They both stare.

"Do you think I'm the Federal Reserve 'cause I play ball? And pick up the crumbs you spilled on my floor. You know I don't play that up in here."

"You know it's not like that. How was I supposed to know I was gonna blow out my hitting shoulder? I wish I could pick them up but I can't bend down."

"Instead of throwing away your money when you were on the football field, you should've saved and invested, Malik. You've got a pension coming, so spend it wisely. Now is not the time for this. Can't you see we have company?"

Malik looks at me like he doesn't care if I'm company or not. The volume of his words increases like his emotions are getting heated up. He continues, "You know I was a rookie and only got to play a few games this season before shit went wrong. I'm popping perkasets 'cause I have to, not 'cause I want to. The specialist said my rotator cuff is torn and I need to get my shoulder operated on, so that's what they got planned for me next week. Whether I like it or not they pulled me from the roster. Pension? After all is said and done I may not be worth enough to be an NFL to veteran who can collect one." He pulls a fifth of whiskey from his pocket, throws his head back, and drains the small brown bottle. When his head returns to its normal position, I notice his bloodshot red eyes as he crams the bottle in his pocket.

"Stop your whining. You should be grateful you made it as far as you did since only three hundred and ten of nine thousand college players make it to the scouting combine. You're old to be getting started, and you may have raw talent but not enough to beat out the draft picks. Instead of trying to be like me, you should've come up with alternative plans when this little charade ended because it was guaranteed to come to an end, Malik."

"I can't believe you just said that shit, Wes," Malik says, slurring his speech.

"Don't be using profanity and drinking in my home on Sunday. That's it. Give me my key back. Get out. And go clean your funky self up somewhere. You can't be representing my family name looking and smelling like you're homeless. I don't want to see you again until you make a decision to be a man and straighten out your life," Wes explains.

His twin takes off his hat and pushes it down on top of Wes's head. Then he answers, "Whether I'm in a slump or not, I'll say what I want, motherfucker. One injury could ruin your career. I hope your cartilage wears out and your knees go bad so you see how it feels when the crowd's not screaming your name. You'll see how it feels when you can't come out of the tunnel or do those damn reverse dunks, just one last time. You don't feel my pain—all you see is you washed-up twin brother. I heard about the Christmas party you had last night that you didn't even invite me to. Every since I lost my contract, niggas been carrying me, acting like they don't even know me. My own brother don't wanna see me no more 'cause we can't go out flossing and get spotted as the powerhouse Montgomery brothers who had football and basketball on lockdown. Excuse my French, ladies, but fuck you, dawg. Take your damn key and kiss my black ass once on each cheek. I don't need you anyway, Wes." Wes smacks Malik's hat off his head and snatches the key. Malik kicks one of Wes's kitchen chairs and stumbles out of the house. No one says a word about the incident, but Shawn is looking at his two-way like he wants me to hurry and finish eating so we can roll out.

    I shamelessly devour my meal and decide that Shawn and Wes's lives are their business. I concentrate on being thankful that I didn't have to pay a dime for a hot morning grub, wondering if I can break away for two minutes to collect my food stash from under the couch in Tomi's lounge. After seeing how Malik was dissed although he was in need, it scared me into telling a tale about having to use the rest room so I could collect my grub.

    About a half an hour later, Shawn and I are dressed, Tomi is hugging me like she's my big sister and really bonded with me, Wes is shaking my hand good-bye like he'd never suffered a major case of the wandering eyeballs, and I'm trailing to follow Shawn who I anticipate will be driving like a speed demon to meet up with the love of his life who doesn't even deserve him giving her the time of day. Now I've seen a whole lot of shit out on the streets, but big timin' in Mitchellville is one strange experience that can scare my curly naps permanently straight!

6
DEHYDRATION

"Are you going to be all right?" Shawn asks me.

"Of course. Big girls born and bred in Baltimore City always hold it down," I tell Shawn as he puts his Olds in park in front of my motel room. I manage to squeeze out a smile.

"Need some change?"

"No, Shawn. I'm good but thanks for looking out for a sista."

"I would stay for a while, but, you know, Jackie's waitin' and all."

"I know. Do you want her presents back? I'll understand if you do."

"No way. You enjoy them. That's what she gets for actin' a fool," he says. I grin.

"You watch yourself, here?" I caution him.

"I will. If you ever come this way again, this is the 1-800 number to my two-way."

"I don't think Jackie will be allowing any calls from people she doesn't know," I tease. Shawn drops his head and confirms my suspicion that she controls his every move and thought.

"Well you know where I work. And oh yeah, Wes said to give you this." He hands me a piece of paper that is folded over several times.

"Jalita?"

I carelessly shove the paper into my pocket, then say, "What is it, Shawn?"

"Don't mention last night to anyone. What happened stays inside of those walls. It's sort of an unspoken rule."

"I'm a quick study. The kid already figured that out hours ago."

"I knew you weren't lying about those street smarts you said you had, ma. The thing is there's a hell of a lot more to you than the outside piece, so don't let Wes get you all wrapped up in some dysfunctional shit. There are hundreds of cons that go along with Wes being able to test-drive a car for a whole weekend or sleep with as many freaks as his king-size bed can hold when he's on the road. As you saw last night, even the married ones can't keep their attention on one woman."

"You're aiight, Shawn, but I'm grown. I know what the deal is. I don't need convincing to stay away," I say, playfully punching him in the arm.

"I can't tell a grown woman what to do, but I know you don't need any drama, so watch it. As you can see by the way Wes treated Malik, he's not exactly the nicest guy in the world."

"Drama is my middle name, but I won't be adding any more by tryna get thick with Wes, so save your worries, Shawn. It won't and can't be like that, and you're *not* my keeper."

"I remember what you said in the bathroom about your moms. It's not your fault. None of your life. Drama doesn't have to be your middle name anymore."

"That goes for you, too, Shawn."

"Maybe or maybe not, but that's another story that's too long to explain. Peace, ma."

"Oh no, you don't," I tell Shawn.

"No I don't what? What are you talking about?"

"I'm talking about you forgetting to hand me that snob's box of things. I know whatever Tomi's got in there can't be all that bad." Shawn laughs. I grin.

Then he adds, "Tomi's gonna question me about what became of her old goods, so I've gotta think of how to manage to stay out of the middle of this one. Last time it was two boxes of belts. This time of year she changes all of her purses."

I open Shawn's back door, slide the box off the seat, then announce, "That figures, but I'll still take it off her greedy little hands. You better not rat me out, either. Now I'm ready to roll out. And you didn't have to offer to carry nothing."

Shawn looks astonished, then replies, "My bad. I'm coming to help you, Jalita."

I balance the box on my knee and open the mint-green motel door, telling Shawn, "Don't bother getting out of the car. I know you've got some other things on your mind, like Jackie. Peace, Shortie Shawn."

When I turn around and look Shawn in the eyes for the last time, I read the hurt in them. For the first time in my life, I'm missing someone who deserves to be missed by me. All Shortie wanted to know was who was gonna love him. Unfortunately Jackie was the last one to be able to give him reciprocity, compassion, and the ability to help him shed the fears of his past.

$

Tomi's stash was exactly as I'd expected. I've never seen authentic Coach bags up close before, but I know these are it. The writing on the knockoff purses is crooked, but these words are straight as a line. So what if everything is in perfect shape though? To hell with accessories, I need clothes and drawers before I think about matching one of the phat Coach bags. After pulling through one of the large bags from Shawn, I locate a pair of sexy, fresh panties that were meant for Jackie, but I have the pleasure of removing the tags to put them on my backside. Thank God Shawn thought of everything that a woman could possibly want on her gear wish list.

Although someone's made it into this sucker to change the sheets, the second set is as abrasive as the first. I can't complain though because bad could always be worse. I fold my hands behind my head and stare at the poorly painted, chipping motel ceiling. I feel like I'm hollow inside and crave someone or something to fill me up. There's nothing. There's no one. I feign for more drugs, but don't know where to get any. Even if I did, I'm not about to waste one dollar bill on a habit I can't support. My mind drifts back to that wonderful sniff, and I fall asleep to R&B music I pretend is jazz 'cause all this cheap motel clock radio can receive is a weak signal of something I really don't want to hear on HOT 99.5.

A few hours later, my stomach is growling, and I hate to do it, but I put on my gear so that I can make the hike to that Chic-fil-A Shawn passed on our way back. If I had a dime for every time I had to walk somewhere, I'd be rolling in ends, but I'm not a pampered Tomi type, so I make that hump until I see the red-roofed building that's got a hot, greasy chicken sandwich waiting inside, just for me.

I say, "Give me a number one meal plus a large lemonade and a small side of fries."

"That's a number four meal, a large lemonade, and one large fry? That'll be $5.10 please," the boy says, then looks up at me.

"No, I said a number one meal, plus a small side of fries and a large lemonade. Don't you hear good? I said plus, meaning in addition to the number one meal."

"That's a number one meal, a small order of fries, and a large lemonade."

"It's about time you got it right. How much?"

"Ahhhh, $7.10," he replies. I give him the money and watch him turn his back, cough over my fries, scratch his left cheek, then put them in the bag.

"Oh no you didn't. I don't play that. Get the manager."

"What?"

"Do it, shortie," I demand. I see a pair of eyes peep between the divider, then they disappear. I know they belong to some employee, so I don't give a fuck. I want the head cheese of the establishment to take notice.

About thirty seconds later, a woman who is taking drive-through orders in the corner area walks in my direction.

"Yes, what seems to be the problem?" the manager asks. She's large and looks like she hasn't washed her uniform in at least seven days. I don't expect her to agree with me that she's got a nasty, funky little worker on her hands.

"First your employee got my order wrong twice, then his nasty butt coughed on my food and he scratched his gross-looking red, pimply face, too. I want my money back."

"They're learning, and it's hard to get good help."

"That's not my fault. Let them learn for free then. I want my money back."

"I tell you what, miss, how about a sandwich on the house?"

"No. I want all of my money back, and I asked for a freaking number one, plus a side of fries, and a large lemonade. I didn't ask for a free sandwich," I say even more irritated.

"Okay, so the original order is on the house."

"Fine, as long as I get my money back, and I don't want that boy to touch my food. I might need to call the health department."

"Look, don't do that. I'll dump the fries, cook fresh ones and have him do some mopping."

"Whatever. That part's your choice."

"Thank you for your cooperation."

I taunt the manager and say, "If you really want to thank me, hire clean help who can just punch pictures right. It's not rocket science."

"Well, until I get more help, this is the crew I've got," she answers.

Before I know it, I shoot off my mouth and say, " I can do better with my eyes closed."

"Are you interested in a position?"

"Maybe, if you give me another free order for my troubles."

"You drive a hard bargain."

"No, I'll just turn out to be your best employee and make you look good to the franchise owner and corporate," I announce with a cocky smile.

"Junior, one extra number one! John, you've got floors."

"So what time you want me here?" I ask, sipping on my first lemonade.

"Night shift. Five P.M. I'll get you an application and uniform before you leave."

"And you will be paying me how much?"

"It's $6.25 to start."

"I told you that I can work fast food with my eyes closed. I've got experience. Is that all your best worker is worth to you?"

"Okay, eight dollars, and that's as high as I can go. If you don't turn out to be what you say you are, it's back to $6.25."

"That'll work. I'm Jalita, and I'll see you tomorrow, boss," I say, reaching out to shake her hand. I own so much pent-up frustration over being constantly dissed and broke that I want to squeeze her hand to death, but I don't. I keep my grip light and pretend like I'm happily gonna make frying chicken my career. The dumb broad who probably has an IQ of a mop is clueless that Jalita Harrison can run her ship real tight, but is only willing to stick around long enough to get a little something something more in her purse.

I'm so tired of pretending I've got my stuff together and so sick of having no one or nothing stable in my life that I give in to my urge to smoke and drink until I fall asleep in my lonely, cheap hotel room. I spot a place called the Starting Gate Lounge. I want to make sure I don't get hit tryna cross the street while lusting after Newports, which I've never had the pleasure of puffing and some kind of cooler that I've seen the college kids get a buzz off, so I remember to look both ways and proceed with caution this time. I open the door that's begging for a wash so badly that I can't see through the dirty film and scan the store for the fridge. I pull out a box of Smirnoff Ice coolers, then set them on the counter so hard they make a rattling, clunking sound.

"I'd like a pack of Newports, please," I say, tryna sound like I've been puffing on cigarettes for years.

"I need to see some ID," the man with an Indian accent says.

"For what?" I ask, beginning my ploy to get my way.

"Read the sign," he says, pointing to it.

"I'm old enough. I've been old enough for a minute," I say, smiling at him and leaning on the counter.

"I've got to make sure I abide by the law, miss."

"Mmm-hmm, I feel you," I say. I slowly unzip my stadium coat and my sweat suit jacket just enough to advertise my two fleshy mounds of size D breasts.

"Now where did I put that driver's license? Maybe I dropped it. I know I had the damn thing when I came in here," I mumble, bending over and putting my rear in clear view, pretending to scour the floor. Just as I finish my snake charmer routine, I come up and see two familiar faces.

"Well, well, look who's here. Sharon Diggs, and in Laurel of *all* places. I thought you would be in Boston watching your mom get out the old pots and pans right about now," I tell Sharon, my former friend from Bentley.

"Jalita. Oh, I uhh . . . Hi," she stutters with embarrassment.

"Lost your words and your ticket home, huh? Now that's bad luck for ya," I say.

"My mom is still tripping over me changing my major from political science to theater. She says they won't pay for next semester if I don't change my mind about choosing a starving profession. You know the drill from home. What are you doing here?"

"The same thing you are . . . save it, Sharon. I guess you've forgotten you told me your mom supported you fully and got over you not wanting to join your dad's law practice. You said you have personal issues with your dad, not your mom. If you're gonna lie, remember your script, because I do listen . . . *even to my so-called friends*," I tell her.

"You remember my boyfriend, Darren, right?" she asks to change the subject.

"Yeah. Hi, Darren. Nice to see you again," I say, throwing up my hand unenthusiastically.

"What's up?" he answers. Darren has an attractive face, but is about ten pounds overweight.

"Oh, that's his sister, Chante, over there with her head stuck in the fridge."

"Can you believe someone put pictures of paper liquor up in the refrigerator? You'd think they'd want to keep stuff stocked. Man, you can get whatever you're looking for in D.C., including a good funeral procession," she complains. Chante is sporting the kind of look where you can't tell which way she swings.

"You can't even buy liquor on Sunday up in D.C., so you need to check yourself on that," Darren reminds his sister, while turning in her direction.

"Whatever. I guess this will have to do then," she mumbles, pulling something out of the fridge.

"Oh, so you live in D.C., Chante?" I press casually.

"Yeah, I love it. I'm smack dab in the middle of everything worth being around. That new convention center is the bomb, too," she answers. I notice her tongue ring, but try not to stare at the tiny silver ball.

"Stop talking about my hood," Darren says.

"You'll get sick of it one day, baby brother. Thirty years of this small town was enough for me. Someone turned up floating in Laurel Lake last week. The crime is getting as bad as in the city."

Darren turns to her and says, "So why you visiting me then?"

"That's a good point. I do have better places I could be," she teases.

"Who are you here visiting, Jalita?" Chante inquires.

"No one. I've got a room for the night. No big deal," I answer.

Darren chimes in and says, "So why don't you come over to the crib and chill with us? It's just me, Sharon, Chante, and her man."

"Thank you, but no thanks. I don't want to be the tagalong. It's obvious that Sharon wanted some time away from me," I say, looking at Sharon dead into her eyes.

"Oh, I didn't mean it like that," Sharon interjects.

"Well from what Ebony said, you had plans up in North West last night. How did you mean it then, since you plain lied to me about leaving town?" I say.

Darren gives a confused look, pauses then says, "Chante lives in North West. I thought she and Maxwell did some last-minute shopping together. Sharon told me she was getting food baskets together for that community service project at school. How could that be?" Sharon doesn't answer Darren. Chante giggles.

"What's up with that, Sharon?" he asks again. Chante giggles louder.

"I-I well . . . I'm busted, all right. I was out buying the gift I gave you. I needed an alibi," she lies. Chante sets the bottles down on the counter, then does a slow jog around the store. I feel the tension building between Darren and Sharon. I want to crack a smile, but I keep wearing my poker face.

"I thought we said we weren't doing gifts this year until the after-Christmas sales to save money. I was confused about why you gave me something so fast. I'm not being ungrateful, Sharon, but come to think of it, you had that Lagerfield Photo cologne in your closet three months ago. You said you were saving it to give to your dad for his birthday," Darren says.

"You know you're always making me account for every second of my time, and I'm sick of it. I have one daddy, and you ain't him!" Sharon snaps. I give myself permission to smirk because I know why Chante has been a giggle box.

"You don't give her much space, Darren. Give the woman a fucking break, boy," Chante says.

Darren snaps, "Why don't you mind your own business? What do you know about our relationship? And I'm all man, I'm not a boy."

"More than you think, *boy*," she says to her brother defensively. All signs of the giggles leave.

"Can't we just let this drop? It's the day after Christmas, y'all. Shouldn't we just be satisfied with spending the holiday together?" Sharon says, tryna skirt the issue.

"Hell no. You've been acting funny all semester. I'm going to get to the bottom of this right now. And what's Chante doing knowing where you are when I can't even get the truth?" Darren presses.

"None of your business. You don't own me, nigga. Who you tryin' to keep on a leash? Ain't no ring on this finger right here," Sharon says, holding up her fingers in his face.

Darren sighs and tells her, "I don't know what just happened here, but I don't like it. I've never seen you trip like this. You're hiding something."

"She sure is. Just tell him about your creeping and be done with it, Sharon," Chante says, turning to Sharon and rolling her eyes.

"Will you stay out of this?" Sharon snaps.

"Oh, I've been deep in it," Chante comments.

"I said shut up," Sharon snaps again.

"What is going on here? Tell me what about creeping?" Darren asks.

"Nothing, Darren. Just mind your business and let this drop, that's all," Sharon tells him.

"Well my girl and my sister are arguing, so it is my business."

"The problem is you aren't taking care of business, so your woman creeps through the day and night," Chante blurts out, then laughs. I finally lose my poker face, and I feel my cheeks moving upward to form a smile.

"Excuse me?" Darren says. "I've got her back at all times, down to buying her books every semester and keeping her freezer full. I work hard to take good care of my Sharon. That's my boo. You don't know what you're talking about."

"Let's buy the drinks and just leave, please," Sharon says, walking toward the counter.

"Well, nice seeing you all. The pictures Ebony took of you, Sharon, were off the damn hook. I imagine Darren will enjoy looking at them as interesting as they are," I say.

"What pictures, Jalita?" Darren asks.

"Oh, you haven't seen them? Oops, my bad. Creeping, creeping, through the day and night," I mutter.

"Bitch, you need to mind your own business, too!" Sharon yells at me.

"I would say 'your momma,' but that would just be too ghetto for my style. Any time a woman has her ass hanging out for the camera, I assume it's to turn her man on, but now I know what I heard about you being confused is true," I spit back.

"I can't take it anymore," Chante announces.

"Don't do it, Chante, please!" Sharon pleads with puppy dog eyes, then shakes her head.

Chante turns to her brother, clears her throat, and says, "Darren, Sharon and I are lovers. She was with me Christmas Eve. Now, that it's out in the open, can we just move on? Damn, Sharon, I've been telling you this could happen if you didn't break up with him." Chante shakes her head, too. She walks to the counter, pays for the Moet minis and Coronas, then watches the Indian man bag the bottles.

"What did she just say?" Darren asks Sharon.

"You know she has a sick sense of humor, baby. She's always messing around and doesn't know when to stop. Let's go. Don't pay her any attention. She's just trying to upset you," Sharon says, pulling on his arm.

"No, no, no. See one of my boys who's a bouncer told me he saw you two all hugged up in a gay club last month during that Gay and Lesbian Pride Festival Weekend in D.C. I told him he was mistaken since he met you both just that one time I threw the New Year's Eve party last year. I swore to him it was a case of mistaken identity. I insisted that neither one of you would betray me like that," Darren says, nodding like everything has come together.

"I've never been in a gay club in my life. You know I was raised strict.

I could never be seen walking around with some proud gays and lesbians. Someone might mistake me for being funny. How ridiculous is that?" Sharon insists.

"Please! Just stand up to my brother. He ain't nobody. Your ass had a blast that weekend. I'm tired of this shit. This is why I don't like creeping with other bisexuals. Y'all always want to be all secretive. I'm going to the car. Don't take all day. I'm ready to get my drink and eat on, so hurry your asses up," Chante says, holding the bag in her left hand.

"Me, too. I'm not putting my business out in the street," Sharon says with no sorrow in her voice.

"You haven't been breaking me off too much either. Damn. It is true. This is the worst day of my life," Darren says, standing on the sidewalk.

"All right, fine, nigga. Since you wouldn't leave it alone, I'm gonna give you the 411. I like the way Chante makes me feel. She listens when I need her to. She takes me out when you want to run the street with your boys," Sharon belts out, then pauses.

Darren asks, "So what, now I'm not good in bed?"

Sharon explains, "Me cheating on you started out as a convenient sexual thing. I love you, Darren, but what I feel for Chante is a stronger sexual desire. She even isn't afraid to lick my pussy. That's more than I can say for your missionary-man ass."

Darren angrily blurts out, "What are you saying? I let you get on top. I handle my business." He balls up his fist and bumps his chest three times.

"Chante's twice the man you are. I didn't want to say anything before, but getting on top of you is like floating on a waterbed. You stink like a toxic garbage dump when you come home from work. My future is standing over there. I'm her freak and her whore, so just live with it already and accept that you're history, honey."

Chante tells her brother, "Face it, she gets on her knees begging for it. I provide for her in ways your ass can't. See this ring I'm sporting, boy? It's a promise ring from my future life partner, Sharon," Chante explains while holding out her left hand.

"I looked up to you. How could you do this to your own brother?" Darren asks Chante. His eyes begin to glisten.

"You never looked up to me. Mom and Dad are paying for your college. No one sent me. You think you're better than me? Now I've got something you don't and never will have."

"It was never like that. You didn't want to go to college. You ran off and got married at eighteen, and got divorced by twenty. That's not my fault you chose a different life path. So this is about getting back at me, I see."

"I really do like Sharon. She likes me better than you even though I work at the post office and never saw a day of college, Mr. Honor Society, Mr. Momma and Daddy Has Every Trophy You've Ever Gotten for the Debate Team Up On the Shelf."

"Okay, my sister hates me, and my girl betrayed me. Ain't this a bitch?" Darren says, crying.

"Don't blame Chante; now that's a damn good woman," Sharon says.

"The only thing I have to say to you, Sharon, is you didn't take the time to talk to me," Darren shouts, pointing at her, then letting his arm fall. Sharon turns away.

"And you two sick-ass bitches can walk. Don't find your way to my crib, so have dinner somewhere else. Maxwell and I are going to have a talk, Chante. If y'all want to be together, you can put your two Judas heads together and find a fucking ride. As of right now, I don't have a sister or a girl. You trifling asses need to forget that I exist. I am through with the both of you for this—and I mean for life. I hope it was worth it to the both of you." Darren slams the door to his green Mustang. He speeds off, throwing his middle finger up at both of them.

"That boy is trippin', but he'll get over it. My cell was on his backseat. Shit. How are we going to get back to D.C.? I have no communication right about now, and I just spent all my money on this liquor," Chante mumbles.

"See what you did, Jalita. I hate your ass!" Sharon yells at me with tears in her eyes.

"Oh, so now you know me or something? I don't think so. In fact, I've never seen you a day in my life. It must be a case of mistaken identity," I say then walk past her, smirking.

"I'm going to ruin you for this. You just wait until school starts!" Sharon says with a thick cloud of snot dripping from her nose.

"Ebony already laid that groundwork. I ain't coming back anyway. Get yourself a Kleenex or something, baby girl. That snot is nasty as shit," I shout.

"Jalita, you're on foot, so you must be staying somewhere close by. You think you can help us out?" Chante asks.

"I would if I could, but no can do when two heads are better than one. Now I can say I want no part of mistaken identity of being like y'all. I'm sure the two of you will figure out something. Now that Darren's out of the way, Sharon can get a matching tongue ring. Bye, freaks and hos.

Have fun creeping, now that you both can be open about it." I walk into the store. I turn around one last time and shake my head. I see Sharon bury her head in Chante's chest. Just like she said, Chante is busy listening to her, comforting her just like a man would do a woman. If I were a betting sista, I'd take my money to Vegas and plunk it all down to bet they'll be sucking each other's toes and licking holes.

"Now I know I need a drink," I say out loud, looking for some liquor.

I'll buy the coolers for you. I'm old enough," the store owner says, picking up where he and I left off. His fingers fly to ring up the merchandise as I hold his gaze, playing with his head, arousing him into an idiotic zone until he pushes the brown paper bag toward me. I've forgotten that my breasts are still hanging halfway out.

"Thanks for helping me out," I say as I wink at him.

"What's your name?" he asks.

"If you really cared, you'd know from making it a point to eavesdrop when the others gave away the clue you're asking for," I tell him, grinning flirtatiously.

"Were those your friends?"

"Not hardly. I wouldn't claim them if someone paid me."

"Those ladies were wrong to do what they did. I guess they never heard of karma. In my country, you don't do things like that and not expect bad to come back to you."

"I hear you, Mr. Sexy. Well I'm about to get out of here and mind my own business 'cause I've got my own problems to contend with," I say, stuffing my breasts out of sight, then winking at him.

"Good-bye, miss. Come back and see me. Maybe you'll tell me your name next time," he says.

I chuckle as the door closes behind me, thinking that getting what I wanted to numb my pain was easier than I thought. I was finding out that I had the power to turn completely intelligent men to mush and sometime soon, that might come in even more handy than an accidental talent. And since that's the case, I may not be showing up to sling chicken parts around for a few dead presidents the next day. My circumstances leave me dehydrated enough, and it's a mandatory thing that I work my way up to hydration before I wither up like a dead leaf and die. There are three ways to get what is needed: earn it, steal it, or have it given as a gift. It's time for me to contemplate feelin' the groove of option three. With a little fine-tuning, I bet that I can collect cash and a stash of shit that will revive my ass and bring me back to life, good as new.

7

CABIN FEVER

Although I'm dressed and heading toward Chic-fil-A, I find myself crossing the street and heading for the liquor store to replace my cigarette and liquor stash. I have about thirty minutes to kill, so there's no harm in swinging by the Starting Gate Lounge. Ever since I snorted that line of coke, I fantasize about getting high, on any level. The relief I felt when I serviced my emotional issues with a synthetic solution, was all that.

Just as I sashay in, I spot an attractive White dude. He's got a thick Southern drawl, and my palm starts itching like it rubbed up against four vines of poison ivy. I'm sizing him up and decide to change the flow of my plan 'cause he seems like the type who would walk sixty-seven New York blocks to help a woman if he received a distress message and had no other means of getting there. You know, a loyal motherfucker who's got so much love for people, you can always see his angle, even before he makes a move. Men like him are dumb enough to let everyone peep his whole hand 'cause he's got no real street smarts. Big mistake. Big mistake. Huge fucking mistake on this cock sucker's part.

I linger close by to eavesdrop. "Do you cash checks here?" he asks the dirty old Indian man I met the other day who is still rolling heavily accented syllables from between his rotting teeth.

"How much?"

I determine what detour I'm about to take, after my potential client replies, "Two thousand dollars."

"No. We don't have enough to cash that right now. Try the check cashing place about two miles down, then a right. It's called Fast Cash,

I think, or something like that."

My guy says, "Thank you, sir," and turns to walk away.

"You're welcome," the Indian man replies.

I dart outside, sit on the curb, and strain to make false tears flow. I put on my burnt orange hat, unzip my coat, and begin to act like I'm up for an Academy Award.

"You okay, miss?" the man bends down to ask me.

"I'm not okay, but no one cares!" I say, wiping my cheeks dry.

As predicted, he questions, "Well, what's wrong?"

"I don't want to bother you with my problems. Thanks for tryna calm me down though," I say, crying even harder and rocking back and forth.

"I can't leave you sitting alone on a curb like this. Please talk to me," he says with sincerity in his voice.

"What's your name?" I ask, sniffing dramatically, making my shoulders jump for effect.

"John. What's your name?"

"Ste-Ste-Stephanie!" I manage to belt out as I take off my hat and sling it across the lot.

"Why'd you do that?"

"Because I was fired!"

"Fired?"

"Yeah, you heard me . . . let go, terminated, given the big metal boot. The damn boss got mad because she found out I'm in college and will be goin' back to school soon. She said she can't give me part-time hours 'cause the district manager will jump on her ass. This is what I get for tryna do right and save money for my education. I get hated on, and all I got a chance to build up was forty-eight cents in my pension plan! Ain't that a bitch?"

"I'm sorry to hear that. What a bad break around the holidays."

"You're sorry? My parents are dead. I need to pay my own tuition, or I have to sit out a whole semester. That's half a year down the drain, then on top of that, most students who sit out never make it back. Walking across that stage was so important to me. I wanted to be the first of my seven brothers and sisters to go to college. Now it looks like it won't ever happen," I mutter.

"Oh, don't do that! You're much too pretty to cry. Would you take a short ride with me? Maybe I can help you figure something out."

"Well, you aren't gonna chop me into little pieces or anything, are you? The way my luck runs, you're some psycho. No one's ever nice to me. No one. On second thought, thanks, but I'm fine, John. I'm not tryna be rude, but I just want to be left alone right now and just deal with my anger over this. Shit, as if this isn't enough, my coat zipper just broke, and I feel like I'm gonna catch pneumonia. It was a pleasure meeting you. I think I need to fall apart in my own space."

"You're not fine. Aww, come on. I just want to be nice to you. You're having such a hard time right now. It's not safe for a pretty girl like you to sit alone in front of a liquor store, either."

I look at him like a wounded puppy dog and say, "Do you mean it?"

"Sure I do. Take this. It's clean. It's just been in my pocket," he says, handing me a neatly folded Kleenex.

"Thanks," I say, wiping my eyes and blowing my nose.

"Get in, and no more crying," John says.

I pretend to shiver for added sympathy points, then explain, "I don't know if this is really a wise thing to do."

"It's just a ride. We're not even going far. Besides, you need to get out of this cold and warm up."

"Screw it. This is the worst day of my life, so I'll take my chances that you're as sane as you claim to be," I say, hopping into his shiny Dodge pickup, which hums an expensive song.

"Where are you from?" I ask, holding my hands in front of the heating vents.

"Alabama."

"What are you doing out here?"

"I do road contracting work, and I go wherever I'm sent. Right now I'm getting double time and a half per hour to work here in Laurel."

"Oh. So where are we goin'?" I say weakly to reel this green sucker closer to my web.

"To find this check cashing place. I don't have a bank I use around here. I have checks I haven't even cashed."

I pull my hands from in front of the vent and let them fall to my sides. Then I respond, "Okay then. So . . . do you have a wife?"

John answers, "Me? Oh no. Who's gonna put up with waiting for me to come home? I'm gone more than I'm in Alabama." He chuckles like a goofy kid.

"Some women would. There's someone for everybody, so they say, at least."

"Do you think so?"

"Most definitely. And it's not like you're ugly or anything. You're kind of cute, and you're all tanned and shit. Women love that, but don't go getting a big head on me 'cause I gave you a compliment, though."

John begins to blush and can't stop his Howdy Doody grinning. After a pause, he says, "If what you just said is true about me, let's go on a date tonight. You don't need money or anything. I'll take care of whatever you need, Stephanie."

"I don't know. I'm not in the best of spirits. I just feel so bad, I wish I could just shrivel up and die. I wasn't tryna put myself in the mix, I was just saying, that's all."

"Come on, it'll be fun. Maybe I can raise those spirits. You don't have to feel so bad."

"Let me think about it then. I just don't think I can be much fun. I just want to sleep and forget this whole day. I think you should step out solo, so you can test my theory about someone wanting to be with you, John."

"I'd rather get a smile out of you, and a yes to follow it up. I really want to spend some time with you, Stephanie. All I'd do is think about how you're feeling all night."

Since this sucker was dumb enough to let me see him walk out of the check cashing place with a fresh bulge in his wallet, and sympathy for someone who didn't even deserve it, I consider it a sign that I'm supposed to pass on showing up for my shift at Chic-fil-A to practically run things.

I sit in the passenger's seat schemin' on how I'm gonna spend a good bit of his check and get him lit up to give away a little more that night. Now that I'm holding the remote to determine which ending I wanna see, I know I'll be picking out a full-length coat to get John's spending mood warmed up. After I play helpless, "Stephanie" will laugh all the way back to her raggedy motel room before he realizes he's been set up.

Just as I'd planned, I break John down like there was nothing to the shit. It's 6:00 P.M., and I'm exhausted from lying my ass off, shopping at Laurel Mall, and eating some decent Italian food from Olive Garden. The more I reminded John of my amended hard-luck tale while we were munching on bread sticks while the pasta was boiling in the kitchen, the more he kept peeling twenties, fifties, and a few hundreds off that pretty fat wad he cashed when we made our way past stores in the mall.

I almost tripped over taking him for a ride until I decided I couldn't feel sorry for him. Regardless of what my beer-guzzling, racist stepdad said, John can seize an opportunity to easily make more in his White man's world. I'm not taking food out of his mouth; all I'm doing is letting him put some in mine. There's no real damage that I've done, so I won't even trip like that over me gettin' a piece of some hand-me-down action from the Federal Reserve. This isn't racial, it's business.

Unless I find a chiropractor to run some game on, I better invest in one suitcase before I leave this town. I refuse to keep up with all of these plastic shopping bags while carrying a load of books on my back anymore. As much as these dead trees with covers set me back, I'm not dumping them off anywhere just yet. Who knows, they may even prove to be useful, somehow.

I've got exactly two hours before John is gonna come a-knocking to pick my butt up. He'll be back, that's for sure. Even nice guys want to collect when they give something for nothing. In other words, there's never a something for nothing, there's always a something for something. Quid pro quo is how everyone in this world rolls. I've never thought about lying on my back with a man who had all cream in his heritage though. Tonight will not be that night, but maybe another time. John is good practice for me to understand a White man's psyche. I think of him sort of like a prequalifier to get to the reward. I have no idea what scripted scene I'll use, but I damn sure know that I better transform myself into a sexual vixen and look the part of being a college girl fantasy. I'm about to lay it on thick, so I can turn him into a blithering idiot who's deep into the "Stephanie" trance.

I turn on the tinny sounding clock radio, hop into the shower, rub a new bar of motel soap over my body, and touch myself in ways I've never bothered to do before. I caress my own neck, rub down my legs, then allow my hands to slowly travel to my fleshy brown breasts as I stroke them as gently as a tender lover. I close my eyes, wishing I had someone to care to touch me that way, but I don't. I move my hands toward my vagina, and wonder what all of the hype about a G-spot is about. My wondering is short lived 'cause when you don't love yourself, you can't pleasure yourself for long. The only way I can allow it is to escape my reality, and only if a man's hands are doing it.

I step out of the shower, wrap myself in a towel, walk over to the mirror, and just stare at my brown face. Funny thing is people have always told me I was a pretty little girl, then a pretty teenager, then finally a fine and phat-butted woman. I never saw myself as attractive. All I could really see was the ugly that covered me, the ugliness of familial rejection, unstable homes, and street life. But today, I must admit that I see it. Even if my momma hated my brown, curly-haired ass, I am beautiful as they come. Men want me. Many of all races have tried to buy me.

Some have tried to worship me. See, Momma's wrong about this right here. I'm worth a whole lot of attention and get my fair share of thumbs-up. At least in this fantasy world, I'm somebody special, even if I don't feel like I'm worth as much as a tin can on wheels.

I'm use to cheap makeup, like Wet-n-Wild you throw in the cart at CVS in a pinch, only to be set back a dollar or two. John informed me that I deserved some Mac cosmetics. He told the saleslady to find suitable colors for me, show me how to apply the basics, then he paid for some really pretty lipstick, a tube of sultry lip gloss, and a bottle of smooth foundation. I'm not into makeup much, but nights like this, I appreciate having some lip gloss to slide across my half moons, so when I decide to turn on the sex appeal, it will sure enough stand out and fuck up some man's mental clarity.

Now that I'm finished doing up my face and sliding into my Victoria's Secret bra-and-panty set, I'm feelin' like a nubian goddess. I'd rather be sporting my classic raggedy look, but I know it's been retired, so I throw my everyday jeans and T-shirt in a dirty clothes bag in the closet and pull the tags off of a fire engine–red silk mini-dress.

I've never had the pleasure of picking and choosing what I want, deciding what fits best behind the door of a ladies' fitting room, until today. These pantyhose alone were ten bucks, and these suckers better last more than one time, costing that kind of money. I slide them on, and they feel smooth, light, and strong enough not to run on my first night wearing them. My stilettos are my last stop before I reach divaville, so I slide my size eight foot into these fly shoes we got from Hechts, and I feel like a sultry, sexy, legit bombshell. I peep at a reflection of myself by looking over my shoulder in the mirror, and yeah, now I see what the fellas are talking about. I do have a phat ass. I'm hoping it's not too phat for John 'cause he's probably use to tiny White women booties, and all I'm interested in right now is his taste, his opinions, and what floats his Southern boat.

I hear three taps at the door. It's got to be John, so I clear my throat, spray some Glo by J.Lo on my neck and wrist, and breathe deeply twice to center myself. I'm ready to con him like a motherfucker. I squint through the peephole, and the Southern sucker who's about to lose control of his wallet is standing tall. So what if I don't have a plan? That's what improvising is for.

"Stephanie!" John says, looking me up and down.

"John," I respond, realizing how much his Southern twang hurts my ears.

He tells me, "You look, you . . . well, you . . . Here, this is for you." He hands me one of those ultra tacky plastic red roses that mostly all gas stations carry, looking me up and down over and over.

I play dumb and respond, "I didn't quite catch what you were tryna tell me, but thanks for the pretty rose. Come on in. It's freezing out there."

"Well, I was just saying that you look absolutely, positively like moonlight on a clear night—simply stunning and beautiful," John says. I hold in my laughter 'cause one little chuckle will lead to me peeing on myself. That was just too damn corny for my style.

"Thank you," I say with a fake shy smile. I really want to notify him that I already know how good I look and how fine I am.

"So where would you like to go?" he asks, still staring at me.

"Actually, John, my mood is still kinda low, and I was wondering if we could alter our plans and stay here. I don't feel like being around a crowd of happy, laughing people."

"But I would love to take you out and show you off."

"I'm truly not up to it, nor do I want to discuss my problems at a pleasant time like this."

"Stephanie, if something else is wrong, please share it with me."

"I don't have a place to live, school's up in the air, and every time I look at my book bag over there, I just get preoccupied all over again. That first-generation college student dream . . . all of it gone down the fucking drain. I can't shake that thought. I go from honor's student on the dean's list to being just homeless and hopeless. I guess I better get use to scrubbing toilets or something similar. Do you see why I want to leave the topic alone for the evening?"

"I understand how you must feel. Gee, no place to live either?"

"Not if I don't get a car in a hurry so I can commute to save on housing fees, and that's if and only if I'm lucky enough to get my spring tuition paid. You know I was thrown out the day before Christmas? That's why I'm here. All because someone framed me and made it look like I did something I really didn't do," I say, mixing truth and lies for added sympathy.

"Wow, I'm so sorry. I wasn't expecting to hear something like that."

I take one look at John's electric purple polyester suit that he has ironed so many times it's shining, then I decide there's no way in hell I'll be caught in public on his arm. He'll have to pay a female escort for that. I think fast on my feet and tell him, "I tried to warn you that I have too many issues. Anyway, can we order in because I truly prefer to hang out here?"

"Stephanie's wish is John's command," he responds. I'm relieved the cornball complies. "What do you eat?"

"Food."

"You've got to be a little more specific, sweetie."

"Good food would be a plus. I've gotten so use to missing some meals that I'm use to hearing my stomach growling," I tell John, hoping to prevent him from considering something like Popeyes popcorn shrimp and a smile.

"Well since I've been here, I haven't been able to find too much good carry-out, but I've got an idea."

"Which is?" I say, batting my naturally long, curly lashes.

"Give me about thirty minutes. I'll be right back."

"Promise you won't stand me up? I don't need one more thing to be sad about."

"Are you kidding? I'd walk back here if I had to."

"Just checking because no one wants me anyway," I say. I knew he was the dumb, chivalrous type, talking about he'd walk back in this fucking thirty-degree temperature.

"I want you to have something decent to eat, so stay put. And for the record, I want you."

"If you say so, John." I sit on the edge of the bed, kick off my stilettos, and reach for any book that will serve as a prop as I pretend to read.

"Boy, you really would miss school, wouldn't you?"

"Yeah, I would, but who cares about that?" I say slowly.

"Do me a favor."

"What?" I ask softly, wrinkling my face a little.

"Close the book. We'll deal with that later. I think you had it right at first, when you said you wanted to relax your mind for the evening."

"Whatever. It won't take away my problem though." I pretend not to notice that he said *we'll* deal with it later, not *you* can deal with it later.

"I have a feeling that things will work out, so stop that, Stephanie," John says with a slight smile.

"I don't know about all that, but I did forgot to tell you something."

"What's that?"

"I eat everything but extremely greasy food, artichokes, anchovies, olives, beets, and unidentifiable meats," I tell him, then chuckle. He bends over to kiss me on my forehead, then leaves in search of some real food, just to please little ol' me. If I had a conscience, I'd bring my ploy to a screeching halt, but I don't believe in feelin' bad if I'm feelin' good. Instead of getting all wrapped up in my lack of morals, I begin to strip and replace my dress with a sexy cream teddy. I look over my shoulder in the mirror and give myself a crash course in ass jiggling. When John gets back, I want him to see what he's about to fantasize and salivate over: juicy, black booty! Now "Stephanie" has a plan.

    Almost thirty minutes later, I hear three familiar taps. I squint and look through the peephole. As expected, John returns with two armfuls of something that smells as good as what use to make my mouth water when I was busing tables, sweeping floors, and doing dishes at Still Hip on the Inner Harbor.

    "Seafood. Shrimp. Lobster. Hot butter. Cocktail sauce. I hope you're hungry, Stephanie."

    "Mmm. Sounds delicious," I say. He finally bothers to notice I'm barely wearing any clothes, and his eyes gloss over worse than the first time. I'm sort of fearing for his health. I don't need no White man dying on my turf.

    "Is everything okay, John?" I ask.

    He struggles to find the words and stutters, "Yeah, yeah, well yeah!"

    "I have a little confession to make. I use to strip to put myself through school. I was so angry today because I tried to give it up and work fast food instead. I told you the rest. You've been so kind to me that I wanted to tell you the truth and give you a little show for old time's sake," I say, looking him dead in the eyes as I arch my back and run all ten fingers across my hips.

    "I'm not here to judge you. You really don't have to thank me," he says nervously. Sweat is starting to pop off his construction-tanned forehead, and I know that he's about to like what I'm about to pull.

    "But I want to, so why don't you sit over there and enjoy brown sugar's show," I say, motioning for him to seat himself in the only chair in the room.

    I finally managed to make the tinny radio cooperate while he was gone. It took me all thirty minutes to do it, but I found 92Q, which is gonna help me out if he's got a dirty mind, and I know that all men except gays have one of those when it comes to gettin' a piece of pussy.

    When I hear Beyonce's "Crazy In Love," I start doing the booty bounce like I'm a backup dancer in her video. My butt cheeks seem to develop a mind of their own. John's eyes are glued to them, and I like being a magnet. Every now and then I make my ass jiggle until it stings.

    "Wow. You are a good dancer. Umm, Stephanie, can you umm, do a striptease for me?"

    I drag my fingers down my neck, smile with my lips pressed together, then say, "It all depends, baby."

"On what?" he asks, wiping sweat from his brow.

I jiggle my ass again, then say, "You've got to *prove* that you adore me. If you give me good reason to show all of my nineteen-year-old body to you and only you, John, I suppose that's what will happen."

"Nineteen?"

I stop moving, turn around, then walk toward John. Then I reply, "Yes, too old to tease you, right?"

"Noo, noo! I just, well, didn't think to ask you, but I was thinking about that age. I'm, ahh, well, forty," John mumbles apologetically.

"So? Age is just a number, and young girls like smart, older men. I would love to please this one if he's smart. Are you smart, John? My guess is that you must be because everything you've told me up to now has been wise," I say, nearly burying his head in my cleavage.

"Yes," John answers.

"I can't hear you," I shout.

"Yes," he answers again.

"What would a smart man do to get a nineteen-year-old girl to rock his world? Stand back or step up to the fucking plate?" I say slowly, rhythmically moving my hips to the song.

"Step up to the plate, of course."

"So ask me what it is that I want then 'cause that's what it takes," I say seductively.

"What do you want, Stephanie?" he asks eagerly.

"A reason to remember why I should be nicer to you. Like *you* said, I don't have to do anything major to thank you."

"But what, tell me what!" he says with sweat pouring down his face and wetting his silk blue shirt that's clashing with his shiny purple cheap gear.

"Cash, so I can go back to school or a used car to get me around," I say, licking one fingertip, then licking my lips.

"Okay, okay. I was going to help you somehow anyway. Ummm, I can do that."

"Do what?"

"Pay you."

"And buy me what?"

"A used car I saw down the street, or, or, or just give you some cash to help you out."

"A car sounds good. I need a whip, John."

"What's that?" John asks, looking half confused.

"A car. So can we get my whip tomorrow, or are you teasing me?"

"I'm not teasing you. First thing in the morning, I'll buy you the whipper," John says, messing up the slang term.

"Then I dance, and maybe more. You'll soon find out how I'm gonna give you a bigger thank-you than I planned for all of your kindness and gift giving, if you play your cards right and keep being that positive motivator," I say sweetly. I see him gulp hard as I moved toward him and drop my teddy to reveal my nakedness. I turn around so that I can rub my ass all over his groin, and feel him growing hard as a brick. I'm empowered by his stiffness, so I tease and dance while almost enjoying this game. I suddenly move away.

"Come back. Where are you going?"

"Just dancin' from over here. Chill out, John. Just keep your eyes on me," I casually tell him.

"No, don't do that, please," he begs. John clarifies his position and says, "I mean I want a striptease, up close, not just a tease."

"Now you know this game well. Give me a reason to come back, and maybe what you'll see is something hot like fire, and you can't get that just anywhere," I explain, giving him a sexy look.

"Here," he says, opening his wallet, searching for a bill, then holding up a crisp twenty.

I move closer and tell him, "That's more like it. If you want to get this party started, I knew your ass was as smart as you look.

"When I turn around, I want you to put it in my butt cheeks, then feel this round brown ass up," I command in a bossy tone. I turn around and feel the money stuck where it should be, then I hear John moaning and groaning like he's being tortured as he gropes all over my ass. I want to keep him sucked into his moment, so I keep talking like a money-crazed 1-900 phone sex operator.

"Now take it out, slowly. With your motherfucking teeth," I say.

"With my, umm, teeth?"

"Yeah, you scared or something, John? I'd do worse than this if you were having a bachelor party."

"No, I'm not scared," he says without confidence. I feel his breath on my ass as he removes the twenty with his teeth. I turn around and take it from his mouth and lay it on the bed.

"Good boy, then continue showing me how smart you are, and put your left foot on the fucking plate you said you'd step up to," I say as I run my fingers through his thick, sandy-brown hair. It feels funny calling a White dude "boy," but I guess I just got one back for centuries of oppression. He just looks up at me, dazed and confused, in disbelief.

I tell him, "Now John, I need your final answer on a little matter we've been discussing. Are you really getting me a whip tomorrow, or are you tryna play me? I'm not tryna be pushy, but I'm not up for another disappointment, my friend. Time to confirm or deny our agreement."

"Yeah. For the last time, I'm really getting the whipper!"

"Good, then a deal is a deal. Now I've got two last requests."

"Now what, Stephanie?"

I bend over in John's face and say, "Smack this fat ass right now." He does, then I order him to do it three more times. Then he starts rubbing all over it and kissing it outright like he's growing a Black woman ass fetish.

Then I tell him, "You scratch my back, and I'll scratch yours. If you want me to finish what I started, open your wallet again and show me the damn money you're gonna spend on me first thing in the morning. You better have at least three thousand in cash . . . one thousand for every smack you just gave your little honey Stephanie. And have you got the juice for me to put these juicy dick-sucking lips to use, or are you just talking shit, Mr. John from Alabama?"

John lays down three thousand dollars in cash on the bed. Then I gloat, telling him, "In that case, I won't be showing you the door. Now gimme that cash."

After I stuff the fresh money into my purse, I watch John shed his clothes. After he gets butt naked, he throws his entire wallet to me, and says, "Here, catch this. I'm not going to blow my chances of being with the girl of my dreams. If you give me what I think you will, I'll take all of my money out, and you can consider the bonus a late Christmas gift."

I look in his wallet, and tell John, "I'm about to ride that dick so hard, I might tear it off your body."

He replies, "I'm willing to take the chance." John grins as his penis grows taller.

I grab it, then announce, "When we finish, I expect that bonus. Now who do you prefer on top, you southern devil?"

I awaken to find that John's Southern self is missing. I look at the pillow next to me that's turned sideways with a head print, then I scan the room, and it appears that we trashed it together. I discover empty bottles of wine coolers, condom wrappers scattered on the floor, clothes and shoes littered throughout, and dinner that is still neatly packaged and never eaten. I try to make out everything, but I can't recall the middle of the events of the previous night, only the beginning that led to me staring at the end. My vagina is sore, my lips feel sensitive, and I feel like I was hit by a train. Well even if John pulled a fast one, and doesn't make good on the car deal, I did take him for a good thirty-six hundred dollars already. What I do remember is him promising me car. I never forget things like getting what I've earned.

I lay my head back down on the pillow and stare at the same ol' chipped ceiling. What I refuse to do right now is to clean this mess up, so I guess I won't push myself to be neat just yet. It's nice to realize that someone's gonna have to wait on my butt for a change.

Just as I begin to drift back to sleep, I hear a horn blowing, and it seems awfully close to the outside wall of the room. I push the heavy, dusty, musty curtains back, and see John stepping out of a gray Toyota. I awaken quickly 'cause I know he wouldn't have traded in that pretty truck for a little Yota so it's got to be my reward for the night before. Before John can give his usual three taps on the door, I fling it open and greet him with a warn, genuine smile.

"Surprise," John says, expecting a hug or some degree of thanks. I run past him in nothing but a robe I'm holding shut with my right hand.

"For me?" I say, opening the car door, plopping behind the wheel, then looking up at him.

"I promised. I told you I was going to help you," he says, opening his arms again. I don't budge and hop out to walk around the outside, looking for dents or rust but I can't find even one cosmetic flaw.

I jump up and down, asking, " So what year is she?"

"An '88, but if you take care of her and keep the oil changed, she'll last you right through school. There's only 80,000 miles on this little baby," he says, knocking on the hood lightly with his knuckles.

"It's perfect!" I scream as he opens his arms again, only to find that I've hopped back into the car.

"And the tags?"

"After thirty days, I'll get you permanent ones."

"*You'll* get me?"

"Yeah, I'm going to see you again, right?"

"Well, you better just give me the registration, and I'll figure out a way to transfer the title."

"The registration is in the glove compartment," he says. I check to make sure he's not misleading me, and he isn't. I know I can get the paperwork done as long as I've got thirty day tags. He's sounding like he's got plans for an us though, and I'm not having all that couple shit!

"This is great and all, but I feel like such a rude fool for forgetting to thank you," I tell him. I reach out to embrace him.

"I know you were excited and everything. It's okay," John tells me.

"Thank you. You're the sweetest man I've ever met in my life, John. I'm sorry you keep catching me in crying spells, but I'm very sensitive," I say, then kiss him on the lips.

"Don't apologize. I like a feminine woman, and you're welcome. You deserve something good to happen after all you've been through. Walk across that stage with the rest of your class, remembering that John from Mobile, Alabama, loves to see a happy female. It was the least I could do for you."

Now that his phat pockets are flat, it's time to roll out. I drum up large tears and prepare for my sudden departure by announcing, "Thanks, but this means—"

John replies, "What's wrong now?"

I sigh heavily, and say, "Unfortunately, I've got to cut out of here today."

"Leave today?" John asks.

"Yes. I've got to hurry and see if I can get my old job back, so I can get ready for school. I don't have long. I hope they haven't hired a replacement girl at the strip club yet, but there's only one way to find out."

"Can't you just call for a status report or get a job here? I thought I gave you enough to get started."

"You said it right . . . get me started. I didn't want to be greedy but tuition is twice the amount you gave me, plus, I still have to buy books and supplies. Stripping down in Virginia is the only way that I know how to come up with the balance in one week, but thanks to you giving me this car I can commute from my aunt's house so I don't have to keep paying to live in the dorm or pay for a meal plan. I wish I could be in two places at once and I also wish I could stop shaking my ass at the club, but Stephanie has to do what Stephanie has to do. You understand, don't you?"

"Awww, I'm gonna miss you. I really like you, Stephanie. I wanted to take care of you, and maybe even ask to date you. What if I helped you out a little more?" I wrinkle my forehead, pretending to be touched.

"Now, John, I'm flattered but I'm the independent woman type. You've done more than enough for me. I don't want to feel like I'm taking advantage of a southern gentleman. That just wouldn't be right. I wasn't raised like that."

John asks, "Well can I at least have your aunt's number? I don't mind driving to Virginia sometimes. Plus, we can go to that Virginia Beach place when the weather breaks and all."

"Well I'm not staying there for sure, and she doesn't allow me to use the phone when I visit. She's a bitch, but that's another story," I tell him, then sigh like I'm reminiscing about a pistol of an auntie. What I wanna talk about is my damn bonus, so his ass better recall that.

"Awww, darn! Well I'll give you my information, and if you come back this way—"

"I'll take it, but who knows when I'll be able to come back. I'm gonna be so busy that I'll have to make a reservation to take a pee," I say. Then I add, "Why don't you take last night's dinner? I can't eat that on the road anyway, and it would make me feel good to know you got a decent meal."

"Are you sure?"

"Yeah. Don't be silly."

"I keep telling you you're such a sweet girl, for a reason. I'll just get it and a few of my things I left in the room."

"I'm really gonna miss you, and you just remember that someone out there is gonna like you as much as I do. She won't care how much you live on the road, so keep your chin up, and don't give up on the social scene. Damn, I hate letting such a good catch go. I can't believe I'm telling you to look for another woman, as hard as it is to find a decent man these days," I say, wiping my last fake tear.

He pulls me close, and whispers in my ear, "Last night was the best experience I've ever had in my life. You take this bonus, and buy yourself something nice. I really wish we could do this again, but I understand why you've got to go. Take care of yourself, Stephanie. The first Black woman I've been with won't be forgotten." John crams more bills in my hand, then embraces me.

In return, I whisper in his ear, "I wouldn't take the bonus if I didn't need it. I should be paying the first White man I've been with. You were off the hook. Take care of yourself, too, John. Remember one thing for Stephanie."

"What's that?"

"*Adventure is alive*. I know neither of us realized what we were getting into, but I'm glad you gave me the privilege of remembering that all work and no play is no good. Now go ahead and get your things before I break down in tears because I've got big issues with saying good-bye."

As soon as John's naive butt gets out of my room, I'm gonna pack my stuff up without even folding it all neat and pretty, pay the bill for this hell hole, and get the fuck up out of this town.

8

ARE YOU BEING SERVED?

Oh shit. I got lost. Well really, I wasn't paying attention to where I was driving. I'm so happy to have some wheels that I got carried away speeding and singing off key so I end up in Baltimore County when I meant to take the Baltimore exit off B/W Parkway to check out some restaurant and lounge on East Preston Street called Center City. I had my lips set to scheme for a sucker to buy me dinner and dessert by letting him believe I had a reservation and my trifling man stood me up. I'm all dressed for the part, too. I know I look damn good in these heels, tight jeans, and tittie top that accentuates my firm breasts. Oh well, maybe another time—no need to stress, I'll just turn off on the next exit that leads to Baltimore County.

I'm assuming that fate has me taking off my stilettos and putting on my tennis shoes to go in to this all night Laundromat 'cause all of my new clothes are almost dirty, and I'm not tryna hand wash all my drawers and other shit. I guess I should make use of my time, but I can kill two birds with one stone since there's a man in the house. It seems like everybody's got a to-do list, no matter what time my butt ends up where. The somebody I'm eyeballing is a man stuffing pint-sized crumb snatcher socks, grass-stained boy's jeans, big bright bloomers, and a bra that looks fit to be a slingshot into the washer. Somebody's wife has him trained like an obedient dog. I like what she's done with the brother who knows that his proper place is right under a woman. That gives a new definition to the phrase "bottom bitch." Who would've thought I woulda managed to find a potential client in a brightly lit, isolated

Laundromat, at an hour when most people are home fussing and fighting, looking at dumb TV shows, or fucking their brains out? Given the hour of what I've seen and observed, I know there's a great chance that he's not gettin' sexually served, and I'll be all up in his pocket soon.

I think of a hook-up opener and ask the stranger, "Excuse me, where can I get a real box of Tide around here?"

He points to the right, not bothering to look up, and replies, "Over there."

"I can't use some little box of Tide like that. I tried them all, and only could get one little box out of the thing," I say.

"That's all they've got in here. The machine supply sells fast and stays empty awhile after it does," he says.

"Oh, well that's typical. *We* must be running this business 'cause it damn sure shows," I remark, rolling my eyes.

"Here, this is my last load anyway. You can have this if you want," the man says, shaking a large Tide box.

"I can't take your washing powder," I say apologetically. I know he is eager to help me because of my good looks.

"Really, you can have it. I don't need to lug this box home with a corner left in it anyway. Go on and use it up."

"Well thank you. I appreciate it," I tell him with a wide smile. I can't leave the kind gesture just sitting in a land of innocence and decide to pry into his personal life.

"What are you doing here this time of night?" I ask, pouring soap powder into the washing machine.

"Washing clothes."

"I can easily see that."

"How about you?"

"Washing clothes."

"I can easily see that, too."

"I guess we're here to do the same thing then. Imagine that, in a Laundromat of all places," I say.

"Yeah," he says, easing into a seat that looks like it can hurt anyone's back problems. I finish stuffing my small loads—one light, one dark—into two machines and plop down one seat over from him. He looks preoccupied and has a double set of king-size luggage bags sitting underneath his eyes.

"So what did your momma call you when you were born?"

"Cleveland, I suppose."

"Your last name isn't Ohio is it?" I say, chuckling. He rolls his eyes like he hates me and all women. It makes me press him harder.

"Sorry about that, I couldn't resist."

"I'm use to it. Women like to give me a hard time," he says, sighing hard. Bingo, Cleveland's wide open!

"Why would you make such a broad statement like that? We're not all alike, you know. I know you've got better sense than to believe that hype," I say sweetly.

"Just because, that's all," he says, propping his elbows on back of the chair and gapping his legs.

"Well since you don't want to talk, thanks for being so nice, Cleveland. I'm sorry if I offended you. Have a nice morning," I tell him in a low, calm voice, moving about three seats over. I let Cleveland believe I thought he and I were finished kicking it and pretend I'm feelin' what Andrew Lesko is saying about free government grant money on his TV infomercial.

I snatch a lollipop out of my jacket, throw the wrapper on the floor, and start making slurping noises like I don't give a damn either.

In less than two minutes flat, Cleveland says, "It's not you. I'm sorry, miss. I'm just having a rough night. What's your name?" He moves next to me and smiles gently.

"Jalita is what my momma named me," I say, fidgeting and hoping it's okay to be bold enough to serve up my real name.

"Don't get carried away with that sucker, Jalita. You might go and eat the stick, and I don't know CPR."

I suck hard with suggestion in my eyes, and reply, "A sucker is made to be sucked, don't you think?"

"I'm not going to touch that with a ten-foot pole," Cleveland answers, grinning like a Chesire cat.

"You must not get out much. I think they were talking like that way back in the sixties."

"No, I don't."

"It shows, but it's all good. So why won't you touch that?"

"It puts inappropriate thoughts in my head."

"About what?"

"Thoughts I shouldn't be having."

"What, are you running for politics or something?"

"No."

"Then fuck inappropriate. Loosen up. It's just us up in here, and this may turn out to be the night to make some wrong things right."

"That would be too good to be true. I better keep it to myself.

Getting slapped is the last thing I need," Cleveland says, looking at me shyly, then looking away.

"Life is too short to hold things in, don't you think?"

"Like I said, I don't want to disrespect you."

"I'm not easily insulted or shocked, so drop the matter of concern. The only way you'll get slapped is if you do it to yourself."

"Well, it excites me. There, I said it, so now you know," Cleveland says, nervously bouncing one leg up and down.

"That's all? So go home and take care of your excitement then," I order him.

Cleveland shakes his head slowly, and explains, "There's nothing like that waiting for this fifty-year-old man."

"I saw your laundry. A set of lips and butt cheeks are waiting all right. Tap her on the shoulder when you get in bed tonight and tell her it's time to get her freak on."

"I can't do that. It's not what you think."

"What, you're washing clothes for your sister and her rugrats? Come on, now. Don't try to play me," I say, slurping again. I know I'm about to get to the core of his problem, and now I'm excited that he's sittin' smack-dab in the middle of my web.

"No, that's not what I mean. I'm married."

"Well I knew that already. Why aren't you wearing a wedding band?"

"I took it off to wash clothes. It's in my pocket, but I told you, it's not what you think."

"Unless the ring is so cheap the gold plating is gonna start chipping off when it hits water, I'm gonna need you to help me out."

"No, that's not the case. I paid a good amount for it," he says, smiling a little.

"So spit out what the case is before your clothes finish the damn spin cycle."

"It's no real marriage, just a paper thing. A formality to keep me on lockdown."

"So why are you washing her clothes then?" I ask.

"To keep the peace with the monster I share my house with."

"What in the hell are you talking about?"

"You don't want to hear all about my problems. I guarantee it. I'm a living example of truth being stranger than fiction."

"Yes, I do. It may help you to talk about it. That's why I keep asking you twenty questions," I say convincingly.

"Are you hungry, Jalita?"

"You must be reading my mind. I haven't eaten all day. My stepfather and I split the last cup of Tropicana orange juice, and I never went grocery shopping. It's not like I have a fine man to wash my dirty drawers."

Cleveland shows off his nice smile, then tells me, "I've got an idea. Since you just finished that sucker and all, maybe you could use a bite to eat and some company."

"Woooh, wooh, wooh, Cleveland. I don't want any trouble with your wife. I respect other people's relationships, even when the other party isn't around," I say like I'm not about to take him up on a free meal.

"No trouble. I have a spot where we can talk until the sun comes up. No one will see us, including my wife. It's as private as it gets."

"I don't have plans or anything, but are you sure about this?"

"Come on. It'll be fun. It's my thinking spot, and it's only about five miles from here. We'll be there before you know it. All I want from you is your company, no more."

"I'll go then, but no funny stuff," I say. I want to ask him what a thinking spot is 'cause I don't know what he meant by that.

"When our clothes come out of the dryer, we can head on out then."

"Dinner's on you, right? I'm fresh out of funds. Spent my last gettin' clean clothes, and I'm in between paychecks. A sista's on a strict budget these days," I lie.

"My invite, my treat. I'm going to run next door and get us some Chinese from Yung's Carry-out. Does that sound good to you?"

"Sounds like a plan to me. Don't let them cheat you out of duck and soy sauce. By the way egg rolls and shrimp fried rice are my favorite. I'm not too much on Chinese folks tryna cook American food," I reply, then smile. Cleveland cracks up laughing as he walks out of the Laundromat.

I won't have to burn much of my gas to get in his head, plus, he's gonna feed me. Oh hell yeah, I'm down with that. Whatever Cleveland has in store for me will be better than getting drunk alone in yet another motel room. I don't want to be alone tonight, and I'm about to get a free meal and maybe more. I'll get my belly full and will let him bare his soul until he gets tired of tellin' me what I really don't give a shit about. If he doesn't turn out to have investment potential, I'm rolling out after thirty minutes of licking the grease off my lips. At least if I'm feelin' full, I'm feelin' something. That might turn out to be my favorite part of the evening, if I can't take control of his damn wallet.

9

TEMPTIN' MR. MARRIED MEAT

Most women don't know the difference between a man and a walking hard-on, but I've seen enough bullshitters to make a clear distinction. A strong man has a cautiousness about baring his soul. He never falls to pieces, allowing just anyone who comes along to pick him up. A walking hard-on is someone like Cleveland, who takes on the appearance of a real man and even a responsible family man, but isn't, if you manage to analyze below the surface. He can switch to hard-on mode with a moment's notice. For example, he has no shame about a woman who may give him some following his dark blue Astro minivan while sporting a MY CHILD IS AN HONOR STUDENT bumper sticker. He's somebody's daddy who will shame his dependent leeches, his Prozac-needing wife, and generations of his last name, goin' through the trouble of goin' to a spot so isolated, it looks like Mother Nature had the blackout of 2003. Cleveland is a dead giveaway. I know what he's capable of.

Since a hard-on has no conscience, a woman in my position is risking that his sexually frustrated ass won't decide to turn into a mass murder or rapist when he discovers his weakness is no secret. Although my nerves are typically strong as freshly brewed black coffee, I'm starting to get a tad bit nervous. The final destination is nearly surrounded by all woods, and I had to drive like five miles per hour down this narrow, dark dirt road before I realized the potential danger. I'll keep it cool though and slide my trusty pocketknife in my shirt pocket just in case the brotha does a 180 on my ass. When he steps out of that minivan, I hope he won't call my bluff to slice or dice his out-of-control dick. He better act right 'cause I can handle anything Cleveland hands me until I get the 411 to see if I can get anything promising up and running. No man will never breathe up on my neck again, unless I say so.

I give myself a pep talk, thinking, *Deal the cards right. Work that shit, Jalita. Deal. Deal. Deal but keep your ace in your hand.*

"We're here. This is it," Cleveland says as he hops out and slams his minivan door.

"What the hell is it?"

"My empire."

"Did I miss something, Cleveland? I can't see shit. Where's your house?"

"Oh, let me shine the bright lights on peace and tranquility, so you can see her."

"What in the hell are you talking about?" I ask, but he's gone. I hope some animal isn't about to eat me 'cause I can't see the hand I'm holding up in front of my face. Suddenly, I'm able to see this huge boat sitting up on cement blocks so high I've got to look up. It's partially painted, looking like it's in the middle of getting a construction makeover.

"Here she is. Inside of here is where I put my thinking cap on and get my peace and tranquility when I can't take the madness at home. I'm remodeling her myself. By summer I hope to take her out for a cruise on the Chesapeake Bay," he explains, knocking on the outside like he's a proud papa who just birthed his progeny.

"Maybe I missed something. I thought you put boats in water if you want to cruise in one."

"Well that's the normal use but my nagging wife drove me to get a ladder, hook up a generator, and sleep in this ol' baby many a night. I was forced to use my imagination. It's not so bad if you concentrate on the good. Let me get the ladder so you can climb up."

"You didn't tell me that we were on our way to stuff our faces and talk in some broke down boat. What are we gonna do, sail around the woods?" I ask, chuckling.

Cleveland shakes his head, and tells me, "This is what I'm talking about. Women just tear men down all the time. I'll lead you out, if you want to leave." He's high-strung for some reason, and I know he's telling the truth about being in a stressful, messy marriage.

"I'm sorry, really. It was just a bad joke. Most people don't think so, but I'm shy, and sometimes I say dumb things when I'm nervous. It's a defense mechanism I've had since I was a kid. I'm working on it though," I say.

Just like that, my smart remark rolls off Cleveland's back. He steadies the ladder for me, then says, "Climb on up." I do. He follows me, then pushes a small door open. We walk through half hunched over. I hear him connecting what better be heat and light 'cause I'm not tryna shiver to death all night just to bump gums in the dark with a married man with home issues.

"There, all set. In a few moments, it will be good and warm in here. Have a seat anywhere, but watch my fishing poles and my daughter's Disney princess scooter though," he tells me. I look over at the three-wheeler. I can't believe he drags his daughter out here to keep him company in the woods.

I sit on the bed and look all around. I know it sounds crazy, but his spot isn't all that bad, minus the growing stack of pizza boxes. If I had one like it, I wouldn't be galloping from motel to motel meeting up with chance.

"So talk," I say.

"Give me a chance to get comfortable first. We've got plenty of time for that."

"You bring me way out here and have me climbing in an arc that's got no water underneath, it better be good, Cleveland!"

"Dag, you called my baby an arc?" he says, half offended.

"Well let me help you out. What do you do for a living? I'm a poor college student on break," I say to get the ball rolling.

"I work at Social Security. I've been there fifteen years. It pays well, and I don't wear myself out. I'm fortunate because a good-paying job with decent benefits is hard to come by. I've forgotten what percentage the unemployment rate is, but it's at an all-time high. Uncle Sam is contracting out most government positions. He'd have to pay me a big severance package to get rid of me though. I'm a grade thirteen."

"I hear that," I tell him, pleased to hear him admit he makes good money. Now I'm motivated to be emotionally available for Cleveland and only Cleveland.

"You know, no one knows what I go through at home. I'm so ashamed. It might be easier to talk to a stranger about my screwed-up life."

"Well what's so terrible about it?"

"I love my kids. They're great . . . five and seven. I'd do anything for them, including lay down my life. That's why I put up with living the way I do. What a life, though. What a life."

"And what kind of life is that?"

"I don't know what's wrong with my wife. She won't touch me, she won't make love to me, kiss me, or even throw a smile my way. The woman has it in for me. Don't ever get married. It's a sentence of hell on earth. I wish I'd figured that out when I was single and happy."

"What do you think is up with the Mrs.?"

"She says it's menopause. I don't think she's going through no menopause. She hasn't done anything with or to me since the five-year-old was born. I use to be her cuddle monster."

"Maybe she just can't manage to get any private time with you because of the kids."

"That's not it but I can't tell you anymore. It's just too embarrassing. You'll think I'm stupid."

Based on what Cleveland's told me thus far I already think he's stupid, but I shake my head and say, "Well if you want to keep this all bottled up inside, suit yourself."

"You'll laugh at me if I tell you. I've never told anyone these things," Cleveland says, hanging his head low.

"Now look, you've got nothing to be ashamed of. The people who don't think they have problems are the ones who have the biggest issues. I'm not a fan of beating around the bush, so since you admitted you have a problem, we can either continue this conversation like two mature adults or talk about what color trim you'll use on the boat, how many square feet it is, and what kind of things your daughter puts in her scooter basket. I imagine that will last all of five minutes. I don't beg no man for cooperation he should be giving me from the get-go. Patience is something I stay short on. Ya feel me?"

Cleveland looks at me and belts out, "It really does something to a man when he works all day long and can't watch *Monday Night Football* and his favorite shows on a big screen he paid for because his wife says the best TV in the house burns too much electricity. And don't even mention trying to have a beer in peace."

"Damn, now that's cold."

"Yeah, I pay the bills. I tell you all I've got is those kids."

"All?"

"Yes, all. I only have two friends left, thanks to her bullying me around and chasing them out if they come visit and we get to talking man stuff in the basement past eleven on the weekends. After the kids go to bed, I'm stuck in misery."

"She sounds like a controlling somebody. You need to stand up against this woman. She sounds more like your mother, not your damn wife."

"I know."

"If you know then I don't understand why you take orders like you're a fucking short-order cook. Maybe you do need your head examined at that mental health joint, Sheppard Pratt. I hear they have psychiatric in-patient hospitalization set up. I know about it 'cause my roommate at school had to get shipped to the place for a while."

"Jalita, I stay married to my wife for the kids. My parents got divorced when I was a kid, and I just would hate for mine to go through that. Who I chose to make babies with isn't their fault. Plus, it's cheaper to keep her."

"So, until your younger kid is eighteen, you're gonna live your life using a ladder to run up in a boat that can't take you anywhere?"

"I don't know. I guess I haven't thought that far ahead," he says, sighing like I usually do. Too bad he owns a penis. I almost start to pity his situation. Then Cleveland says, "I don't know what got into me. When she yelled at me saying all I was good for was cooking, cleaning, and paying the bills, I had to do something about the way I was feeling, so after the kids went to bed, I disappeared the other night and watched a stripper with track marks on her arms move around. I spent three hundred dollars drinking with a stripper who didn't even turn me on. The one I wanted some attention from wouldn't even make eye contact with me. It seems like she took every guy in the back room for a private dance, but me. Maybe she thought I looked cheap because I wasn't dressed up. All I wanted was to be reminded of what a woman looks like under clothes. I face twenty nasty voice mail messages at my work extension every day and walk in on her lying on the phone telling someone how no good I am. So why don't I feel any better since I had my night out?" Cleveland asks, grabbing his head and squinting hard. I can tell I made his blood pressure fly on the high side, so I better calm his uptight ass down.

"Enough about the dancer and your in-house fool. Quite frankly, I've heard enough. Now that you've explained some things to me, I understand your predicament," I say, reaching over to stroke his head and calm his voice. If he spent three hundred bucks to watch booties shake, I can take him easily. He just gave me an incentive to become his surrogate fantasy giver.

"That feels good. She won't even hug me."

"She just made a big mistake 'cause I'll hug you. Now, how does this feel?" I inquire, rubbing my plump breasts against him, and squeezing him like he's the last man on Earth.

"Good. No, better than good."

"Your bald head is sexy, Cleveland. You look like a nubian warrior from the African terrain," I say, giggling seductively and stroking it again. Then I add, "Big daddy, I just want the best for you. Nice guys don't have to finish last; not all women are the same. I told you that before, and it's the truth. It would be like me saying all men are the same, and I know I'd be wrong to say that."

"You care about how I'm feeling and don't even know me?"

"I must know you, if I'm in your corner of peace and tranquility. You think I'd just run after a strange man I've never seen if I didn't feel some sort of concern and connection? I'm sure you listen to the news. There are some crazy maniacs out here who don't mind killing people for next to no reason and I'm sure my family wants to keep me around awhile, ya know?"

"You've got a point. I've never let anyone other than my kids up here either."

"See, it's because you know you can trust me. That's your instincts working for you, Cleveland. I try to make mine work for me, too," I say.

"Jalita, I'm horny as hell. I had to blurt it out like that before I lost my courage."

My palm starts tingling and itching, and I say, "Don't tell me. You need to do something about what you see. When the moon slices through the clouds out here, you'd love to beat up some pussy under the stars after you get your dick sucked. In fact, I bet you dream about the shit almost every night you go to bed with a hard-on."

"How did you know all of that? I couldn't have explained it any better myself."

"You haven't been living under a rock, so unless you're into butthole bandits hitting your back door, you've got to have had those thoughts. You need to get a girlfriend and drop the visits to the see the teasing tricks. All that'll get you is an expensive hard-on. This is the new millennium, and you have every right to blow the Mrs. off. Who *doesn't* cheat these days?" I say to test the waters. I want to see how faithful he is.

"Thought about it a few times, but I don't know. I always thought it was supposed to be one person for life. I told you, I'm a nice guy. I could never cheat and feel good about it. It's just not my nature."

"Well let me give you an incentive to consider getting down like that. Unzip your pants, take off your shoes, and show me what you're working with. Don't think on the shit either, just do it right now," I order. He does eagerly. I take off my shoes.

"What are you going to do to me?"

"Give you a little push to let me watch you love yourself and feel good about it."

"Love myself?"

"Yeah, play with that luscious thing. I wanna see it get hard like when you take that fine body of yours on to bed."

"Okay, but I've never done it before."

"There's a first time for everything. It's yours, isn't it? Or does she schedule your hard-ons, too?"

"Hell no. I'll try it then," Cleveland says. I can tell that I've fired him up.

"I'd touch it and help you get started, but you said you're not sure about—"

"Please touch it. I don't know why, but I do trust you, just like you said," Cleveland says eagerly. I reach through his boxers and feel him harden. He's packing at least nine inches, and I'm wondering if his wife is more interested in someone from Venus than Mars. No woman in her right mind would turn down a thick, long, black cock from a man who was truly a sexy fifty, even on his worst day. Cleveland was hot. He just didn't know he had the power to make a woman's pulse quicken, or perhaps forgot due to a confidence lashing by his wife.

"Feel good?" I say, stroking it gently.

"Yeah, great," Cleveland says, half dreamy-eyed.

"Now you do it yourself. This is the first step of you taking control of your life. I never thought I'd tell a man this, but start by using your little head, instead of your big one." I withdraw my hand. I'm not giving him too much for free.

"This does feel good, but it feels better when you do it."

"Well, if I were a stripper, what would you do to make me make you bust a nut you've been waiting to shoot all over the ceiling of this boat for two years?"

"Pay. I'd want all of the attention from you I could get."

"Well since you put it like that, would you pay a girlfriend? Would you take care of her if she started taking care of you, on the real?"

"Why not? It's cheaper than a stripper, when all I can do is look."

"Cleveland, I've got some good news for you."

"What is it?"

"I'm your new girlfriend, that is, if you can hang," I announce, sticking my left hand in my shirt and stroking my breast to rope him in.

"Uhh, okay."

I know that Cleveland is fantasizing about what my breasts taste like while I completely bare them and knead them so I make my move and ask, "Do you have your wallet on you because I've got financial needs."

"Yeah, I do."

"Good. Open it up. Money inspires me to think of sex under the stars, too."

"That's what I'm talking about, Jalita ... sex."

"Start building some credit with me by taking care of this. Let's see how serious you are, big daddy." I move closer to him, squeeze his muscular arms and eye his huge penis like I want to do more than he hoped for.

"I haven't been to the bank, but here, you can take this," he says, laying down two hundred dollars on the floor of the boat.

"That's a good start. Is there more where that came from without you messing with your 401(k)? I know you have one since you're so use to thinking with your big head."

"You cut to the chase, don't you?"

"Baby, excuse my lack of manners, but I've got to do a little credit check to find out if you've got potential as a good daddy, with no stress or strain," I explain, batting my eyelashes and grinning. "Now are you good for more than a down payment, or what?"

"I've got the credit, baby," Cleveland blurts out quickly.

"Then close your eyes. It's time to get what you need and have waited for."

"I can't wait. It's been too long. Oh shit," he says.

"Calm down and sit back. We don't want no premature ejaculating. I'm your girlfriend now, and I like it long, strong, and all night long, so you gotta learn to represent, big daddy. Control that stick, you hear what I'm telling you?"

"Yes, I'm calm. I'm calm," he says after his rapid breaths slow. I know I'm not giving him much for no piddly two hundred dollars, but I'll give him just enough to make him think there will be a future with me. I stroke his penis with the care and precision of a porn star until I feel his Mount St. Helens yearning to explode. I kiss him gently between his penis and his balls, then stroke faster. He's moaning and groaning like I'm fucking his brains out, when all I'm doing is teaching him what to do when I'm long gone. After a good sixty seconds, I start talking dirty to him.

"Is this pussy good?"

"Hell yeah!"

"Remember how I looked while I was sucking and licking that sucker?"

"Mmm-hmmm," he says, nodding. He's starting to look all shiny and glossy in the low light. I know I won't have to talk dirty to him much longer, and I'm glad. I hate seeing men get any degree of pleasure, even deserving ones like Cleveland. It's time to rush his needy ass along.

"You want more time with me, big daddy? Do you want me to do to you what I did to that sucker?"

"Yeah," he says, panting.

"Well shoot me one mandingo-size nut a mile high. Cum so I can open wide and swallow it like a sleazy, cheap ho from the hood!"

"Ohhhh. I'm about to cum! I'm about to cuuuuuum," he screams.

I look at his throbbing penis and say, " Got dammit, if you think I'm fine and you want to stick your new girlfriend next time that dick gets hard, you better represent by shooting some unborn children all over the walls and ceiling of your boat, like you're excited, you nasty, old Negro!"

His eyes widen to the size of saucers, then Cleveland looks at me and shouts, *"Yes, I think you're fine as shit, and I do want to fuck you."*

"Good, now cum right now, so we can set a time and date for you to bang me on your lunch break. Shit, I'll even fuck you on your boss's desk after everyone leaves. We can do this, Cleveland. All I gotta know now is you're okay with signing up for this fuck fest with no guilt," I say harshly.

"I'm cumming. I'm cumming. Oh. Oh," he screams as he follows my orders. As I watch cum fly through the air I think that although he kept his end of the bargain, I knew good and well I wasn't gonna eat it so it was a good thing it flew out of my mouth's reach.

Cleveland got what he craved, only by self-lovin', which he should have learned to do a long time ago. That stupid ass paid me two hundred dollars to tell him to do something that comes as natural as breathing. Oh well, I guess this consulting fee was to help a dude untangle himself from some hang-ups about goin' blind if he touches himself or whatever. The next step is to maintain this "I care" 'tude and convince him that I'm the real deal.

While he is still breathing heavy and coming back down from his little sex trip, I find an old towel and clean up what he blew from his penis. I know doing this and letting him sleep with his head in my lap will earn me extra points. Cleveland sleeps as peaceful as a baby after a meal and wears a smile on his face to match. About thirty minutes later, he awakens in a jolly ol' mood.

"That was fantastic. I never role-played like that."

"You ain't seen nothing yet," I announce as I kiss him on the forehead.

"I want you to see something."

"What?"

"I'll grab the fishing rods. Follow me. Put on your coat though."

"Okay," I say, following him on the top deck, sliding my arms inside of the sleeves of my stadium coat.

"Look up there."

"Wow. I feel so close to the stars. It looks like, with a little reaching and stretching, you could touch them," I say, like I'm fascinated by Mother Nature.

"I thought you'd like it. I sometimes lay on my back up here, and just fall asleep thinking of the life I'd rather have."

"I see why. You're so sensitive and romantic. I like that about you, Cleveland."

"Ever been fishing?"

"No."

"We're going now."

"What?" I say, wondering if I made a mistake heading to his spot. This shit is getting stranger by the second, and I'm tryna play it cool, but he's working me up to a mild worried condition.

"This is how you cast," he says, throwing the line outward.

"Fine, Cleveland, but it's cold out here, and there's not even any water. Save it for after the restoration project."

"Just try once. Be spontaneous. You just taught me all about that," he says, handing me the other rod. I do, just to shut him up. He already gets flack at home, and I won't give him more. I want to be his perfect little girlfriend fantasy, for at least about a good ten minutes more until I make it clear I've got to roll out. I won't burn my bridge, in case I decide to come back.

"You're a fast learner. You're right, okay, I'll practice what I preach. There, I did it!" I say.

"Let's get you out of this cold. Wind it back up like this," he says.

I mimic what he does, then I say, "That was kind of weird and all, but it was kind of fun. No one ever showed me how to do anything like this. I almost feel special you shared that with me."

"You *are* special. The more time you spend with me, the more I'm going to show you my credit check is good on all levels."

"You're too much. I wish I was the one married to a man like you. You know, you're the total package, Cleveland. Kiss me. I want to remember this night for always."

"Mmmm. Don't mind if I do, Jalita," Cleveland says, reaching over to smooch. When he tries to kiss me on the lips, I correct him and say, "Ahh, ahh, ahh, on the cheek. Save the kisses on the lips."

"For what?"

I grin at him, wink, then say, "The day you divorce your wife and come home to me. Remember that I'm the one who's willing to take care of every hard-on for life."

"What are you saying, Jalita?"

"This may be hard for you to understand or believe, but I think I just found my husband-to-be. I really didn't intend on saying all that since I don't want to scare you away, but I know what I feel, and that's love at first sight. Now I don't know where all this can go, but I'm just putting my cards out on the table 'cause something is leading me to be honest and upfront with you this early on."

"In that case, I'll kiss you on the cheek while I wish under these stars that maybe there was a bigger reason you ran out of Tide. By the way, I'm not scared of that thought one bit. If I had a wife like you, I wouldn't be using the boat as my convertible sofa," Cleveland says like the romantic he is, then kisses me on the cheek, just like he promised to do.

We settle back down inside of the belly of the boat, talking, laying around while I stroke his arms, back, and bald head. I wonder what time it is, but we end up passing time as Cleveland tells a thousand stories about his kids who really do sound like gems. About twenty minutes later, I hear movement outside. Cleveland tells me that strange animals sometimes roam around his spot, and that's all it is. He lays his head back down on a dark, balled-up blanket and keeps on talking until we hear footsteps.

"Cleveland, Cleveland. Answer me. I know you hear me," a husky, transvestite-sounding voice says.

"Oh no, it's my wife," he says, sitting up.

"I thought you said she never comes out here," I snap. I suddenly wish I would've followed my intuition and rolled out after my thirty-minute time limit passed a while back.

"Big Shirley usually doesn't. She was raised in the country, but doesn't like the animals and all the darkness."

"Well unless she's got a clone, she changed her mind tonight. You better handle this and get rid of her," I tell Cleveland. I should be concerned that he described her as Big Shirley, but by the looks of those bloomers in the wash, I can imagine the size of the woman outside.

"I'm up here," Cleveland says.

"I've got a bottle of wine, the kids are with my sister, and I'm alone for a reason, Cleve."

Steps are getting closer to the boat, and I hear her starting to climb the ladder.

"Throw this blanket over your head. She's coming up," Cleveland whispers. I crouch down in the corner farthest away from the front of the boat and throw an assortment of junk on top of myself. I feel the boat vibrate as she takes each step, and wonder if they ladder is gonna give while she's climbing it, but luck is on her side, and her egg-looking self makes it on up.

"Cleveland, they say the truth will set you free. I need to be free. I just need to let out some things on my mind."

When I hear, "But what's the BB gun for?" I make it a point to peek through a slit I created in my shield. The neckless woman holding a rechargeable lantern is wearing electric blue eye shadow, orange lipstick, and her hair is dyed the kind of blonde that doesn't fit someone with a brown complexion, let alone midnight black. Damn, she reminds me of a gorilla with makeup on. I wish her light would go dead so I can't see her face. The wide gap in her teeth sets the shit off. No doubt, one of those people from *Ambush Makeover* TV show needs to get a hold of her ass and work their magic.

"You know I'm scared of these animals. I gotta have it just in case these critters come visiting. I don't mind making me fried rabbit or deer steaks. They can make my day if they want to," Shirley says.

"Why don't you give me that?" Cleveland responds, tryna convince her to hand it over.

"No way, Cleve. This is my protection. If I hear anything even move, I'm shootin'," she responds. He laughs nervously. I gulp hard.

"There's really no place comfortable for you to sit up here. Let's go home and talk there," he says.

"No, this is the perfect place for me to come clean. I've got wine for after, and everything."

"We don't have glasses. Come on, honey, let's go home and do this."

"Nonsense. I've got paper cups in my other pocket."

"Oh," Cleveland says, half stunned and disappointed.

"Reach in," she says. He does. Next, I hear Shirley giving him wet, sloppy kisses like a damn labrador retriever. It's enough to make my stomach turn the Chinese food rancid.

"Open my coat, Cleve."

"Well, ahh, okay, but I don't know why you want me to," he says. He does. I hear him scream,

"Ahhhhh! What's that on you?

"Lingerie, fool. You need an eye exam now or somethin'? I found it at Lane Bryant. They started carrying big women's sexy stuff. Ain't it nice?"

"But you don't wear that kind of sexy stuff."

"I do now, startin' today, and always. Just call me Super-Sized Mrs. Sexy!" she says, then giggles, and exposes her breasts, which look like at least ten kids were fighting over sucking her tits when she had milk.

"What's gotten in to you, Big Shirley? Cover yourself up before you get a cold. You know we're out of vitamin C at the house."

"Don't be tellin' me what to do, Cleve. This is what you been lookin' at, so I thought you'd like to see it on me. You didn't tell them hos to do no covering up, so shut your mouth. This summer I'm wearing bikinis, midriff shirts, and letting it all hang out when you take out this boat on the Chesapeake Bay."

"Whaaa-Whaa-What?" Cleveland says in a row of stutters.

"I know you went to see some strippers. They ain't got nothin' Big Shirley don't, and Big Shirley don't have nobody temptin' her man! Go over in that corner and close your damn eyes," she says.

"For goodness' sake, calm down, Big Shirley. I don't want to," Cleveland protests.

"You won't what? I don't know where all of this backtalk is coming from, but I don't like it. The day I married you is the day you became my property," she says, placing her hands on her hips with balled-up fists.

"I don't care what you say anymore. I said no, I won't do it." I watch Cleveland turn around to walk up on deck when Big Shirley hits him square in the right ass cheek.

"Oh really? Well that's for spending my hard-earned money in some raunchy strip club! You knew better than to think you could get away with slipping out on our anniversary. I guess you thought I forgot, huh?" she asks.

"Ow! What'd you go and do that for, you big abusive bully? I'm tired of you smacking me around, bossing, and taking all of my money! Every payday, you start something. I can predict it like clockwork, and I'm sick of it. And you put me out on our anniversary, remember?" he says, rubbing his butt.

"If I've told you once, I've told you fifty times, I'm the ruler of our home, and you won't do a thing without my permission. I never told you to go to no strip club. You'll do what I say, and I say your eyes better stay on this right here. Your money is suppose to go straight to my hands. You have the guts to call me a big bully now, huh?" she says, aiming at poor Cleveland. This time she's aiming at his penis. Most people talk about domestic violence against women, but today I'm learning firsthand that there are some men roaming this Earth who catch it, too.

"Sorry," he says.

"No, say it right!" she replies, still aiming at him.

His tone changes, and he tells his wife, "I won't go anymore. I'm sorry, love of my life."

"And?"

"I'll come straight home as soon as I get off," he says. His knees fold inward like he's in pain. He's shielding his crotch with both hands.

"And?"

"I don't know what I left out, Big Shirley."

"You love me, and you're where you need to be. You know the drill. You better tell me somethin'!"

"I love you, and I'm where I need to be!" Cleveland parrots back.

"Come here, lover. You're so beautiful. I don't need to look at other women. I was wrong, and I knew it. That's why I planned to bring home Chinese for you. It's in the car. I know what you like, and I know how to listen to you for my own good," Cleveland says. Big Shirley stops aiming the gun but still holds it in her right hand. Cleveland puts on his shoes.

"Awwww, you were thinkin' of Big Shirley?"

"Yes your Cleve was. Now come on, let's go. Sexy ladies first," Cleveland says. He thought fast on his feet and thank God he and Big Shirley make it down below.

I lift the blanket from my head. I hear them talking and Big Shirley nagging just like Cleveland told me. She's pushing out hot air with complaints about no egg rolls and why he forgot the pepper steak and didn't put fabric softener in the eight loads of clothes he washed and folded. Big Shirley locates an extra plastic fork and beings to shovel the food in her mouth like it's about to hop up and run off the damn paper plate. I roll my eyes and keep peeping out of a window.

"Cleve, what's that over on the other side of the boat?" Big Shirley asks with her mouth full.

"What? Nothing. I don't know what you're talking about. Let's go."

"Well *nothing* is a car!" she exclaims. I hear her revving up her violent tendencies. She drops the Chinese food container and shoves the fork in her pocket.

"Maybe someone broke down. Cars do that a lot in winter weather, you know. Let's go," Cleveland says.

"Why would someone go down a clearly marked private road to

break down? You not telling me somethin'. I'm going to my car to load more BBs. I'll get it out of you since you want to play games!"

"No, no, no. I'm telling you the truth!" Cleveland says, watching Big Shirley open the car door to find her bullets.

"Then you won't mind me shootin' the trespasser," she says bending over and loading her ammo. I can't risk crossin' paths with Big Shirley's strong grip, so I bolt down the ladder in my socks, run to my car, hop in, and reverse it like a maniac. I back into a tree, put the car in drive again, and make dust fly as I bolt down that narrow, dark road. I hear Big Shirley screaming and threatening Cleveland and me.

As I bolt past, I knock over the yellow recycle trash bin. Bottles clank and spin everywhere. By the time I hit the large metal trashcan, I hear, "You had the nerve to invite one of those slutty strippers down here? Open your damn wallet. All my money better be in there. I know it's payday!"

"You're the one who needs an eye exam. That was Gus."

"That was a nondriving woman, you lyin' worm. My money's missin', too. I'm shootin' her clumsy ass, and you will clean up every shred of that trash! I been telling' everybody you're no good. I can do bad by myself, you know. Nobody pulls one over on Big Shirley!" she says, hitting my back windshield. I begin to disappear over the slight hill. My head hits my ceiling from movin' too fast on that rocky road, but this is not the time to creep. I manage to get away and sigh with relief.

When I make it to the intersection, I can't decide which part of my body hurts worse—my head or my feet. I vigorously rub my head, wondering if I need ice to keep a knot from growing. Just as I reach down to pick these round prickly gum ball–looking things that appear in the winter from off the bottom of my socks, I hear one last bang.

Cleveland should stand up to Big Shirley like a man, take out a restraining order and run to the nearest strip club, or better yet speed to a divorce lawyer. How can a piece of married meat that fine be the captain of stupidity when he hasn't even been getting served? If his boat or balls gets shot up, it's not my fault I disturbed the distribution of household income just once. Shit, I invested all of that talk in him, and it all went down the drain. I don't appreciate getting cut short or being right about him not being a real man.

Cleveland left his wedding ring in his pocket at the Laundromat for a reason. Now he's got a reason to drink a six-pack of vodka miniatures, put the ring back on, and shut up his damn complaining 'cause I'm not the one to listen.

10
TAKIN' IT OFF THE TOP

I stuff my two new bills into my cigarette tray, considering how lucky I am that all the damage that was done to my ride was two small BB marks on the back window. I can live with that since the BBs didn't even break the glass, but I'll take this warning as serious as a heart attack: no more flirting with other people's married property for me. That Cleveland wasn't worth me losing my damn head. I would have gotten smoked over a small cut over next to nothing had that bullet made it in me. That alone is a good reason to break it off with Cleveland. Between Tony, John, and him, I've discovered that older isn't always better or more mature. Sometimes it's just, well, older.

By the time I cross Washington Boulevard, PSI Net Stadium looks close enough for me to reach out and touch it. I'm reminded of how much money men who bat balls for the Orioles and chase a football for the Ravens make. A homeless man dressed in filthy army fatigue pants holds out a cup and squeezes a dollar out of the moral conscience of a driver, two cars in front of me. He happily runs to the curb and throws up his hand when traffic begins to move. *I can't be him. I refuse to be him.* Broke. Destitute. Satisfied with insulting, pathetic, measly handouts. After all I've been through in life, it's time for me to roll with premium-grade men and take my cut for my troubles off the top.

As I'm coming off the Russell Street South ramp, I'm thinking that I now see no justifiable reason in shooting for the mid-grade quality, when I don't have to aim low. Wes's nutcase woman, Tomi, was right about one thing: Why fool around with broke men with no real assets when they're gonna turn out to be dogs anyway? Might as well get played by ballers and shot callers who earn their paper the prestigious way. Anything short of that is effectually a waste of time. Perhaps Tomi was wrapped tighter than I originally thought. Maybe that's why I'm vibing that her bark is probably no more than a territorial threat. Now that I don't fear being bitten, I'm salivating for landing a sure shot. I know a sure shot, and his name is Wes Montgomery.

I pull into a Texaco gas station at the bottom of the hill, unzip the inside pocket of my Coach purse and unfold the piece of paper Tomi's man sent to me. It reads: IF YOU KNOW WHAT'S GOOD FOR YOU, HIT ME UP ON MY CELL @ 301-215-6317. When I realize his number is long distance from the 410 area code, I spring for a five-dollar calling card and put it to use.

"Hey, Wes. What's up?" I ask when he answers.

"Who's this?" he says, sounding confused.

"It's Jalita. You've got so many hos you don't know which one you're talking to, huh?"

"I didn't recognize the number on my caller ID, smart ass, but it's about time you called. You're late, beautiful. My holiday break doesn't last forever, you know," he says like he's been expecting my call.

"You tell me why I need to call you, if I know what's good for me? What do you know that's so damn good?"

"My house, my cars, my motorcycles, my job, my title, and best of all my looks answer all of that," Wes says.

"Aren't you full of yourself to the brim?" I comment, rolling my eyes.

"Why not be? I'm Wes the best from the east to the west, baby girl. Women of all ages stand in line to get the digits you were slow to use."

"And how long did it take you to think up that one?"

"Are you outside or something? The reception's bad. I can barely hear you."

"Yeah, well I'm in Baltimore on a pay phone. I'll hold my mouth closer to the receiver, but getting that close to germs freaks me out. Who knows where these people's mouths have been?"

"That's better. I can hear you know."

"If you can't, you're out of luck. I'm not getting a millimeter closer."

"Pay phone? No one uses them any more. No cell?"

"If I had a cell, do you think I'd be touching a germ-infested pay phone?" I say half irritated.

"You are living in the dark ages, beautiful, but it wasn't meant to be an insult."

"Well not everyone has money to live large, Wes," I explain. I'm laying the foundation for whatever he's willing to build.

"That's what I hear, and I didn't always live this large."

"I had that feelin'. It shows."

"What's that supposed to mean?"

"People from money don't usually flaunt the shit out of it, like it's goin' out of style. Only hustlers and men who didn't have it like that growing up get off on that bling-bling shit," I tell him.

"Whatever, Jalita. Where are you headed in Baltimore?"

"To a cheap motel room," I say.

"How come?"

"Long story. Nowhere to be Christmas break."

"Damn, girl. You're making me feel guilty for living large."

"No need to be sorry 'cause it's your world, and you told me you always didn't live large. Look, I just wanted to say hi. I'm tired, and I wanna get a room. Last night was kinda rough, so I prefer to get off my feet instead of yapping with a star who can no longer relate to roaches, rats, and damn near getting a heart attack just tryna live from day to day."

"Would you like some company? Better yet, would you like room service overlooking the Harbor . . . that is if you can stand a taste of my standard of living. It would give you a chance to get off those feet, too, beautiful."

"Suppose I do like the sound of that, what about your other half?"

"Tomi is out of town for at least another day, and she's not my other half. I'm a whole person with or without her, so you better put that in the front row of your memory bank."

"Come on up then, if you're sure she won't mind you flaunting your cheese to impress me a little bit, although you try to act like you run things at home. Boy, have I met some pretenders lately. Their balls are just empty. No weight in 'em whatsoever," I tease.

Wes becomes blatantly flirtatious, and tells me, "Girl, you need to be spanked to have some discipline smacked into you. I don't know about those weak-ass niggas you've been running across, but I can run a whole lot at one time, including you and my woman."

"Tomi, did you hear that? Your man is getting fresh with me. Put your boxing gloves on, girrrrrrl," I tease.

"I never slip up. She'll never hear what I don't want her to. Just stop wasting my valuable time and tell me where to meet you."

"I'm at a Texaco gas station just as you come into Baltimore, off the B/W Parkway. You can't miss it. It's the second station on the right."

"I know where you are."

"So get here then."

"I'll be driving a black Mercedes SLK coupe. What are you driving?"

"An '88 Toyota. No need to mention the color. You'll spot me right off."

"Damn, you've got to upgrade. You're too fine to drive some busted piece of shit."

"That was an upgrade, so stop hating on me, Wes."

"I'll see you in about an hour."

"If I had a watch, I'd tell you you better not be late, but I don't even have one of those either."

"Don't tell me anymore. You're the bomb, and there's no reason to be going out like that. Let me get some stuff together and secure things."

"What am I supposed to do for a whole hour?"

"Hold tight, that's what."

"To what?"

"Your heart because I'm coming to Charm City to steal it from you. I assure you that I'm worth the wait, so turn on the heat and stay put. Bye, beautiful."

One thing about ballers . . . they're so spoiled they ain't gonna spend time with a woman in a substandard atmosphere. First of all, they want to show off and ego trip. Second, if you're use to a Mercedes kind of room, why would you ever settle for shacking up in a Toyota one?

Fuck the candles, wine, slow dances, and all of that sappy bullshit. Money is my aphrodisiac; romance and love have no place in my heart no damn more. I was winding up to feel Wes out later by laying the foundation well. I intentionally pulled over next to The Comfort Inn, which I knew wasn't good enough for Wes to park his ass and told him that would be fine for me since he'd be leaving and all. He took one quick glance, turned up his nose, and insisted on moving on to the best spot he'd laid his head down while spending overnighters in Baltimore in the past. So less than ten minutes later, Wes and I are having our cars valet parked at the best hotel on the Harbor. I don't know the statistical odds of a 1988 Toyota being valet parked at a place like this, but that's what just went down. I guess the truth is sometimes stranger than fiction. Some dude should be collecting a nice fat tip for parking one 2003 SLK and one Toyota that might be headed toward the compact car hooptie list, but I notice Wes leaves him hanging, with no regret for being cheap.

After we check in, we take a trip up to the eighth floor in an elevator that's shaped like a time capsule, surrounded by a patterned lighted design, and tinted ever so slightly so you can see where you're goin', but those looking in can't see who the hell you are. I'm guessing people with money have a thing about anonymity, when privacy counts most. Wes walks in front of me, and I notice his bad leather coat, Tims, and the smell of his Sean John cologne that tells me he has expensive taste. The only way my ass can identify the shit is 'cause I remember smelling the tester at Hechts when John took me shopping at Laurel Mall. Just one sniff of that potion, and my vagina grew slippery. If I get one whiff of it if and when money talk comes up, I might be in for a repeat performance.

Wes sets down his bag and inserts the key card to open our door. He pushes the door open and begins to walk in while I'm still struggling to get a better grip on one of my heavy, tacky plastic shopping bags that he went on and on about being ghetto the whole trip up the elevator. I knew I should've invested in a suitcase, but it slipped my mind.

All of the sudden, I hear a woman belt out, "You're going to fuck me right now, Wes Montgomery. Come and get it, number twelve!"

"Bitch, you better get off my sheets!" he responds as he moves farther into the room.

"You know you want this. Stop playing hard to get, hop in this bed, and fuck me! You won't regret it, so come on over here and give me some basketball dick!" she insists.

"You might not think so, but you are about to get your feelings hurt."

"Come on now. I won't tell, if you won't. I know you're long winded 'cause I see how long you can run around chasing that ball without working up a sweat. You're my kind of man, number twelve. Am I your kind of woman?" the mystery woman says then giggles.

"I deal with the finest of the fine, and that would not be you. Get your cruddy, homely ass out of my bed while I call the manager," Wes says angrily.

"But, Mr. Montgomery, please don't call the manager. I'll lose my job if my boss finds out I broke the rules," the naked woman pleads. Her voice changes from sex siren to a stunned and quivering shrinking violet. I push my way past Wes and stand in full view of her.

"Let me explain something to you, ho, you should've thought of that before you ran up here to get butt naked in my room," Wes reminds her.

"I'm begging you, please don't tell my boss, please," she whines.

"You just wrecked my program, and I don't appreciate you insulting my honey," he says, looking over at me.

"I thought you were alone. I'm truly sorry," she says. Her eyes being to tear up.

"Well, as you see I'm in good company. Now this beautiful lady with me is what you call a dime. Take a long look, so you understand what it is I like. Turn around, beautiful," Wes says to me. I look back at him in astonishment and find my feet moving as requested.

When I stop and face the woman, Wes says, "I saw you winking and blinking at me at the front desk. If I wanted to know who you are, don't you think I would have let you know? You damn groupies get on my last nerve sometimes. You wouldn't be going through all of this if I was flipping burgers at the home of the Whopper, that's fo' sure!"

Wes dials buttons on the room phone, then shouts, "Y'all better get this stank-ass ho from the front desk out of my shit I paid for before I go off up in here and let everyone know what kind of operation you're running. Come collect your help, and the manager better be running to straighten her out like he's the one on the court."

The slamming of the receiver makes the woman shake like a leaf. She hops up and struggles to find her uniform. I can relate to her, but I can't request that Wes cut her some slack. She ain't in my league and should have known better than to pretend she had it goin' on like that.

"And one more thing," Wes tells her.

"Yes, Mr. Montgomery?" she says, kneeling in the middle of the floor, crying her eyes out.

"Are you sorry you offended me?"

"Yes sir, I told you that I am."

"Do you want to keep your job?"

"I need the money. I've got a car payment, rent, and a one-year-old to feed."

"Well if you mean it, stop that crying bullshit, and prove that you want to keep your job."

"How, Mr. Montgomery?"

"Simple. Give me a kiss, sweetheart," Wes informs the woman. As she attempts to get up to kiss Wes, she smiles, then asks, "That's it?"

"Yes, but don't get up. Bow down and kiss my feet, ho."

The woman's smile leaves, she slides off one of his Tims and socks, then performs what I feel is humiliating. After she nervously pecks Wes's foot, she looks up at him.

He says, "Now number twelve is about to give you some vital information. Let my foot serve as an example of how yours should look, after you use some money out of your last check to get a damn pedicure to saw those corns and crusty heels down. While you're at it, lay off the twinkies, and get acquainted with a damn treadmill. Oh, and trim that damaged perm hair, and just hang on to that new growth. You'd be better off sporting short, nappy buck shots!"

The woman bows her head and begins to cry all over again. We watch her wail as she covers her face, until a knock on the door makes us all turn toward it. The woman hops up, looks around for an escape route, but there is one way in and one way out. Wes opens the door and begins to shout an explanation of the chain of events, leaving nothing to the imagination, breaking his promise to the woman. The manager is appalled at his employee's behavior, fires the woman on the spot, and offers Wes a month's free stay with room service.

Now the funny thing is the rich get shit for free when they can afford to pay and the poor get no love from anyone, mistake made or not. I see what Tomi means. Being around people with money will teach you some things you'd never think of demanding, and seeing what people will do to get someone with money will make you file that shit away for years to come and fantasize about being rich your damn self.

After all the drama ends, we are moved to the penthouse suite overlooking the very place where I use to scrub toilets, bus tables, wash dishes, and occasionally cut potatoes while people barked orders at me. Me, Jalita Harrison—I don't have anyone who loves me—is laid up in an eight-hundred-dollar-a-night suite eating prime rib, tiny potatoes with red skins, long string beans fixed the way White folk like them, with a star basketball stud who's feeling me. I don't think I've done too badly for myself in learnin' the fundamental rules of survival of the fittest so quickly. Even if Wes isn't gonna love me, this makeshift version of the script will do just fine.

"Would you like something to drink?" Wes asks.

"I have some coolers in my bag. Want one?" I ask, still pulling more sympathy from his wallet. I hop up from the table and pretend I'm about to produce two warm, low-alcohol-content drinks knowing they're in my car.

"No way. I'm ordering the best champagne."

"Well okay, but it's not necessary. I don't want you to go through any trouble. I'm a simple girl with simple tastes," I lie. He's in deep belief.

"Pleaaaaaase! They're paying. If they don't treat me right, they know I wasn't lying when I said I'd tell the whole team what the ho did. Talking about putting a dent in their business. I could be the man to get that done with one phone call. With this economy the way it is, they would want to handle their business in the customer service department."

"Want a cigarette? I've been wanting to try these Newports," I say, handing him one.

"Newports? I've got something way better than that planned. You'll see soon," Wes says, then looks at me like I'm stupid. "You never *smoked* before?"

"Nah," I respond, shaking my head.

"How old are you, Jalita?"

"Nineteen, last time I checked my birth certificate."

"Well it's a good age to learn some new things. If you ask me, you're overdue."

"Who's gonna teach me how things work?"

"Who do you think?"

"I don't know. I just asked you, remember?"

"Well, you saw how I handled that little situation, didn't you?"

"Yeah?"

"Looks like you found yourself a twenty-five-year-old teacher. I can teach you everything you need to know about life," Wes says, motioning for me to join him on the couch. I slide my shoes off and sit on the other end.

"Why are you way over there?"

"Someone named Tomi, that's why."

"I'm not married, Jalita. I do what I want to do, so stop bringing her up."

"Well aren't you engaged or something?"

"Tomi's not here, and you need to leave it alone," he says. I move closer. Our legs touch. He runs his right hand down the fabric of my hiphugger denim jeans.

"Stop fantasizing," I tell Wes.

"I plan to do more than that. Where the hell is that champagne?" Wes says as he hops up and dials room service. I hear him jumping on someone's ass, reminding them how important he is and how late they are after the first fuck-up not so long ago. Within six minutes we're sipping on Cristal. I'm officially impressed. I like Wes's style. It's a refreshing sexiness after dealing with Cleveland.

"Do people always kiss your ass like that?"

"I am a star, you know. There are privileges for running the show," he says casually.

"You don't run no show. You just contribute to the show," I say, grinning to tease him.

Wes's face turns serious, then he corrects me by explaining, "Only stars in the show never stand in lines, half of the time pay whenever they feel like it, so yeah, it's true: money talks. And this point guard does run the show. I've got a multimillion-dollar contract so phat you can't even count that high. I'm tired of the press broadcasting my financial business because I don't like to get too specific with the dollar amounts, but let's just say I do more than all right for myself. In case you don't know, I participated in the NBA All Star game last year. I hold the highest points-per-game average in All Star history, at twenty-three points per game."

"I believe you. I was just messin' around."

"That's right, you better be giving a nigga some props then," he says, smiling back at me.

"Too bad that girl lost her job. She didn't have job security, and who knows what she'll face tomorrow. I can see her little Geo Prism being repossessed right now."

"So the fuck what? You don't do shit like that. Real hos would be smooth about it. That just wasn't the way to go. She wasn't even supposed to get personal with me—house rules for employees when athletes come through—so she made the boldest move since she's been warned."

"Your ego must be feeling good since she blatantly bucked some authority for a shot with you."

"I see all types of shit all the time. I'm sorry we had to get started on that note."

"Shit happens. No need to apologize for someone else's actions."

"I could tell you some stories about how athletes are roped into some real bad situations, including rape allegations that were nothing but set-ups. I remember last time I was here with my teammates the ho who jumped in my bed was in the hotel bar with some other bitch who works here. The fine bitch slipped something in my boy's drink. We caught it before he agreed to go up to the room and hit it though. Most likely someone would've taken bizarre pictures of him while he'd be out cold, maybe even in bed with a man, then tried to blackmail him with embarrassing photos. If he agreed to pay up they'd split the money. That trick is old now. It all starts with looking up a baller's salary on HoopsHype.com to see if his paper is long enough to be in the top few or simply following contract negotiations in some sports section of a paper."

"For real?" I ask in astonishment.

"Enough about those trifling hos. I sent one packing, remember?"

"Only 'cause I was standing there."

"Not hardly. That shit irked me. My most important passion is basketball, although my second is women. Ain't no ho worth losing my contract. I've got the most important offensive position on the court, and I plan on keeping things that way. Her type is trouble. The team has someone to try and drill warning speeches into our heads during camp to remind us of what's out here."

"Mmm-hmmm. You would have hit that. Men don't turn down no booty, and that talk you all get is a waste of time. Athletes can't keep it in their pants. Regular men can't even do it."

"How do you know? You're not a man."

"Through what I see and observe, smart ass."

"And experience?"

"Maybe that, too."

"Do you like me, Jalita?"

"Would I be here if I didn't?"

"I mean, I meet all types of girls when I go out, and I've got Tomi and all, but from the first time I laid eyes on you I felt this weird connection. It's almost like I knew you in another life, and I don't even believe in that kind of reincarnation shit."

"I know. Me, too. I have a boyfriend back at school. He and I've been inseparable for the last year. He even buys my books and keeps the fridge stocked but something in me still wanted to see you," I lied. "So what do we do about it?"

"Roll with it, and don't analyze. When you think too hard, it fucks shit up. Who cares where it's coming from? And who cares about your nigga? You're not married."

"True that. Have any parties lately?"

"Not this soon. I don't like people trailing in and out of my main crib too much. Only people really close to me have an open invitation. Enough talk."

"Isn't that what we're here to do?"

"I think you know better than that. I've got a different type of show to run, right here," he says, kissing me all over my neck and sucking on my nipples. He takes a strawberry from the fruit bowl, dips it in champagne, takes one bite, then sticks it in my mouth. I feel moistness between my legs, and I discover that Wes is right. We do have this synergy goin' on that I've never felt with anyone I've been around in an intimate setting. Just like he said, I decided to roll with it. Every step of getting in Wes's wallet would be a pleasure. I was already addicted to chasing him and planned on making up for lost time. If he's packing a big dick to match those big feet, the big mansion, and the big account balance, I will just fucking pretend Mr. NBA is gonna love me like it's the real love deal.

$

"So how do I smoke it, Wes?"

"Inhale. How else you gonna enjoy the shit, beautiful?" he says, sucking up on the joint. "Try yours."

"I can't," I say, looking at it like one inhale will earn me a trip to the morgue. Just like when I was with Shawn, I remind myself that I've seen many junkies in my day, and using drugs has been a no-no for years.

"You did the line of coke at the party."

"That was an accident," I lie. Me being depressed over my life, my pains and reaching out for temporary joy was what made me indulge. I'm thinking along those lines again, and since I can't talk to Wes about my past, I'll tell it to the power of the joint.

"Coke doesn't accidentally fly up your nose. You enjoyed it, so don't bother to front on me," he says, still puffing away, becoming more relaxed with each inhale and exhale. I hold the rolled joint up to my lips and mimic him as the voices of my past rise and face me.

"That's more like it. Take your time though. Savor that good shit, beautiful. It's not going to run away from you," Wes tells me.

"Okay," I reply as my eyes grow heavy. I feel lightheaded, but I don't fear the buzz. I keep puffing to invite more of the mellow sedation. Wes turns to me all spaced-out looking, and tells me to take off my clothes. I set the joint in the ashtray. I move slowly, wobble here and there, lovin' the smell of the pot, and manage to peel off everything that covers me.

"Damn, girl. Your body is, is—" he takes a puff— "the bomb! You know it, too, don't you? Long, thick legs; big ass; nice tits; and a tight, little waist."

"Whatever, Wes," I say slowly, still getting my smoke on, drunk off the highness as my thoughts run in circles.

"Jalita?"

"What?"

"Do you like to fuck?"

"I haven't been fucking my man long, due to his religious issues. It's okay I guess."

"So are you telling me you've got halfway virgin pussy?"

"Sort of. It's more virgin than you might think," I explain, gapping my legs open, still puffing away.

"Can I touch it?"

"Shit yeah," I say in a sedated giggle.

"Damn, you're wet and tight. It is just like virgin pussy. You gonna give me some?" Wes asks, fingering me.

"Depends."

"On what?"

"If you're gonna treat me right. I ain't no little cheap groupie like you-know-who. I don't need to brag to my girlfriends that I know what you're like in bed."

"If that's what I had planned for you, I wouldn't be high in this suite, drinking the best shit in the house, and me risking shit with Tomi by taking my overnight bag out of the house. If you're cool as I think, I've got plans for you, girl."

"I like you, too, Wes," I announce, stroking his erect penis and exhaling like a pro.

"Get in the bed, beautiful."

"And if I don't?" I say with slurred speech.

"You'll never know, I suppose."

"About what?" I say, half smiling from my buzz.

"The possibilities of anything we talked about. I'm bored with being chased by groupies in clubs, hotel lobbies and ones trying to catch my eye when I come out of the tunnel at games. Cleavage for days and short skirts are nice but I want something on the down low. I want a girl who can keep her mouth shut. Someone sophisticated, sexy, and with sense would be nice, too."

"Since you put it like that, I'm in bed," I say. I crawl on all fours.

"Lay on your back though," he orders me.

"Oh, doggy style is reserved for Tomi, huh?"

"What do you know about that, if you don't have much experience?"

"I'm not dumb, just haven't been around much. There's a difference."

"Well before we leave here, you're going to be very experienced. See all of this?" he says. My eyes fall on his long, thick penis that is looking me in the face. I grin as Wes opens a yellow condom wrapper. He rolls it down so smoothly it heightens my arousal.

"Mmmm. You've got good pussy, girl," Wes says as he eases inside of me, thrusts slowly, then slightly faster as my vagina adjusts. "Squeeze my nipples, but not too hard," he says.

"Okay, Wes," I say. I do. I feel him stiffen. My vagina grows even more slippery since I now know he's packing. I close my eyes, enjoying the moment, then I hear Wes say, "Yeah, beautiful, I'm willing to pay for this stuff." I smile, start to moan, and simply imagine I'm on some island like Fiji with a tall, dark, and handsome native who loved me from the second our eyes met and locked on the shoreline.

Before I know it, I find myself telling Wes, "See, I told you athletes can't keep it in their pants."

He replies, "Maybe you have a point when it comes to trying to resist wanting to fuck a fine sista like you. I'm guilty as charged, but that's not necessarily a bad thing 'cause this ain't rape . . . it's a consensual good fuck."

In between moaning while Wes is pumping me, I breathlessly respond, "It's consensual, all right. You don't have to worry about me telling tales. If you give me my props and lace me real lovely, I'll be the best pick you've ever thought about getting with."

What was supposed to be one night of keeping Jalita fed, watered, and entertained turned into three days and three nights of Wes and I getting high as two kites, getting laid, running the legs off some overworked, high-paid cook, and getting to know each other better. I didn't have to sucker Wes in to my web though. He walked through it and needed no prompting to get tangled up with me, missing his New Year's Eve plans with Tomi. We brought in the New Year doing shooters and Wes sucking Absolut out of my belly button. I didn't request that he turn off his cell and pager; he made that move on his own. That made me give everything I had to him better, more, and with full desire to give him whatever he decided I was worth. He even held me after sex, massaged my shoulders, and told me all about how he secured his ship to prepare for life after b-ball. Not only was Wes a star, he was nobody's fool. Come to find out he was an honors student, attended a top-ranked college, and earned his grades, even though he was top draft pick bound. Tomi chose well; her momma must of taught her some things worth knowing while they probably held two mugs of cocoa and sipped slowly between discussing gold-digging pointers. Those smart fuckers know how to work a paid brotha over.

And speaking of Tomi, I'm sure she was hitting the pretty chandelier right about now, 'cause her man stood her up for some bourgeois candlelight supper with her stuck-up gal pals and their anal hen-pecked sissy other halves! Wes is greasing my palm, making arrangements for my new cell phone, gonna put me up in his spare place, and hinting around that I may have a better ride by my birthday if I'm a good girl who stays on his A list. Tomi's stupid butt is thinking she's the queen bee who can't be knocked off her golden throne. Like I told her before, my name is Jalita, and she never should have insulted me without finding out if I was trash before accusing me of it. For her information, her man likes the touch of my tongue and fingertips so much he's willing to put up some green stuff to keep me using my tools. Now who's the queen bee, bitch?

$

"Now you're good for longer than I want you to be laid up in this hotel," Wes says from around the corner in the bathroom. I hear the toilet flush. He emerges carrying empty ashtrays. I like the way he walks. It's not a bop. Wes is sexy without even tryna push the issue. He just is.

"Getting rid of evidence, huh?" I ask.

"Not that I'd get in trouble, but people don't need to know everything."

"Why don't you leave me a blunt. I'd like to try it again."

"Now don't get addicted to weed on me, Jalita."

"I won't. I just want something around that makes me feel half as good as you."

"Good answer. Just one though. The media loves shit like this. Some things don't need to be seen, so don't leave anything laying around. My reputation makes my money. I'm up for some endorsement deals, and I'm looking forward to saying a few words about cereal and cell phones."

"I've got good sense. Your image will be just fine," I say, taking the joint from Wes, burying it snugly inside of one of my bras in a drawer. As I close the drawer, I remember that less than one week ago I would have cussed someone out for just letting me get a whiff of secondhand smoke. Here I am feigning for weed and coke, and schemin' to get paid for having my hole stretched out. I hate to admit it, but my R.A., Ebony's ass was on point about me having a price.

"It better."

"I understand more than you think. I happen to know some things aren't to be talked about either."

"Now what are you talking about?" he says, zipping up his overnight bag.

"The party. The next morning you and Tomi acted like the perfect God-fearing couple."

"Hey, I still give God the glory. Sundays is off limits for getting down with hedonistic principles."

"Big words for someone who takes it to the hoop for a living."

"Don't judge a book by its cover, or you'll never learn a thing from reading that book."

"I guess you told me. I'll be a good student, Mr. Montgomery."

"Will you wear short minis to class and sit in the front row?"

"Every day, and with no panties either," I say, capturing his eyes and holding his gaze by running my tongue across my lips like he did while he was screwing Tomi in the pool.

"You remembered me doing that, huh?"

"It was a little hard to forget, under the circumstances," I tell Wes, fondling my breasts.

"I'm getting hard, and there's no time for a quickie, so I'm not even gonna go there. If you have any issues while you're here, don't hesitate to hit me up on the cell. When Tomi cools down, my place will be ready for you. It's like that. You'll enjoy staying there."

"Okay, Wes. I'll put my quickie on hold."

"You better. Now give your nigga some sugar," Wes says. He bends down for me to kiss him. I press my lips on his left cheek.

"On the lips," he complains.

"I don't kiss men on the lips," I tell him. I mean that shit 'cause swapping spit turns me off.

"I'm not just a man, I'm about to become your sponsor to better things. Now let's try this again," he says. This time, I not only kiss him on the lips, I nestle myself in the middle of him, close my eyes like I'm about to dig deep for my first teenage kiss, and stick my tongue in his mouth. I kiss his soft, full lips, slide down his long legs, unzip his pants, steady his penis, and suck him into a stiffness for a good twenty seconds.

"Now that right there was a kiss!" Wes says, shaking his head.

"Thanks for everything, Wes. Our time together was perfect. These were the best three days of my life," I tell him. Manners are an essential ingredient 'cause it's a part of ego stroking. I'm bent on giving him the precise dosage of consideration he needs. "You're welcome, You're very welcome, but everything was on the house this time," Wes says, smacking me on the butt then grinning.

"Not everything. Dick didn't come on the house, now did it?"

"True that."

"Freak," I tease.

"Freakette," he teases back.

"I'll miss you," I say. I lay nude on the bed, prop my head under my left arm, and bat my eyes like a sex pot in a pin-up magazine.

"I could just look at you laying there all day, but I've got to go. Jalita, you're addictive. Starting tomorrow it's back to the routine for me. Thank goodness we play a home game. I'm not up to flying on the chartered plane with a bunch of men."

"Will you take me with you if I kiss your feet, number twelve?" I tease.

"No, smart ass, you're so beautiful, you can get use to sucking my big dick," Wes says then makes a kissing noise and pulls the door shut. I laugh and smile at his corny talk, then I hear the lock click. I roll on my back, not feelin' used like Tony made me feel, but purely enjoyed, adored, and savored like a vintage bottle of wine collected from a cellar and poured for a special occasion.

I turn on the stereo, turn the dial, and hear James Brown's song "The Big Payback" cranking through the speakers. I turn it up a notch and feel the words. I start dancin', light up my blunt, and smoke myself into feelin' real nice. I feel like I'm so relaxed I'm halfway floating, and remember I do have someone in mind to deliver a big payback to.

11

THE BIG PAYBACK

"Tony, I was so wrong. I really need to see you. If you don't forgive me, I don't know what I'll do. I just want to see you so badly, and I'm hoping we can get some things resolved to make that happen. I feel so humiliated and embarrassed that I'm begging like this, but I crave being with you. Please hold on. My nose is running. I'm just a complete wreck," I say, putting on fake tears and honks in Kleenex. I know Tony's eating up my lies 'cause his dumb butt hasn't grabbed a hold of a clue and slammed the phone receiver down in my ear, like a pissed-off man would.

"Well, I don't know. You did a lot of damage. I told you to lose my number."

"Every night I masturbate, wishing I could touch you, kiss you, and just experience you one more time. I crave you physically and emotionally. You've always been there for me, and I can't forget that, so all that I want from you is your forgiveness. I'm only nineteen, and I've got a lot to learn about life and people," I add, sniffling and whimpering.

"My baby is gone."

"Where's your child? Did Charlene go off and take the baby somewhere?" I press.

"*They* haven't moved out."

"So what do you mean your baby is gone?"

"I lost my Escalade."

"Oh shit. Sorry to hear that. Accident?"

"No . . . it was repossessed. I got behind on my payments when the dumb people in child support court didn't listen when I told them I wasn't making the kind of money anymore Charlene showed them on paper. Do you have any idea how I felt when I saw my baby being chained to a tow truck? See what you've done?" Tony says.

"Oh no. I'm-I'm, soooorry, Tony! What a raw deal!" I burst into another forced cry.

"I wasn't really going to get no part-time job because working in my business drains me enough, but now I had to go out and get me a job at 7-Eleven to fill in. You know how humiliating that shit is? One of my main competitors saw me bagging cigarettes. It's getting so no one in the business is taking me seriously 'cause that shit got around fast."

"Look what I've done to you. This mess is all my fault. I'm just no damn good." I break out into another fit of tears but I'm really holding back a belly full of laughter and ridicule.

"Yeah, you ought to be facing this music, not me. You came over here throwing your shit at me. I'm no faggot, what was I supposed to do?" he says bitterly.

"I know you said lose your number, but I think I'm falling apart. I realize you're the only one who can put me back together. I polished off a bottle of E&J last night, and I'm working on some vodka and cranberry juice today. I realize that I fucked up, but decided I had to let you know I'm aware of what time it is. There's no use in me pretending I can quietly walk out of your life. I can't. I don't want to go nor do I want you to leave."

"You think you're falling apart? I'm the one who works eighteen-hour days and gets one day off. This is it, and it's not even a whole day because of Charlene's demands," he says just as bitterly.

"Tony," I say, whimpering more and breathing hard.

"What, Jalita?"

"Look, no one can ever replace you because you're my first. I miss you so much. Words can't explain the level of shame I feel for my behavior. I acted like a hood rat, and you know I worked hard to escape poverty and the games it invites. I'm not saying I can erase what I did, but I can offer you a back massage, prime rib, all of the room service you desire, and the opportunity to lay up in a big, beautiful bed, and look at sports all day long on a big screen. What I wouldn't give to spoon-feed you ice cream and maybe give you some lovin', too. I know what a man needs now, Tony. If you just come to me and let me embrace you with my heart, I'll be good to you and give you a day you'll never forget."

"I don't have no big screen anymore, if that's what you're looking for," Tony complains. I really want to tell him to shut up his whining.

"Well what happened to that?"

"The witch gave it to her mother for spite. Now she's enjoying my TV, probably looking at dumb soaps and shit while she's soaking her damn dentures."

"That's how we are. Women can be so mean. I think it has something to do with hormonal imbalances. You know we aren't wrapped too tight. I wouldn't admit it to another woman though."

"You're telling me. By the way, you can't come here anymore. Plus, at five, I've got to pick up Charlene from work with her car, then pick up the baby from child care. So even if I wanted to, I just can't see you."

"Oh, but you can. A friend put me up in this suite at the Hilton and everything is on the house. I just want to make amends with you, in some way, if you'll accept my effort to squash the ugly scene of what happened," I say sadly.

"That would be impossible. I can't risk Charlene getting on my ass for one more thing. You know, she hung up a sign above the bed. She really flipped out over what happened."

"Sign?" I say slowly, but sympathetically.

"Yeah, it says, 'Tony is a dumb ass who's going to learn to keep it in his pants. I'm engaged to Charlene.' Every time I buy her a big present and go down on her, she takes a letter down. Do you now how long I've got to kiss her evil ass to make this stupid shit end?"

"Now that's foul and sick. You don't deserve that abuse. Why not leave her ass?"

"She's blackmailing me with more. If I don't keep her happy, she says she's going to turn me in to the IRS and talk them in to an audit."

"How far would she get with that, Tony?"

"Too far for me to risk since I had to let my accountant go. I can't see you, Jalita."

"That's cool then, but at least you know I'm sorry and you whipped me so good all I think about is you making love to me under better circumstances. I tried, so there's nothing I can do.

"I'm gonna go order some room service, take in a movie on this bed, and take a long nap to sleep away the thought of this conversation. I just want to forget the fact that you're gone and completely out of my life. You know what they say: you never forget your first. That shit is too true. I know you've got your own life and all, and I'm not tryna confuse it anymore, but despite it all, I'm still feelin' you, but that's my problem, not yours." I sigh like I'm let down and crushed.

"I'm burned out. I do wish I could take in some quiet time."

"Then do it. Come to the Hilton. You know we've always been close. Nothing is supposed to come between Tony and Jalita. No one either. Maybe I can give you some ideas on how to cool Charlene off a bit. I'll make sure you're in the parking lot of wherever she works by 4:30 with a few fresh flowers I'm looking at in this vase. I promise, Tony, so please consider every word I've told you, because they were from the heart and not easy for me to put out there."

"And you're really sorry?"

"Every second, since our last call. Can we start fresh? No one has to know about us. We can spend some quality time on the down low, but that's on you. I told you that I'm not tryna confuse things in your life."

"I'm coming, but I've got to be out of there, on time. No fuck ups or drama when I've got to roll out."

"No, I told you earlier. Trust me, boo. Have them ring room... no, scratch that thought. I'll be waiting in the lobby, so I can see you, first thing."

"Whose room is it though?"

"It doesn't matter. I'm alone for three whole days, and like I said, straight up, all I want is you, and I've got your back. I'll stand in the lobby and wait for you and everything. I'm that excited about seeing you."

"I'll be leaving in fifteen minutes. I've got to forward my calls from the studio to the cell and wrap some things up right quick."

"And don't eat lunch."

"I won't."

"This means so much to me. For the record, Charlene needs to give you a break 'cause a good man is hard to find these days, and she's got one staring her in the face, but doesn't even see it. And Tony..."

"What?"

"I'm sorry for the loss of your baby," I say, smirking.

"Thanks. I miss my ride already. Charlene's Chevy Cavalier doesn't cut it."

"I can't wait to see you, Tony. Hurry up and get your fine self on over here. I'm feigning something awful to give you a big hug to let you know everything's gonna work out, boo. I need your energy like I need food and water. I'm straight up addicted, fly ride or not."

"I won't be long."

I hang up the phone and squeal with laughter. I know he'll be here fast as a bolt of lightning. That's good though 'cause I want him to get what's waiting on him while it's piping hot out of the Jalita oven of revenge.

$

Dropping a bomb on Tony's universe is all of the motivation that I need to grab hold of Tony's hand and grip it firmly in the elevator. I slide a scarf out of my pocket while I hit the close button.

"What are you doing?"

"I want this to be the best time of your life. Role play, work with me, baby. Cover your eyes with this and tie it, please. Don't give me grief, just catch the vibe of this intense energy flow I'm feelin' with you and for only you," I say, handing him the scarf.

"This better be good," Tony says as he follows my request.

I use the key card to take us up to the eighth floor. I don't want him to see the floor or room number 'cause I have to cover my tracks as best I can, considering the way I plan on him departing from the scene.

As soon as we make it inside of the door, I uncover his eyes and abruptly drop my full-length, tan Evan-Picone coat. Tony pulls a yellow contraption with a red canister out his jacket pocket before he even notices me.

I notice he's disturbed my flow, so I ask him, "What in the hell is that?"

He answers, "My puffer. My asthma came back, and I've got breathing problems again. The walk from the parking lot had me wheezing up a storm."

"Oh," I respond. Then I add, "Are you sure you and your burning lungs can hang with me?" I spin around seductively in three-inch midnight black stilettos and the same cream lace Victoria's Secret teddy that turned John's brain to mush. Tony takes one look at me and starts wheezing something awful. He wraps his lips around that damn puffer and treats himself to three squirts.

While he's tryna get his breathing shit together, I give him a private once-over and notice that he's already gained a couple of pounds since I saw him a week ago, but I hope he develops a three-month pregnancy pudge before it's all said and done. I privately gloat, empowered by the damage of his misery at home.

"Damn, Jalita, you didn't have no clothes on under there. You know how to fuck up a nigga's head. You look great!" Tony says with lust in his eyes.

"And? I know that, man, but you don't have to go and hyperventilate from looking at me," I say confidently, then laugh. I feel his eyes burning a hole in my butt as I head for the couch. I know he's mesmerized 'cause he replies, "Stress brings my attacks on. You gave me some good stress. I'm okay now, though. I definitely can hang with you, boo." Tony puts his puffer away.

"Is that smell coming from your goatee?" I ask, leaning toward the edge of his face.

"I don't know."

"It is," I announce, scrunching up my nose.

"It must be the Just for Men," he explains, lowering his head in shame.

"What are you doing using dye?"

"Stress since, well . . . you know why. I guess you noticed my cornrows are gone, too. I couldn't afford to keep them looking nice, so I shaved them off. I'm not the one to be walking around with raggedy-looking braided hair. That signals to the whole world you can't afford to get them redone. Back to doing my hair myself. Good thing I have a little barber skills."

"The only thing you've managed to talk about since you've been here is stress and financial problems. Let's not talk about the past. It's a new day, and I'm glad to see you. Don't fall out on me or nothing though." I want to laugh, but I hold it in. I'm happy the fucker is also graying prematurely and almost bald head, revealing the pit bull fat rolls in his head. Short hair does *not* hardly suit Tony. I'm wondering if those scars and nicks in his head came from Charlene's wrath.

"Look, I'm going to be just fine. It's good to see you, too, Jalita. Damn, this penthouse is phat. Who do you know who's got money to put you up here?" Tony says to skirt the issue.

"Wouldn't you like to know? Stop asking me that," I say, winking at him.

"You didn't just get a man or married or no shit like that, did you? I don't want the hint of trouble."

"Me? Come on now. I can't keep a man to save my life. No one wants me. Thanks for coming, Tony. Just remember that we don't need to get all into things that aren't important," I say, batting my lashes and leaning forward to show my cleavage.

"Uh-huh," he says with lust still in his eyes.

"How about a massage?"

"That would be great."

"Strip."

"What?"

"Down to your boxers. I've seen what you've got before, so don't be shy."

"Oh, okay."

"Lay down flat on your tummy," I say noticing his half-bleached blue dress socks haven't been retired to the trashcan, so I guess he managed to salvage what he could. I straddle him and rub his back like I give a damn for his abundance of mental aches and physical pains.

"That feels sooo good," Tony moans.

"So, you like my hands all over your back, do you?"

"Mmm-hmm. Yeah, this is great. Can you get down low?"

"There?" I say, letting my fingertips touch him gently on his lower back.

"Oh yeah, right there. You've got such a gentle touch."

"You know, I'm really sorry, and I hope you'll let me make up things to you. You're way more to me than a man, you're a best friend for life," I say.

"I believe that means something now."

"I'm glad to hear that. Are you getting hungry?"

"Yeah. No time for breakfast this morning. All I had was a biscuit left over from dinner last night."

"Good, 'cause a great big, sizzling porterhouse and sides are on the way."

"Really?"

"Would I lie to you? Look at all the times you fed me, back in the day. It's my turn to look out for a brotha."

"This is too much."

"So what would you like to watch on the idiot box?"

"ESPN would be great."

"ESPN it is then," I say.

"Can you keep massaging my back? I never knew you knew how to do this."

"There's a lot you don't know I can do. Perhaps you'll find out, over time."

"That would be nice."

"Maybe so," I answer, pressing my lips gently on his back, then resuming the massage. He'll gain another dose of Charlene's wrath 'cause I'm gonna keep him indisposed 'til waaaaaaaay after five!

All through lunch, I smile and wink at Tony as I pour him wine and get him feelin' good, but not drunk. I want him to be able to remember the boiling vat of hot water I've got waiting on him. Tony is so relaxed that he says yes when I ask him to turn off his cell phone, and when he makes that move, I know I'm home free to seek revenge.

"Are you enjoying yourself, Tony?"

"Yeah, of course," he says, his eyes glued to the commentator on ESPN.

"Good," I say. I pull his hand in my lap and guide him to rub my legs.

He moans lowly, still lounging and listening to a brown-haired man yap about which football player made the most mistakes on a game and who turned out to be a Pro Bowler.

"You know, Tony, we can have some more fun," I whisper in his ear.

"I haven't heard that word in a long time."

"Well you're hearing it right now," I tell him. I lick his neck, then pull on his boxers.

"You want me to take these off?" he asks.

"Only if you want to. It's your decision," I say, laughing inside. He takes them off and turns to me as I watch his soldier rise to attention and salute me. We share a long gaze, and I crawl across the bed, licking my lips and stroking my breasts.

"I want to try something different, that is unless you're scared. No, that was silly of me to think of that. Never mind," I say, hopping up and stretching like I was never in the mood to please and tease.

"Whaaat? Why'd you stop? Get back on the bed."

"Does Charlene ring a bell?"

"That witch? I don't want her. I want you. Get back on the bed. You can't leave me like this."

"Only if you're sure, 'cause I'm no virgin anymore and sometimes I like to do erotic things. My sex drive has been in overdrive every since you opened me up and put it on me," I announce, looking at him seductively.

"Try me. Try me, Jalita! You're turning me on. Please don't stop," he begs. I lick my lips, sway my hips, roll over, arch my back, then talk dirty to him about thirty seconds longer.

"See these?" I say, grabbing the scarf and a pair of jet-black pantyhose.

"Yeah," he says half confused.

"I want you to fuck me in these heels while you're tied up," I explain, handing them to him.

"I don't know, I never—"

"Scared of adventure, huh, negro? Just as I suspected. Maybe another time. I understand if you don't have it in you to make room for fun," I say, taking off my heels.

"No, no, I'll try!"

"Good, Tony. This is one experience I'm sure we'll never forget," I tell him, winking at him then sliding back on my stilettos. "You hold the blindfold, and I'll tie." I kiss his rising penis gently. I watch it stiffen as the veins bulge, then I grin.

"There," Tony responds. I double knot the scarf in back, then push him backward as I tie what seems like miles of pantyhose around his tanned arms. I turn the TV off and summon the stereo to belt out seductive jazz.

"Now what?" he asks, smiling.

"Relax, boo," I say, then kiss him on the cheek.

"Relax, boo," I say, then kiss his belly.

"Relax, boo," I say, then kiss his penis.

"Relax, boo," I say, giving a fake moan and rubbing one finger across his lips.

"Are you relaxed?" I ask sweetly.

"Oh yeah. Really relaxed. No stress at all, Jalita."

"Good, boo. We're gonna do it all around the suite after I put some of this body butter on your back. A good-smelling man just makes me want to live out every fantasy I've ever had."

"Make me smell good, then," Tony says. He groans with pleasure as I rub some Garden's Gate Mint Body Butter into his skin.

"Am I driving you crazy?"

"You know what you're doing to me, Jalita."

"Good. It's all in the fingertips. Come on, my first love. The bed is the last thing. I want you to stand against the wall while I suck your dick to get you hard for your turn in this fantasy. Do you like this sex game?"

"Oh yeah."

"First, I'm gonna feed you a special snack, then I'll grab the condoms, and we'll do it my way, then we'll switch up to your way. How's that sound?"

"You know how it sounds. Look down if you're not sure."

I softly stroke his penis, then say, "Mmm, that thing is ready to be used, don't you think?"

"I stay hard for you, Jalita. I hope you don't expect this little game to be quick and to the point. I'm ready to make love to you until I have to force my legs to carry me out of that door. I'm feeling you, too."

"I don't enjoy no two-minute brotha, or even a thirty-minute one, so we're on the same page. That's why you're my boo."

"I was hoping you'd say that."

"So you really want this pussy, huh?"

"I'm gonna tear that young booty up to prove it," Tony tells me.

"Okay, well taste this, and let me see you eat it in a real erotic way. Pretend like you're me licking your cum. Can you do a little role play?"

"Hell yeah."

"Okay, here it comes, now work that tongue for me," I tell Tony. What I failed to disclose is that the whipped cream I should've squirted on his strawberries is more like TRESemme extra hold styling mousse. I know the directions say it's not to be tested on animals, but intentionally misusing it this one time ain't gonna hurt nobody. I won't let the dog lap up too much 'cause I need that stuff; it gives me real good curl definition, fo' sure!

I watch Tony stick out his tongue and show me his oral powers of seduction. All of the sudden, he pauses and says, "Jalita, why does this cream taste so different, baby?"

I respond, " 'Cause it's a diet brand. Is that okay with you that I count calories for my figure's sake, boo?"

"No problem. Can't fault a brother for asking. I'll eat it anyway because I like this game."

"Good. Now bite into that strawberry 'cause you need the last boost of sugar. I'm not gonna let you up for air, water, or food. You know what I'm talking about?"

"Damn sure do!" Tony answers, chews, then swallows the strawberry.

I stroke his face, and tell him, "Don't worry about a thing. I told you this will be an experience you'll never forget, and it will be just that. You know what I'm talking about?"

"Hell yeah to that, too!"

I caress Tony's head, then guide him by his wrists, which are still bound. I walk that asshole Tony right out of the door. I open and close it so easily behind me, he doesn't hear it click. I quickly press a Super Sticky Note Post-it on his back that reads, "I did it again, Charlene." I'm thanking my stars that the elevator is a few feet down the hall, 'cause all he's wearing is a hard-on, and I'm sending him down to the lobby dazed, confused, and wondering what happened to his little fantasy role play.

He hears the ding of the elevator as the door closes, and says, "Jalita, Jalita! Why are we in the elevator?"

I reply," We, nothing. You're alone, boo. I realized it was getting late, and I promised you'd be on time to pick up Charlene, so have a nice trip going down. I'll let the lovely fiancée know you're running late though! Bye." The elevator doors shut, and I can hear traces of Tony gasping for air.

As promised, I turn Tony's cell phone back on. I plan to answer it nice and sweet when Charlene calls to yell at Tony for leaving her standing in some cold parking lot. I know she's made of the spunk that I think she is, so I'm willing to play a brief waiting game.

In less than three minutes, I hear, "Tony, where the hell are you with my car? Do you know how many times I called your cell? Do you know how long I've been waiting out in this winter weather? Why was your cell off almost all damn day? Why didn't you return any of my messages? I lost count of how many I left. You better say something, and it better be good. This is no way to act when you're on probation with my ass," Charlene says.

"Well, hiiiiiii, Ms. Charlene the butt-whipping machine. Would you like to leave a message?"

"Who the hell is this, and why are you answering Tony's phone?"

"Oh, just a close friend of the little family," I say, twirling a small curl around my index finger.

"Put his ass on right now."

"Tony said you were a witch. Sounds like he's right. Where're your manners, girlfriend? I know your momma raised you better than that," I say, wiggling my toes on the bed, noticing I'm due for a polish.

"If I find out who this is, your ass is mine. Get my man on this phone!"

"I can't do that. All things in due time, Charlene. Patience is a virtue you need to rub elbows with, starting right now. I'm not big on orders, so I'd appreciate it if you adjust your stank attitude and turn the channel to something appropriate for me to listen to."

"What are you talkin' about, bitch? I'm gonna find you, and I'm gonna tear him a new asshole!"

"Well, maybe you're all upset 'cause it's six o'clock, and Tony was supposed to pick you up in your Chevy Cavalier at five. I can understand why your voice is escalating. Mine would be, too, if I were in your predicament. On second thought, go on and let it on out, if you need to, girl."

"How'd you know that, bitch? I don't want to talk to you! Get Tony right now!"

I begin talking fast and hysterical, so Charlene won't have time to interrupt me. I tell her, "Now let me see, what would the best way to explain this be. Okay, I think I've got it together now. I'm real fine, and Tony is a very weak man . . . the type who's an easy target. He took his clothes off when he hit the door, ordered food without asking to put it on my room tab, threw drinks down his throat like the shit was free tap water, and spent all day with me in a fancy hotel room doing things I consider tacky to repeat. I don't ever want to see him again. Even if the man can fuck my brains out, he just has no class, and now I'm too through with him. My guess is that your car is parked on the street somewhere near the Harbor in a lot 'cause you're bleeding the poor man dry. I know he didn't have money to pay for all-day parking in the hotel underground lot to keep it safe during our lunch date 'cause he asked me to spot him for that, too. Shame on you, Charlene. You're really stressing him out. He had so much tension in his back, he begged me to massage it. I'm sure it's gone, since I was nice enough to work the kinks out while he griped over your finances. If I have to hear one more thing about your finances, I'll scream. No wonder he ran over here in thirty minutes, after I called. It really didn't take much power of persuasion to get him in bed with me. He seemed so attention starved and depressed. I know that was a mouthful. I know I had *my* mouth full today. Did you follow all of what I said? I tend to ramble when I'm upset. It's a bad habit I'm working on losing."

"You psycho bitch. What's goin' on?"

"I know you're not the brightest woman in the world, but isn't it obvious? Once a cheat always a cheat. No matter how many ways you try to keep these men out here on lockdown, it just can't be done. They're pleasure seekers, not promise keepers. Kiss the baby for me. Tony said he's glad it came out looking like him, not your sea monkey–looking ass. Toodalooo, *boo!*" I say then push end on the cell.

Now I almost feel the need to grow a conscience, but I don't feel sorry for Charlene. I see no good reason to cry no rivers for that broad. I keep doing her favors to show her that a man can't be forced into obeying like a dog to be trained. Those who think like Charlene shouldn't be so freaking gullible. Just when you think you can trust men again and maybe even turn your head for longer than a hot minute, they'll go roaming off to run the streets to play with another kitty cat. Meow.

12

DANCIN' ON THE MOON

    I hit the lobby and hear the concierge and security guard chuckling and saying, "that" was the best thing they've seen. They hold their sides, laughing about the crying guy who got hauled off by the boys in blue. Guess who feels like she's dancin' on the moon? Me, Jalita. The baddest, boldest chick up in this piece is actually cheesing and can't stop. The icing on the cake is laying down Tony's fully charged cell phone on a bench facing the Harbor. I'm sure some dishonest somebody will snatch it up and call everyone from here to Malaysia, so he'll get his shit shut off and find himself being forced into a payment plan. I don't appreciate having to waste my gloves, intended for my color touchup on this little job, but I know that wiping down prints just isn't enough these days. Charlene will bail Tony out of whatever slammer he ends up in any time now. Enough about Tony. My work with him is *finito*. I think I'm gonna head for the Aquarium 'cause I've always wanted someone, just anyone, to take me there as a kid, and no one ever bothered to make it happen. It must have been too much for me to ask.

    I know I'm supposed be watching fishies, but if I've missed taking a tour of the Aquarium this long, a few minutes isn't gonna be that critical. I just set foot up in the Aquarium to chill out and I'm already cocking my ear to hear what some man's flapping his gums about at the information desk. I hear, "Yes, thank you very much for the information. I'll try e-mailing him." He turns around, picks up his attaché case.

    "Excuse me. I hate to bother you, but may I ask you a question?" I say.

"Sure," the man says warmly. Then he asks, "Jalita? Is that you? Do you remember me?"

"We met in Mitchellville when you were raking leaves. Seth, right?"

"Yes," he confirms. We both smile. This time Seth's got this dressy casual thingy goin' on that I like. I don't know how it's possible but he looks even better than the first time. The only problem is my freaking palm isn't itching.

"It's nice to see you again. Is this place worth the walk-through? I mean I've never been here before, and if it isn't, I can go over to the Science Center and play with static electricity or something," I say, cocking my head slightly and smiling to show off my straight teeth and light brown eyes, which I know must be sparkling right about now. Since my agenda is different these days, I don't care if he's obligated to a live-in pussy. I'll get his digits before we part this time.

"It's nice to see you again, too. Yes, it's worth the trip. I think so anyway. Plus, a new experience is worth having, right?"

"True," I say. This one has this magnetic vibe that's pulling me and holding me like a tango partner dancin' cheek to cheek.

"Are you visiting Baltimore?"

"Oh, no, I'm a native of Charm City."

"And you've never been to the Aquarium? You're definitely overdue. It's a must-see."

"That's what I've always heard, but I just never had the luxury of getting here to do this before. When I was growing up, I moved around a lot. I'm a military brat who finally decided to leave Dad and Mom in Germany to attend college in the states," I lie.

"Well it's never too late for anything," Seth says. I want him to shut up on the spread-your-wings-and-fly vibe. I'm not tryna hear no Les Brown speech right now but there's something about Seth that I've never picked up from anyone else on this planet.

"You look like you're busy doing business, so I'm not gonna keep you, but Seth, I think you do something nice for the decor of this place."

"What do you mean?"

"You make it a bit more interesting."

"Well I don't know about that. I'm just clean this time," he says humbly.

"I do," I tell him.

"Thank you, I think," Seth tells me.

"Oh, it was a compliment, and take it wherever you're goin' and hold on to it all day." I bat my eyelashes. I turn around and know that by my fifth step, he'll chime in and consider staying if he can adjust his schedule.

"Say, I could use a break for a while. Would you like me to walk through a bit with you?" Seth makes his offer with charm and class. *Bingo, I'm almost in there.*

"Since you left so abruptly last time, I'd be highly insulted if you didn't and could," I reply, batting my lashes one more time for good measure.

Seth picks up his attaché case and follows me. I like that he's not making *me* follow. It says a lot, given that most people with penises are control freaks.

"So what brings you in and out before you've had a chance to say hi to the fishies, Seth?" I press.

"Business."

"Oh, I see." I want to ask more, but it's too early to pry.

"Are you off today, or were you on business somewhere nearby?" he asks bluntly. I like his style. He wastes no air flipping the script.

"No, not exactly. I hope your briefcase won't be a pain to carry since you've got all your important stuff in there."

"If you want to know what I do for a living, Jalita, just ask me."

"So Seth, what is it that do you do for a living?" I say. Seth is good. Better than most. I can't believe he just saw straight through my mountain of bull crap!

"I'm a writer," he answers.

"Oh, a writer, huh? I've never had the pleasure of meeting a writer before," I say. I need to remember to get his last name out of him this go round so I can research what he's written. He must push a pen mighty well if he can afford that crib in Mitchellville.

"Freelance really isn't a pleasure, so you may have some misconceptions."

"What's that? It still sounds exciting."

"Not really. It's sort of like earning your place to become a full-fledged writer," Seth explains. Now he's got me worried that he ain't got shit.

"You mean you're sort of like a feature writer, but not as high up as an editor?" I press.

"Neither. I've got to sell myself enough to do short write-ups and hopefully someone will want to buy a blurb or a story. I'm working on my portfolio to get some tear sheets. It takes a while to even become a feature writer."

"So, who do you write for, and when? A magazine in New York?

The Post. The Sun? Please share."

"More like *The Word, First Impressions, Eating Wholesome*, and any other magazine, card company, or website that's in the need of a wordsmith, on an as-needed basis."

I wrinkle my forehead, scrunch my nose, and tell Seth, "I never heard of those."

"I hadn't either, until I got some leads off the web from a writer's job site."

"Is what you do stable?" I ask.

"If you're asking how much money I make, Jalita, I don't earn much. In fact, as an aspiring writer I earn anywhere from five dollars to twenty-five dollars per article. Beyond that pay scale, you're fortunate. It's no secret that a career in writing can be one of those starving artist professions. Sometimes you don't even get paid. It's more like a chance for exposure and building for the future," he says, stopping to observe some small, circling sharks who look more cute than harmless. Then again, they all have teeth!

"I wasn't asking about—"

Seth cuts his eyes at me, then interrupts me by saying, "Yes you were, but it's perfectly all right. And while I'm at it I want to clarify something. I was in Mitchellville doing yard work for someone who hired me for the day. That wasn't my house or my car in the driveway. My boss wanted me to get back to work, instead of talking to you. I've been doing odd jobs on the side this past year to help fund my main writing project. I could only get a modest loan from The Small Business Administration, so I've had to scuffle so I can wrap things up to pay my printer in a few days." I've never been read so well. I don't understand why Seth keeps peeking at my ace, but he's doing a good job of it. Since he's broke I feel like leaving his ass to walk through the Aquarium alone but I know that Wes is busy, so it ain't gonna do no damage to kill some time with Seth. I can exercise my legs and fuck with Seth's head at the same time.

"Instead of telling me your personal business, why not tell me something like what made you want to try to become a writer," I say to mask my shock.

"Everyone has a dream and a passion. We're on this planet for a purpose. Ultimately, I will become a best-selling author, helping heal some people with my positive words, and maybe more. I sometimes dream about what I'm going to say when Oprah has me on her show. So what's your passion, Jalita?"

"*Passion?*" I ask him like I'm confused.

"Don't you have something you crave doing, or are you already doing it right now?"

"No. I don't have one." I want to crack up laughing at his assuming Oprah's people will call him to be on her show. Unknown Seth would go straight to the no pile. In case he hasn't been keeping up, she's the first Black woman in the nation to achieve billionaire status. Her interview Seth, pleaaaase.

"You need to find one. What do you do for a living, or do you go to school full-time?"

"I *was* a college student on break," I say while checking out a stingray. This little interactive experience is more than I thought it would be.

"Was?"

"I haven't decided if I'm goin' back when the winter break is over yet."

"So you're just going to give up on yourself? You must have worked hard to get accepted."

"I did, but there's no reason to put up with all the studying, people's bad attitudes, and all that stuff that's only important if you have a cheerleading section in life."

"Well, if I were waiting for a cheerleading section, I'd be sitting on the curb with a sign, begging for food. What I have to do to make it is hard, but isn't the journey always worth a struggle?"

"You don't know you're gonna make it. You might go through all of this and end up shortchanged. That doesn't make much sense to me. Call me a pessimist, but life is too short for holding out for a long shot."

"Oh no it's not. I'm going to make it. My self-published novel is going to make it on the *New York Times* Bestseller's List someday. I'm going to add something important to this planet, and I'm going to be able to stop deferring my student loans. Guaranteed. Everywhere we go in life, we should travel with dignity, not giving up on the hope of great things materializing."

I can't resist snubbing him and say, "If you say so, Mr. Warwick and Psychic Friends."

"I know so, so you really shouldn't make light of it," Seth warns me.

"Says who?" I ask him with a snotty attitude.

"First of all, I believe in myself and trust my spirit. Second, I was an underdog growing up, and I didn't go through all of that rejection for nothing. Third, my mom is lending me her spare car, not giving me a hard time about living in the basement, and tells me she knows I'm going somewhere big. I owe it to her to push for the best result possible.

Fourth, something happened that changed my life forever."

"You have quite an imagination—I mean sense of determination," I say, walking a little slower. I stop to watch some seals balance balls on their noses. I don't care if I've insulted him. Money over looks. Money over looks. Money is what counts to get this honey.

"Oh, you said what you meant all right. And yes, I do have an imagination. What I imagine will become a reality because I'm one determined somebody," he says, clapping while the seals do some fancy trick.

"Well a whole lot of people want to write, and whole bunch of other people went through special programs and training to learn how to do it, yet they still can't get published. Who doesn't want to write the great American novel, or a memoir or something? I'd say everyone with a computer or a pen. Now how can someone like you compete with all of them?" I say, tugging at his confidence enough to make it fall and shatter. I'm wondering who in the hell this Seth brother thinks he is!

"Well, Jalita, if one person out there did it against the odds, so can I. I work hard at this, sharpen my skills, work on my craft. Don't assume I wasn't trained in some classroom. I was. I majored in English and earned a B.A. degree from Morgan State. I even won the Zora Neale Hurston Writing Award. Only one is given a year. I know I'm good and have potential."

"Oh," I say flatly.

"I don't date right now because women won't take men like me seriously. They want the smooth-talking guys with bad attitudes and money to flaunt and flash. My payday is coming, and when it does, I'll remain humble and plain ol' Seth. Always," he says, clapping for the seals again. Then he says, "By the way, you're truly beautiful and all, but stop batting your eyelashes like that. Be yourself, Jalita. You're so much more on the inside than the great shell on the outside."

"What are you talking about?" I ask.

"We're supposed to be having a serious conversation, but your mind seems to be on trying to look sexy," he explains.

"So what's your dad think of your ambitions?" I say, changing the subject.

"He died suddenly when I was four."

"I'm sorry," I say. Did I just apologize to someone who owns a penis?

"I was, too. Times were hard. But then I realized it all could be worse. What if I didn't have a great mother to teach me customs of her people and love me with all she had? What about yours?"

"Missing in action since I was a little girl. I never tell anyone that."

"It is what it is. It's not your fault. Nothing to be ashamed of. Hey, want to go into Mountains to the Sea?"

"Okay," I say. I follow Seth. He's leading now, but not in an "I'm the man" sort of a way. I secretly wish I own five grams of his confidence. I just can't tell him that.

"So what happened that changed your life?"

Seth's face lights up, when he says, "Jalita, you'd think it's corny if I told you."

"Maybe so, but please share," I tell Seth. Did I just hear myself say *please* to a man? *Damn girl, he's got you trippin' without even strippin' down to your thong!*

"I read a book about something that happened to this young African-American woman who was trying so hard to attain success in America that it almost killed her. It was so moving, I cried at the end. It was just what I needed to read. I use to never cry. I mean, when I put it down, the words stuck and became real."

"I don't read books like that. If I read a book it would be a page turner like the new street fiction titles, not a yawner."

"Well this book is about so much: depression, racism, family, hurts, romance, healing... I mean it covered it all. I picked it up by an accident, and I'm so glad I did. Those other books are entertaining, but no matter what the story line is I think they should teach something or give you something to ponder."

"One little book did all that for you? Don't you think you're exaggerating?"

"Well, it's a thick book, and yes, it did all of that, and no, I'm not exaggerating. I no longer live in the past. I'm going for mine, and I'm convinced I can get there if I do right."

"Well goody for you, home boy!" I say. The conviction in his voice makes me say something stupid. I hadn't even read this Black chick's story, and I'm already spooked out by Seth's outlook, which he swears was brought on because of it.

"I can read you, Jalita. Me being myself makes you nervous. You considering that you, too, can have with you want by the labor of your brain and own two hands frightens you. I was where you once were, that's why I get you. Just in case you change your mind about testing my book review claims, it's called *4:17 Vinegar Blues* by Andrea Blackstone."

"Andrea who? It sounds like an unknown author tryna get paid to me."

"Oh no. It's the real deal, but in a serious and heartwrenching way. In fact, when I part with you, I'm going to interview her main character,

Dr. Brenda Brown, in her office not far from D.C. Ever heard of Chevy Chase?"

"Don't all rich White folk who stick their noses up like they smelled something bad live out there?"

"Some, but not all. Be careful about generalizing. In fact, I want to be early in case I get lost. I can't wait to meet Brenda. I went to one of her seminars, and man, she's an awesome lady. To think she said yes to me doing a story on her."

"Maybe she needs the PR. Public relations sells books. Especially boring ones. Don't be so gullible," I tell him, rolling my eyes. I'm really feelin' like a like a hustler could sell Seth the Brooklyn Bridge.

"Oh no, she's famous now and has been interviewed by people all over the world. Despite all of that, she's still approachable. By the way, here's my card. If you ever would like some quality company, I'm the one. Maybe we can go to a pow wow or go dancin' or something."

"Thanks for offering, Seth." I reach out to take it. Between it being flimsy and having perforated edges, I can tell Seth printed it out on his home computer. He looks down at his watch, then looks into my eyes. I read the e-mail address on the card. Hotmail, huh? I'm thinking he just lost fifty cool points.

"Jalita, I've got to get some energy before I make my drive. How about a quick lunch? I can't afford anything fancy, but I was just about to head on over to Boardwalk Fries when I met you."

"I don't want you to be late for your interview."

"Not to worry... nothing is going to make that happen. If you don't want to go, just say so. My feelings won't be hurt if you want to do something else."

"I'll come along for a quick minute then," I say, although I'm no longer use to meals in big foam cups. Damn he's broke. I knew he was too good to be true, but I'll go along with the shit 'cause I might as well let this play itself out with manners.

"Okay then. Shall we?"

"We shall."

He's beat. The other half of Seth's cool points just went flying out of the window. This is one broke motherfucker. To add insult to injury, my feet are tired from standing at this circular wooden table 'cause Boardwalk Fries is so low budget they supply no booths or chairs.

After we finish "eating," we walk to a lot. Seth unlocks the trunk of his momma's banana-shaped yellow whooptie, then hands me the dumb book he raved over. He says, "Here, Jalita. I'd like you to have this. Read it, okay?"

"Thank you," I respond. Although I don't intend to read one damn page, I add, "I'll be sure to read it." I notice the change jar nestled in the corner of his trunk and a dollar store bag holding something cheap.

"It's been a pleasure," Seth says.

"Likewise," I reply.

Seth gets into the whooptie and the damn piece of shit won't turn over. As I twist up my face in disgust, my eyes fall on the doughnut tire and rust on the bottom panel of the car. Seth jumps out and sprints across the lot to ask a brotha to give him a jump. I watch Seth slip him a five. The man pulls his car in front of Seth's momma's whooptie. Seth connects the jumper cables, then attempts to restart it. Apparently, he's forgotten that I'm standing here.

He shouts, "She wasn't supposed to do this again for at least three days more. Thanks, man."

When he leaves the door open, I see duct tape holding the seat together and the right handle of the passenger door is also missing. Seth breaks my trance when he walks over and announces, "Now I can get the show on the road. I hope to speak with you later, Jalita. I'm really off to my interview this time." He gets in and slams the door.

I tell Seth, "Don't let me keep you. Thanks for the book and fries." He smiles back, then backs up to do a three-point turn, exposing the busted headlight but still having the nerve to blow the horn good-bye. As a new member of The Gold-diggers' Association of the Baltimore/Washington Metropolitan Area, I can't earn my top-dog spot as CEO if I hang around men who are faking it until they make it. Attention all broke asses, Jalita's time is valuable. I no longer believe in giving it away for free. I'm not interested in spending it on a man who shops in a dollar store. He can't do nothing for this right here. Poof, just be gone.

13

BAD TO THE BONE

Wes got caught up having to practice extra hard and attend lecture after lecture since the Blitzers lost their away game in Los Angeles–Eagles, 103, Blitzers, 81. He said the new head coach was extra pissed 'cause he felt the team was distracted by the pretty L.A. cheerleaders and A-list movie stars that were perched courtside, but that was a bullshit copout 'cause flexible pretty women with implants who need their roots bleached come a dime a dozen and the Blitzers are bigger stars themselves. Wes says his coach needs to lay off the caffeine in the coffee he's addicted to and quit bullying players by threatening to trade them and give the rest of the coaching staff a chance to coach guys they've known way longer than his grumpy, graying ass. He also says he yells too loud, and when he yells too loud the players rebel and feel justified to play lazy. Please. I bet the Blitzers are guilty of what the coach said 'cause from what I saw of them at the Christmas party, they are some horny motherfuckers with swollen egos.

As a result of him placing that call to me on the room phone, I spent an entire week alone in the penthouse, but I'm not complaining. Wes was courteous enough to wire me one thousand dollars to a Western Union so I could have some spending money to shop at stores on the Harbor and eat something in Little Italy or wherever else I wanted to go for a change of pace. That put a smile on my face and an understanding that butt kissing will pay off. It did. I can say good-bye to the Hilton. Wes's haven is now *my* new little haven. His beach house is at an undisclosed location, out of Tomi's earshot and off the press's itinerary. And lucky it is, 'cause I plan to scream plenty and fake orgasms on the regular, as long as he's treating me well and putting me up in this phat crib.

I'm finally discovering that my downfall in life has been my inability to swallow my pride and kiss someone's crack who knows more than me, has more than me, and can do something substantial for me. I'm stubborn as a mule, not dumb as a squirrel. I'm gonna knock out the fat of saying what's really on my mind and lock in the flavor of what Wes wants to hear and listen to shit when he wants me to listen. My kitty cat is extra wet 'cause I increased my output mentality since my sex drive comes and goes, as needed. Now, I'm on the same page as most women who know how to get ahead, in search of a decent paycheck or a decent relationship. I'm learning. Jalita is getting there. Life is too short. Since it is, if you wanna lay up with the kid, you better hand me something worth having when you hit the door I'm sitting behind. I wouldn't be giving it up to Wes if he didn't have it all. This hookup situation is a no-brainer so long as he doesn't get traded to some crappy city.

"Slide your knee up, beautiful."

"Like this?" I say, looking back at Wes.

"That's good. Stay there," Wes tells me. I can feel his wrapped penis moving in and out of my wet vagina so much that I'm guessing he's using those extra-thin Life Style condoms.

"How's it feel, baby?" I ask as he strokes me doggy style.

"I swear you've got the best pussy in this town."

"You would know. I'm sure you've had your share of kitty cat in this town. How's Tomi's? Does it meow better than mine?" I say, grinning.

"No. It's nothing like this one."

"And how is this one?"

"Young and gushing like Niagara Falls!"

"Oh yeah, daddy, oh yeah. Your dick feels soooooo good. Don't tease me, work me!" I lie. He's pleasing himself, not me. Wes doesn't want to be a magic man right now. He wants to work on bustin' a quick nut, and that's about it.

"Who's your daddy?"

"I don't have no daddy. I don't know where his ass is."

"You say, 'Wes is my daddy!' Let me hear you say it."

"Wes is my daddy?"

"It doesn't sound like it. Say it again, you horny bitch," he says, making my butt jump and jiggle with a smack.

"I said Wes is my daddy," I say louder, moaning extra loud for flavor.

"And whose good pussy is this?"

"Wes's pussy!"

"And whose phat ass is this?"

"Wes's phat ass!"

"Ahh hahhh. That's right. Turn over on your back, ho," he says. In a way I'm his paid-for trick, so I do, and don't bother to protest against his lack of tenderness.

"Lick your daddy's nipples," he says. I do. He starts making some strange noise. I want to laugh, but I stay with the moment, and grind with the motion of his hips.

"Who's gonna love me, Wes?"

"I'm gonna love your ass. I'm gonna take care of you. You're my paid-for, hand-picked bitch. You're mine, you got that?" He smacks me on my ass yet again. In fact, if he wasn't paying me to put up with the shit, I'd smack him hard on his ass and then ask him how he likes it.

"Yeah, daddy. I've got that. I'm head ho, and I'm gonna take care of you, too."

"How ya gonna take care of your daddy?"

"Fuck him, fuck him, fuck him the way he can't get fucked at home by his upper-class prima donna. Me, I ain't got a problem with getting buck wild like a project chick," I say, breathing hard, then beginning to moan loud enough to wake up the dead.

"I'm gonna cum. I'm gonna cuuuum," he whines. I'm thinking, *So the fuck what? Go ahead and cum, negro, 'cause you ain't getting me off. And why you negroes gotta announce the shit like it needs a formal introduction? This ain't no term paper, just get on with it, and do what ya gotta do already!*

"Aaaah," he says, vibrating like someone electrocuted him while he was on top of me.

"How was it?"

"That was some good shit! Whew!" he says, springing up, wiping sweat from his brow, and leaving me with nothing to shout about. I guess today wasn't my day to cum with Wes, but come to live with Wes.

"I've got to shower up and roll back on out to Mitchellville."

"Got plans?"

"Tomi insists on me taking her to some play called *If These Hips Could Talk*, then shopping in Georgetown, and anywhere else she can think up for my missing person stunt I pulled on New Year's Eve. I've got to keep her happy and quiet, so I've gotta go put in my overtime at home."

"Whatever, Wes," I say, lifting my legs in the air to show off an anklet that I deliberately put on to suck him into my web.

"What's that?" Wes says, wiping his sweaty face with a white terry-cloth towel.

"Nothing."

"Don't play games. Who gave you that?"

"The old boyfriend I told you about," I lie.

Wes moves close to me, looks me dead in the eyes, points at me with his index finger, and announces, "I don't want you to wear it anymore. I don't like it, and you know better, Jalita."

I shrug and respond, "Why?"

"Because you're with me now, so take it off," Wes demands, then puts both of his hands on his hips.

"It's just an anklet, no big deal, Wes." I press my body behind him and wrap my legs around his waist. I kiss him on the cheek as I laugh inside. I'm about to set myself up to get some of whatever he's willing to buy to replace what I won't wear anymore. I snatched the dumb thing up when John took me to Laurel Mall, but Wes doesn't know I only wore it to make him open his wallet and want me more.

"It is a very big deal. I'm your daddy. When your daddy tells you something, you listen and cooperate," Wes complains.

"But it's my favorite, and it's all I have. If you really want me to, I'll take it off though," I tell Wes, reaching down to unfasten it. I sigh hard and pretend that I'm heavy-hearted as I place it on the dresser.

"That's better."

"But now I don't have any jewelry. What's my damn daddy gonna do about that?" I complain.

"You'll have way better than that cheap plated shit. Your daddy is going to see to that. I might even see something in Georgetown that has your name on it. If I do, I'll get it later, when Tomi isn't with me."

"Don't worry about it. I was wrong to disrespect you like that. I apologize," I lie, sighing hard again.

"It's nothing to buy you what I want you to wear. I'm dressing you from now on. No nigga drives my car, touches my money, or tries to unzip my ho's pants. He was just trying to work his way back into your life. Don't let it happen again, and don't be stupid. You belong to me, and I take care of you. This is my pussy, and I mean that, so don't take the shit for a joke. What you need to do is call that nigga and let him know it's over. The next time I see you, you better have squashed it. Don't give him dialogue, just let him know and hang up," Wes informs me.

"If you really feel that way about it, I'll do it," I say, hugging and squeezing him from behind. I know I've just upped the ante and can expect way better than a fourteen-karat gold anklet. When you let a man believe he's running the show, he'll go out of his way to provide and please. I see no reason not to be as sweet as honey when batting my eyelashes and acting soft earns me loot.

"Look, I've got the place stocked with plenty of food. Start unpacking, because this will be your home," he tells me, walking from the room.

"Okay, Wes," I say. I unzip my new matching suitcases and open oak drawers. I reach to move a cute, medium-size teddy bear from the dresser. Wes stops me and places his hand on top of mine.

"No, don't move that. Tomi will flip if anyone touches that bear. Her mouth will take off until the next century," he tells me.

"But she's not here, and you say it's my home," I quickly remind him.

"Please, Jalita. I never know when I'll have to send you out for air so she can see I'm not pulling anything here."

"But you are," I say with a grin.

"But that's our little secret."

"Sounds like a big secret to me."

"I'm going to clean up. Remember your daddy's rules about cooperation? Use that as your road map and follow that shit to a tee," Wes says. I want to tell him he's too much of a dirty dog to ever get clean, but I decide not to risk getting thrown out just yet. Instead, I continue to unpack and get use to the fact that I may be here for a while. Within seven minutes flat, Wes emerges with a towel around his trim waist, ready to lotion and cologne his trifling behavior away. He smells the same way as he did when he stepped in here. Only a true player would remember to go home smelling the usual morning wash way.

"Don't forget to plug in the cell phone charger I gave you. It's charged now, but make sure you plug it in every night. I expect to be able to reach you any time of the day, so pay attention."

"Okay, Wes," I say again. Damn do I feel like he's laying down the law to me. No happenin's dawg. Jalita's still gonna do what she wants to do as soon as you're gone.

"You remember how to work all the locks, and which key goes to what? Make sure you lock up every time you leave out."

"I've got it, Wes," I say. Now, I want him to go running to Tomi.

"I'll be back tomorrow after practice. If you need me, call."

"And what if you don't answer 'cause Tomi's got you occupado?"

"Now Jalita, you knew about Tomi when we hooked up, so stop that."

"I know I did," I respond politely.

"So leave me a sweet, sexy message so I can listen to it tonight. And if I don't answer, and something is on a serious note, leave a message and mark it urgent."

"Mmm-hmm. I'd love to," I respond, nodding once. I refuse to be a hundred percent beholden to him and refuse to say another fucking okay to his ass today. Even ass kissers should have limits.

"Time for a quick tour. Stand in the hall while I point because I'm almost running late," he says. I do. Now he's completely dressed, looking and smelling like new money.

"Kitchen's down there, living room across from that, bathroom through the door in this bedroom, second and third bedroom right next to each other, entertainment room down the hall to the left, and that about covers it," Wes says.

"You call *that* a tour?"

"Yes, a quick tour. Look, I've gotta go. Make yourself at home, but don't let any strangers in my crib. Don't even answer the door if it's a nigga knocking on it. Oh shit, I know that's Tomi ringing the cell. Damn she's impatient," Wes complains, looking at the flashing caller ID. I roll my eyes with disgust.

"Give me some sugar," Wes says, bending down. I do, just like he likes it, smack dab on the lips.

So what does this fool expect me to do out here? I'm making good progress with getting my stuff and all, but I'm no Laura Ingalls Wilder from *Little House on the Prairie*. Shit, my ass is use to bullet holes in the sides of houses, not baby deer running around in circles playing with each other. You can't take someone who slept on city streets and abandon them in a damn summer cottage and expect them to be satisfied with the view of the waves swishing and swooshing, long term.

My eyes land upon the dramatic beams, pale blues, sandy whites, turquoise, and shades of green. Every room has some quality that stands out and adds to the serenity of the natural setting that would make anyone stressed want to breathe easy. The fireplace with slate around it is the focal point of the living room, but a large paper lantern hanging over the dining room table reminds me of something I'd see giving off light somewhere in Okinawa after the sun goes down. Seashells, bright paintings, an assortment of candles, soft chenille throws, rocking chairs, stacks of CDs, DVD player, big-screen TV, and hardwood floors with a perfect polish you can almost see your reflection in add to the carefully coordinated decor. And the master bedroom is off the hook, with the wall of glass overlooking the meditation garden, or whatever it's supposed to be with those teeny trees and oddly shaped shrubs that look like they belong in *Better Homes and Gardens.*

I guess I didn't need a tour from Wes 'cause it seems like my gold-digging self noticed everything important. And sorry, Tomi, I won't put my paws on your teddy weddy bear no more, and I'll be thanking you for the nicely decorated crib, every time your man busts a nut in me and runs home to you, the queen bee. I know one thing for sure, I'm the one who's bad to the motherfucking bone, and I'm gonna prove it to Wes by making his head spin.

14
TRICKS AND TREATS

"So how ya been doing, Shawn?" I ask. I decided to surprise Wes's cousin on his job.

"Jalita, what are you doing here?" he asks.

"Surprised?"

"That's an understatement."

"So . . . I see you're still working here, huh?"

"Oh yeah." Shawn says, ringing up a customer's bag of Utz chips.

"How's Jackie?" I say. I feel like prying.

"How should *I* know?"

"What do you mean by that?"

"She left again."

"Shawn, Shawn, Shawn, I'm not even gonna comment."

"Don't."

"You still love her, don't you?" I ask, point blank. He's quiet and lowers his head.

"Never mind, don't answer then," I say. I'm feelin' like Shawn and Jackie could earn a spot in *The Guinness Book of World Records* for breaking up and getting back together. I want to tell him so, but I decide to spare the brotha since Jackie's got his mind twisted in enough knots.

"Hey, what's all that in Hefty lawn bags I can see in the back?" I ask.

"I don't know what you're talking about," Shawn says, but I know he's lying.

"When a man says that, it means he does know what you're talking about. Since you don't know, I'll make it a point to find out myself, so I can let you know," I tell him, pushing my way past Shawn and walking into the small area of the store.

"No Jalita, only employees are allowed back there. Please don't."

"Too late, chum," I say, untying one of the bags as I feel Shawn's breath on my neck. "I knew it was bullshit! I can't believe that bitch brought this kind of drama down on your job. I'd bet my last two pennies she made a scene when she dumped your clothes from the crib you're paying for, didn't she?" I ask Shawn.

"Just come out of there before someone sees you."

"I've got my info. I'll gladly step out of this hot armpit. You don't have to ask me twice," I announce, returning to the front of the counter.

"It's not what you think, Jalita, so just let it go, will you?"

"You men need to learn some new lines. I heard that one too many times before, too. It's your life. All I've got to say is, damn, you're one weak Negro." I shake my head.

"So where ya staying now?" Shawn asks, tryna shift the subject.

"I can't say."

"Can't say? What's that all about?"

"I don't wish to speak on the grounds it may incriminate me," I inform Shawn, pretending to zip my lips.

"Awwwww. Jalita!"

"What?"

"Awwww, girl, no you didn't!" he says as his eyes widen. "You got with Wes."

"I didn't say that, you did. That NBA star stuff don't impress me. Big shit if he can get behind a velvet rope. That ain't nothing important. He puts his pants on one leg at a time like everyone else."

"Well, if you were saying it—but you didn't—watch out for Tomi. I think she's got some screws loose."

"And Jackie doesn't have one too many screws crowding up her little toolbox? I can't even call your tail to say hi, and our relationship is one hundred percent platonic."

"So you are seeing Wes?"

"Like I said, I didn't say that. I'd be happy to have a good man who'd serve me his last glass of flat Coke, if he really was gonna love me, so can we talk about something else?" I say to throw him off.

"So where'd you get the Toyota?" he asks, craning his neck over the counter.

"It's a rent-a-wreck. Satisfied? Now when are you gonna grow some balls and put your foot down with Jackie," I say. Just when

Shawn is about to think up a lie about how he intends to let Jackie go for good, I feel someone cover my eyes.

"Who the hell has got their hands on me?" I ask.

"Steeeeephaniiie!" the voice answers.

"John? How did you find me here?" I say half confused.

"Easy, I saw your car outside," he explains. Shawn props his elbow on the counter. It's his turn to dig all up in my biz.

"Oh, well hi!" I say with a false smile.

"I thought you went back to school?"

"I did. I'm here half a day visiting my brother, Shawn," I say, winking at Shawn to signal him that he better cover for me.

"Hi Shawn, I'm John. John from Mobile, Alabama!" he says, sticking his hand out.

"What up?" Shawn says.

"Ahhh, the sky's up, last time I checked," John responds. I can't believe he actually said that. Shawn snickers.

"Your sister's a real nice girl. I'm kinda sweet on her."

"Yeah she is, and I bet you are. Who wouldn't be?" Shawn says for spite. I playfully punch him in the arm, wanting to slug him for real.

"Stephanie, can I take you to lunch before you leave town again? I'd really like to spend time with you."

"Shawn and I were supposed to—"

"Oh no, you go right on ahead with John, sis," Shawn chimes in.

"But really, Shawn, who knows when I'll be back, and we have some family stuff to take care of, remember?" I say, smiling and gritting my teeth at the same time.

"Oh no, really Steph, I'm caught up here for a while anyway. You may as well make some use of your time with your friend here," Shawn insists.

"All righty, little lady, I'm taking you on a lunch date then, and I won't take no for an answer." John locks his arm in mine. I turn back and mouth to Shawn: *I'm gonna get you. I'm gonna get you for this.* All he does is wiggle his fingers.

John is so mushy and fucking annoying. He's some kind of hopeless romantic who always is opening the door to the truck for me and even fastening my seat belt like I'm five years old and still legally required to sit in a booster seat. My fingers ain't broken in case he hasn't noticed!

It's his idea to go to some Arundel Mills Mall place and let me get my eat on and shop. And shop I do, first thing. His gums are flapping, but I don't do much listening. I do what men do to women—appear to be listening, but not doing a very good job of it. Everything he says, I respond with a standard, "mmm-hmm, is that right?" I see why men do it 'cause getting in this frame of mind is easy and sometimes necessary so you won't go and say somethin' you really think, like *shut the fuck up* or *will you stop running your damn mouth so I can have some peace and quiet?*

I wasn't born with a shopping gene, but I must've grown one. I snatch and grab, but John pays again and again. Loading up Johnnie boy's arms is becoming a pattern I won't ever get tired of creating. As long as I pretend like John is worth my time, he keeps peeling those pretty dead presidents off his fat roll, very liberally. It's funny how I feel like goin' crazy with spending the funds since I'm not paying. Shit, I don't even wear glasses and had that dummy waiting on me while I got an eye exam from Dr.'s Vision Works, just so I can see if the optometrist is gonna be honest and tell me I've almost got 20/20. Even though he did, when John overheard the salesman pushing sunglasses to make a sale, he insisted I indulge in blocking out those harmful rays. He told me something about wanting to keep my beautiful eyes bright and healthy, dumb ass, but I picked out some silhouette sunglasses that actually mold themselves to the shape of my head, using my body heat. That's $125 John just wasted 'cause I don't even like wearing sunglasses, even if the shit is high tech!

Fuck the sun's rays issue, what I'm lovin' is the fly clothes. I did deviate from my pattern, just because I needed to collect a variety of goods. I threw in some crystal birds and an automatic vacuum so I don't have to lift a finger, for the same reason I got the glasses—just because he was being nice and didn't tell me to put anything back. Shit, what do I need with that stuff? Wes's place is already nicely decorated and Jalita ain't gonna be the one to vacuum it even with an automatic vacuum. Maybe I can sell it and keep the cash since I just snatched it for the hell of it. I will be keeping the Nexxus hair products, CDs I like, Bath and Body Works shit, and shoes, shoes, and more shoes though. Getting a slew of heels out of him on this trip was easy. All I had to do is keep reminding him of what I did last time when I was standing on stilettos. I'll be showing off my calves for someone other than John, but he's too dumb to think ahead like that.

We're about to take in a movie at this huge Muvico place that's got this Egyptian theme thing goin' on with huge white columns and everything. The least I can do is let him make one stop for himself and let his wallet cool off 'cause it's smoking from all the friction of him sliding it in and out of his back pocket. Hey, I don't feel guilty for swindling John. I mean, he's got on a real strange get-up. Who wants to hold hands or even walk next to a man with bright yellow pants, a sweatshirt with a beaver on the front, a blue skullcap, and a nice black leather coat? Unless a blind man dressed him, John does need to compensate me for just walking beside him. It's an even trade since he wants to be a living rainbow today. As long as he's treating me to the best there is to have up in a whole lot of stores, I'll be his makeshift boo who won't even ask him why his clothes don't match.

"Are you having a nice time, Stephanie?"

"Yeah, real nice, baby!" I say, batting my eyelashes at John.

John invades my personal space enough that I can clearly detect his breath smells like a backed-up sewer system. Ironically, that's when he says, "Kiss me, right here, right now. You bring out the animal in me, brown sugar!"

"Just 'cause I strip doesn't mean I'm into that display of public affection thing," I tell him. The smile falls from his face and shatters. I change my mind after looking at the four hundred dollars worth of stuff he's toting in all those bags.

"There," I say, giving him a quick peck on the cheek.

"Naaaw, shoot. I mean one of them long movie-style kisses like the actors give them pretty women like Halle Berry and that cute Nia Long," he insists.

"Now John, Stephy will give you even more than that in private, if you're a patient little boy," I tell him, batting my eyelashes again. Even if John cures his halitosis, I'll kiss the fool like that when hell freezes over and the devil starts serving ice water to all his damn guests!

"Oooh," he says like he's picturing it.

"Like that thought?" I tease.

"Oh yeah. I remember last time."

"But this time, I'm gonna do more wild stuff! I'm gonna dress up in these new pretty clothes and model them just for you when we're all alone."

"Stephanie."

"What?"

"Ever since you left I couldn't stop looking at brown, round booties. Is that how you say it, *booties*?"

"Yeah, that would be the way."

"I like my baby with back."

"Where've you been hanging out?" I ask, wrinkling my forehead.

"Nowhere. I did invest in that BET channel though. They even have a Black movie channel, and my favorite is the music videos. Those girls sure can shake, but not as good as you though. I've been learning a lot about your culture. I'm renting a house now; the motels got to me."

"Well, John, I'm gonna be your video girl tonight. I'm gonna let you enjoy this brown, round bubble 'cause you've been taking good care of me today. And when you take care of me, I'm sure to take care of you," I say, grinning and pinching his cheeks.

"Stephanie, I think I love you," he says all dreamy eyed. I pretend like I don't hear. I want somebody to love me, but nobody from Andy Griffith town! Where are all my hip all-coffee-and-not-an-ounce-of-cream brothers?

"So here are the movie choices. You've treated me so good, so you choose," I say.

"See, that's why I like you, Stephanie. You're so sweet and considerate," John tells me, grinning.

"You're the best, John! A woman can't help but to try."

"Aww, shoot. You're gonna make me blush."

"Save all your blushing for our afternoon of love. Now hurry and pick one before you miss the beginning. It's no fun watching a movie if you miss the first few minutes."

"That one looks good."

"*Peter Pan?*"

"Uh-huh. It's got all of the makings of a good movie—action, adventure, and fantasy. This one's the newest adaptation so I can't wait to see what new stuff has been done to it."

"*Peter Pan* it is then," I say, wondering if I need to ditch John and pay for a taxi back to Laurel, but I'm too cheap and he's a sucker, so I decide to agree to the movie. It will be a perfect time to catch a much-needed nap.

I rear my head back to take a nap, while John is pointing and enjoying the latest visual effects, including Peter Pan leading some crumb snatchers over rooftops to some freaking jungle. When I slide down in the seat just right and drown out watching stuff I never had the luxury of watching growing up, John nudges me.

"Wake up, Stephanie. You're missing the best part," he whispers.

"Yeah, that is funny as shit. *Hahahahaa,*" I say with a dry, forced laugh.

"Oh no, fly Peter, fly. Don't let Captain Hook catch you. Keep going. You can make it! Watch out," John screams. I feel people's eyes fixed upon us. Who wouldn't if a grown man with no kid around was doing all that yelling about a boy who won't grow up? I'm glad he's a condom wearer 'cause the prospect of him having progeny scares the shit out of me.

"You're really into this, aren't you?"

"This is classic stuff. I love it," John says. I can see the trace of his face in the dark. He can't see my eyes, so I roll them hard and sigh 'cause John's annoying the shit out of me. At my highest point of irritation, he puts his arm around me and asks me to lay my head on his shoulder.

I begin let him know his little requests have gone far enough, saying, "Now look you're—"

I'm interrupted, when wetness gushes from above my head. I look up, and John looks over 'cause some splashed on him, too.

"Here, have a drink on the house!" a woman screams while ice falls on my head from a large soda cup. It's Big Shirley. I gulp hard and nudge John to grab the bags. We scoot on out of an aisle, then break out into a run faster than the animated boy John was just cheering on would fly.

"I'm gonna get you, you Jezebelin' man thief. You won't get away from Big Shirley this time," she shouts. Her voice carries although she's trailing behind quite a distance.

"What's going on? Who's Big Shirley, and what's she want with you?" John asks. I'm glad he's in shape from construction 'cause it just might save us from destruction.

"My aunt. There was a big misunderstanding; she thought I was flirting with her man. I moved out of her house in Virginia before I got a chance to pay the last Verizon long-distance bill. Word got back to me her phone was disconnected because of it. I'm in big trouble with her," I lie.

"No offense, Stephanie, but she's a whole lot of woman on two legs."

"I know, that's why I don't want her to catch me—I mean us. She's a shopaholic, so I guess she drove up to raid this mall."

"What are we gonna do?" John asks as the bags bounce off the sides of his legs. I know they're heavy, and I'm concerned about him losing the grip on my loot or breaking my crystal birds.

"Run to the truck and leave this mutha!"

"Okay," John responds quickly.

"Get her, Little Harry. If you catch her, Momma's gonna give you thirty dollars."

"Oh boy, I'm gonna be rich. I can get her. I can run fast, Momma.

Mr. Turner says I'm the fastest in all his gym classes," Big Shirley's son says. We fling the mall doors open, but have to pause to take a quick breather. I see glasses coming at us, sitting on the face of who I assume to be that damn determined, greedy Little Harry.

"Why are you slowing down? Keep it moving," I shout, looking at John.

"Just pay her what you owe her."

"No way. That's not good enough for Aunt Shirley. Take my advice and run!"

"But I'm tired of running, Stephanie! I'll pay. Just tell her I'll take care of your bill so we can get out of here in one piece," John says." He starts to huff and puff.

"Didn't you hear what I said? You talk too much. Keep that ass in gear and run!" I scream like a maniac. We make it to the truck. He pops the locks, we hop in, both panting with fear. I pound on the dashboard, then scream "Go, go, go!" I look around and notice that John can't back up 'cause some people are standing behind the truck. I feel sweat under my arms.

"Shit. Here comes my aunt Shirley!" Big Shirley taps on the window, nearly kissing it. Her face is so close, I can see why her husband, Cleveland, runs to that boat on cinder blocks. I would, too, if I had to answer to that.

"Roll it down!" she screams. I tell John to obey.

"Get out, man thief," she yells. I do. A crowd from the movie theaters surrounds the car. I'm glad no one knows me 'cause this shit is getting thick and kinda embarrassing.

"Pay Little Harry thirty dollars," she yells. He grins. He's got two teeth missing: one on top and one on the bottom.

I answer, " The hell if I will. No happenin's. I ain't giving no little jack-o-lantern-looking boy my hard-earned money. Besides, he caught up to me but he didn't stop me, now did he? I say his gym teacher was saying he could run fast to boost the little nerd's pea-sized ego." Little Harry looks up at me, begins rubbing his eyes, then cries. Big Shirley puts her hands on her hips.

"How dare you insult my boy. Big Shirley's gonna kick some ass," she says, backing up and balling up her chubby fist. The boy is still crying, and the people are still watching. Big Shirley swings once like Tyson and misses my head. She pisses me off with how far she's carrying the shit. Before I know it, my temper flares up, and I snatch her auburn wig off her head and hurl it across the parking lot. Half of the people in the crowd are laughing so hard they've fallen onto people's cars while Big Shirley is grabbing onto her tight, linty black wig cap, ordering little Harry to retrieve her matted coif, which landed on top of someone's car antenna.

"I should put you in the ground for everything you've done," Big Shirley screams at me.

I shoo some nosy asses away, hop in John's truck, position myself in the passenger's seat, then scream back, "Not today you won't, Big Shirley. Snatch some money out of Cleve's wallet and invest in a good wig that matches your dyed and fried blond hair, bitch. It was nice to see your ugliness again, but I prefer Sprite over Coke. If you're gonna treat me to soda, at least get what I like," I say. John drives slowly since some onlookers are still taking their time moving out of our path.

Little Harry is holding up his mother's wig, points at me and shouts across the parking lot, "I'm telling my daddy on you. I don't like you, you're mean!" He stomps his foot and grits his teeth.

I smile then say, "Thanks for the compliment. Now get your little drawers out of your crack, Little Harry. We're cool. I really hope your teeth grow in. I gotsta roll out. Now be a good boy and help your momma put back on her wig and maybe your daddy will give you thirty dollars for that." I stick my hand out of John's window and wave good-bye.

This has been a day of tricks and treats, and I've got one more trick to pull off before I snatch my treats and haul ass. If I do the damn thing right, I might even get to see a grown man cry. That's the kinda movie script that would keep my ass awake. It's time for Jalita's feature show.

15

THE PERFECT PUNCH

"When you said you liked doing stuff together, I didn't know all you wanted me for was sex, John. I never want to see you again. To think you just took advantage of my vulnerability. You don't want a companion, you want a whore. Why don't you go pick a cheap one up off the strip in Baltimore?" I scream.

"I have no clue what you're talking about, Stephanie," he answers.

"My aunt always told me this would happen. She said my tits and big ass would be all a man could see in me, so I better keep these thighs closed until my wedding night if I wanted some respect. Me, I go shake my ass for some tuition then fuck up by losing my virginity to you. See what I get for ignoring a woman with some damn experience under her belt? Now I feel bad for snatching her wig off in public. *It's your fault.* You never should have suggested two adults look at some damn children's movie. Had you not done that, we wouldn't have seen her."

"I didn't know you were a virgin, Jalita. I would have been more careful with my mouth, if I had. I'm truly glad you chose me, brown sugar. I'm sorry about me picking *Peter Pan*. All the critics said it was so good."

I work up two eyes full of tears, turn to John and say, "Don't you think I get asked out at the club? I never go so it really hurts when I waited for someone special, and you turn out to be a selfish snake in the grass. I never should have put myself in this position. I feel like a complete idiot for thinking that fate brought us back together at my brother's store. Now I find out you were on a mission all along. Of all of the choices of people I had to pick from, I've got to pick some asshole like you who can't grow up."

"Please don't say that because I—"

I interrupt John as I make my voice shake and belt out, "Save it. Let me break it down for you, homeboy. I never want to see you again."

"Never?" he says as his eyes begin to glisten. "Whatever I did or said can't be *that* bad, can it?"

"You mean to tell me your ass still doesn't know what you said to offend me? I thought you were a gentleman. All that's on your mind is sex, you horny pervert. I told you I was tryna get away from being a sex object. That really does it. Your apology means nothing, for sure now. You can't apologize for shit you don't know you did wrong. That shows you don't give a damn right there," I say.

"I'm not a pervert. I hadn't had sex in a whole year."

"Whatever. I'm no sex machine, you motherfucker! Go to a sex toy shop and buy a blow-up doll. Fuck her until you poke holes in her. It's time for me to accept the truth that you're no good and move my ass on. Dick ain't nothing but a headache on layaway. I knew I should've stayed to myself when I was sitting on that curb," I say and turn away.

"You've got it all wrong. Come back, Stephanie. I'm sorry," John says while motioning for me.

As I slide down the length of the seat, I make my voice shake again, and announce, "I'm sorry, too. I thought you liked me for who I am and what I stand for with my studies and goals. I'm smart, too, you know. I've got a brain, or have you bothered to take time to notice? When will just *one* man notice there's more to me than just what he sees?"

"I'm him. I do. I respect you, brown sugar. I know you've got a good brain to go with that pretty face and nice body," John says convincingly.

"Then why'd you insult me by tryna get me to do you on the side of the highway on our way back here?"

"Oh, so that's what this is about. I wasn't trying to be no octopus. I was just trying to be romantic, when I said let's pull over on that spot and have some fun."

"Oh, I know your type. And I know why you've got a truck with seats that fold out and a horn that plays that 'Rhinestone Cowboy' tune. I'm not a backseat or front seat chick. I'm classy. My standard is big beautiful bedrooms with fresh rose petals on the sheets. I refuse to be used by you anymore. You just ruined a perfectly good day. You've done enough damage with your nice guy act. I just can't believe how naive I was. I don't blame you, I blame myself for allowing this shit to go this damn far," I say, shaking my head, then hopping down from the truck.

"Come back, Stephanie. I said I was sorry. We don't have to do nothing right now," John says, leaning over and reaching out toward me.

I snatch the merchandise from the truck, then get real ignorant on him and say, "Right now, right now? I hate you, John. Give me my damn bags. And go visit one of your other lady friends while you've still got the fever for fucking. Hurry up and make your backup connection before your erection goes down."

"There's no one else. I swear it. I haven't been with anyone since you, Stephanie."

"Yeah, right. That's what they all say. Check your answering machine messages at your new town house and dial the next woman on the list. I'm sure you've got plenty of takers to satisfy your needs when I'm gone."

"I'm falling in love with you, Stephanie. I really am. You're the most special girl I've ever met in my life. Your aunt is wrong."

I break out into a run, head toward my car, turn around to get one last look at the fool, and shout, "Bullshit, you're falling in love with what's between my legs like the rest of the slime buckets at the club. I just made one of the biggest mistakes of my life. You humiliated me."

"Please come back so we can talk about it," John hollers out of his driver's side window.

I don't bother to turn around and say, "You need to think about what you've done to me. You don't love me. If you did, you'd treat me right, like I was good company. It's about what you do, not what you fucking say."

"I thought I was. I tried to be good to you. Now that I know you're the sensitive type, I'll choose my words better. I can't replace you, so please don't do this to me," John insists.

As I begin to start my car, I tell John, "I'm cold, halfway wet from what my aunt did to me, and all you can see is me in those heels with my legs gapped open on the side of the road. You call that being good to me? Hmmmph. Men, you're all the same. You couldn't choose your words better because the little head rules the big head to fuck some pussy. When will you people learn? I can be replaced by anyone with a hole, I'm sure."

"No, you've got me wrong. I'm not like that. This is a big misunderstanding," John says, hopping out of his truck.

Just as he begins to run toward my Yota, I pull up next to him, look him square in his eyes, spit in his face, and say, "I'll give you something to understand. Good-bye! And don't come around my brother's job tryna stress him out. He's got a murder record, and it was hard for him getting that so don't risk him gettin' fired. Got that?" I pull off like a bat out of hell and leave him wiping spit off his face, running and shouting, "No, come back. Please give me one more chance, Stephanie."

I'm so into playing my part that I don't realize that John is way out of earshot. I'm still arguing with air, saying, "Get back in your truck and leave me alone. All White men wanna do is experiment with a sista so they can talk about it in private or something. Take your one more chance and go to hell with your pack of lies. Falling in love with me, yeah right!"

After I finish the sentence, I look around and laugh up a storm. All I'm really gonna do is sit around the corner for about ten minutes, then come back to talk to Shawn before I head on back to Wes's part-time spot. Boy, that was a good little impromptu haul-off. John didn't even see this one coming. BET, huh? Fuck that. I got enough of what I wanted. My current desire is to take a hot shower, wash Big Shirley's soda out of my hair, and get my ass to bed. It's been a long day, and then some. Speaking of some, I'm horny. I notice that money does make me all wet and slippery down below, and John did nothing but get it hot for Wes! I'm gonna douche with some Massengil, and wash the coochie extra well just in case Wes swings by early. I won't even care if I've gotta role play. I'll take it any way I can get it.

So long, sucker, Johnny boy, and thanks for the nice pile of things. Sorry about spitting in your face and everything, but I had to make sure you understood that I really don't want to see your ass ever again. If I don't say so myself, I just delivered the perfect punch.

16

SEX ON THE BEACH

I'm a firm believer that if you don't spend time putting some knowledge in your head, you can easily work your way up to becoming a stupid person with a partial view of the world. I know that I should at least be watching *Nightline* or listening to WOL, where information is power, but to hell with current events. The kind of dirt I'm doing requires sex appeal, not a plethora of miscellaneous knowledge. Maybe I'm changing or my circumstances have changed me. Getting to the bottom of it really doesn't matter much because I can't dictate the details of how this I-have-a-sugar-daddy game should be played. Now that I've finished putting away my goodies from my haul with John, I'll pick up my cell phone to stiffen Wes's dick. I need to think of something to say that will make him swallow deeply and nearly shit himself from unexpectedly processing my bold words.

"Wes, baby, um, guess what I'm doing right now? I just took a long hot shower, and I'm playing with myself, fantasizing about having sex on the beach with you. I'm butt naked, looking through the glass right now, staring at the ships far away, wishing I could wrap these thick brown legs around your waist so we can cum together. They're freshly lotioned and shaved, and they feel so soft to touch. Mmmm, Wes, I hope you can slip away from home and finish what I've started. Do you think you can tell Tomi you have to run to the store to get some milk? It wouldn't be a lie 'cause I need my tits sucked so bad, I'm licking my pretty-ass titties myself. Don't fuck Tomi's pussy too much; save some stick action for me. I'm gonna love you right on up, like it was my last time I could get stroked, if you know what to do, following this message. Good night, honey. I wish it was me in Tomi's spot, but all you gotta do is close your eyes and pretend she's your baddest chick." I make a kissing noise into the receiver of the cell phone.

    I'm not even gonna give the brotha a chance to call back. It's about game not a return call, so I'll let the cell phone rest and charge until daylight comes—if Wes doesn't make it here first. Before I go to bed, I think I'll put this CD player to use and find out if he and Tomi listen to more than smooth jazz and loud gospel. It's a shame to have a romantic spot like this and no man to keep me warm tonight, but that's the life I'm stuck living. Tomi's gotta take hers directly off the top, before I can get mine. I know I can't have everything I want.

    I slip into a new short nightie, throw the tags in the bamboo trashcan, and slip into soft, silk sheets. I take one look around, smile, and sleep away my loneliness. REM isn't far behind. While I'm resting, calm and secure, I feel some hands in my dream. I feel caresses, kisses on my lips, licks down on my vagina. I flow farther into this zone. It's delicious in a way I've never felt before. It's erotic. It's soft. It's kind to my womanly curves. The hands take their time with me and respond to my moans with a desire to please me, too. I like being here. I've longed to find this place. The hands aren't too busy to cater to my needs. Consideration is what I've lacked for as long as I've had the memory of life. The touches aren't rushed. The kisses are gentle as a summer wind. I smile. I feel complete. I'm not goin' anywhere. This is a good thing; I feel like my soul has been revived.

    It's funny because I never sleep this deeply. It's like my dream is as real as living color. I don't examine what is. I just feel the hands as they lift my gown from my head, hold me close, then suck on my nipples and massage my breasts. No man has ever done that this way—none. I'm so happy that my body feels loved. I feel my legs opening, not in a forced way, but purely natural and freely. It isn't for the money; it's for the way I'm being dealt with. I can appreciate this vibe. It's hypnotic. Fingertips tease my vagina before goin' straight to it again. I gush. I moan. I feel more soft licks and the twirling of a tongue. I gush again, but it rises and mounts into a wild orgasm that is as sweet as honey poured straight from a honeycomb. I'm happy again. I hear the waves crashing against the rocks outside of the clear window across from the bed. My mind is free. My soul is resting peacefully. The lips return to my vagina. They make me tingle all over. This time I cum, but I'm exhausted and physically depleted. All I can do is curl up in a peaceful ball as the arm of the one who made me feel as beautiful as the glow of the sun lays on top of me. If I had a soul mate,

I'd hope that lovin' him would make me feel a lot like this. Damn, that shit would be the bomb.

The light shines through the soft, white curtains. It's so radiant, it hurts my eyes. I feel better than usual, like my soul was satisfied with the richest of foods. I think I had some kind of a dream about . . . Wait a minute, Wes came in. I wasn't dreaming! I'm gonna put my head under the covers and suck his dick into a hardness of Mount Rushmore to thank him for what he gave me last night.

I close my eyes, slide way down into the covers, press my head against his middle, and prepare my mouth for taking Wes to a place he claims Tomi can't. I reach to grab it, but there's nothing there to yank and suck. I throw my eyelids open. I fling the covers back. The bright sunlight illuminates an unfamiliar face. My lips begin to move as a rush of confusion invades my mind.

I sit up in bed and shout, "What the fuck is this shit? Who the hell are you?"

Ms. Anonymous White Girl smiles brightly, plucks sleep out of the corner of her eyes, reaches over to shake my hand, and says, "I'm Wes's publicist, Patty Bingham. You must be Jalita. It's nice to meet you. I've heard so much about you, girlfriend."

I wrinkle my forehead, look her up and down and tell her, "I ain't shaking your damn hand like we're in a business meeting. Your ass is laying up in this bed with me, and I asked you what you're doing here, so you better say something and explain this shit real fast, Ms. Patty." I gulp hard, and my heart begins to race.

"You *are* as sexy as Wes said. He sure knows how to pick 'em!"

"What?"

"For us, you know, for our fun-filled fantasies."

"Oh no, I didn't with you!"

"Mmm-hmm! You sure did," she assures me.

"Oh shit," I yell, getting up, pointing at the blue-eyed, blond-haired skinny broad who's got no problems with being in bed with another girl. I'm shaking, and I can't stop. I'm in extreme shock and can't pull myself together yet.

"Relax. You really enjoyed last night."

"What is your definition of enjoy?"

"You came at least five times. Do you know how many women have trouble just having one orgasm? You're a natural, Jalita. This is definitely a good match. I'm going to enjoy hooking up with you more than the last one."

"What? How'd you get in? Why are you here? And tell me this is a joke!"

"Wes lets me slip in the back door when he gets a new girl. I've got a key. He told me all about you the other night after the Celebrity Bash in D.C. when we were, you know . . . Doesn't he have the prettiest dick you've ever seen? I love me some brothas. They're hung like mules and as passionate as they want to be," she says, pushing a patch of hair behind her ear.

"I don't swing that way, and Wes shoulda revoked your key privilege when I moved in. This is some trick you two pulled on me, and I don't appreciate it," I say, moving toward her. She is all White for sure 'cause she's sitting nice and calm like she did me a favor instead of seeing she should be running.

"But what's the problem? You enjoyed it," she insists. I don't appreciate her pushy attitude. It's making me want to beat that ass.

"So you did all of it to me last night, and think nothing of it, huh?"

"Your pussy tastes real good, Jalita. I can't wait for our threesome. It's gonna be hot. Can I lick it some right now?"

"Get the fuck out you gay White bitch!"

"What?"

"What, nothing. I'm tired of running into this I-like-pussy-and-dick shit. Is anyone completely straight in the D.C. Metropolitan Area? Damn, not another freak of the week," I scream at her.

"But Wes said that we—"

I cut her off in mid-sentence and say, "Ewww, and stop looking at my tits like that, you bisexual ho. There is no *we* nothing. You've definitely got it twisted, and I'm about to straighten it out right now," I say.

"Wes is coming soon. He'll get mad if I leave. Like, calm down, okay? I'm sure he was just trying to surprise you. He and I do this all of the time. No offense intended. It's all in good fun, girlfriend."

"Calm down? Calm down? You just fucked me, and I don't have sex with no one who's got what I do. *Get the fuck out, and don't be calling me girlfriend!*" I scream again. This time I find my pocketknife and brandish it in her face, which reminds me of the inside of a raw ham. Now she gets the point. Her smile leaves.

"Is that how you thank me? You want to hurt me for giving you a whole row of orgasms? That's foul," Patty announces, reaching for her clothes and shoes.

"I'm gonna count to ten. If your pale, flat, Somalian-looking ass isn't out of here by the time I count to one, I'm gonna cut you for raping me!"

"I didn't rape you! You didn't tell me to stop nothin'!" she says. I move closer with my knife. Then I begin to count, "One, two, three, four." Patti fumbles and trips, losing half of her clothes.

As she looks back to see if I'm bluffing, I keep counting. "Five, six, seven." By the time I make it to ten, Patty breaks out into a run down the hallway to make it out of my sight.

After the back door slams, and I hit ten, I'm so fuming mad that I'm gonna have to call Wes before I can take my morning pee or guzzle some H_2O. If he doesn't answer, I just might have to take me a trip to Mitchellville and let him know what I think of his stunt, even if it might get me kicked out for good. I mean, he's lacing me and all, but I'm not gettin' no ice and real thorough shit, *yet*.

I grab the cell with rage in my heart and pound Wes's number. As my heart begins to race, I try to breathe more calmly as I once suggested to Tony's girlfriend, Charlene, and say, "Look you freaky deaky Black motherfucker, don't be sending no hungry-looking White girls over to keep me company and turn me into no lesbo. I don't have nothing against gays, but I don't want to be one either. If you haven't noticed, I'm into dick and only dick, okay? I don't play that shit. Does your ass understand that? You better call me in the next ten minutes or you'll be sorry for the day you laid eyes on this soul sista whose wheels will be rolling toward route 301."

Within five minutes, the cell rings. The caller ID shows me it's Wes answering to my wrath. I don't even get to say hi before he sounds off.

"Now let me explain somethin' to you, Jalita. I don't need no lip or stress from you. I got that right up in here. I jacked off in the shower this morning, and a nigga was feeling good until I found out you went off on Patty like that. All you had to do is calmly hit me up and ask me what the deal was. Yes, I sent her over. Yes, she and I have threesomes. Yes, I wanted you both to spend the night together. And yes, I thought my publicist would be good company for your ass. You left me that nice little erotic message that turned me on so much, I wanted to get down with you and her today. You turn me on for your looks and she turns me on because her creative angles keep me visible and remembered. If I'm remembered then I'm worth more. Her ass is connected and I need to keep my media contacts tight. Now look, if you don't act right, I can find someone else who will easily cooperate. And if you shut your damn mouth, I'll bring you the surprise I was planning later, too. Don't you *ever* make my dick go limp by threatening me with telling Tomi shit. Get with my program or pack your shit and hit the highway. If you want to do that right now, be my guest. As for myself, I've gotta go eat my breakfast because Tomi's waiting in the kitchen, and she hates it when I take my time getting to the table, and the eggs get cold because Mary can't keep standing there keeping my meal warmed over. Peace."

17

DAMAGE CONTROL

I stand in the middle of that great big, romantic bedroom and decide that there's no use in arguing with a rich man. What Wes wants, Wes gets 'cause he might as well have all the money in the world. I need to be a leech on his back, to build myself up a stash, and he's still got plenty of what I want. So what if he loves Tomi, and I'm just his toy? Wes isn't gonna be the one to love me, so I might as well shake off that thought. But Wes is gonna make me earn my place in his world, and I'll treat that NBA negro just like a king then. It's time for a little damage control.

"Yeah, Wes, Jalita here. Um, got that message from you. Now that I've thought it over, I realize that I acted like a stupid kid. Look I'm only nineteen, and I've got a lot to learn about being around a VIP. Please tell your publicist that she just freaked me out the way she came in, but I'm sorry I scared her. I realize you don't need the stress and drama. I know you need some lovin' with no questions asked, so I'm gonna sure 'nuff stop tripping and enjoy our little no-strings-attached arrangement. And Wes, spend some quality time with Tomi, because she's your boo, and she's got needs, too. The next time I see you, I've got a surprise for you, too, and I'm not just referring to the make-your-back-so-sore-you'll-need-a-rubdown-in-linament makeup sex you've got coming your way. I promise you won't be limp for long. Peace and apologies. Smooches, baby, and please don't be mad. I'll be watching you do your thing on TV."

$

Three days later, I light about fifteen beautiful candles around Wes's Jacuzzi tub and wash him like a Geisha girl. I went to some freak shop and bought a sexy schoolgirl uniform—a short pleated skirt, thigh highs, a tight cardigan sweater, and some body lotion that warms up when it's massaged into skin. I even thought to buy two ponytail holders and squeezed my blow-dried hair in them, on both sides of my head. I dry Wes off, massage him, then wrap him in his robe and lead him to the dining room table.

"What's all this, Jalita?" Wes says, grinning.

"A home-cooked meal, candlelight, and I've got presents for you."

"Presents? You went shopping for yourself today?"

"No, Wes. They're for you, silly," I say, grinning and batting my lashes.

"You didn't have to do that. Your daddy doesn't want you spending money on him. You bathing me while wearing this sexy costume after a hard practice is a big enough treat."

"But you're always paying for everything. That's not right. It was worth it, and just a little something, but not what you're use to, I'm sure," I announce. "Sit down, and let me serve you. I know what you eat on the road can't rival with this," I say, sliding out the chair for Wes. I parade in the kitchen and dish up some fake home-cooked food, although I did warm it myself. It was worth me taking a trip to Levi's in Mitchellville to find some Southern seasoned greens, honey-cured ham, corn bread, and macaroni and cheese fit for the President of the United States. Wes won't know I didn't slave over a hot stove though 'cause I was smart enough to drive the containers all the way to a trashcan in the park down the street. I'd rather starve than slave over a hot oven for myself, let alone a damn hungry man.

"You did all of this for me? And you look fine in that uniform and those stilettos, baby," Wes says, inhaling the savory steam from his dinner plate.

"Well who else was gonna do it?" I lie.

"Let's say grace. Bow your head," Wes says. I do. I can't believe how Wes and Tomi are on that same page to honor God, then turn around and act like God's got His eyes shut. They better hope God doesn't have VCRs in heaven 'cause if He does, He's got lots of tape to play back while deciding if He's gonna let those two into the pearly gates!

"Dear Lord, bless us for the food Jalita and I are about to receive. In your precious, holy name. Amen."

"Amen," I repeat. We lift our heads. I never say grace, but pretend I usually do.

"Go ahead and eat, I'll catch up with you," I tell him, making my plate.

"Oh, damn, this is the best! Girl, where'd you learn to burn like this?"

"Well it's not that good."

"Not that good? You know what to do with some pots and pans. This is the best food I've ever tasted. Most of these hos can't even boil water good," Wes says, chewing and savoring every morsel he balances on the fork. Well they say the way to a man's heart is through his stomach, maybe it's the way to dig up a nice shovel full of gold, too.

"So what are you drinking, Wes?"

"I'll take water from the cooler."

"Water? But I made freshly squeezed lemonade for you," I lie. I bought that from Levi's too.

"Bring it on, then. I'm supposed to be on a strict four-or five-meal-a-day schedule and you've got me cheating like a motherfucker." I get up, pour Wes a tall glass of lemonade and set it in front of him.

"Oh, baby, you've got a little macaroni cream around your mouth. Let me get that for you," I tell Wes, picking up his cloth napkin, wiping a small speck of yellow from his face while pushing my breasts all up in his face.

"Jalita, you know how to take care of a man. I like your style. This exceeded my expectations."

"Good, 'cause I don't mind being a submissive servant sometimes. Plus you handled your business in Boston. You came behind number seven who missed shooting that free throw and tore it down with those trick shots. My baby's got skills," I say, winking. "Oh, I almost forgot, I've got something to show you," I say, springing up from my chair.

"It's nice to know you watch me play. That's sweet. Eat your food. It can wait, beautiful," Wes says.

"But I want to see if you like it," I say. My food can wait. Shit, he'll be out of here in under two hours, and I've got all the time in the world to feed my face.

"What's all this?" Wes says when I return. He continues as I push two gift boxes in front of him.

"One for you, one for Tomi," I explain, massaging his shoulders.

"What?" he says, patting his stomach.

"See, I realized how wrong I was a few days ago, so I just wanted to, want to—" I say, then walk to the other side of the room and begin to conjure up a false cry for sympathy.

"What's wrong, Jalita?" Wes says, walking over to comfort me.

"I hate that we had our first official fight. Now you won't want me anymore. I'm aware that I'm no master of relationships, but I accept how I am and want to explain that I don't want to chase you away by pissing you off."

Wes strokes my cheek, looks in my eyes, and tells me, "Oh no, everything's cool. I got you a surprise, too, but later, okay?"

"You mean it? You're not gonna kick me out 'cause I need to find a job or decide if I'm gonna go back to Virginia to school when the break's over? I don't have anywhere to go but some crummy motel that gets so damn expensive," I say, sniffling and keeping my head low.

"You're not going anywhere. I want you to stay. I want you. I even need you now. Relax, beautiful."

"Really, Wes? You're not just telling me this to make me stop crying?"

"No way. I told you your daddy will take care of his pussy, remember?"

"Thank you, Wes. You're the best," I say.

"Well, you know it," he jokes, wiping my tears with my napkin.

"Open your gift please," I say.

"Sure, but only if you stop crying. You're too fine to be encouraging fine lines and premature wrinkles. You better take care of my face. Now let's sit back down," Wes says. We both do.

I smile and tell him, "I hope you like it." Wes unties the bow, tears the paper, and pulls out three different types of antibacterial hand formulas from Bath and Body Works.

"This is nice. I can really use this. Thank you, Jalita!" Wes says, then bends over the table to kiss me.

"I know how you feel about germs, so I knew I had to get it for my baby when I saw it. When you can't get to a sink, that stuff will keep your hands super clean. Oh, and the other is for Tomi. One is Mango Mandarin Foam Burst body wash and the other is Orange Blossom Purely Silk body lotion. When I met her, she told me how much she likes her pampering stuff, so I did my best to mimic her taste. I know she's use to designer and boutique everything, but if you give it to her out of thoughtfulness, she'll eat that up," I explain, batting my lashes. Little does Wes know that I didn't pay for nada. Both gifts are compliments of John from Alabama, from when I was shopping on his dime in Arundel Mills.

Wes looks up at me, good and confused, then says, " But I don't get it."

"Well I understand things, where we stand, and if you've got to keep her happy, I'm gonna be more considerate of what she needs. If Wes is happy, I'm happy, and I'm here to make life easier for you. So when you go home, I want you to write a nice, sweet message on the gift card and give it to Tomi. She'll feel secure that you do love her, or whatever arrangement you two have," I explain.

"This shit doesn't come along every day. You ain't going a damn place, girl. I must be dreaming 'cause, not only are you phat as shit, you're a genius and think just like me. I think we're going to get along just fine," Wes says, then sticks his tongue in my mouth and guides me to the bedroom.

"I think so, too, Wes. I think so, too."

Wes humps me like a dog, as usual, but this time under candlelight, with those tiny ships in the background that are so small all we can see are the glow of the lights. It's something that happens in a man's brain chemistry when a woman gives him what he needs with no protest and all smiles. I'm figuring out a woman needs to emphasize the good and omit the bad. Men appreciate that upbeat, keep-your-real-damn-opinion-to-yourself approach. Wes is playing me and I'm playing him, but while we are touching, moaning, caressing, and getting all freaky deaky, it just doesn't seem like we're playing a game.

The whole time I'm getting poked to death, I'm thinking of my surprise, which better be some expensive, impressive shit, or else I'm gonna sniff out a higher bidder who wants my thong to keep hitting the bedroom floor. I don't know a lot about designer clothes, expensive perfumes, and all of the other things I should be demanding, but I'm gonna start educating myself by watching *Style* on cable, reading *Elle* and *Vogue*, and eavesdropping on high-maintenance hos when Wes invites me to sit in the bleachers. As far as I'm concerned, Wes is getting off light, but that's just a temporary matter. My itching palm tells me so.

About thirty minutes later, after Wes gets his strength back, I watch him slide into a pair of jeans and throw a long-sleeve FUBU T-shirt over his head. He always heads straight to the shower after fucking me, so I wonder what the hell is up. After I slide a thong over my ass and stuff my titties into a matching push-up bra, I suddenly realize that Wes must be reading my mind about increasing my net worth.

He walks over to his leather coat, puts it on, and tells me, "I had a real nice time with you tonight, beautiful. Now it's your turn to get something you need. Look in my inside left pocket and pull out what you find." My heart starts to pound with excitement. In silence, I pull a gray key with an alarm gadget from his pocket.

He announces, "It belongs to you, Jalita."

In shock, I ask, "Does it?"

"Yeah, unless you don't want your brand spanking new Lexus," Wes says proudly.

I slide my feet into my stilettos and bolt outside in my underwear, pretending that I've forgotten it's wintertime. I leave the front door wide open. A stylish candy-apple-red ride is parked behind my Toyota, and I can't believe I've been upgraded this high so quickly. I jump up and down like I won the showcase on the *Price Is Right*, then prepare to rattle off some lies by the time Wes is in earshot.

He says, "You better put a coat and something more on all that ass and tits. Have you forgotten we had flurries this morning?"

I respond, "I know, I know, but I'm so excited. Now I can return this fake rent-a-wreck to my aunt in Virginia. This piece of shit wasn't worth the fifty dollars a week she was charging me to use it, but I had to have something to drive. No one's ever given me anything. Not even my family. Thank you, Wes! I can't believe you did this just for me. You are my daddy, just like you said. You don't talk about it, you *are* about it. You take such good care of me."

"Looks like I picked out the perfect surprise then," Wes comments coolly.

"I'm freezing. How do I get in?" I blurt out quickly.

"Hit the button on the left. You're crazy," Wes says, grinning. I know my almost nude stunt is making him feel like the man, so I block out the cold and play on his ego.

"Yeah, about the car," I say, running in the dark, then opening and slamming the door. I turn on the engine and fumble until I find the dome light. By the time Wes gets into the passenger side, the heat is blasting, and I'm running my hands up and down the black leather seats. I'm intoxicated by the fresh, new smell of leather, and almost feel high.

"Jalita, I need to give you the rules now," Wes says. My smile turns serious.

"Rules for what?" I inquire.

"Your Lexus SC 430 car rules, that's what."

"If it's really my car, why do I have to honor rules?" I ask. I really want to say, "*If you're giving me the car, why can't I fuck it up, if I please? All John did was remind me to change the oil in the Toyota.*" Instead, I suppress my comment and pretend to respect him.

"Remember what I said about having your full cooperation?" Wes reminds me.

"Yes, daddy," I say obediently.

"Good, so listen up. One, never take the ride through a gas station wash. One fuck-up with a bent brush bristle, and there goes the paint. I have a brotha I use exclusively to keep the cars clean. He hand washes the Hummer, the two SLKs, and even details my BMW bike. Two, be sure to take up two parking spaces whenever you take the whip out and floss. Three, you're now a bona fide Blitzers fan, that's why I set a Blitzers hat in the back window. Don't remove it. That'll piss me off in a major way. Four, I'll keep up with the maintenance schedule. I don't even want anyone lifting the car hood to check the oil. Five, put on my coat, remove what you find in the trunk, and get your half-naked ass back in the car, real quick."

Wes is getting on my damn nerves with his bossy shit, but since he's a finalist in my take-care-of-Jalita-right competition, I comply. After I put on his coat, get out, and pop the trunk, I find a pretty green box sitting in the middle. I grab it and run back into the car, then I give it to Wes with a fresh smile.

He asks, "What are you giving it to me for? That's yours, too, beautiful. Open it."

I rip the packaging open and find a jet-black purse.

"Thanks for the purse, Wes, but I don't understand," I say, looking bewildered.

"I peeped Tomi's old Coach bags in the hall closet. There's no need for you sporting secondhand merchandise, and I know that you took them from my cousin Shawn after Tomi told him to give them away. Congratulations, you've made it to the next phase. I plan to keep you around, Jalita. That's why I've taken the first major step of investing in you. Now open the damn thing." When I do, I discover a wallet with $500 in a Prada bag. Before I can ask another question, Wes says, "This is rule number six. Keep the Lex fully gassed with premium petro. Nothing less. When you're running low, give me a holler. I didn't want to give you too much at one time because I'll be keeping up with your whereabouts."

I egg Wes on, and inquire, "What's rule number seven, daddy?"

He replies, "When you want to roll out, I want to hear about it first. Let me know something. Now number eight is crucial. I want you to memorize this shit, and be able to recite it backward and forward in your sleep."

"I'm listening."

"Don't ever let another nigga put one foot up in your car. Don't ever go see another nigga in your car. Don't ever let another nigga pull over your car so he can holler. You're my bitch, and I'm the nigga who feeds, clothes, and shelters you. Got it?"

"That goes without saying, daddy. I can't even force myself to look at another negro. It's all about you, from sunrise to sunset. *Now do you have any real rules left?*"

"That was it, but I do have some big news."

"What is it?"

"My agent called, and I've got a new sneaker that will be coming out by the end of next summer."

"That's great news, baby. I know how we can celebrate," I tell Wes, hugging him around his neck.

"How?"

"I'll elaborate later 'cause Tomi might be busy reading *Modern Bride* magazine in her flannel pajamas, picking out the color invitations and dreaming about you settling down with her for good. I don't want to keep you out too long. Your woman needs to stay in a good mood."

"Actually, I already missed Bible study, so let me be the judge of that."

"If you say so. I better work quick, fogging up the window with thank-you kisses 'cause you-know-who will be tryna find out why her dick didn't show for Bible study." I open up Wes's coat and push his face in between my breasts.

When he unfastens my bra and begins sucking on my nipples, I tell him, "Christen my ride before you go home. Starting tomorrow, you deserve as much sex on the beach as you can handle. If you transfer the title in my name in the next thirty days, maybe I can get to know Patty better, if that's what you really want."

"Damn, you're killing me!" Wes exclaims. I know that I scared Patty so badly that she won't come back. Even if she's got more guts than I think, we won't be taking that shit too far 'cause all I'll allow her to do is stare at my phat ass while I earn every dollar laying on my back. I know better than to get caught up in the game.

As far as the "orders" go, I don't care if Wes is an anal retentive. He's rich and about to have his own sneaker out in the fall. Mo' money, mo' money, mo' money for this gold-digging honey. Shawn may still be living in a one-bedroom apartment because his cousin hasn't done a thing for him, but when it comes to me, I'll get mine.

18

A FOOL IN LOVE

Although Wes is only twenty-five, he's my daddy 'cause a daddy is supposed to provide, and does that shit so well. Shawn is my boy 'cause I finally understand him being a fool in love is all the proof I need that he's not interested in taking my pussy for a test drive. And since Jackie's got him shook up half the time, the least I can do is check on Shawn since he seems to catch it from so many angles while I'm getting my way every time I turn around.

When Shawn answers his work phone I say, "Shawn, it's only 10:00 A.M. Do you know where your Jackie is this morning? Whaaaat's crackin'?" I tease.

"Jalita?"

"The one and only."

"How'd you get this number?"

"I ain't no rocket scientist, but I do know how to use the alphabet well enough to look it up in a phone book."

"Okay, smart ass."

"Jackie isn't gonna quit you for good for taking my call, is she?"

"Why you always teasing me about Jackie?"

" 'Cause you let her treat you like a dumb chump, that's why!"

"Then how come we're engaged?"

"Oh, so this week you're engaged again?"

"Okay, Shawn, that's why I don't bother to put my two cents in most times. Talking to you is like communicating with a Martian. You don't understand the words coming out of my mouth or anyone else's when it comes to that girl. You may not be rich, but you've got things to offer."

"So how was your date with Mr. John?" he asks, snickering.

"Oh, yeah, I owe you for that."

"So who is he?"

"He was nobody. Just some fool I was nice to when he lost his job."

"Seemed like more than that to me."

"Mind your own damn Jackie and call me in the morning."

"And what am I gonna call you on?"

"I've got a cell now, with free nights and weekends, I might add," I say, giggling.

"Where are you gettin' all this stuff from so fast?"

"I told you about your nosiness. I almost like you, even though you're a man and all, but I do have my limits. I work for mine, just like you say you do."

"Jalita, I hope you're stayin' away from Wes. I warned you. If you never listen to me in the future, listen to me now. Leave that boy alone," he cautions.

"I'm not even in Maryland. I went back to Virginia. I'm calling from the dorm. I keep telling you that Wes's flashy self doesn't turn my head. If you must know, it's a turnoff."

"Oh, really?"

"Yeah. Don't play no Inspector Gadget on me. Make better use of your time, and play it on Jackie."

"I just have a good memory, that's all. Some things you've told me about school aren't matching up."

"Well remember that you have some balls. Stop being faithful to someone who doesn't give a constipated shit and four wipes of toilet paper about you."

"Love is love, even if it isn't perfect. If I want Jackie, why would I go running off with anyone else? Some stuff that comes out of your mouth is unbelievable, girl."

"You're sucked in so deep in the Jackie current, you're just a fool in love. My story matches up, you just weren't paying close attention to my words 'cause what Jackie says is all you notice. I don't know how I always stray back to tryna hammer sense into your thick head."

"So you're back in the dorm, huh?"

"Yeah. I just went to administration and put my foot down about that promise I was given. Having a big mouth pays off sometimes. I cleared the resident assistant fiasco. They fired Ebony for what she did. Nobody messes with Jalita."

"Hmmm," he says. Shawn suspects I'm lying. "Oh, I almost forgot. Guess what happened to me."

"What?"

"A few things. The first one is that someone cut the gas line on my ride."

"Whaaaaaat!" I say.

"Yeah. Lucky for me, I know about cars. I happened to be doin' some repairs and found it."

"Oh, shit."

"I also happened to check my wheels and noticed all of my hubcaps were gone."

"Why would anyone do that to you?"

"You think *I* know?"

"It was probably Jackie."

"I really don't think she's the one to blame for this."

"I know, *she* can do no wrong."

"Jackie wouldn't do something like that."

"You still got that little bathroom habit you showed me at Wes's?"

"Naw. No more of that."

"Right. I hope you've got that thing under control. I won't say over the phone but you know what I'm talking about."

"I said I took care of it. I was just feeling like shit that night. No more."

"Whatever."

"Oh yeah, the other thing was the chain letter."

"Chain letter?"

"I got some letter in the mail talking about, 'Dear friend, you have one week to talk some sense into someone you know who needs it or a whole lot of people will have bad luck for eternity. Pass it on to all your family in Maryland.' It was typed in bold and all caps, too."

"That's twisted."

"Tell me about it."

"You think the same person cut the gas line?"

"I have no idea, but I do think the same person stuck a potato over my tail pipe."

"What in the hell?"

"I know. Why would anyone take the time to carve out a hole in the middle just right so it would fit?"

"To either make the car cut off or kill you from carbon dioxide."

"Exactly, but that means they'd be singling me out. I haven't done nobody wrong. I live a clean, simple life."

"What about the return address on the letter?"

"None."

"Postmark?"

"No town, no date, just a postage stamp."

"Boy, you better watch your back. It might even be Jackie's ex tryna get even."

"I hadn't thought of that. He is still real possessive of her."

"I just did, considering that he went through the trouble of sending someone to pay you a visit once already."

"True that."

"Or it might even be some bozo tryna scare you. Then again, it could be those ten-year-old kids that have been goin' around stealing cars in the District and some parts of PG County."

"Those are all possibilities. Well I gotta go. Some customer has a question. What's your cell number? Maybe I can hit ya back later."

"Oh, well, I just got it and I can't remember the number by heart. No one has called me on it, you know? I'll give it to you next time," I lie.

"So look it up in your paperwork and give me a ring back?"

"I'm getting ready to leave out to go to choir rehearsal."

"Since when did you get into the church?"

"Wes and Tomi served as two examples that gave me a push to join one, if you must know."

"Mmm-hmm, well bye, girl."

"Bye, Shawn, and be careful."

"I will. You can even pray for me since you say you're a church girl, now."

"You must have been reading my mind. I'll be on my knees tonight, on your behalf."

"Please do. I'm don't know why, but I think I need it."

19
OPERATION PUNK ASS

It's January 20, 2004. I just realized that registration for spring semester at Bentley University is tomorrow. I could pull a Kate move and clear out all my shit I've been collecting, leave the Lex behind, and drive the Yota and use the money I've been saving, although I'm about $200 short on my tuition, or stay here and live off Wes's ends until it's time to pink-slip him. I wouldn't even consider goin' back if I knew I couldn't scrounge up the remainder of my tuition, but now I know that I can do it. One visit to a pawn shop and my ass is back in the running and can even spring for off-campus housing this time. Negative. I think this option is conceivable but unnecessary. To make sure that I keep schemin' I'm gonna tear up my roundtrip bus ticket that I've been holding. Shit, my newly spoiled ass wouldn't be caught dead smelling farts on the bus now anyway.

Things are goin' so well here in Maryland, there's no need to make a last-ditch effort to hightail it to Virginia, now that I know Wes is serious about our arrangement. How serious is he? After Wes left, I whipped out my cell phone to find out how much "my" cute Lex is worth. When I hit up this website called fantasycars.com, I nearly fainted. I guess I've got mad whip appeal skills if my daddy spent $63,640 on my whip just so I can floss in style. That in and of itself gives me license to be nasty. Every man with some ends and every woman with a man with some ends can say good-bye to the rookie. Jalita La Shay Harrison is an official player and gold digger. Most people hate to get up and go to work in the morning, but that's 'cause they're too dumb to learn how to work less and earn more.

The baddest chick's got mad privileges to learn to get rich the lazy way. Instead of fighting rush-hour traffic, working my blood pressure up while keeping an eye out for road rage, it's just me, peace, and quiet in Wes's spot, giving this Best Buy circular a once-over. As I scan the pages, I start mentally writing my wish list. There's no way I'd be stupid enough to write out my list and risk Wes finding out how much I calculate and scheme. He wants to think he's in control of what he dishes out, so that's what I allow him to believe. In his mind, Jalita don't know which way the world turns. Wrong. Wrong. Triple wrong, you presumptuous, cocky, motherfucker.

I still have priorities. First, I must set up shop in Maryland and get a P.O. box for private mail that Wes shouldn't find. Second, I need to collect a Toshiba processor notebook to organize my grand finale gold digging plan when I flush out the details regarding goin' for mine. It's only gonna set Wes back fifteen hundred dollars, on sale. Shit, he can save one hundred dollars if he mails in the rebate, but something tells me he's a baller who doesn't care about being cheap to have more for a rainy day, or just more, period. Fuck all that considerate shit. That's Tomi's job to be his adviser and complain about coming down to financial reality. Let her ass be the worrywart. She's good at it—no, an *expert* at it. She's in it for the long haul, not me.

My immediate problem is that I can't ask for anything major since he did just park that pretty Lex in the driveway. I know who I can hit up, if I do a little research to locate him: *Cleveland.* So what if I did say Cleveland was history? I reserve the right to see his mug one last time, especially if he's gonna be the victim of Operation Punk Ass. If he was stupid enough to tell me he worked for Social Security in Baltimore, then I'm bold enough to stand in this lobby and flirt with this guard to pull up a last name and floor to locate him. Why wouldn't he tell Cleveland's niece who flew in from L.A. where her uncle is? Family has a right to know, especially ones who hit the scene rocking designer gear.

After I take a trip to the post office and pay seventy-eight dollars to rent a P.O. box for a year, finding the whereabouts of my favorite timid punk is a piece of cake. I'm guessing that Cleveland stepped out of the office to take care of one thing or another. I relax my brain, spin around in his plush black chair, cross my arms behind my head, then cross my legs, and put my high-heeled Giuseppe Zanotti boots on top of the papers on his desk. Cleveland turns the corner while reading something, and doesn't look up immediately.

When he does, I say, "I have some unfinished business with you. Are you aware that your wife and son chased me down in Arundel Mills Mall? That he-woman bitch tried to body slam me in front of a whole crowd who was watching a movie. I expect to be compensated for my emotional distress, Cleveland." He jumps. Papers fly from his hands. All I can see is a cloud of white until they hit the floor.

"How did you know where to find me, Jalita? Keep your voice down. In case you haven't noticed, I'm at work." He looks at me like I'm a stalker.

I point my finger in his direction, and say, "Look, if you don't start talking about things I motherfucking want to discuss, I'll stand out in the hall and scream that you raped me on your boat and tearfully announce that I'm about to file charges. Do you want me to go there to wake some overpaid government workers up?"

"Of course not. I'm sorry about what happened at the mall. She told me all about it. Life hasn't been cushy for me either, so could you cut me a break?"

"Fuck you and your problems. What is happening to you is your damn choice. You don't deserve a break," I say coldly.

"I told you, it's about the kids," Cleveland whispers, then tramples on top of his papers. He nearly slips from running to shut his office door in a hurry.

When he returns, I stare him down and say, "Do you realize you broke my heart? You said you'd be my man on the down low. You used me. I thought we could have a special bond."

"I'm sorry, Jalita. It's not like I planned on getting caught. I still would love to be with you," Cleveland responds.

"Hell no. I'm not getting smoked over your married ass. You put me in a dangerous position, and I don't appreciate your carelessness," I complain then kick a large stack of papers off his desk with my right heel.

Cleveland sighs, sits in the chair on the other side of the desk, and asks, "So what can I do? Please don't wreck my desk, Jalita! Those papers are for important reports."

"Fuck your desk and the papers on it," I say, picking up a picture of his family. I kiss the glass, hold it out in front of me with both hands, then laugh.

When I put it down, I open a can of Sprite sitting on Cleveland's desk. I take three swallows, then slam the can on top of a folder. After it splashes, I say, "Aaah, that hit the spot. Now back to the topic at hand. I've decided to start a small business. I need a laptop so I can organize some things on the go. You can purchase one for me as a parting gift. I think everybody in that picture would approve to keep Daddy Cleve out of trouble."

"You're blackmailing me now? I thought you liked me? We talked for hours about me deserving to be treated fairly, Jalita."

"That's Ms. Jalita to you. Maybe I decided that I liked you more for what you could give me after I thought about your liability factor."

"Damn, not another one."

I lean over Cleveland's desk, grab him by the tie, and say, "Shut up the fucking whining, you pussy. Now should I get ready to scream at the top of my lungs or what?"

In a raspy voice, Cleveland says, "I can't breathe. I'll get it if you let me go."

"Good," I say. I release my grip, then add, "I'd hate to make my throat sore. Now go tell your boss you got an emergency call from the school nurse about a vomiting Little Harry who needs an express ride home. You can't take care of this on your lunch hour because you're gonna follow me to the Best Buy in Annapolis. I'm taking no chances that your wife is lurking around somewhere in B-more." I smile, then tilt my head.

"Fine," Cleveland replies bitterly, coughing and rubbing his neck.

"Fine, who?"

"Ms. Jalita."

"Now you're talking my language. Hand over your wallet as collateral. Don't remove anything. You ain't getting away from me, and hurry your ass up, too. Traffic is a bitch, and if I have to burn too much premium gas sitting in traffic, my shopping trip will turn into a shopping spree," I announce with confidence. Cleveland rolls his eyes and drops his wallet in my Prada bag.

I'm feelin' the melodic flow of a Missy Elliot cut, having the nerve to sing off key but sparing the whole world from discovering that I'm completely tone deaf since it's too cold to roll the windows down. I smile and sing, driving eighty miles per hour all the way to Annapolis until I exit off into the town near Westfield Shopping Center. When I turn on to route 450, I slow my roll to adjust to the speed of traffic. I look in my mirror to see if Cleveland's still following me and he is.

About two hours later, I'm standing next to Cleveland in the line at Best Buy. I return his wallet to him, then he slides out a Master Card. After his credit card is verified, I snatch the box from him and head toward my Lex with the energy of a speed addict. Just as Cleveland walks over to my car, I whip my Canon Power Shot S400 Digital Camera out of my purse and snap a picture of him before he has time to throw his hands up to block his face.

He asks, "What was that for?"

I tell him, "The mistake of being married. I came prepared to remind your forgetful ass."

"But you knew I was married, so why are you doing all of this to me?"

"I was testing you to see if you'd cheat on your wife. Since you were game, I saw fit to play games," I respond in a nonchalant tone.

"I can't even get my dick sucked? I just spent fifteen hundred dollars on you, Ms. Jalita."

"You have to be kidding me. You better go home and beat all that meat. I'm focused, now that I've got what I need. This laptop will be used strictly for gold-digging purposes. I'm down with investments, but I don't need no Charles Schwab in my life. What I need to do is to start being aware of my financial future, which is in the hands of men who need Charles Schwab in theirs."

"If those are your qualifications, that's me. Now how about sucking me off?" Cleveland begs.

"I ain't no prostitute. How dare you insult me like that."

"I wasn't implying that you are."

"No thank you, Cleve. I need to get busy organizing my single candidates. I'll keep every detail straight from the physical description, what a brother does for a living, the size and color of the whip, to how many credit cards I've seen him slide out of his wallet to pay for my treats. I can stockpile some real cash."

"I don't know how or why, but your ruthlessness is turning me on. I want to be one of the men on your list. I'd be honored to be your first customer, Ms. Jalita. Why are you making me beg?"

"Hell no. I only deal with VIPs now. I have single boyfriends who pay me for my company, not married customers. That Ms. Jalita shit is getting on my nerves, so stop it. And there's no need to beg 'cause my lips ain't sucking nothing that's attached to you, shortie."

"But why? I tried to explain that I'm still willing to pay you for your time," Cleveland says, scrambling to redeem himself.

"I can roll with ballers and not feel intimidated by their title or get played. Now that I'm growing accustomed to my new lifestyle, I'm not even willing to settle for a short ride in a limo, bragging rights about letting him hit it, or being taken to restaurants like Fridays. I consider restaurants like that to be high-grade fast food. So even if you weren't married, would you be able to afford me?" I ask.

"I do have a fair amount of investments, but I can't touch them right now. It's my kids' college funds."

"I thought so. It's time to say good-bye then, even if you are balancing a sexy head on top of that neck. Just to clue you in, I'll share Jalita's rule number one, which is meant for the female hos to hear: I'll take your man just because I'm fine and I can. But if he's broke and can't find his way behind a velvet rope, he will be returned to sender with express delivery. Jalita don't do shit for free, so don't look at me, accusing this right here of tippin' with your king. If he doesn't have the money, he'll never get my thong off me, so collect your walking papers and try the cheap trick next door who might be entertaining his sorry, broke ass for his last glass of flat Coke and a cheap smile."

"Don't you think you're being a little extreme with that hard-core attitude?"

"Extreme my ass. I don't have to pay a ten-buck cover charge to pull men in clubs. I don't have to make myself look cheap in public by switching too hard, hiking my skirt up for anyone and everyone. I'm not loud and obnoxious and can easily fit in at some social affair anywhere in the country. I'm fine as shit, and I'm a baller's best accessory. Hell no, I'm not being extreme by only dating men who make at least seven figures. There's no reason why I should accept a pittance for my pleasing," I say, unzipping my coat.

"What have you become? You're not the same woman who held me in your arms on my boat. She was sweet, loving, and gentle."

"I'm a shrewd vagina owner now. I understand the game and the rules that must be honored if I wanna be the down-low boss. It's not just what's between these legs, it's all about how to get inside a dude's head, letting him think he's all that I need when I'm not even considering having it. No woman can raise no man. If the tables were turned and the ladies were in charge and they had to take the brunt of the gender laws we laid down, you people would find a way to manipulate us out of our ignorance. When you weren't up in Big Shirley's grill, you were with me, explaining that she's a nagging bitch who expects too much from you. I'm not the naive kind. I know what time it is, even in my sleep."

"So you're telling me I can't even get a little time and affection?"

"You haven't even hit it, and you're this pressed? Shit. I feel sorry for your needy ass. I'll give you something good. Get in so I can suck your dick. On your way back to Baltimore, you'll have plenty of time to think up a lie to tell your wife when she discovers your Master Card bill."

Cleveland complies, shuts the passenger door to my Lex, rears his seat back, kicks off his shoes, drops his slacks, pulls out his dick, then closes his eyes. Just as he's sure he's gonna get a sympathy suck, I whip out my digital camera again. I throw a small plastic bag of fake cocaine in his lap, then snap two pictures: one of his face, and one of the clear bag sitting next to his stiff dick. The bag holds nothing more than powdered sugar that I picked up from Giant, but Cleveland won't realize I'm bluffing. He springs up.

"What are you doing?" he asks.

"How many times are you gonna fail your fidelity test?" I ask Cleveland, snatching his shoes, grabbing his slacks, then throwing the slacks out of my driver's side window.

"Jalita, I need my pants and shoes! I can't believe you're treating me this way! What's this powder you threw at me?" Beads of sweat cover his forehead.

"It's cocaine. There's your something good you asked for."

"I don't do drugs and never will. I don't want that stuff."

I tell him, "First you said my ruthlessness was turning you on, now you're whining again. Take your cocaine and get the fuck up out of my new ride. And while you're at it, go find your pants before I find a cop. I see what that woman of yours is talking about. I'm developing these pictures in case you get out of line again. Don't put it past me to find out where to mail them to your faithful wife. I'm sure she'll be glad to read the letter about your drug habit. You know I'm good for constructing the facts as I see them. Now get gone before I scream."

Cleveland tosses the white powder in my direction and nearly breaks his neck getting out of my car. I discover that his wallet must've dropped out of his pants pocket when I threw his slacks out of the window. I can't help but to rub it in while Cleveland's getting dressed in the middle of the Best Buy parking lot faster than anyone I'd ever seen.

I shout, "I think you forgot something. Here, you pussy!" I snatch all of Cleveland's dead presidents out of his wallet, stuff them inside of my bra, then toss the battered leather thing in his direction. Then I add, "You should be thanking me I didn't keep it, but don't underestimate me 'cause I have a photographic memory. I read your license and I've filed away where you lay your head. I'll mail the letter there, if I feel like it!"

"I want my shoes. My shoes are missing. What did you do with my shoes? And I don't have enough gas to make it back to Baltimore. Could you at least give me one of my ten-dollar bills back?" Cleveland asks.

I reply, "Damn you're pathetic. Why can't you learn to stop whining?

Take the coke and put it to good use. Try selling it to a junkie who needs a fast hit. And if you really want your shoes, they'll be in the woods off 97 North," I tell Cleveland, then throw the bag of powder his way.

As he's running away, he slips on a paper Big Gulp cup and falls flat on his face. I laugh as he curses me out and limps over to his minivan. My degree of cruelty doesn't move me. If you play games you shouldn't be playing, you better be prepared to suffer the damn consequences. If Cleveland didn't understand that, he just found the shit out. Fuck it if he got the message or not though 'cause Ms. Jalita done got over on the Negro.

20

READING THE RIOT ACT

Since I reside in Wes's spot his mail is now my mail. I open the first letter and find a woman's panties and naked photos. After I conveniently dispose of the proposition to lick him everywhere and drawers that look like fancy dental floss, I roll my eyes and rip open the other piece of mail. It reads:

Wesley Antoine Montgomery,

After you were traded two years ago I had a time finding a personal address for you. It doesn't matter how I tracked you down, so stop wondering how I did it. I'm writing to remind you that it's been two years since you've seen your daughter, Dominique. In case you've forgotten how to count, that's twenty-four months. Our daughter is asking questions about your whereabouts. I'm sick of lying to her about her daddy. I'm going to put it like this: You have one week to call or get your ass to Florida to set up child support arrangements and spend some time with your daughter. If you don't express a desire to make her a priority I'll be forced to do something I should have done long ago. I'm prepared to take a day off work to find a lawyer who would be happy to take my paternity case. I have no qualms about submitting DNA to a lab—you and I know this six-year-old girl is our daughter. You're just a boy in a damn man's body but I'm a real woman who isn't afraid to stand up to you despite your newfound success and notoriety.

Word on the street has it that you're in Maryland acting like a spoiled fool. Reliable sources tell me that you're throwing orgy parties, drinking and driving, and even put that greedy Tomi bitch up in a mansion in

Mitchellville. Yes, I know you dumped me for her, but it's all good. I've come to feel that you'd rather reward Tomi with Prada, Gucci, and a new Mercedes because her phony ass feeds your inflated ego. You are one of many athletes who value a gold digger instead of a real woman who helped you get what you've got in the first place. Had I not been there to wash your sweaty uniforms, feed you after practice, and pray with you over your torn ligament you'd probably still be stuck in the hood with the rest of the trash talkers who watch TV claiming they could put some NBA player to shame. I was there when you made your first basket on that raggedy court. You kissed me for the first time, that same day, remember? It's hard to imagine that you use to carry my books and that I'm the same high school sweetheart who is writing you a letter like this. Now it's one thing that you didn't make good on your promise to come back for me after establishing yourself after college, but it's another to leave me to raise Dominique alone for the last six years. A uniform doesn't make the man who puts it on.

What did your daughter do to you, Wes? Nothing. Why is it that you can waste your money on people who wouldn't be there if you lost everything but you deny your flesh and blood who should be your everything? This is not about us, it's about an innocent child who is developing self-esteem problems because her parents were young, foolish, in love, and didn't use protection. You're not there to wipe her tears over you. I am. It breaks my heart, and it should break yours just as much. You should be ashamed of yourself. I know the Blitzers were in Florida not so long ago for a game. You could have called or something.

Don't mistake this letter as a ploy for me to get my claws in to a paid brother. I'm not looking for a kickback. I married a real man three months ago and feel that it's only right for you to contribute to your daughter's daily care. Another man is working two jobs to buy clothes, food, dolls, and going to PTA meetings for your kid. I told him all about the situation and he says don't worry about it because he'll raise Dominique as his own but that's not his responsibility, it's yours. If you don't want to build a relationship with Dominique, I'll just have to explain it to her. Your daughter needs an identity, Wes, even if another man is willing to be a father figure to her. Not that you'd care but she and I moved out of the condo shortly after I saw you last. I lost my good job due to downsizing and had to accept a substantial cut in pay elsewhere. When I met my husband, your daughter and I were living in the projects. Luckily, our Section Eight housing came through after waiting what seems like forever. My husband and I hope to move our family out of this area after I secure a job on a decent *payroll, for at least six months. I'd rather have a loving black king who's a school custodian and barber on the side, than an irresponsible, low-moraled basketball dud who doesn't have enough gumption in his big toe to get his head straight for the sake of his daughter. This would make a good news story, don't you think?*

Word on the street has it that you fucked a stripper with a bad weave and big tattoo on her breast in the VIP room of a club in Atlanta and she's itching to tell that you got her pregnant. You would think you would have used two condoms with a woman with a rep for fucking every athlete who rolls through her spot, but then again I see you're promiscuous, living carefree like you're invincible.

In closing, if you don't call our number that's been the same for the last two years very soon, I'm going to light your ass up by proving that you're not above the law.

Marquita Lewis Johnson

Yeah right. Wes's daughter. This Marquita chick is probably some jilted groupie who's using reverse psychology to get in Wes's pocket. She ain't getting shit 'cause she'll have to get five hundred feet behind me. I'm the queen bee, and I say this letter needs to be shredded and flushed down the toilet. Back to business. Shit. I can't believe the words I'm hearing fly out of the commentator's mouth. Now I'm pissed over something real. Wes is supposed to be in Milwaukee hooping it up on the court not fighting with fans who came to watch the game.

If the knucklehead fan of the other team threw an empty soda can at Wes while he was sitting on the bench, he should've said what he had to say and let it go. Had it been full or he spit on him, that would have been another story but Wes made fifteen points in the game, that's why the guy was hating in the stands and Wes should've remembered that. I guess he forgot about our talks of how athletes are often perceived as violent, overpaid dummies who don't have common sense to stay out of trouble 'cause now the big news at half time is how Wes Montgomery acted like a certified fool up in the piece. I also remember him saying that if someone sees incidents players will be fined. No doubt Wes will pay for throwing a water jug he grabbed from somewhere and hurling it at the fool's head. Shit, that was money I could've had in my purse. I haven't seen him for a few days but I'm in no rush to now. When he gets back in town I hope he doesn't come straight to my ass. I hope he wants to fuck Tomi instead.

21

A COOL MORNING

Since Wes made a dumb move, I'll call Seth and mess with his head. If Seth paid his phone bill this month, maybe I can fantasize that he's got Wes's loot and Wes has his personality. Now there's somethin' that would make me turn in my player's card. But I never will 'cause that combo doesn't exist.

"Seth, it's Jalita," I say when he answers his cell phone.

"What a pleasure. Why hello there, Jalita."

"I'm surprised to catch up with you."

"It's good to hear from you. It's been a while."

"Yeah, too long, in fact," I tease. I don't mean it.

"So why didn't you pick up the phone earlier, if you were thinking of me?" Seth asks.

"Work, that's why. Some people have obligations to meet...like me, for instance. We can talk right now, if you have a few though. I've been working so much overtime, my boss gave me the day off. Something about budgeting issues, blah, blah, blah."

"Sure, I have a few minutes...for a friend," he says.

Oh, so now I'm your pal, Sethie? I don't think so! "So what ya been up to, Seth man?"

"The usual."

"You mean eating Boardwalk Fries while taking a stroll around The Inner Harbor? That's the usual, right?" I tease.

"No, I'm just taking care of business. Nothing exciting. I do work hard, contrary to your opinion."

"How's the usual goin'? I hope it defies my logic since it doesn't seem to involve a steady schedule."

"If you're asking if I've gotten any new assignments, things are going slowly."

"If you don't have plenty of work, what do you do all day long?"

"I don't lay around watching TV, Jalita. I'm working, whether I get paid or not. Last time this woman I did work for got over on me, and I didn't get paid or have my work published. She didn't credit me for writing my article and put it on her website."

"Why don't you just get a real j-o-b like everyone else? You think you're too good to work or something?"

"As long as I'm trying my hardest, *this* is my real job. I refuse to fight with destiny. I know I'm doing the right thing. Writing is my calling," Seth says firmly.

"I bet you don't have anything coming in. Your calling won't put food in your mouth and gas in your tank. So far it sounds like what you're being called to is the unemployment line. You need to stop wasting your time and making excuses why a nine to five isn't for you. Don't you think your mom is tired of taking care of a good and grown-ass man?"

"She helps me, but she doesn't take care of me. There's a difference."

"Men like you will never change."

"I'm not shiftless, and it's really not my place to have to defend myself to you. You're not putting up anything on my behalf, so you need to be satisfied with me telling you I will complete all things in due time. This is just a lesson in patience that has nothing to do with you or your opinions of me," he answers. Translation: Sethie is still broke and hasn't learned his lesson.

"Damn, you don't have to get all uptight like that. Sorry to hear about what happened," I say, holding back the laughter. I ain't sorry to hear shit.

"Thanks, but don't go feeling sorry for me. My day is coming."

"When? Next century? Crack open the classifieds and get a j-o-b."

"Like I said, I can't predict the day or hour, but I know it's just a matter of time and putting some extra elbow grease into my plan. I have a strategy mapped out, so leave me alone about it. I'm not hitting you up for any loans," he says with confidence. I sigh. He's such a bore when it comes to his dream-catching speech.

"I get the point."

"Positive vibes, positive thinking, positive results. That's my favorite motto," Seth informs me.

"Did you get that interview with that scam artist author, Brenda Brown? You sound like you've been talking to her."

"Don't call her a scam artist, and yes, I did. It went well. I got compensation and the privilege of meeting her. Now I've gotten one more tear sheet to add to my portfolio."

"Well isn't that special," I say to poke fun at him.

"You don't need to put your insecurities off on me. I'm getting tired of it, Jalita. You've been negative this whole conversation. Why is that?"

"Excuse me?" I say, sitting up. Seth is bold. I do like that he's no spineless jellyfish.

"You just have issues with me because I'm living my dream. I know that I've got skills. If I fall down the first time, I'll get up and attack the problem until I get it right. I'm not afraid of failing because I know that taking a risk is a part of the process. You don't have to believe in me, but *I* do. I have the guts to take a leap of faith to go after what I really want, and you can't stand me for it."

"I don't have issues with you," I lie.

"You do. I told you before, I know where you're coming from."

"Just because you carry an empty briefcase and wear a halfway decent-looking silk tie every now and then, you think you know everything now, don't you?" I snap.

"Not hardly, not even about myself. I never said that."

"Well you implied it."

"Look, Jalita, I'm not trying to argue. This is supposed to be a pleasant conversation, and I'm going to see to it that it is. Life is too short for playing games. I'm tired of your snide remarks."

"I'm not into playing games, but since you're so touchy about your work status, we can talk about something else," I say.

"That would be a good idea. Have you decided anything about school? Hasn't spring semester started?"

"Yes, but I'm looking at my options first."

"Like what?"

"Hitting the lottery, goin' on some reality TV show and winning the prize, I don't know."

"You need to stop making light of your future and get empowered. You have potential, if you would just remember to make things happen like you use to."

"How'd you get to be an expert on how I need to run my life? You ain't no damn role model."

"You're so defensive and condescending. I'm just trying to help you."

"Well I've got things under control, so don't go feelin' sorry for me either."

"Whatever you say," Seth says, sounding like he doesn't believe me. "Did you check out *4:17 Vinegar Blues* yet?"

"Is this woman paying you a commission to promote her book or something 'cause you keep cramming it down my throat, and I'm sick of that."

"You know the answer to that, so why ask?"

" 'Cause it's damn annoying."

"Well I'm sorry if you find enlightenment annoying. I'm going to talk about things I believe in, and I'm not going to stop doing that for anyone, including haters," Seth says. His spunk almost makes my nipples harden, at least until I remember his little financial deficit.

"See, this is what happens when people want to run from the truth."

"You assume too much."

"Oh no, I don't."

I whisper in the phone. "Your momma still washes your shit-stained drawers when you don't wipe good enough, doesn't she? I bet I'm not assuming that."

"Did you say something?" Seth inquires.

I laugh and say, "Not a thing. You best be checking your hearing during your next physical, boy."

"Well on that note, I do have to go. I've got to get on the job and pound the pavement."

"How's the old clunker putting these days?" I say, holding back my laughter.

"As a matter of fact, I've got to go to the junkyard and find a tire. The car's been running rough all week but changing the plugs should straighten that out as soon as I can get to it."

"Go ahead and handle your business then."

"Always. Always. Good-bye, morning flower. Take care of yourself. Don't hesitate to call me if you ever need me. I still can make time for you. Remember to smile. It makes life easier to live," he says gently.

"Bye, Seth. Take care."

Call me if you ever need me. What? The day I need Seth's help is the day pigs fly better than birds. How can I ask you for anything if you're living off lint in your pocket? I probably just blew your whole paycheck with that one call. And that good-bye, morning flower shit. I mean, he's so nice he makes me want to throw up and run and smack his momma he's bleeding dry. I hope he doesn't make her pay for the old, used tire.

Momma's boy. She's the whole reason his head is all up in the clouds in the first place. Now that ain't right!

$

"Hey, Shawn, what's crackin'?" I say in a really relaxed voice.

"Identity theft, that's what the fuck is crackin'," he says bitterly.

"Is that any way to say hi to your good pal-sy wal-sy, Jalita?"

"I just opened my credit card bill this morning, and some asshole charged five thousand dollars worth of shit. I been on the phone all day tellin' people I ain't do it, and all I'm getting is the bureaucratic runaround. I missed near six hours of pay foolin' with this bogus shit!" he snaps.

"More problems so soon? Maybe Jackie did it."

"Nah. Jackie didn't know I even had this account."

"Maybe it had something to do with Dumpster divers. I hear they'll go through trash to get bank records. Do you shred your financial documents?" I ask.

"No. I didn't think I was in the category to need to."

"Maybe it's a random act, but perhaps it isn't. If it involves green bills, a woman's gonna sniff it out. I'm leaning toward you-know-who."

"She didn't. I got it when she was gone last time. I bounce back from a damn sorry ass credit rating, and now this, mutha—"

"Calm down. All ya gotta do is order credit reports from Experian and TransUnion to find out what's on there, and get the names of the places so you can dispute the charges. Don't forget to call your bank and credit card company, too," I say like it's nothing.

"I *did* call my bank and credit card company. They're just trying to carry a brother."

"Well order a credit report tomorrow, 'cause you've done all you can do today."

"And if that ain't enough shit, some fucking idiot keyed my car on both sides."

"Did you and Jackie have it out again?"

"Well yeah, but it wasn't that bad of an argument. All it was was not being able to agree where we're having the reception. She came back the next morning and apologized," he says, then sighs.

"Here we go again," I say, rolling my eyes.

"She said she didn't do it."

"And you believe that?"

"I believe her. That's not Jackie's style either. Someone else is behind this."

"If that woman is capable of the shit she's been pulling since I've known you, she's got a whole lot of devil in her. If you ask me, it sounds like she crawled out of a crack in the walls of hell, so get a clue and accept it. Why don't you just send her back to her freaking ex and find some new pussy to whip your butt."

"This is no time to be raggin' on Jackie."

"Look, I'm sorry for you, Shawn. If men were nice, not that you all are totally capable of it, I'd say you were on that short list," I say, really meaning it.

"Thanks, Jalita. I hate to cut this conversation short but I'm sorta pissed off and want to get off the phone."

"I understand. I would feel the same way if someone I loved was stealing from my ass and lying about it."

What started out as a cool morning has turned out to be a strange one. What Shawn just told me is making my stomach turn. I mean, between him taking Jackie back and her running up his credit card, it's a wonder he can lay his peanut head down and sleep at night.

22

TAKIN' A FLIGHT OUT

Today is February 14—it's Valentine's Day and also my birthday. That's why I'm back to see Kate, or at least spy on her family. The way I've had to wire my life plan together is a result of the undue burden she stuck me with. Dumping me off on others is finito now that I'm twenty years old, but it's not over until I say it's over. Thanks to her I was born fighting a losing battle on a day people celebrate love. She hasn't been a mother. I wonder if she's ever thought about the good in me she destroyed. I doubt that shit. I don't think she could have that much concern for Jalita La Shay Harrison, even on her best day.

Damn, the woman lost quite a bit of pounds since I saw her cellulite lumpy big butt. Maybe she can try to get a spot on that Weight Watchers commercial. If money is tight as I think for her, she can hit 'em on up and fax over a before and after picture to their creative director. On second thought, the way she's dragging those feet tells me her energy isn't so high. Scratch that shit. I wonder what's goin' on with Kate. Perhaps I stirred things up a bit too much with my scandalous appearance.

She better deal with it if that's the case 'cause Wes's ex, Marquita, started my wheels turning in regard to Kate's disappearing act in the welfare office when we were supposed to meet with someone about the government keeping us covered for food and shelter. That bitch may have escaped by lying to me that she had to hit her boss up on a pay phone in the lobby on the bottom floor but I'll be mailing Ms. Thang a riot act she can't escape from on my birthday. Kate's fortunate that I'm letting her off the hook by not putting this glass Ocean Spray juice bottle to use.

I had my "use condoms or be a parent" message all prepared, written in my best handwriting, but I don't need it now. A letter would give Kate more stress. And since you get back the energy you give in this world, I'm about to give her something that'll prove I'm willing to fight toe to toe until she breaks down and acknowledges me.

The boy wearing three earrings in his ear and fish heads on his feet must be my teenage half brother. Interesting character. He sort of looks like he might worship the devil. And there's my stepdad, the racist son of a bitch. He should stop carrying that toddler and make her walk. My half sister's cute though, I must admit. Good looks must run in our genes. Speaking of genes, excuse the fuck out of me. I guess Kate didn't see fit to go on birth control after she slipped and had me. Happy birthday, Jalita. Happy birthday to your damn self. No one wants you. As Cleveland once told me, what a life. Shit, what a life.

My cell rings. "Jalita, happy birthday and happy Valentine's Day, boo! Should I sing both verses, bring your ass chocolates, or what?" Wes says.

"I'll go with the chocolates. Don't even hum one bar with your tone deaf self. How'd you know?" I say.

"Never mind that. Twenty. The big 2-0. I remember those days."

"You can remember that far back?"

"Oooh, so you're bolder, too, I see."

"Maybe."

"For the record, I'm only twenty-five."

"Like I said, you can remember that far back?"

"Since it's your birthday, Wes the best from east to west will let that one slide. I have somethin' real special for my favorite young honey."

"What is it?"

"Now, now, now, patience is a virtue."

"I don't believe in virtues, but I do remember telling someone real flustered that once," I say, then chuckle as I think of my conversation with Tony's fiancée, Charlene.

"Well you better start."

"Whatever."

"So where are you?"

"Visiting my momma."

"Your *moms*? You never mentioned you had family around here."

"Well, we fell out because I broke the tradition of becoming an attorney. I changed my major last semester, and all hell broke loose, but that's a story I don't want to get into on my birthday. She did at least bake me a cake before she started jumping on my back again though," I lie.

"Wrap your visit on up and carry your twenty-year-old phat ass on over to the beach house."

"You're there now?"

"I will be in about thirty minutes, and with your big, nicely wrapped present."

"What is it? Tell me! Tell me, daddy," I say.

"Me, with a bow on top, all nude with edible undies on and shit."

"Ewww, I thought it was supposed to be a good present, not something that would traumatize me on my birthday."

"All right now. Watch yourself or else I'll give your stuff away."

"I mean, yeah, Wes, baby. I'd love to eat some edibles off your b-ball playin' body!"

"Now that's what I'm talkin' about. Total appreciation for perfection."

"Perfection? Now don't push it too far. That shit might fall off the cliff."

"Ahh, ahh, ahh! What'd you say?" Wes playfully cautions.

"I was saying not to lose your perfect body and captivating charm."

"I thought that's what I heard. You know every minute of my time is supposed to be accounted for so don't take your time seeing what Wes picked out just for you."

"Okay. As soon as I pick up my little brother from the park and drop him off, I'm out of here," I lie again. If I don't have a normal family life, I may as well make one up.

"And let me know when you're stepping out next time. Remember the car rules?"

"Mmm-hmm, my bad. See ya shortly," I tell Wes. I hang up the phone. My palm starts itching, and I smile like I already know what Wes picked out just for me. No one's ever surprised me on my birthday before, so today is real special, and I'm not even gonna let Wes's stupid-ass statement steal my joy in this moment. Who does he think he is, telling me to ring him up when I'm rollin' out? He's not my man *or* my keeper. Slavery is over. He's just my sponsor to better things.

See, I don't want no man for real. While most of you dum dums are sitting home waiting for that one guy you really want to return the call you placed on Friday night, he's out doing what he wants to do. Go whip out that three-speed mixer and bake a cake or something 'cause he ain't thinking about you until he takes the I-had-sex shower.

I'll say it a million times: Women need to take lessons from the players and play the damn song right back. Enough of that though. I can't get all wound up and shit 'cause I've got a present to collect, not a damn seminar to teach.

$

"If you want to take the trapeze lessons tomorrow, go ahead. You only live once, beautiful."

"I don't know. What if I'm scared while I'm up there? Are you gonna come rescue me? I think not."

"You got that right, not if I have some Jamaican rum in my hand!" Wes says, showing all thirty-twos.

"For real, Wes, this is the prettiest place I've ever seen. Thanks so much for this surprise. You take such good care of me. I can't believe you managed to shop for my new clothes and fold them in the Samsonite luggage. You're too much," I say, looking at the tropical sun dip down.

"Well you've been holding up your end of the bargain for a while now. I'm happy. I'm relaxed. The coach is going to notice me for making a record number of baskets this season. That incident with the fan threw me for a loop, but I paid the three thousand dollar fine and learned my lesson. You'll be traveling with me while I'm out on the road next season, so you can keep me straight. You won't have to watch me work on the boob tube because you'll be seated in the VIP section," Wes announces while pretending he's shooting a basketball.

"I won't argue with that."

"You better not."

"You know something, Wes?"

"What's that?"

"Only a freak would choose for us to go to some Hedonism II resort in Jamaica on Valentine's Day. There's romantic spots like Paris, Italy, Milan. All kinds of exotic places in the world that have some substance and history, and you pick somewhere where a fuck fest goes down," I tease.

"Well you've got nerve to be calling names and placing blame for taking your ass away from contaminated water and muggy conditions. Have you been hanging around Tomi or something? That sounds like some shit she would come up with. I flew in straight from Chicago to do this for you and I've got practice for a home game the day after we get back. I like history and culture, too, you know, but this was an impromptu short trip for your birthday, so it'll just have to do," Wes snaps.

I tell Wes, "I was just kidding with your ass. Don't get a foul attitude with me. Look at all these freaky deaky people walking around nude and feeling each other up. And did you notice the mirrors on our ceiling in our suite?"

"Who are you calling a freak? And I happen to like those mirrors. Gives the place a nice ambiance," he teases. I'm relieved my comment didn't escalate into an argument, so I return to my playful tone.

"Well you're not complaining when you're giving it, ambience or not!"

"I know that's right. I guess we're both on the same page," he says, playing with my nipples.

"How ya gonna do that all out in the open?" I complain.

"That's what Hedonism's all about. Being hedonistic. Anything goes. All day, every day, for as long as you're here. This place is the shit."

"I'm not use to being naked on nobody's beach. Can't these people walk their horny asses to their rooms?"

"Loosen up. Enjoy yourself. Have a new experience to think about when you're eighty," he says, admiring the sunset. Wes pats his feet in the sand, then picks some up and watches it slowly slip through his fingers.

"The last time you said something similar, I saw you lose your mind in a pool poking Tomi like it was your last porno flick."

"Well, I love women," Wes says. I want to blurt out that there's no need for a man with money to be faithful when women are seen as a smorgasbord of bitches. It's all about tasting variety and moving on to the next dish. Even if athletes are Troll doll ugly, or their breath is in need of a glass of Scope, the women will be there throwing the panties off like their dicks are gold and laced in diamonds and cultured pearls.

"You better not love men."

"Is there anything wrong with a dog chasing some cat?"

"If I thought so, we wouldn't have hooked up," I say.

"True that."

"So when's Tomi coming home from the Baptist convention?" I say in an attempt to kill my thoughts of how men rule the world with their cash stashes.

"This afternoon. I'll buy her ass something impressive, and she'll get over me not spending Valentine's Day with her."

"Does she go to these things often?"

"No. This is the first time. Her dad's been on her case to get more involved in that stuff 'cause he's a preacher in Louisiana and he says she's too wrapped up in my career. He forgets she's my personal assistant who is being paid well."

"A preacher's daughter from the land of red beans and rice. That's a laugh."

"Now don't go making fun of Tomi. She's okay."

"Mmm-hmm, yeah. So we're here for just tonight and part of tomorrow, right?"

"Well we need a little time alone to celebrate your birthday, however short it has to be. Don't we, beautiful?" he says, licking on my right ear.

"That tickles," I say, giggling. I raise my left shoulder toward my ear. Being tickled gives me goose bumps and turns me on at the same time.

"It was supposed to."

"So you've been here before?"

"Now don't go asking questions you already know the answer to."

"Freak, just like I said."

"And so what? I work hard, so I need to play hard. I'm not a sexually repressed brother. Never have been, never will be," Wes tells me with confidence.

"I bet you work that stick as hard as you work on the court, huh?"

"No. Getting it up is natural for me. I plan to prove that while I'm here."

"With me, I hope."

"Oh no you didn't."

"Well if you stray, just remember to use a condom."

"It's not like that, and even if it was, no bitch is getting half of my money through having a kid by me."

"Okay, honey," I say, kissing him on the lips.

"Lay on your back, Jalita. I want to give you a real birthday kiss, right here on this nude beach in Negril. A beautiful woman under a beautiful sunset can make a man just feel like he'd trade everything material in his life for just a few moments like this," he says, lust heavy in his eyes. I watch his penis harden, and he looks like a sun god, slightly illuminated by a disappearing red, orange, and yellow streaked sun.

"If that's so, I hope I'm the one who has that power over the man who brought me here," I tell him. Thanks to my growing hatred for the "privileged" Wes, the only way I can grant him any degree of affection is to pretend this is my honeymoon and he really loves me.

I feel his penis rub up against my clit, and I quiver. I look around. All I see is people doing the same thing, but they're spread out for the sake of privacy, I'm sure. Wes reaches in his backpack, tears open a condom, rolls it down, and I feel like I'm dreaming again, but this time I'm sure it's him. I moan with waves splashing in the background as a gentle, soothing breeze makes my curls dance. Wes pushes my short curls back from my face as he straddles me between my browning, thick legs. All I feel is a whole lot of goodness, which is enough to make me forget that I'm in this world, alone . . . and completely unloved on Valentine's Day.

$

"Good morning, Wes," I say slowly, smoothing my hair back with both of my hands.

"Good morning," he mimics, then sighs.

"Is everything okay on the home front?"

"Tomi is really getting on my nerves. I swear I love her, but she really just irritates me. She goes over and over the same things, again and again. It drives me nuts," he says.

"Come here and sit next to me, daddy," I tell Wes. I begin to rub his back.

"Thank God for you. I'm starting to seriously rethink some things."

"Look, just relax and enjoy our trip," I say, kissing him on the right cheek as my hands move up toward his shoulders. I rub and knead his muscles some more.

"You're right. She's not going to mess this up. Tomi is too spoiled for her own good and isn't thankful for the good life she has with me. That girl never even made her own bed a day in her life, so I should expect her to behave like she's entitled to my world. Thank you, Jalita. I needed this arrangement with you and this time away," he tells me. I'm happy I'm his crutch 'cause the more Tomi's ass is gettin' on his nerves, the better he'll treat me.

"Relax, baby. Who was it that told me thinking too hard fucks shit up?"

"That would be me," Wes quickly credits himself, then gives me a half-cocked smile.

"So why don't we go get some breakfast. Hey, look where we are. No need to get dressed," I say to make him deliver a full smile. He does. We laugh.

"Good idea 'cause it's over at 10:30. Tomi usually cooks for me at nine when Mary's off, so I'm ready to get my grub on."

"Well, let's take quick showers. You can go first."

"Jalita, this time I want you to come shower with me and watch me shave, too. I don't want you to say a word, just be near me."

"Whatever you want, baby, you've got it," I tell Wes. I know this is a couple's move, so I'm shocked. Since Wes is feeling vulnerable or just wants me to soap up his back and scrub, my depression and episode of bitterness leave. Even if men do rule the world with the paper chase, it doesn't mean their asses are automatically happy or fulfilled. Plus, I'm here having a blast in Jamaica, and Tomi's I don't know how many miles away.

23

CHANGIN' LANES

I'm standing in line at a quaint boutique in uptown Manhattan. My arms are loaded down with Roca Wear, FUBU, Lady Encye, and some accessories by some new fashonistas called Sistahs Harlem New York. Just as I'm about to hand the saleswoman Wes's American Express card, I observe a young girl stuffing sunglasses, earrings, and a denim wallet into her purse on the sly. I make an excuse to step out of line, discreetly walk up to her and quietly whisper, "Sometimes the biggest chance you can take is not taking a chance at all, but I assure you that this one isn't worth taking. Put it all back, right now before you get caught."

The girl throws the goods out of her purse, then prepares to bolt out of the shop. I firmly grip her arm, and softly whisper, "Get a fresh start, honey. Sell your tight little pussy to successful men. It'll get you far more. Stay away from copping a shoplifting charge by landing a side hustle with one of the one percent of Black men between eighteen and thirty-four who earn $150,000 plus. That would be a good start for you. Here's my card. Give me a call, and I'll explain everything. If you're wondering who I am, I'm the CEO of The Gold Diggers Association of the Metropolitan Area. I'll consider waiving my consulting fee because you remind me of myself when I was your age."

Just as the young girl scrutinizes my card then looks into my eyes, I awaken to Wes saying, "My baby is tanned and even finer. Damn, Jalita, every day I look at you, you get finer and finer. You're like that. I could fuck you right here on this plane."

I flinch until I realize that I'd drifted off and had been dreaming. Even if my conscience about gold digging wasn't hitting me in the heart, it was apparently creeping in, through the back door of my mind. That moral guilt shit lasted all of one minute more, then I was good to go again.

I laugh, then quickly take my cue and tell Wes, "I've heard of the mile high club. Let's go for it." I wink.

"We better not chance it."

"Chicken butt. I knew you were all hot air," I tease.

"It's a nice thought, but I better keep it in my pants right now," Wes says. I laugh as he grabs my hand and holds it tightly.

"Suit yourself," I tell Wes, shocked that he could ever desire to let his dick stay asleep.

"Girl, you need to stop. You couldn't hang with that. You'd get us kicked off here for moaning, alerting everyone you were getting some. You make way too much noise."

I pitch the perfect ego-building response, when I tell Wes, "That's because you have way too much dick, and ain't no woman that deep. Anyway, that trip was awesome. Thanks again, baby, although you've left me sore . . . and you can guess where."

Wes chuckles, then says, "You don't have to keep thanking me. I know you appreciate it, beautiful. You show me and my big dick daily."

"So can you stop wearing those dumb baseball hats now? I'm tired of you having to disguise yourself. I'd like to see more of you than your chin."

"It just goes along with the territory of what I do."

"I know that's right."

"I get tired of it sometimes. But how would it have been if I were constantly mobbed in Jamaica when that beautiful sunrise came up?"

"Terrible."

"See what I mean?"

"You're right, as always."

"I can't wait until the day I can retire, be a regular guy, enjoy my investments, and use my real name," he says.

"Well that's a long time coming, so you better keep on moving that ass up and down the court while the gettin' is good."

"I know. Don't get me wrong. I'm fortunate and grateful to have my spot on the team," Wes explains, reaching over and squeezing my breasts through my shirt.

"Now just keep that frame of mind every time you want to complain—and I'm referring to the frame of mind that doesn't involve feeling up women."

"You're right about a lot, too, you know that? So young to be so wise. I still want to feel you up though. You're so damn sensual and sexy, Jalita," Wes says as he smiles and looks me square in my sparkling eyes.

"Well I don't know about all that," I say, stealing Seth's modest line he threw my way once.

"You are. You know how hard it is to find a good woman without a botched boob job, a good brain, and willingness to treat a man like he's something these days?"

"No harder than it is to find a good man who doesn't have to walk around sucking in his stomach, isn't addicted to Viagra, afraid of a full-time job, and doesn't live with his momma," I say, pinching his cheek.

"Damn, what a list of complaints and objections. So, you think I'm a good man?"

"Would I have flown all the way to Jamaica to be with you and only you if I didn't? And what about me?" I say. I want to tell him, hell no, you horny-ass motherfucker.

"Would I have spent all that money and gone through all that trouble to make your birthday extra special if I didn't think that you are the best?" he says, throwing back the same line to me. Mmph. I guess Wes and I are finally equals. Both of us are bullshit delivery experts.

"We never did make it to that reggae show."

"Maybe next time. Hedonism ain't going nowhere."

"So you plan on there being a next time?"

"Fo' sure, unless you really want to do the Paris thing. You keep acting right, and I may be able to take your ass abroad off-season," Wes says, kissing my hand the exact way he did the first day he laid eyes upon me.

"Your generosity must have been inspired by the way I made you sweat on the dance floor when Lil Jon & the Eastside Boyz 'Get Low' came on," I say, moving my head from side to side, then up and down.

"Now that was something. You got so low that I thought you were gonna break something important, girl. I don't know if you noticed, but you turned a whole lot of heads. I've got to remember you're so flexible the next time we do our thing," he says, grinning. "Tomi says she doesn't dance. And she sure would never dance like that, if she did. She's more into tennis, sipping on cocktails at a piano bar, and running her mouth to her girlfriends about new shoes, designer dresses, and how she plans on spending my money. And that high-pitched whining she does is enough to ruin my whole day sometimes. Bitches need to stop that damn mess," he complains, shaking his head. Then he adds, "That's why athletes get roped into fooling with groupies and hitting the strip clubs to pay a dancer a few thousand to shut up and work the pole."

I'm wondering why Wes feels the right to be comfortable enough to refer to females as "bitches," in my presence. We're cool, but not that cool. I know I use the word *ho* all the time, but to me, it's not in the taboo category with what seems to be Wes's term of endearment for those of us who own vaginas. Hasn't Wes noticed I don't believe in using the word *nigga*? Black people have been called bitches and niggas so long that I feel like it's a taboo thing to throw around those words like terms of endearment. I mean, I really gotta be sent into orbit to call a man a nigga, so the way I see it, they shouldn't call us women bitches, unless that shit is absolutely necessary to say because of living up to the word.

I keep cool and reply, "I was just thinking, just like men are different, so are the sistas. You can't measure everyone the same. Tomi likes to express what she thinks. You've got to admire her honesty," I say, tryna defend her. I know it will make me look good in the long run so the explanation is worth concocting on a whim.

"I see what you mean. Yeah, she has her good points. She's good with keeping the finances in order and stuff like that. She majored in accounting, and she's good at what she does," he agrees. I want to tell him that's because she likes money, just like I do. All females are good at counting ends.

"Well from what I saw you doing to her in the pool, I think she's good at little more than just number crunching," I say, nudging him.

"That stuff was for show, to keep the groupies and others from trying to get to me. Also to help me stay popular with everyone on the A list in this town. It comes in real handy."

"Well look at you, who you are, the house, and your stardom. She's just protecting her relationship, Mr. A List. Who could blame the woman? She'd be a fool to let down her guard," I say.

Wes skirts the issue, and says, "Jalita?"

"That would be me," I answer.

"College classes have started at all universities. Do you intend on going back to Virginia?"

"I guess so, but the way I left kinda left a bad taste in my mouth. I'm not feelin' Bentley like I use to so I figured I'd take off for the semester and get a job instead," I say, sighing. My preoccupation is real.

"You don't want to really go back at all, do you?"

"No, I don't. From what the R.A. said, all my stuff will be gone when I get back. How am I gonna start all over again? I'm sort of tapped out on funds, too. I don't even want to talk about it. I'm so frustrated."

"That's not the only school in the world, you know. There are some better ones than that right here in Maryland. They look very impressive on a résumé."

"Yeah, I know, but they're more expensive."

"What if I were to get you a hook up so you could attend my alma mater?"

"What, you'd do that for me?" I say, truly shocked.

"Well I wouldn't be doing the work for you, and Tomi's draining me anyway. I hate to say it, but I'm certain that I don't want to marry her anymore. When you and I were in Jamaica, I realized how much she and I have grown apart. What would you say if I offered for you and Tomi to trade places in the near future? Suppose I told you that Jalita would be front and center and there would be no more sneaking around after I break off my engagement? I'm too young to get married anyway."

"I'd say, hand over my front door key," I tell Wes, opening my left palm and grinning from ear to ear. He kisses me on the lips and sticks his tongue in my mouth, right there on the plane. It feels more like sealing a bond, not swapping spit for lust's sake.

After we part, Wes tells me, "As soon as I collect Tomi's key, I'm changing the security codes, and I'll tell you all of the vitals. I have certain rules that I think you can put up with."

"Like?"

"Parking shoes and street clothes downstairs. Changing into robes before entering the main part of the house. Taking a shower in the morning and in the evening before putting booty up in my covers. Leaving the bar stools in the exact place I put them, lining up perfectly with the furniture across the room. You know, shit I've developed as protocol for a laid crib. I've always had this fear of dirty and disgusting things. Believe it or not, I have a weak stomach."

"Neat is my middle name, boo, and my hygiene is exceptional. I'm with you on every point."

"That's what I'm talking about. Hey, beautiful, are you breaking out on me?"

"Are you talking about those four bumps on the side of my cheek and one on my neck?" I ask.

"Yeah, those," Wes replies.

"They sprouted because of the oil in the suntan lotion. It's the price I had to pay for this butter pecan tan you can't stop salivating over," I explain, then wink.

"Well we're going to get that shit right and tight. Perfection is the name of the game. I want niggas to break their neck tryna look at my woman. It's time for a new hairstyle, a facial, and a new closet full of clothes that look good on all of that ass and suckable titties."

I say, "Whatever you want, you'll get. I can be talked into being a spoiled, high-maintenance chick from head to toe."

"Good, because you're beautiful now, but I'm about to make you into one of baddest bitches from coast to coast."

I close my eyes to kiss him long and passionately. When I do, all I see are dollar signs standing tall and pretty as trees in the country. I think Tomi's gonna need a storage bin 'cause there's no way in hell that diva can round up all of the shit she collected on moving day. As soon as Wes gets a live reminder of her bitching and whining, she'll be notified of a sudden lane change. When she does, I'll say, "Hit the road, sista, and don't let the doorknob hit ya where the good Lord split ya 'cause your ex is happily sprung over this kitty cat, worse than an addict on the corner up in the hood needs a hit of that addictive crack-a-lack-a-lack."

24
SOMETHIN' SOUR IN THE MIX

Just as Wes and I step off the plane at BWI airport, his cell rings. He stares at the luminescent light green screen, and I know he's fretting after staring down his caller ID. It's Tomi calling. I can tell by the eating-sour-dill-pickle look on his face. We step over in a corner. I stand with my back turned to appear as though I'm giving him privacy, when all I'm really doing is cocking my ear like a cable satellite dish to get the latest scoop. This game is easy to figure out, if a woman learns to do more listening and less talking.

"Tomi, huh?" I ask when he gets off the phone.

"I don't even want to talk about it. I've got to cut our after party a little short. Tonight I'm going to have to tell her it's over. I can't take one more day of her shit," Wes answers, then sighs heavily.

"So cut our time short then. I can live with a rain check. You know I'm not hard to please. Now let's walk out of this airport with good memories on our mind. You work hard, and all you deserve is some peace and tranquility," I say, rubbing him up and down his back.

Wes had no idea why we have the pleasure of rolling back to the beach house in a white twenty-two passenger stretch Navigator limo when all he requested was one that held up to twelve. He's so preoccupied with "the talk" with Tomi, he doesn't say a word about the mix-up with his reservation to the limo driver. I don't give a shit about the extra room 'cause it's all good to me. This ride has tinted windows, two stocked wet bars, a fish tank, stereo and CD player, mood lighting, intercom, TV and DVD player, plus some. In fact, Wes basically doesn't have much to say the whole way back until I kick off my shoes and use my bare feet to rub his crotch. I feel him harden, then I unzip his zipper then dim the lights for privacy.

I tell him, "We can't part with you wearing that serious face, Wes."

"I'm okay, Jalita, just preoccupied over what I'm about to do," Wes answers soberly.

"But something's gotta be done about my baby looking like that," I say seductively. I work my way in his head by becoming sweet music to his ears. While I'm waiting for Wes to respond, I'm revving up my hormones. I think fast and tune in WPGC. Ludacris's new cut blares through the speaker. It's one of those songs that can bring out the freak in people who aren't even freaks and make freaks ultra-freaky. Being that I now fit into the latter category, I grab champagne from one of the bars, pull Wes's shirt, socks, and shoes off and do what I feel I need to do to make sure he won't back out of kicking Tomi to the curb.

"I've got this. You relax. I'll give you something better to feel than preoccupied. I know what you need, negro, and don't you ever forget that shit either," I tell him boldly, carefully pouring Moet on his chest and dick.

I push open his long, toned legs. "What are you doing? Got damn! Mmmm, yes," Wes says as I put my head in his lap and suck him on beat to the music with my head bobbing up and down like I've done it a thousand times before.

"You like a woman who knows her place, don't you? Don't you, *motherfucker*? Answer your ho right now," I say, coming up for air, then goin' back down to nearly swallow the head of his dick, then lick on his chest.

"Yes, yes," Wes answers as he grabs a handful of my curls from the back on my head.

I come up for air again, and say, "That's what I thought, you fine-ass negro!" Wes pushes my head back down to suck his dick again while he's breathing heavy. I pull my head away as his arm falls limp to the side of his body. I wipe my mouth on my arm 'cause he ain't paying my ass enough to swallow sperm — yet. He is paying my ass enough to suck those toes though, so that's what I do, still working with Ludacris's baseline.

"You make me feel so good. Damn! I think I'm dreaming. Yeah, this is just too good to be true. Got damn you, Jalita. The shit you do makes my head spin," Wes moans and mumbles as I lick his toes, kneeling on the deep pile carpet. Bingo. The man just admitted I make his head spin. Now I know I can get deep in his pocket. All I gotta do is say something to keep him in this frame of mind.

I look up at him and belt out, "These are *my* motherfucking toes, that's

SOMETHIN' SOUR IN THE MIX   215

my motherfucking chest, and that's *my* motherfucking dick, not Tomi's so don't you ever act like you're disturbed by her static. The bottom bitch is the most important one. Now you go home and handle your business."

"No one's ever done that shit to me before," Wes says as I get up off the floor. When I sit next to him, I can tell his heart is still beating hard, and he's still good and excited. Then Wes adds, "You know how to blow my mind. I want our next after party to be at my mansion. I'm ready now, Jalita. Tomi's got issues. I'm going to ask for my ring back. The bitch will have to move by next weekend, and I'll put her up in a hotel until we sort out the residence issue. Unfortunately, I fucked up. By law, I can't just dismiss her since she's been living with me for two years."

I don't want to appear like I'm gloating. I lean over and lick the remaining drops of liquor off Wes's pecks. Then I tell him, "We're almost back to the beach house, and I think you got the point about things. Let's put your clothes back on. I need to lick and suck on those toes more often, too."

Wes gets sentimental and says, "Girl, you're crazy. You're so easy to get along with. I'm really glad we met. Moments like this are pretty nice. Maybe we'll get to have more of them, you know? I can see us doing quality things someday. I may even be catching real feelings for your hot ass. Thank you, Jalita, for the best time I've had in years."

I wink, then say, "When you lay your head down tonight, remember you're the best from east to west. Don't hate the player, hate the game. Being a famous athlete isn't an easy bag of goods. All some women understand is the fringe benefits of your title. I want to understand you 'cause I may be catching real feelings for you, too," I say. I can't wait to gargle, brush my teeth, and unpack my neat souvenirs from Jamaica but I don't let it show. Instead, I gently kiss him on the cheek to make him believe he truly did strike gold by pushing up on me. I know our deal is sealed.

When we reach the beach house, the limo halts, and I'm ecstatic that the trip was productive. We sit, waiting for the driver to open Wes's door, but instead the privacy divider comes down and I see Tomi wearing a wedding dress and headpiece. She stares at us while holding a gun in her right hand and a tabloid in her left. Our eyes scan the headline that reads, WES MONTGOMERY AND HIS SEXY HONEY, EXCLUSIVE PHOTO SPREAD AND STORY INSIDE.

Tomi says, "Well, well, well . . . I've been expecting the two of you. Welcome home from Jamaica."

The next thing I know, some goons fling the limo doors open, cover our mouths, and throw burlap bags over our heads. This is one time I'm the one who's scared 'cause I doubt my silver tongue will do much good.

25

ALMOST SIX FEET UNDER

"You didn't have to get some eight-foot goon to throw no damn black burlap bag over my head, gag me, and tie me up. I keep telling you that Wes and I are just friends! " I say, rolling my eyes at Tomi. She's dressed in a white, low-cut, floor-length wedding dress that's form fitting at the waist and embroidered in gold. White matching heels make Tomi statuesque; she looks at least six feet tall. Her hair is pulled back into a smooth, freshly permed looking ponytail with a fresh gardenia pinned on the side. Tomi's swaying with her legs slightly bent and keeps kicking her legs out like she's a kid who's got to take a pee. I don't appreciate the fact that my initial instincts were right on the money. The girl ain't wrapped too tight, and her rubber band just snapped. She's got the gun pointing at me and Wes, who just so happens to be tied up in brown, thick rope. We're both sitting up by force, on the bed where we usually work out his little anger management problem with Tomi.

"Shut up, bitch! I heard the whole conversation in the limo," Tomi screams at me while I look down the barrel of a Smith and Wesson.

Wes tries to appeal to Tomi's sense of reason, even if it's a lie, and tells her, "Now Tomi, you look beautiful in your wedding dress, but come on now, honey, let's be reasonable; this is ridiculous. I told you over and over that Jalita and I are just friends. Now, baby, you know I love you and only you. I gave my life to the Lord and gave up womanizing. I was just doing the Christian thing by looking out for her over her college break since she didn't have a place to stay. You don't want to do this. Why don't you think about what I could buy to make you feel better.

I know you've been under a lot of stress. Just put the gun down so we can all forget this little nasty outburst, and go home," Wes says.

Tomi's not buying the Brooklyn Bridge he's tryna sell her, and replies, "There's nothing worse than a cheap whore and a man with money. Since I won't get to wear my dress at my dream wedding, I'll show it off right now at this little ceremony." Tomi's still rocking side to side. I can tell that this is gonna be a long-ass night, if I live to see the sun come up as usual. She adds, "I'm not to be played with this time, Wes. You can't buy your way out of this one. I've got everything I want now, but one thing...and that's your heart. Don't you patronize me; I'm not your baby!"

"But I love you, and I don't want things to get out of hand. So please, Tomi, give me the gun, if you won't put it down," Wes pleads.

"I've got PMS, cramps, I'm retaining water like a camel. This Vera Wang dress is tight as a body stocking, and I didn't take my ketoprofin pain pills this morning, so, so, so you people better shut up and do what I say without all of the lip," Tomi announces.

"I know how cramps can be, Tomi. Maybe when they're gone we can laugh about this someday . . . please don't kill us," I tell her.

"Bitch, you talk when spoken to. Oh, God, my ankles are swollen, and I need to just go on and shoot so I can get off my feet and soak them in an aromatherapy blend," Tomi whines. She begins walking toward me.

Tomi runs the gun down my right cheek and tells me, "You stole my man, and I told you when I first met you that he wanted you. I gave you fair warning that I was capable of putting you six feet under. In case you didn't notice Wes stood me up on Valentine's Day to be with you." She hits me upside the head with the pistol. Next she says, "Lord, forgive me, and please don't tell Daddy." Tomi returns to her original spot on the floor.

"Tomi, I've never seen this side of you. What's gotten into you, boo? I can't believe you just pistol whipped Jalita and put that gun in her face like that. I've never even heard you cuss before. Someone can get hurt here," Wes says.

"Years of your infidelity. The cheating with the groupies chasing your limo, throwing cheap nylon thongs, and sneaking into your hotel rooms. The disrespect I've endured has made me a bitter, nasty bitch. I plan for two someones to get hurt! This is the real me, motherfucker, so enjoy yourself. I'm not your boo," she yells.

"We're not married. What are you talking about, infidelity? And I told you Jalita is not a groupie, just a poor college kid with nowhere to go," Wes replies innocently. He tells that lie so well, I almost forget it isn't the truth.

"Well I'm here to tell you I'm prepared to go to jail tonight. I've been practicing at the range four times a week, preparing myself for this day when I can stomp out this type of legal prostitution. Jalita will put her mouth anywhere for some cheap gifts, a car, and a quick trip," she says. Tomi walks over to me and smacks me in the head with the gun again. My head begins to hurt like I have a hangover.

Wes replies, "You're making a fool of yourself. She honestly doesn't know what you're talking about."

"You both do," she yells to Wes, wiping her face.

She turns in my direction and asks, "You want something to look at, cheap ho? Look at this shit. One tabloid, two tabloids, three, and four. The whole world knows Wes cheated on me with his sexy honey. I guess you two didn't count on paparazzi taking pictures, me checking into your travel plans and sending over a phony limo driver since all of my friends all around the country will think I'm a laughingstock. I can't go out like that. My image has been damaged, and my self-esteem has been shattered, so now I'm gonna bust a cap in two asses. Since you two are so close, you can die together," she says as tears begin to stream down her face and wet her neck.

"See, I can explain. Jalita is a theater major, and she wanted this part real bad, so I said I'd be her acting coach," Wes says. I look at him like he's an idiot for tryna deliver that weak line to Tomi. Now she'll really fucking lose her last marble. I wish he'd shut up 'cause he's supposed to be the man and can't even wear the pants. What a wus. Now I know I don't wanna be with his butt no more.

"Okay . . . I know what it looks like, but it isn't what you think, honey," Wes says.

"Well, what is it then? Some special mentoring program where you go down to Jamaica and get butt naked in the sand with a homeless girl as community service for the team?"

"No, it wouldn't be that either," Wes answers.

"I should blow your head off with at least ten shots, Wes. You never tell the truth. All you do is expect me to turn my head while you fuck your dick off," she screams.

"Wake up, sista; he paid you off for his hoing habit," I mumble under my breath.

"I heard that, cheap ho. I should blow your head off right this second. You don't know what it's like to have agents throw women your man's way, his boys encouraging it, and then him going in that direction on his own. I do and I have for two fucking years," she says, nodding and rocking.

"It was a joke. She's trying to calm you down, boo. Come on. Put the gun down and untie us, please. For our future, our children to be, your parents . . . everything you want and we talked about after you march down the aisle in that gorgeous dress!" Wes begs.

"Fat chance. So it's not what it looks like, huh?" she snaps.

"I was just about to tell you which invitations I liked. I'm getting older now, and I'm ready to get married and have that good Christian family. Now's the time, if you just stop this madness and think about what you're about to do."

"You didn't care about that or the orchestra a few days ago. You didn't even know I picked out my dress because you were too busy taking care of business in other places. Fuck you, Wes. You're a lying bastard who needs to pay. I know what you are, and I'm tired of pretending that I don't. Today is a new day, mister. You like being a star. Your ass is starring in my show on primetime Tomi-vision!" Tomi says.

"I do care about you, Tomi. I do want to get married. Just stop what you're doing and imagine our baby's first smile, you telling me our child lost its first tooth. All of that will and can come true if you just let us all get through this safely. How many ways can I ask you to marry me, right here and right now? Will you marry me, Tomi Montague?"

"Don't you dare insult me! That's no real motherfucking marriage proposal. You told Jachita you wanted the ring back you gave me, so here," she yells, grabbing Wes's hand, tryna force it over one of Wes's large knuckles. It stops on the end of his finger.

"Ouch, Tomi! Take it easy. That hurts. You know I have big fingers. You've made this whole thing up in your head, boo. You've always had quite an imagination."

Tomi grins with a sinister flavor and says, "Do you think I care if it hurts? I'm your woman, your personal assistant, and your accountant. Did you forget I was on your payroll, honey? Did you forget we met because I landed you as a client? That wasn't by accident. I was determined to wiggle in your life. I explained my plan to that trashy woman of ill repute the first time she visited our home."

"But I met you by an accident at the grocery store in Mitchellville."

"Please, Wes. I'd been studying you for months before I made my move. I know when you're lying to me because I know more about you than you think. I researched you on the Internet. I found out all of your likes and dislikes. I spied on you in restaurants. I sat in the bleachers and watched you come out of the tunnel in different cities. I even had a lawyer get some information on Lexis-Nexis. I set you up because I just had to have you. Every gold digger knows to go to that Safeway in Mitchellville to pick up a baller. Tapping the fender of your car was a setup. That miniskirt I was wearing that barely covered my ass was planned, thanks to the power of pussy. I hunted you down and captured you. I had you in the palm of my hand until this cheap ho showed up," Tomi shrieks.

"Well got damn," Wes says.

"And I've got news for you, playboy. I've had a tracer on your car these past months. I've got phone records that match a cell phone on your account. I've been watching this house, especially this room over the Internet. And I handle the books, remember? I've got hotel receipts, perfume receipts, dinner receipts, clothes receipts, and damn paperwork on the Lexus in the driveway. You want to play, learn the rules and pay cash, you bold, cocky, insensitive motherfucker."

"We're in neck-high doo doo," I mumble under my breath.

"Shut up, cheap ho. I watched enough of what sluts like you do. I knew you were trash when you stepped into our happy home."

"With all due respect, you don't know what I do with whom," I say.

"Oh really, cheap ho? See that bear on the dresser? Well there's a camera in it. I saw it all. While you all were here having your fun, I was home fuming, crying, ordering voodoo dolls, putting ground-up glass in Wes's breakfast and my menstrual blood in his favorite decaffeinated coffee on the maid's off days. Where I'm from they say if a man drinks your blood, it'll keep him faithful. They call it shift tale tea, but I'm sure you don't know a thing about black magic, voodoo, roots, working spells." Tomi's eyes light up like stars.

"You fixed me coffee last week. Shit!" Wes leans over and vomits on the rug.

"Shut up. You drank it up and even told me how good it was. I guess I shouldn't tell you about the pubic hair I put in the spaghetti sauce. Now you know why I didn't eat any," Tomi mumbles, laughing. Then she continues, saying, "I'm from Louisiana. We are not to be messed with. I didn't go to some church convention, but to have some roots worked on the two people sitting on this bed, right there. The voodoo priestess said it would be way more powerful and destructive than just shooting you as I had first intended," Tomi says while pointing at us with the gun.

"Voodoo priestess?" I belt out.

"Oh yeah. Mother has great spiritual powers. And understand this: Since you two wanted to play games, I can, too. That's when I sent Shawn a note, scratched up his car, and messed with his credit card account. The dumb motherfucker couldn't figure out what he was supposed to do. Since he was so dumb, Wes, this little habit of yours didn't stop. He introduced you two, so I held him responsible, too. He invited the tempting devil into my home to meet Wes. I didn't appreciate him befriending Lucifer's daughter, at all."

"No one wants me, Tomi. You told me yourself at the party that Wes wants a woman who's close to White, like you. Look at my brown ass— I'm not even his type. That pile of vomit is stinking. Do you think we can open some windows up in here?" I ask her, scrunching up my nose. I'm buying time, or at least I'm tryna while I think of what to do. I know Tomi wants attention, so I know our gooses won't be cooked just yet 'cause she's not finished making a point and didn't shoot me when she could've before.

"Shut up you dick-sucking, doggy-style-fucking, White-girl-flirting dirty ho! Smell your sin. Sniff it good," she screams. Sweat makes the top of her dress wet, and it's clinging to her. She looks like she's been to wedding boot camp on a ninety-degree day.

"You watched over the Internet?" Wes says. He looks and sounds weak from vomiting.

"Every stroke. See, you underestimated me. I got that bear from a spy shop. I wanted evidence that you thought I was such a naive fool. All of the athlete's wives and girlfriends rave about that shop. You all aren't fooling us one bit. We know about all of the dirt you people do before you turn your keys and come home to us."

"You sneaky, psychotic bitch," Wes says.

"Shut up, Wes. So you think I'm a bitch, huh? Well I've got a tape for you to watch. Get in here, boys," she screams. The two big goons guard us while she connects the cables to the VCR, pops a tape inside, then turns up the television volume so high it hurts our ears.

Tomi does her bride's pee pee dance from a corner, so we can see the TV. Then she says, "Don't forget to send a thank-you note to the two people who gave you this present, Wessie. Hmmm, weren't you supposed to be in Jamaica with your bride on your honeymoon? Hmmm, I guess I got left behind and Jachita went in my place as a dry run before it was my turn to go. How thoughtful of you, Wes. Now that you're back in town, take this spoonful of your own medicine."

A naked, sex-starved-acting Tomi says, "Mmmm. Oooooh. Yes! I'd never do this to Wes."

A lusty-eyed man starring in Tomi's personal porn flick has his back turned, but we can hear him commenting, "He'll never know. Give me some head, then I'm gonna put this big cock right up your tight ass, you hot bitch."

"I can take it. Put it in. Put it in. I don't get this at home. Wes won't take the time to satisfy me, Travis baby, that's why I'm so tight. Fuck my man though, 'cause your dick is the bomb! Wait 'til I brag about it at the country club," Tomi says on screen, then turns around and looks into the camera.

"Well in that case, I'm gonna make sure you got somethin' real good to brag about over those cocktails. I been wanting to hit this for a long time, Tomi. The pussy is good as a motherfucker, so I know the asshole has got to be the bomb, too. What in the hell is wrong with Wes? He's got a gorgeous honey with good ass at home," the man says, turning around and facing the camera.

Wes's mouth falls open, then he screams, "You and Travis. My best friend? My teammate. My boy for the last six years?" I can see real hurt cover his face. He starts crying real tears. His voice cracks as he keeps repeating his words. I thought he was a *real* player. How's he gonna get all emotional over this shit? Hello, Wes, women cheat, too!

"Yeah, that's right. Revenge is a motherfucker, isn't it, Wes? See, at first I invited Travis over about his tux fitting and rehearsal, then one thing led to another, and I was thinking, well, as the best man he's supposed to help out the groom. Since you needed someone to take me off your hands for a while, the best man—your best friend—was the perfect candidate to lube up my asshole and fuck me hard-core. Travis was dumb and didn't know I was taping him. He gave me the best orgasms I've ever had. Now you watch this until the tape runs out. Maybe you can learn how to please a woman in bed, you selfish, two-minute motherfucker," she yells.

"Turn it off. I can't take anymore. This is disgusting," Wes says, crying like a baby.

"No, motherfucker. You watch and listen. You're mine tonight. I'm going to teach you about paying attention to one woman at a time," Tomi insists as she wipes her forehead again.

"How could you do this to me? How could you fuck my best friend, Tomi?" he says.

Tomi laughs and grins, then tells him, "The same way you did what you did with this cheap ho and all the other hoochies when I was the one wearing your ring, that's how. I forgave you for every indiscretion, but her," Tomi screams at Wes.

She turns to me and says, "Wes was getting attached to you. This was more than cheating. He wants to be with you. Every time I was ovulating and ready to make Wes a daddy, you were in here fucking your brains out with him. That's the ultimate insult and betrayal. Just think, he dumped me for you, and you're nothing but low-class, street-walking trash."

"Turn it off. Turn it off. I think I'm gonna throw up again," Wes protests.

Tomi is unmoved and yells, "It ends when it ends. Now you see how I've felt."

Wes pleads and lies, "I do! I learned my lesson, baby! I'll act right. I'll give you my heart. We can get through this, if you just stop this right now!"

"No deal. I have to make good and sure, so there's more when this one ends," Tomi screams while nodding her head up and down.

"No more, please Tomi!" he begs.

"Well you're going to hear it anyway. I tracked mud all over the house on your precious, imported carpets and drew all over your pretty walls with red lipstick to remind you of the only lips you had a right to kiss, and how you took your size fourteen feet and stomped all over my heart for years and years."

"No! No! My rugs, my walls, dirt! I think I might throw up again," Wes says, then begins to moan and hold his stomach.

"And those dumb fish of yours in your back pond—"

"What did you do to Frederick, Tiger, and Porsha?" Wes asks nervously.

"The pit bulls down the street told me to tell you they were yummy, yummy, yummy and slid aaaaaall the way down their two empty tummies! I think they want some more, but I only killed the ones you liked the best and told them don't be so greedy in one day. I set the ducks free. I hope they appreciated my kind gesture of returning them back to nature."

Wes screams.

"Well enough about your wild animal kingdom. Godfather Wes, you don't like dirt, do you?" Tomi comments.

"Godfather?" Wes says weakly.

"You better get use to dirt because babies are reaaaal sloppy and love to make messes," Tomi says, shaking her head.

"Baby?" Wes says as his eyes widen.

"Oh, here's a little souvenir for you, honey bun. Why don't you put it in that memory box we started?" Tomi suggests, throwing a pregnancy test into his lap. Wes gulps hard. Tomi throws her head back and laughs wildly.

"Who? Who?" Wes screams.

Tomi grins, then pauses to prolong Wes's torture by putting on her veil. She tilts her head and whistles "Here Comes the Bride" over and over for about two minutes then recites their vows, changing her voice to play Wes, herself, and the minister. The next thing I know, she walks over to the dresser, uncovers a wedding cake, and slices into three tiers with fancy red rose petals sitting between each one. Tomi eats a piece while looking at the ceiling, the walls, and out of the window half dazed, then at Wes.

She finally belts out, "Oh, I was having so much fun at my wedding, I forgot all about what you just asked me. Oh yeah, about my baby's daddy. Would it be you, Wes? No, that's not right. Travis? No, not him either. I remember having my period after I got some from him. So who's left, Wessie boy?" Tomi asks.

Sweat pours from Wes's face, and he nervously says, "My twin brother Malik?"

"Bingo. I used a straight pin to poke holes in the condoms and finally got pregnant by him to get back at you since you were up to your old tricks with this cheap ho! I know you two aren't speaking, but if you run into him can you let him know I'm three months pregnant and I'll be keeping the baby? Since I couldn't have the star, I took the next best thing . . . his blood brother who looks just like him."

"No, tell me this is a joke! This isn't happening. Nooooo! You said yourself that you have cramps. You're bluffing!" Wes screams as tears stream down his glistening face. Tomi calls in the goons who watch guard over us as she puts her gun down on the dresser, then walks over to Wes.

"I did that to get attention and throw you off to see how you were going to treat me. What I have is more like morning sickness. I hinted at that when I called you on your cell and explained I was feeling nauseous. Had you been paying attention to me, you would've noticed that I've gained a little weight and haven't been jogging or using the StairMaster. Why didn't you poke your head in the storage room, Wessie boy? Had you done that, you also would've noticed the baby crib, rocker, toys, and cute wallpaper for the nursery. Oh well, so now you're completely surprised. Surprise. Don't you think I'll make a good mother? I consider myself very nurturing. And maybe I should name the baby Wes, if it's a boy," Tomi says, grinning.

"Bitch," Wes screams as the top of his lungs.

"Oooo, yes, baby, yes. I like it when you talk dirty to me. It turns me on. Just because I've got a baby in my tummy doesn't mean I still don't get horny. It's our special day, for goodness' sake. Didn't you hear the reverend unite us forever? That's no way to treat your wife. Here, have some cake, honey. Everyone's watching. Smile for all of the cameras and camcorders! This is the happiest day of our lives!" Tomi says, tryna shove cake in Wes's mouth.

"Get away from me, Tomi. You're fucking nuts," Wes screams. Tomi was able to shove some cake in his mouth, but most of the frosting ended up on his face.

Tomi walks back over to her spot, then tells Wes, "Oh, I didn't stop there. While you were spending petty cash on your cheap ho, I helped myself to your bank accounts. Your brother felt guilty after the first time we fucked, until I cleaned him up and started buying him things your cheap ass wouldn't share with him. See, watching you fuck this cheap ho and all the others made me horny. I wanted mine, too. After my patience wore out, and I gave up on your ass, I seduced your brother with your cash. Yes, Wessie, it helped him stick around long enough to devise and complete my plan. I paid for his sexual services, just like you did for your cheap hos. Let's just say he was on payroll as my escort. Malik just gives me chills. Damn, he's fine as Denzel, with those sexy pussy-eating L.L. Cool J lips."

"What?" Wes screams with wide yes.

"Oh yeah. All of those glorious spring days, hot summer nights, and cold winter afternoons didn't go to waste for Tomi. There he was in your bed, making me feel like a whole lot of woman, orgasm after orgasm. The baby is going to have plenty of everything, including savings for the best college, thanks to you. One bad turn deserves another, don't you think, Uncle Wes? I said godfather before to throw you off. By the way, boo, all of your accounts except the one you've been using are in the negative balance. I take that back, I left three quarters and a nickel in the second."

"Huh?" Wes says.

"That's right. Now I'm the rich one, and you're dirt poor again. Well, you can always sell your property to raise some cash. After all, it was your signature on the withdrawal slips—or so it seems. I know how to write just like you, honey," Tomi says, then laughs while shooing the big goons out and picking up the gun.

"My money, my boy, my brother, my ducks and fish, my house, a fuckin' crumb snatcher? Shit. My life is ruined," Wes belts out, then begins to cry hysterically again.

"Y'all are some crazy Jerry Springer motherfuckers. I shoulda stayed my ass in that paint-peeling motel room flirting with the man with the rotten teeth," I mumble.

"Yeah, I tried to tell you that, dumb-ass cheap ho," Tomi screams.

"Well if I had a place to go, good parents like you have, and a real life, maybe I woulda, and I don't want your man. If a man will do it with you, he'll do it to me. I don't want no Wes. I was just playing his game so I would have some basic necessities like food, water, and a fucking safe place to lay my head," I snap.

"Oh, so now I'm supposed to feel sorry for you, cheap ho?" Tomi screams.

"No, and you shouldn't. No one ever has. In fact, no one is ever gonna love a half White, half Black kid who was eating out of trash cans. All I've got is a 1988 Toyota to my name. So Tomi, now you know I hate myself and wouldn't even call 911 to come out to 2339 Willow Lane, if I could. The only way I can get some love is to open my legs and play a man. I can't believe I'm admitting this, but my White momma won't even acknowledge me. I lived on the streets and washed up in restaurant sinks. I can't even tell you where my daddy was when my foster momma threatened to beat me with extension cords and my foster daddy was tryna get his rocks off watching me changing my clothes. That sick fucker went farther than I care to explain. Shawn is the only one who would come to this cheap ho's funeral, unless he holds a grudge for me dragging him into this mess," I say, distorting some of the truth.

"Shoot this bastard 'cause I'm just a waste of space I take up in this world that is meant for sistas who have good breeding and had the benefit of the best educations. And Tomi, look at you, runway model material, and you're going to be a drop-dead gorgeous bride. You're the complete package men search for. I guess I hate myself because I can't be you. Just get it over with before I lose my nerve. Good-bye, Tomi. From one bastard to a real woman, I just want to let you know that I never meant to hurt you. I just wanted to be like you, that's it."

Tomi looks at Wes as if she's in a trance, still holding the gun out in front of her and mumbles, "Job 19:19: All my inward friends abhorred me: and they whom I loved are turned against me." I watch Wes gulp hard. Sweat pours from his face, and he's at a loss for words, looking like he's about to go into cardiac arrest. Tomi suddenly points the gun at me.

The fruitcake is scaring the shit out of me, but I reply, "And God, if you're listening, forgive Tomi for what she's about to do 'cause I deserve however many bullets she decides to put in me. Have mercy on my soul. My deceit will be the cause of my death," I say then squeeze my eyes shut.

I hear Tomi's voice start to quiver, as she responds, "Psalm 7:9 and

10: Let the wickedness of the wicked come to an end; but establish the just: for the righteous God trieth the hearts and reins. My defense is God, which saveth the upright in heart."

Wes screams, "No, no, Tomi. Don't pull the trigger. I have something to say. Ahh, ahh, I admit it, I cheated on you, and I didn't do right by you. I'm sorry; I'll never do it again. Don't kill us. You can't do this. You're a Christian, and you believe God's word. God's word also says, 'Revenge is mine, saith the Lord' so let Him handle the revenge."

"If you're going to quote God, make it count with me. If you can tell me the chapter and verse, I'll shoot Jachita and spare your life."

"I don't know. Ahhh, I can't remember," Wes mumbles, squinting.

Tomi calmly replies, "That's it then. No breaks for you, Wes. You don't know because you started standing me up for our church and Bible study dates. You're going to pay for it now. This is your day of darkness, and the time for judgment of the wicked has come. I've found the peace that I need to reward evil for evil. It's too late for admissions and apologies. We've had some good times, but we've had too many bad ones, and I can't get over this. Adios to you and Jachita. Say hi to the devil for me because you two are about to get an express trip to his headquarters."

26

MY SECURITY SYSTEM

I manage to bend my wrist and slide my trusty knife out of my pocket. I'm able to cut my ropes to free myself. Tomi pulls the trigger, but her attempt to shoot me in the center of my chest is futile. She stares at the gun and begins to shake and panic when she realizes something is wrong. During our struggle, I knock the gun from her hands. It spins across the floor and slides under the bed. After we knock over the bear on the dresser, I forcefully pull Tomi by the ponytail then tie her with the extra rope that she left sitting on the nightstand. Within about seven minutes, I'm securing her to the back of the headboard, next to Wes.

One of the goons hears the commotion, so he opens the sliding glass door and sticks his pit bull–looking head inside of the house. He begins moving toward me with his arms outstretched while saying, "I'm gonna get your ass, tie you up again, and throw you in the water with a brick holding you down so you'll drown."

I tune out his words and think of the men in foster care who put their hands on me when I didn't ask. I visualize Mr. Rodell's face and kick the goon in the balls like I'm Bruce Lee's sister. He cries, "This bitch kicked me in the fuckin' nuts. Ow. Ow. Ooow. Shiiiiit." When he falls backward just outside of the door he hits his head on a black Japanese lantern yard ornament statue that's about twenty-six inches tall. I look at him and thankfully he seems to be knocked the fuck out.

The other goon steps over him and tells me, "You're really gonna get it now for starting this static." He chases me. We run through the bedroom, living room, then down the hall. Along the way, I throw anything I can in his path to slow his big, blubbery ass up. He's still on my heels, but my strategy works long enough for me to purposefully dash into the kitchen 'cause thinking fast I recall seeing some black pepper sitting on the spice rack. I quickly untwist the cap, pour a handful out in my palm, and splash it in his face. He fights for his vision, tryna deal with the pain from the hot pepper. I seize the opportunity to pick up a large black cast-iron skillet to whack him over the head with it but as I lift my arm upward he grabs my wrist and I drop it in midair. While he's struggling to find my other wrist I pull away from his grip so hard I lose my balance and fall to the floor. I get up and run when I see him removing the coiled phone cord from the telephone, and I'm assuming he will try to choke me with it.

I run out of the kitchen, down the hall, through the living room, back into the bedroom, and just as I'm about to lock the door behind me. I hear, "I can see now. So you thought this was over, huh, did you, you slutty bitch?"

My heart begins to pound. He looks at me evil and intense, like the devil's son would probably do. When he charges toward me this time, Tomi's gun flashes in my mind.

Wes looks like he's too scared to talk, but Tomi is shouting from the ropes, "You said you've done this before so get on with it and just kill her!"

As I'm reaching under the bed to find the gun, I feel the goon's presence moving toward me while he replies, "You'll have to pay me two thousand more for getting my hands this dirty."

"I'm good for it. Just do it, will you?" Tomi says anxiously.

"My pleasure. I'm not fond of sluts," he replies.

My hand is shaking but by the time I feel the goon dragging me away from the edge of the bed by my ankles, I've got a good grip on the gun. I warn him once, "Stop! Let me go."

He laughs, then replies, "Did I mention I was recently released for murder from Supermax in Baltimore? I can kill you and get away with it. Tomi will stick to my story, and I'm going to kill Wes next, so your luck's run out, my dear. I've been craving the sight of fresh blood, just craving it from somebody, and now that somebody is you."

Wes shouts, "Let her go. Don't kill the girl. What do you want, man? If it's money, I can get that for you. Just let her go."

While the goon in sliding me by the ankles to the other side of the room, the goon replies, "You know why I was locked up, Wes? Because my wife cheated on me with a man like you. A man with the kind of money I didn't have. I blew both of their brains out while they were in bed, and I don't regret a second of what I did. I'm the right man for this job. I'll finish what Tomi couldn't."

Now I know I'm running out of time, so I quickly shout, "This is your last warning. Stop! Let me go."

The goon still laughs. His grip seems to tighten instead of loosen. When he stops pulling me by the ankles, I twist my torso around and bend upward toward the goon. This is one time being flexible comes in handy 'cause I've got to hold my body in this half-twisted position and place my finger on the trigger and shoot.

Bang! The gun sounds off. The bullet lands in the goon's stomach. Blood is flowing like a river.

He releases me from his grip, saying, "Oh God, I've been shot," yet he persists in moving toward me. I manage to stand and aim at his leg.

Bang! The gun sounds again. He collapses on to the floor. When I listen to the thud of his heavy frame fall, I cover my mouth with shaking hands. I back away from his limp body that's spewing blood from his leg and stomach.

I hysterically blurt out, "I shot someone. I shot someone. Tell me I didn't just do that. Damn. What am I gonna do now?"

Wes speaks up, "You saved our lives, Jalita. You had to shoot him. He was going to kill us both. He said so. We almost died up in here," Wes says, half crying. Then he adds, "How about untying your boy, Jalita?"

I feel like a zombie, numb from what just happened. I walk over and untie Wes.

"We've got to get him some medical help," Wes announces while walking over to a phone in the bedroom.

I tell him, "Tomi cut all of the lines in the house. Look." I point to the disconnected wires.

She replies, "Oh, that's right, I did cut the lines, didn't I?"

I explain to Wes, "The police are on their way anyway. My voice-activated cell phone did the job when Tomi had us both tied up." I walk over to turn it off.

Wes replies, "That's my girl."

I turn around toward Wes, saying, "You're not my boy. A negro goes and buys a girl one rib, a bottle of perfume from time to time, a few pieces of Baby Phat clothing, but he's fucking his dick off as Tomi would say, and all of the sudden he tries to own a girl and lay claim like he's got rights to something. I see you'll never change, Mr. One-Way Street. You're just as crazy as she is."

Tomi screams from the ropes, "I hate you."

I reply her, "That's nothing new, you little possessed, hypocritical broke-down diva with an over-priced education. You just had a lesson in manipulation 101. And by the way, your dumb ass forgot to take off the safety. Even I knew that, and I've never been instructed on how to use a gun."

"I should have blown your head off. I would have loved to have watched it roll right off your neck," Tomi replies.

"I've got to have a few words with you, too."

"Like what, bitch?" she yells.

"My name's *Jalita* not bitch or Jachita, okay? I've been wanting to make that pushy request for you to say it correctly since you showed your ass on day one. In case you've forgotten, a man is over there bleeding because you started this cowboys and Indians shit. This is a serious matter. Crane your ostrich neck and look on the floor if you need reminding."

"God, you're such a bitch. It'll be a serious matter if I get rope burn and stain my dress! My skin will never be the same again, not even if I get a seaweed body wrap. I wonder if Julian can give me an emergency appointment at this hour. No, this damage might be so bad that I need to fly to Manhattan for one of those stone and lava facials. I wonder if they can use the stones all over my body. Last time, my skin was left with an amazing glow. Jachita, call this number. Umm, I think it's 212-717-9300. The establishment is called Completely Bare. See if anyone answers," Tomi boldly orders.

"I'm not gonna warn you about fucking up my name one more damn time. I wish the police would hurry up and get here. You're getting on my nerves, and I can barely stand being in the same room with you. All you were scared of is losing your meal ticket. Maybe that's why your little curse drifted off somewhere and didn't work. No wonder Wes cheated on you as much as he could. You're really annoying. If I were into murder records, I'd gladly get one for shooting you, Tomi, but that's not my kind of party. I guess today's your lucky day, too, you overpriced, snobbish ho."

In a shaky voice Tomi explains, "It's my lucky day, only if God has shown Wes he should appreciate a good girl with good breeding and let the freaks like you go. I can still manage to forgive him, if he apologizes and works things out." A river of tears begin to pour from her eyes.

Wes looks over at Tomi and says, "Drop the theatrics. Hell no, I don't love you, you high-maintenance ho! I'm gonna make you pay for this attempted murder shit. Jalita wouldn't kill me for nothing, unlike your Prozac-needin' ass. I want her, not you," Wes says.

I stare Wes deep in the eyes and tell him, "I was playing a game. I don't want your ass. My shirt is torn, I'm splashed with blood, and I'm scratched up thanks to your crazy woman. Enough of this, already."

"Bullshit, you do want me. You didn't treat me like the Federal Reserve 99.9 percent of the time. You listened, caressed, played, laughed, and made me feel like a man. I have you wrapped around my finger. You're falling in love with me," Wes insists.

I roll my eyes at Wes, and say, "Keep dreaming, and don't put words in my mouth, Mr. Basketball. You're just plain foul for knowing this girl was this off and risking both of our lives. I just thought she was bluffing myself. After months of watching you do your thing, I could see how even a sane woman could lose her mind. That was pretty low. You don't love me, and I most certainly don't love you," I say, shaking my head. Then I wave my arm around in the air, and tell Wes, "Oh, shut up, man. Either commit, or be single and play the field fairly. Your charm was so cheap, I wanted to laugh after that plated shit wore off after the first night. A real player like me doesn't need a dime to sucker people in the pit; suckers fall in regardless. I was schemin', that's all."

"Will you please fix the TV, please Jachita? That noise and snowy screen is starting to bother my morning sickness," Tomi whines.

"It's about time you try to use those nice Southern manners you probably *use* to have, but my name is *not* Jachita!"

Tomi carelessly blows off my warning and says, "Yeah, whatever."

I walk about four steps to the TV that's been blank for the longest. I disconnect the VCR and accidentally hit the TV button in my effort to turn it off. A bright smile forms, and my eyes widen, then I scream, "Seth! My baby!" I see a familiar face on the boob tube.

"That's the gardener from next door," Tomi and Wes say in unison as I watch Seth talking to Oprah about his hit book that apparently did climb just like he said it would. The queen of talk just publicly announced his inspirational book is becoming the hottest read around the country. Thank goodness for reruns at odd hours. Now I know I just made a big mistake I'm about to fix.

"Mmm. I never noticed he was that fine when he use to do all that work around the neighborhood. Where does he live? Can I get a last name, Jachita?" Tomi asks eagerly, apparently forgetting she's pregnant. Wes looks at her. He's crushed, too, just for a different reason called ego, 'cause yet another man made Tomi lose interest in gold digging in his newly linted pocket! In a sweet, calm voice, Tomi corrects herself, saying, "I mean, Jalita."

"I applaud you for finally getting the name right and all, but girlfriend, *he's mine*. Get your eyes ready to read some childbirth books or something. I'm about to live the life I really want."

Wes belts out, "What about me? That pretty boy nigga ain't shit. All he does is write words down on paper. I'm the NBA star here. Completely legit."

"The *real* you doesn't even act like a man. You wanted your threesome, I'd say you got it, minus the skinny White girl. Since this has nothing to do with a love thing, Wes, I've just upgraded for the sake of quality control." Tomi laughs as Wes looks at me in astonishment.

I ask her, "Do you find something funny, you violent, shallow ass?"

"Of course I do. You think Wes really wants to be with your ho ass, well he doesn't. As soon as you untie him, he'll go home, have makeup sex with me, buy me something ridiculously expensive, and everything will go back to normal. I'm the type who can pull that Seth if I really want him, *not* you. I keep telling you you're trash. No man is going to commit to you. I know Wes like the back of my hand. Tell her, Wes. Tell her who you're loyal to. Tell her she's nothing but a fling, like the rest of the groupies."

All of the sudden, we hear a deep "Police!"

Our heads swing toward the sliding glass door. I run over to unlock it, then move out of the way as two uniformed police officers pointing guns ease inside while one guards the first goon.

I point and say, "That woman over there tried to kill us. I just want all of this to be over. This is so upsetting. I can't believe what happened. I had to shoot the man because he tried to kill me." As the policemen lower their weapons, I walk over to the cutest one and hysterically sob in the middle of his chest.

He responds, "Ma'am, we have to sort this whole thing out. Until we do we've got to handcuff all of you, then listen to your stories while you're separated."

Wes walks over to him and says, "Don't you know who I am, dawg?"

The officer answers, "Mr. Montgomery, I've got to treat everyone here the same, now would you please hold out your wrists." As the officer handcuffs Wes, Wes complies and looks as if he wants to give the Prince George's County cop a severe tongue-lashing that he'll never forget but all he does is clench his teeth and make the veins on the side of his head I never noticed become pronounce. He guides Wes into another room then another officer walks toward me. I follow Wes's lead and hold out my wrists. As he handcuffs me, I humbly tell him, "I understand you're just doing your job. You have my full cooperation. Easy on my wrists, please, 'cause they're sore from the ropes I was tied up in." I look at Tomi as the officer guides me out of the room.

The other officer is left in the room with Tomi, who's already screaming, "I want my lawyer, and I refuse to be handcuffed like a common criminal." As I'm explaining the love triangle between Wes, Tomi, and myself, I hear an ambulance pull up, I assume to scrape up the goons and cart them off to the nearest hospital.

About thirty minutes later, Tomi discovers Wes is loyal to himself after she finds out he parroted a story identical to mine.

Within a few minutes, we all hear, "You have a right to remain silent. Anything you say can be used against you in a court of law. If you cannot afford an attorney, one will be appointed for you."

After one of the policemen finishes reciting Tomi's rights, she shouts, "I said I want my lawyer!"

At this point, Wes and I are treated as victims of a crime. The cutest officer says, "Ms. Harrison, you and Mr. Montgomery can either follow us in your own vehicle or ride in the squad car down to the station so that we can take written statements."

Tomi shouts, "Baby, you're pressing charges on me? Please don't. Please let it go like you said you would so we can all go home."

Wes ignores her, turns to me, and says, "Let's take the Lex, Jalita. You drive though. I'll transfer the title to your name to help you reconsider moving in to the mansion. As you know, one side of the bed is now empty. I'd love for your body heat to keep me warm the rest of the winter and every winter after that. Don't answer yet, just think about my offer, beautiful. I'll even let you decorate. I never liked what Tomi did to the place, anyway. We can find a new interior decorator and start from scratch."

Tomi walks by cursing in handcuffs, then screams, "This isn't over. You two will get what you deserve for trying to destroy my life. Everything you told the police was a lie, and you know it. When I contact my daddy's attorney, expect trouble for framing an innocent woman. Your arms are too short to box with God, and He saw everything. I'm calling upon his name, right now: O God, do not keep silent; be not quiet, O God, be not still. See how your enemies are astir, how your foes rear their heads. With cunning they conspire against your people; they plot against those you cherish. I know justice will prevail. I'm protected by your blood. Hallelujah. Hallelujah."

I walk alongside of her, commenting, "You can't stop defiling God's name, can you? I'm sure you'll look fabulous in used, dull jail clothes.

The grunge thing is back in. So much for that seaweed body wrap, aromatherapy foot soak, and facial. Now you're the one who's gonna have to take a rain check. And I'll be pressing charges on you too, murderer."

Wes screams, "I was good to you and gave you everything. I put you in front of the line of all the bitches and groupie hos. Look how you thanked me. This never would've happened if I hooked up with a White girl like some of my teammates did. Now I see why they openly cross the color line. Most Black hos get too spoiled and start trying to regulate instead of keeping their lips zipped and their feelings in check."

Tomi loses it and says, "Your pictures aren't pasted up on a website in a Yahoo group where women gossip about if a woman is worthy or pretty enough to be with an NBA player, mine is. All anyone ever saw was you. They looked right past me like I wasn't even there, even when I was holding your hand or eating dinner with you in a restaurant. I was never in front of anything but the line at the bank, holding your checkbook. That wasn't enough, even if I thought it would be."

Confused neighbors gather to watch Tomi being led to a squad car. Two ambulances that collected the goons pull off. I feel justified that I had to shoot the second goon who seems to be injured, but I'm sure he'll recover just fine with good medical attention since he regained consciousness and began talking before he left on a stretcher. As for myself, I hope we don't get tied up at the station half of the night while officers generate a pile of paperwork. As soon as I say what I've got to say, I'm ditching Wes. I'm in a hurry to place a call to Seth 'cause my palm is itching like a motherfucker.

27

A WAKE-UP CALL

"So you saw the show?" Seth asks me.

"Yes, Seth. I'm so happy for you. You blew up the spot. Well done," I respond, scratching my palm and smiling.

"Thank you. I knew my payday was coming. Now that it's here, I can't believe it happened so fast. After I went on *Oprah*, all three thousand copies of my books sold out off my website, and my phone's been ringing off the hook.

"You did say that it was on its way, almost a thousand times. Wow, so you're a bona fide writer with real credentials and everything. I'm honored to know you from back when your goal was just a vision."

"I can finally get my financial house in order and buy Mom some things she deserves. No more rusty Betsy either. We donated her to a nonprofit organization. I'm sure all she'll be good for is parts."

"So what was it like, being on TV and stuff?"

"Although I'd practiced looking Oprah in the eye for years, I was still nervous. The studio wasn't as big as it looks on a TV set at home though," Seth says cheerfully.

"Nervous or not, you were right, and I was wrong. I didn't mean to be so hard on you when we last spoke. Freelance writing is a real job. You knew what you were doing," I admit.

"Well, that doesn't matter. No hard feelings here, Jalita," Seth says in a light-hearted manner.

"So, if you're not busy touring or anything right now, do you think we can go to a powwow like you said? I've been reading up on Native

American history for a week now. It's very interesting. I hear they're building a Museum of Indian Art in D.C. I'd love for you to be my tour guide and explain the exhibits to me when it opens," I say.

"The Morning Star Celebration in Bel Air was a one day event. Since you didn't express interest, I didn't attend. I wanted to take you to the benefit dance that took place afterward, after you saw what I assumed would have been your first friendly Native American dance competition. I won't miss out in April, though. I'll be at the Twenty-first Annual Gathering of Nations Powwow in Albuquerque, New Mexico, which is the biggest in North America. My intention isn't to be rude, but I have to come out and say it: I won't be inviting you anywhere, anymore. You aren't ready for a real man. Still aren't. What about some things called trust and reliability, Jalita?"

Seth catches me off guard. I pause, then calmly inquire, "What are you saying, Seth?"

"Jalita, way down deep, you're a good person hiding who you truly are because you have some unresolved conflicts. You need to find the light within and stop running game. It's tired."

Deception has become so natural to me, I don't have to think hard to concoct a reply. "You're way off base. I may be moody, but I'm as honest as they come. I guess I was tryna protect myself from getting hurt because men tend to walk all over me like I don't have a spine. I didn't want you to be the next one, so that's what the 'tude was all about."

"You're so attractive, but that attitude makes you ugly. Try working on the inside. That's what needs some attention. If you can't be honest with yourself, no wonder you can't be honest with me," Seth says, sounding like he's been sitting on Dr. Phil's stage instead of Oprah's.

"Now Seth, I'm not out to diss you. I explained everything, and just told you why I—"

Seth interrupts me, and says, "Maybe not now, but when I had my mom's whooptie with the temperamental battery and tried to treat you like a lady, all you did was make fun of my dream. You could have killed my spirit to keep going, if I would've let you. Too many people don't realize their full potential because others dictate their worth and what they should be doing with their life."

"What are you implying?"

"Well since you asked, I'll tell say it straight out. You're one of those women who wants to know how much money a man makes right off, when that just shouldn't be the focus. Do you really enjoy gold digging and walking all over people in the process?"

"But Seth, you've got me all wrong. I'm not that kind of sista. I'm not out to hurt you one bit. I swear I'm not a dollar-bill catcher. I just put someone in her place who was that way. I told her how dead wrong she was," I insist.

"The words don't match the history of your actions. I'm not buying it. I bet you didn't even bother to read one page in that book I gave you."

"Only because I was working my butt off to earn some extra money in case I changed my mind about spring semester. Since I didn't go back to Virginia, I was gonna read it since I have a chance to catch my breath and get some r-and-r now. If I were a gold digger, I wouldn't have been getting chicken grease under my nails at Chik-fil-A," I lie.

"That book was really special to me. It has a message in it that I wanted you to extract. I was trying to give you a chance, hoping and praying you would just pick it up and make a U-turn. I was willing to be patient while you were trying to improve, but you didn't care to try to help yourself or consider that maybe I did know something important. The book was autographed by someone I admire and everything. All you could see was a struggling man who couldn't offer you material things. That was a low blow."

"How materialistic could I be? If I were a gold digger, I also wouldn't be tryna get somewhere in life. Instead, I'd be racking up material things or pushing the latest whip. I own a '88 Toyota for God's sake, so how could I have room to make fun of the car you were driving or have some man financing my alleged expensive habits?"

"You say these things, but I know that you're just not interested in the most important things in life yet. I can see right through you, like you're transparent. It's so clear to me in my mind. In a way I wish I couldn't see it."

"But it's not too late for us. I can show you who I really am, and I do know what's really important in life. Why don't you stop accusing me and let me prove what I'm saying," I whine.

"A real man likes and loves a real woman, someone who wants to use her smarts to attract attention, not just her looks. I'm not going to mess up my head and my number two fan's heart by reaching back for a confused you. I can't take that risk now," Seth explains.

"You're willing to cut me off because of a few mean comments I made when I was in a bad mood with men?" I say in disbelief.

"No, I'm letting you know that I wish you the best, but I'm exclusively dating someone now. My graphic artist became my second biggest fan. I think she's going to be the one I settle down with, even if you were my first choice."

"So you're turning me down for someone who probably isn't even as fine as I am? Everyone wants this. Everywhere I go, men stop what they're doing and take notice. No one turns me down, no one," I say.

"One day you're going to realize how silly you sound. You're not all that, Jalita," Seth comments, then chuckles. I know that I've lost my credibility with him when he adds, "It's not about how much attention you get, but the quality of the person that you're getting it from and how you choose to handle why they're giving it. Sounds to me like you think you're the only woman with a pretty face and a banging body. Those things may turn a man's head, but they won't and can't keep his attention for life. I just got finished telling you that you don't understand what life is about yet. You just proved my point yet another time."

"I can't help it if men don't take me seriously. I didn't ask to look like this, and I have a right to be confident. I'm not perfect, Seth. You're blowing this whole thing out of proportion," I say.

"A relationship is not built on sex or a woman's looks. I'm a real man who saw past all of that and took you very seriously. Maybe you didn't notice that either because you were too busy trying to judge me and put me in the same category with those who treated you like your outside is the focus. You had weeks to give me one small sign you could change, and that never occurred. You're good with words, but not that good. You say you were too busy to read the book or even call, but all of the sudden you see me on *Oprah* and can lose the bad attitude, then call the same day it airs. Jalita, you really need to stop this lying. You abuse your looks, and that's a dangerous thing. You're going to miss out on a lot in life if you keep using them as a decoy. What are you going to do when you get wrinkles and things start to sag?" Seth asks.

"I'm hoping I'll still have my looks. Not everyone shows their age, you know. No man has ever loved me. Using my looks is my only hope. Who's gonna like me for who I am if I told him the truth about my past with an open heart? No one, including you."

"You know how they say love at first sight can be. I loved you from the first second you made up a reason to speak to me, but sometimes all of that isn't quite enough. Almost never is, so it seems. I often prayed that God would allow me to meet a true love. I met her while raking leaves in Mitchellville. The problem is I should have a good relationship with someone I want to spend the rest of my life with. I've got to like that person as a person and vice versa. Without that, a relationship can't have a shot to stand during times when life goes sour."

"Love at first sight. You really felt that way about me?" I question.

"Yeah. I'm not into saying things I don't mean. I hate to blow your theory and everything, but I'm a man who did want to be with you, regardless of anything you've been through. I wasn't asking you to be perfect, just for real."

"You say that now, but I bet you would've hauled ass right after I poured my heart out to you."

"I see you refuse to believe the truth, and I'm not here to tell you what to believe. Look, I'm sorry things didn't take shape like I hoped. A little piece of me is always going to wonder where you are and how you turned out. I want you to keep that book as a token of the friendship I tried to build with you. I'll always wish you well and acknowledge you as the woman who taught me I could really love someone. If love hurts more than it feels good, it's not love—at least not flowing from both sides. Love is all about an ebb and flow of action. It can't be a one-sided deal, ever."

"But Seth, I made a mistake. I said I'm sorry. How many ways can I tell you that? I always liked you. You always had my attention, Seth. Why do you think I stopped you outside in Mitchellville in the first place? I was drawn to you right then," I lie.

"You're doing it again, and I know why."

"What are you talking about now?"

"I guess you've figured out that I'm not making five dollars an article now. As I mentioned, my phone's been ringing off the hook. Publishing houses have been competing for me to hurry and agree to a deal. I decided on one and was lucky enough to get an advance so I can have some immediate cash flow. This is what you were looking to hear, so now you know everything you called to find out."

"I hadn't even thought about money. I'm just proud that you—"

Seth cuts me off in mid-sentence, and says, "Nice try. I really hope you make some changes and stop having that limo-chasing mentality. An us could have been the best thing you ever had, if you understood what I meant when I called you a morning flower. Mom and I are at a dealership. She looks good in that Benz she's sitting in. Looks like we've found a car for her. I've got to go tend to my number one fan and do some paperwork with the salesman. Good-bye, Jalita."

"But Seth, now I understand what I did to mess things up. I didn't know you cared. I won't do it again. I'm telling you the truth this time. I really am," I plead.

"I got down on my knees and prayed that I'd know what to do about this. You were the last loose end in my life. Funny thing is I knew you thought I was a momma's boy who didn't have it together, from day one.

What you didn't consider is that a man who loves and takes care of his mother will treat his woman with comparable affection and love. Still, I had hoped you'd see me for what I really am. I finally know it's time to say good-bye to the thought of ever seeing you again. I know I can live with that reality now. Sometimes things just don't work out how we'd like them to, but that's the quirky nature of life, isn't it?"

"Why are you doing this? I've been wondering who's gonna love me for these last few months. I need you. I've never met anyone like you. Please don't go. You're everything I've always wanted. I mean that from a place within myself I didn't even know existed."

"You should have thought about the possibilities of that place every time you clammed up on me when we talked. Every time I encouraged you to get real, you hated on me instead. I learned the lesson I was supposed to learn from meeting you. I want to be accepted as I was before, not who I am now that things are going well."

"If you walk away from me now, we'll never know what could have been. Don't do it. I'm a good woman, Seth. I want to know how it feels to live a dream. I can go back to school and everything. I'll get it together, too. I know I can do it with a good man like you behind me," I say, whimpering.

"Saying good-bye to you isn't easy, but being true to myself is all it takes for me to make myself move on. If you're really sorry, you'll try to change all the way, not when it's convenient to pretend. I told you that I can see right through you, so do a couple of 180s, if you bother to make the effort to try to put one foot forward and get right with yourself."

"Look, I'm in this motel right as you come in off the B/W Parkway. Just see me one last time after you handle your business. Please come, Seth, even if for only ten minutes. Let's talk about all of this in person, baby. This is not the kind of thing that's appropriate to decide over the phone," I say, putting on a false cry with a side order of sniffs.

"Save the fake tears, Jalita. You're not getting me over there to try and use sex as a weapon either. I know all of your moves, and I refuse to behave like a weak man. Maybe I'll see you again if we bump into each other down in Jamaica. Tell Wes to work on his jump shot. There are some new draft picks who will give him a run for his money. All the best to you and him. From what I saw in the tabloids, you're being taken care of. I'm sure you haven't been in that motel room alone for too long. I won't stand in the way of what you and Wes already have going on. I guess he has your back, and that's a great thing. You know, that's really what a healthy relationship is all about," Seth says, then hangs up his cell.

I'm still yelling, "I'm not with Wes. I'm not with Wes. He means nothing to me, John. I mean Seth. Are you there? Hello? Hello?"

I finally hang up and accept that I've been dissed and busted for the first time since I started playing this little game. Shit, I even slipped and called him John when Seth got me all riled up. Thank goodness he didn't hear that noise, just in case the bridge isn't completely burned.

Seth just gave me the best wake-up call I've ever had. I could have enjoyed being his morning flower, but I missed my opportunity to bloom before his eyes. I found a real friend and member of that less than one percent of the good guy club. Now he wants to forget I exist all 'cause I was caught up playing games and not even bothering to find out all about me. For the first time since I was a kid, I think I'm gonna break down and cry me a whole bucket of real tears right here in another cheap motel room that needs a paint job. Maybe I really don't think I'm worth having the best, and I'm not talking about Gucci, Prada, or being with a guy with a built-in fan club.

"What do you want, Wes?" I say, dabbing my eyes with an overused Kleenex.

"How you gonna go and answer the cell that I'm paying for like that?"

"I won't be using it much longer, so get a grip," I say, watching several roaches chase one another up the motel wall.

"Sounds like you've been crying."

"So what. People sometimes do. I'm human, you know."

"You don't sound like yourself, Jalita. Want me to come over and fuck you doggy style? I can get some good stuff and we can temporarily smoke the memory of what Tomi pulled away."

"No, Wes. Don't you think you best be straightening your twisted shit out?"

"Tomi is history. You know that."

"I'm not interested. I've got more important things on my mind," I say. As usual, Wes ignores my needs and continues to rant about Tomi.

"Serves her right for trying to gold-dig and treat me wrong all those years. My lawyer is on my financial shit right now. Turns out that the bank froze my accounts when they sensed something was wrong. Her ass didn't get but so far, mainly setting up new accounts that she can't even access, dumb bitch. I didn't know about it because she'd been burning the mail from the bank. Doesn't she know blood is blood? She can't make me turn on my brother or my boy. She's nothing but an expensive trick. Wait until the media gets a hold of this one. It'll show how gold-digging women abuse us athletes," he says.

"Whatever, Wes," I respond in an annoyed tone.

"Look, I think you and I can really get something going. I mean for real. You're right, I did meet my match. You're like a female player version of me. What do you say to a commitment, beautiful?"

"Hell double fucking no," I reply.

"What? You're rejecting a good life with me?"

"Good life? Isn't it crystal clear to you? I just turned in my player's card, and I'm not interested in being six feet under for no man. You'd do the same thing to me you did to Tomi, and I'm not having it because seeing a man you're with not lovin' you right in a relationship has got to hurt. That groupie shit is the worst deal, and no one ever cares about anything when you're around, except catering to your whims. Do you know how it feels to be treated like you're invisible? It never stops," I say, sniffing.

"What are you saying?"

"Your world sucks and stinks like rotten eggs. No thank you, Wes."

"I'm the best from east to west, and I've got everything I want in life, so stop hating. You're a fool, Jalita, a damn fool for chasing me off. I had no idea you were serious."

"Yes, I am, and the hell if I'm hating. The world you live in is a lie. Team politics. Games. Women throwing booty at you, you taking it like you don't remember what Magic Johnson went through. There's nothing of substance in your world. It's too much drama for me. I was a fool for taking the bait in the first place."

"This act is part of my job. I act, but you act, too. Don't try to play it like you don't know how to work people over. I used condoms with everyone but Tomi so I may as well hit pussy if I decide I want to. That was a brilliant speech you made at the beach house. And that stuff about being abandoned, having the White mother, the knife. All of it. I loved it. It was so real. It was the perfect diversion that bought some time to save our hides."

"Well, I'm about to tell you how real that scene was. I lived on the streets and really did see some things while I ate out of trashcans, so I initially knew she was running short upstairs."

"Well, I had no idea that bitch was crazy. She was really going to smoke us. I can't shake off the fact that I was living with a cold-blooded killer."

"Do you even care about what I've been through my whole life? I just told you something very personal, and you skipped right over it to go on an on about what you wanted to talk about."

"Damn, Jalita, I didn't mean to. I'm just use to people listening to me—from reporters at news conferences on down. What is it that you were saying again?"

"I'm not repeating it for your benefit, but I will say what I told Tomi may have been just a diversion to you, but some of that was the truth. I'm gonna drop off your cell and precious car tomorrow. Let me know when you'll be available so I can put the keys to the Lex in your hand. Keep the title in your name 'cause I don't want it."

"You really don't want to be with me? I can't believe this. No woman rejects Wes."

"Now you're listening. I think I just lost the only person who ever really loved me, so I'm not feelin' like jumping for joy and being your cheap ho. And don't forget to use a condom tonight when you go get some from someone else, Wes. In case you haven't heard, there's something called AIDS out there. I know we were using condoms, but I think I'm due for a trip to get tested just because I allowed myself to lay on my back with you. I need to start facing why I got myself into this mess, misrepresenting myself as a woman who sees people for what they have, not who they are. I just figured out that I've been walking around for the last few months of my life like a zombie. I don't love myself and am due to make some life-altering changes. By the way, I could have fallen in love with someone, and his name is Seth. Later for you and your tired-ass self," I say, then push the end button on the cell phone. I turn off the ringer 'cause I know how players are. Wes will just become more persistent to capture me, then throw me away. I was a player not even six hours ago, so I ought to know.

All I can think of is Seth who probably is genuinely one of the best from east to west. I hold my pillow tight and pretend it's him absorbing my sadness. After I cry another bucket of tears, I'm gonna turn page one of that book he was nice enough to give me, just 'cause a real man said there was something in it that he feels I need to read and ponder.

Now Jamaica and everything else I've conned these men out of was nothing. *4:17 Vinegar Blues* is the best gift I've ever been given 'cause Seth gave it to me from the heart, not 'cause he had the power of a dollar bill over me. To think, Seth could've loved me for real, even though he never even laid one finger on me to get some.

Life is such a bitch, especially when you haven't been living right and have no man, no momma, and no friends to support your ass through a mandatory change. How do I manage to clean up this mess, all by my damn self? Right now, that's all I want to know.

28

A FORMALITY OF COMBAT

Outside of getting one bucket of ice to cool down some V8 Splash juice, I haven't left this room for forty-eight hours to sniff out one crumb, exercise my legs, or brush the plaque build-up off my teeth. I didn't even bang on the wall when I heard some woman getting her brains fucked out until the sun came up. Instead, I dragged the comforter off the bed, draped it on top of the curtains, and covered all signs of sunlight peeking through the window. I lay in bed and tolerated the sound of the moaning and the cheap, flimsy headboard smacking against the wall like it was music coming from the radio. I guess it was okay with me that someone might feel good in their world for the right damn reasons. The darkness kept me sane. It gave me room to think, too, even if my dizziness was growing. I could tell I unintentionally shed at least two pounds from my voluptuous frame.

By the third day, I washed out a pair of underwear in the sink and hung them on the shower bar. While I was up, I heard the door next to me shut and forced myself to pull the curtain to the side. I peeped them kissing, holding hands, and laughing on their way out somewhere. When I saw all of that romantic stuff, I closed my eyes and imagined that Seth and I are doing what the lovebirds one door over were doing in a cheap motel room, and I'm not just talking about the sex stuff. I felt warm and tingly all over, then my heart started pounding, when I considered getting away, spending some one-on-one time with Seth while he lets me know it's all about paying attention to me.

I find the energy to rip down the comforter, then sit on the side of the bed pondering what I wouldn't give to have me some Boardwalk Fries with Seth again and hear the story behind him managing to get invited on *Oprah*, then selling all of his books. Damn, Seth, why did I have to fuck up? Why didn't I realize learning the art of macking is a waste of time? Now I realize I have some thin spots in my character, but I still can't let go without fighting for him. I'm gonna hit him up on the cell and tell him just five words: *I could've loved you back*. If he answers by telling me to put on my dancin' shoes so we can go out and start all over again, maybe there's hope for him being the bigger person, but I won't know if I don't try.

I dial Seth's number and bite my bottom lip. I've never tried to get with a brotha on the begging tip, and I feel uneasy about it, but there's a first time for everything, and I can't be shy now that I realize what the brotha means to me.

Instead of a ringing, I hear, "This number is no longer in service."

My eyes begin to water again. I fall onto the bed and begin to cry another river. I don't know if this is a phase or something that will last for eternity, but I just feel numb to everything. I don't even have the energy to open the soap wrapper, turn the knobs on the shower, and wash the dirt off my body. I guess having the kind of dirt you can't wash is a formality of combat. All I can do is just live through the feeling of owning it. There's no communication left with Seth, and he's gone forever. Although I have a silver tongue, my words fell on deaf ears. Apparently he wasn't messing around or playing hard to get; Seth really meant what he said.

I feel so weak, depleted, and shaky, I think I'm having blood sugar issues like I developed when I didn't have enough food to eat back in the day. Unless I want to pass straight out, I better force myself out of this hermit phase, throw on some jeans, and roll on up to a drive-through somewhere close by. Damn, I hate B-more all over again. Everytime I come here, something life-altering happens, and I'm truly sick of not being able to side step the drama.

I walk into the bathroom and use the toilet before I gorge myself on some junk food or greasy fast food. I flush the toilet and notice the polluted water is getting closer and closer to the top. Damn. Why did the toilet have to overflow? Tell me this just isn't happening. Okay, fine. I'll just call the motel office and let them know someone needs to run around here with a plunger.

"Hello. I'm in Room 212. My toilet is broken. Someone needs to come and plunge it fast because everything in the toilet is running out all over the place," I announce frantically.

As hungry and weak as I am, this isn't the time for this little detour, but what can I do? I've been sitting on this bed for nearly half an hour, and no one has shown up yet. And of all things, I just took a shit, so lucky me gets to watch you-know-what pour all over the floor and flow in front of the front door. I've been nice enough about putting up this long with the liquid toxic, stinking mess, so it looks like I'm gonna have to dress and take a walk to that damn office since the maintenance man is off taking a nap in some utility closet.

"Excuse me, miss. The toilet in my room just overflowed. I called and no one has shown up to fix it," I tell the purple-haired woman when I arrive at the office.

"You can't stuff too much toilet paper in these toilets," she responds rudely.

"I used the normal amount, if you must know," I snap, leaning on the counter.

"Well you can't flush too many tampons in these toilets, eva."

I feel my hostility level mounting, and I find myself belting out, "Look, a shit stain was in it when I first checked in so you are way off base here. You probably need to be grilling the maid, who may have sat her ass down on the seat before I check in, okay, girlfriend? As raggedy as this place is, I'm sure it's happened many times before. And by the way, I'm not even on my damn period, but I see you want to bring out my PMS attitude."

"You don't have to get nasty, *miss*," she says, exposing her gold tooth.

"Well you don't have to act like an asshole. I know how to use a toilet, and I'm tired of using manners of ghetto queens like yourself, who apparently haven't been taught that the customer is always right. Why don't you find a plunger and do something, so we can just get the damn thing fixed and I can get out of your face?" I tell her loudly.

"That ain't my job."

"I guess you're scared you'll break one of your Lee Press-on nails or scrape one of those little painted palm tree designs off. I've got your number, sista. You don't want to have to get those nails done early. If you don't want to work, don't show up."

"You needs to just stay out of my personal business 'fore I get up in yours. We can get something started, if that's what you're tryin' to do now."

"Just give me another room like a person with sense would. I don't know who your boss is, but she must not be hitting on much herself if she keeps your trifling butt on payroll and has the nerve to put you on front desk duty," I say, rolling my eyes, then sighing.

"Let me get the manager 'cause you need to take all of your damn criticisms with her on the way she trained me up," she says.

When she disappears in the back office, I'm thinking it's about time for me to poke out my chest and have someone lick my boots like they did for Wes. I may not have the money he does, but my money spends just the same, and I deserve satisfaction, too. It would even be nice to get a free night for me having to put up with some things that weren't right from jump. At the very least, someone better offer me up a "have a nice day" line.

"What seems to be the . . . I'm gonna whip that ass, you trick bitch," Charlene says while her eyes widen, realizing that she's finally caught up with me.

"Charlene," I say as my eyes widen, too.

"Oh, so you found out where I worked so you could tease me some more, bitch! You won't stop, will you? This time I'm gonna make you stop. I've been waiting for this day, but didn't think it would ever come. Well hot damn, I'm gonna get my wish after all."

"No, I've changed, Charlene. This is a coincidence. I really do have a broken toilet in my room, and I'm not trying to be funny. You can go look yourself, if you don't believe me."

"Yeah, right. I know what you pulled."

"It wasn't what you thought. Tony was the one who lied. He lied to me about everything. I didn't know he had someone in the picture or a little baby. I swear I'm not looking for no baby momma drama," I say, shaking my head.

"Tony told me everything. I'm gonna make good on my promise to whip your ass with an old-fashioned beatdown to teach you about messing over an innocent woman. You just had to pull that hotel shit. You just went too far," she says, running from behind the front desk, grabbing my hair, and pushing me to the ground. We both start rolling around on the floor like we're in a wrestling ring. Charlene is in her dress clothes, and I'm in my favorite faded, broken-in jeans, a T-shirt, and pink fuzzy slippers.

"Stop, stop. Somebody help meeee. Heeeeelp. Heeelp," I scream. Charlene manages to sit on my chest and covers my mouth by pressing down with her left palm. The woman who initially waited on me locks the door and begins popping gum like she's enjoying a feature show. I'm feeling so weak that I can't defend myself much, and remember I left the room without my trusty pocket knife.

"Sheila, call my cousin Mimi and tell her to call Rhonda, Peaches, and Big Tina to come down here right now 'cause I finally found the bitch who messed with me and my man, and we're gonna have a showdown up in this motherfucker. I want you to hold things down for a while. As you see, I'm a little busy right now," Charlene says.

"I got you, Charlene. I see why you want to whip her ass. That bitch be mouthin' off, and she needs to learn how to talk to people," the woman says. I'm even more scared than when Tomi had the gun pointed at me and wonder how brutal Charlene's gonna get. I struggle to get up, but I can't do any more than lift my head two inches.

"Bring me that duct tape and scissors we've got in the back. That'll hold her until my peoples get here, then Miss Thang's going for a ride 'cause she ain't costing me my job. She's taken enough bread and butter out of Tony's mouth and mine. The bitch won't get one more crumb, and that's a guarantee," Charlene mumbles.

In less than five minutes, my arms are tied behind my back with duct tape. Then I listen to every line repeated to me I threw Charlene's way after I paid Tony back. When I was playing games, I didn't realize it would end up with Charlene showing back up with her cut-up underwear, which she says she rubbed between the crack of her ass and will be used to gag and blindfold me. She kept telling me that since I shit on her, she would make me eat my shitty words. Payback is a motherfucker, I tell you. Voodoo from the bayou must be to blame for karma boomeranging right back in my direction 'cause the start of this melee is too strange to think otherwise. All I can do is cry like Wes did when he was bound in those ropes and hope for the best, like that's gonna count for anything at all. My only concern is if I'm gonna live to tell this bizarre story.

"Charlene, what do you want us to do? We've got to work fast before someone sees us back here. This alley is known to be busy, but it was the only spot I knew somethin' about," one voice says.

"I hadn't thought about all of that. I don't know. I've never done anything like this before," Charlene answers.

"Let's just kill the bitch. She can point out every one of us in a line-up. She put you through hell, Charlene."

"Do you want to go back to jail? None of us needs no damn murder charge. I ain't tryin' to be no fugitive felon," a third voice says.

"Well you got a better idea? Why you think we took her ass to this alley?" another voice asks.

"She's a sneaky bitch. I know we got her blindfolded good, but I think we should put some duct tape over the gag, just to be safe," Charlene says. Within seconds, I feel someone go around and around my head and mouth with duct tape, then smooth it down.

"That'll hold her," one of the voices says.

"Peaches, I thought you had a plan. This is your kind of thing. Now what?"

"Don't be sayin' my name out loud. No names. And I did. I said to kill her just like the one I laid to rest years ago," the voice answers. Now I know Peaches's voice.

"But that was different. He was beating the shit out of you for seven years. It was self-defense."

"We ain't goin' nowhere, just round in circles. Let's do something. Charlene, it's your call. What's it gonna be? Hurry up."

"Let's not kill her, but I'll let y'all handle the punishment. I ain't goin' to jail on her behalf and leave Tony scot-free to have some other bitch laid up in my bed and be around my baby. I want to be the punisher in his life."

"That's a good point, but that nigga needs his ass whipped, too," a voice I figure to be Big Tina comments.

"No, if Charlene had him beat down, he couldn't work. She's handling her business with him. Let him stay healthy so he can work his damn fingers to the bone," the third voice answers.

"I heard that. He better pay those bills and stay off the couch loungin' around," Big Tina replies.

"I've got a suggestion," the third voice says.

"What?" Big Tina asks.

"Let's beat her ass, one by one, then throw her in the Dumpster. Let me start things off. Lay her on the ground y'all," the third voice says.

"If I see any rats, I'm runnin' faster than Marion Jones," Big Tina comments.

"Stop being like that. Charlene needs us, and you was raised right in the same house as rats. You whole family was on a first-name basis with them, so don't be tryin' to perpetrate girl," the third voice says. I feel myself raised into a seated position.

"Okay, now what?" Charlene asks.

"Back up, back up. They don't call me Big Tina for nuthin'. There, bitch," she says, letting all of her weight drop in the middle of my stomach. When she gets up, I feel a stiff shoe kick me in my ribs. The pain is so excruciating, tears come to my eyes. Big Tina feels as heavy as Big Shirley looked, and it's a miracle I'm still breathing.

"Now what's that one going to be for, Charlene?" Big Tina asks.

"We said no names," the third voice hollers.

"Part of a good ass whipping is knowing who did it to you, Rhonda," Big Tina says, half laughing. Now I know Rhonda's voice by process of elimination.

"That's for my lights, which have been cut off for the last week, and the candles I had to burn because of the bail I had to put up for Tony from that stunt she pulled. I had to take out a personal loan to pay the damn lawyer's bill. That wasn't right, ho," Charlene yells.

"Now don't you feel better?" Big Tina says.

"I do. I needed that," Charlene replies.

"Good. No one messes over my cuz!" Rhonda yells. I hear the three of them high-fiving.

"Let me go next. You save the best for last, Charlene, so think of somethin' real good," Rhonda says.

"Okay," Charlene says. I feel a row of kicks into my ribs, on my right side this time. Then I hear, "Hold her up, somebody."

"Is that good?" Big Tina answers after they stand me up.

"Yeah, now watch out," Rhonda cautions. I feel wind coming toward my left eye, then I hear, "Drop the bitch!" I feel a punch hit me so hard, I black out for a few seconds, then come to again.

When I come to, I hear, "What was that one for? You tell her so she'll remember."

"Stealing my money out of my purse. You wanted to make an enemy, now you've got one, bitch! I hope you spent it well, girlfriend," she yells.

"Now it's your turn. Handle your damn business, cuz," Rhonda yells out. Process of elimination tells me Charlene is personally about to deliver her wrath.

"Get the damn scissors out of the truck," Charlene says. I feel her straddle me between her legs. Then I hear, "So you think you're all that, bitch? You think all the men want you? You think you're cute? You think you can go around causing people to have records? You know Tony has a record now. You know how the legal system do Black men. He ain't been the same since either. I'm 'bout to butcher up your hair to start with, after I give you another black eye, so you'll look just like a damn raccoon. Ain't no one gonna look at you after this, ho," Charlene adds, then punches me harder than the first time. I feel my ringlets falling from around my face, then I hear laughing which is followed by, "That was better than just shaving her head with some clippers. The bitch looks like she got her hair did by Edward Scissorshands!"

Charlene tells me, "Now, I've got to be leavin' real soon and take my damn nap like you took yours that day, so I've got two things left to pay you back for right quick."

"What's that gonna be for, Char?" I hear Rhonda ask.

"That two-thousand-dollar unresolved cell phone bill I'm still fightin'. That was my cell phone account while you were going around leaving it somewhere so thieves ran up the bill. Me having to pawn my engagement ring so we wouldn't get evicted. Tony, me, and our baby not being able to move out to Baltimore County to the house with the garden tub and finished basement we put the down payment on."

"Give her some more. What you did wouldn't even cover the cell phone bill, baby girl," Big Tina comments.

"Yeah, don't stop, Charlene. Stick it to her good," Rhonda yells.

I feel four slaps across my face, then Charlene says, "That was for me having to stay at that raggedy motel job 'cause Tony's business started falling off. That shit really, really made me mad. Everything started going bad since you showed up and put your ass in my lingerie."

Big Tina says, "Fo' sure! Plus all that shit she was talking on your cell phone. Don't forget how you felt when you called us right after that! It fucked your head up for two weeks, remember? You couldn't even eat, and lost ten pounds."

"Hand me the got damn razor, somebody."

I don't hear anything, but I feel my eyebrows being shaved off like a blind man's doing it. The hairs are getting caught up in the blade, and all I can do is take it.

"Got damn. She looks fuuuuuuucked up. I bet that shit was painful," a voice says. I am so numb from the pain I can't even recall whose voice belongs to whom.

"Good, that was my damn intention," Charlene says. I feel someone search my pockets, but I recall the only thing stuffed in one was my old locket.

"The broke bitch ain't got no funds, just this old, dirty, rusty shit," a voice comments. Her crew laughs. I hear her crush the tarnished locket beneath her foot. I can't believe she destroyed the one thing my father ever gave me, and the only picture I've ever had of Kate that was inside of it. I'm hurting fifty times over the physical pain. Now I'm glad I put the room key in my sock, on the side of my leg, when I was walking to the motel office to complain about the broken toilet.

Another says, "Why you unbuckling your pants, Char?"

"I'm feelin' this shit; now y'all got me hyped. Time to get raw as a muthafucka, so she can settle the rest of her debt with this collector. Y'all might want to turn your head 'cause I've got to take a piss," she tells them.

"This is no time to piss. You can do that when we get out of here. We've got to hurry up. I told you this spot ain't for takin' your damn time."

"I heard you, but I'm gonna make time to point and shoot on her face before we roll out. No money, no mercy."

"Damn! You're going out hard, Char," someone answers. In a few seconds I feel a golden rain shower wet my bald spots and whatever hair I have left. It stings as it runs down my cheeks and neck, and mixes with my tears. After it stops, Charlene makes a hawking sound that comes from the back of her throat, then spits on me and says, "There, that about does it. I had your ass beat and peed on you. You're lucky I didn't have to shit 'cause I thought I did at first. If I had time, I'd smoke me a cigarette and burn your tits when I put it out, but I gotta get home to kiss my damn baby good night and collect my latest gift from Tony. You're lucky I didn't listen to my cousin who wanted to kill your evil ass, but I have my reasons. I'm not completely gangsta. Now too da loo, you baldheaded *bitch*!"

"That was a good one. Nice work," a voice says, half laughing.

"Get her in the Dumpster, quick! I need a cigarette after this shit. Revenge is better than sex. Good thing it is 'cause I haven't been gettin' no dick from Tony anyway," Charlene explains.

"You think we should at least take off her gag so she can scream for help? Ain't nobody gonna look in here and find her," one of Charlene's cousin's says.

A concerned voice says, "But she knows where Charlene lives. She can send the police. Don't do that. Just hope no one finds her, and let's find out what happened on the morning news."

"The bitch is suffering. Look at her. She ain't moving. I told y'all . . . no killing."

Someone checks my pulse and says, "She's alive."

"I dare her to report this shit. If she does, she'll have a hit on her ass for real. Take the duct tape off, but snatch the shit, so it will burn like the hell she put me through," Charlene says.

"Okay, it's your choice," a voice answers. I feel a burning sensation like some of the skin on my face has been ripped off as the duct tape and some of the gag is torn off. Some of my hair is ripped out by the roots too. I feel my scalp beginning to bleed. The foursome manages to pick up my limp body and push me into a trash-filled Dumpster. I smell nothing but an assortment of trash and can't make a sound because I'm in so much unbearable pain.

29

UNEXPECTED CONFESSIONS

I'm watching *Good Day Live* and one of the attractive hostesses is complaining about the java she is sipping being old. Just as she is beginning to discuss sexual assault allegations of Kobe Bryant, I hear a coded knock at my room door. I answer with a "come in" then I see Shawn emerge from behind the door. I'm relieved to see him, so I skip the niceties and move straight into the meat of the conversation.

"Thanks for coming, Shawn. I didn't know who else to call," I say weakly. My ribs are taped, an IV is sticking in my left arm, and my other arm is in a cast.

"You're welcome, Jalita. The doctor said you're very lucky. If that homeless man hadn't been trying to get a free meal out of that doughnut shop's Dumpster, you'd be history."

"I know. I wish I knew where to find the guy who saved me, so I could thank him."

"Yeah, he didn't have to say nuthin'. He could have let you die and gotten his ass out of there."

"It's funny how people the worst off can have the best morals and people with all these folks swarming around them can be the most rotten."

"I'm not naming any names, but isn't that the truth. But there's some good and bad on both sides of the fence though."

"Very few."

"So who did this to you? They say you refuse to talk to the police."

"I'm not pissing anyone off by opening my mouth. It's like this, Shawn: I've hurt a lot of people lately, now bad luck is coming back to collect. I'm not interested in starting anything else by telling the police. I've been warned that I need to call it a truce, and I think I'll take the hint from the sender of that message."

"Damn. I knew you were into some shit when you kept calling, but did you deserve all of this? Look at you, boo. You're real messed up."

"I know. I sort of didn't deserve all of this, but then again I egged it on by instigating and acting trifling. Does that make sense?"

"By the looks of you, it does."

"How long have I been here? I know I was unconscious for a while."

"They say you were out for three days."

"Dag. I didn't expect it to have been that long. To think that all of this madness started at Christmastime."

"Yeah, girl, you've been through some things. I told you to stay away from Wes though. And something tells me your ass whippin' was the work of some other woman who wanted you dead, but didn't have the heart to finish the job."

"You're right. At first I was the victim, then I made some more victims who weren't havin' it. Speaking of Wes, does he know what happened to me?"

"Do you really want to know, Jalita?"

"I asked, didn't I," I say in my classic feisty style.

"I told him, but he didn't seem in a rush to come by and bring you flowers. You know how some people can be when they know you're in trouble. They'd rather be off with three limos of users on their way to a flight out of BWI to a preview of some movie, ready to pay for a first-class section full of people they think are worth impressing," Shawn says bitterly. I can tell he doesn't approve of Wes's insensitivity.

"Figures. I can't say I'm shocked. By the way, thanks for the flowers. No one's ever given me a dozen roses before. I'm gonna save one, press it down, and put it in a photo album when I get out of here. You're a real friend, Shawn, and I never want to forget how good of one you are."

"I love you, Jalita. Now I'll never try to hit it; you're like the sister I never had. I just want something good to happen to you, for once. Tomi and someone else could have taken your smart mouth away from me, and I would have had a problem with that," Shawn says. A tear streams down my cheek.

"The same goes for me, Shawn. I love you, too. I'll never forget you. Never."

"You ain't goin' nowhere, girl. I expect to see a turnaround in lifestyle. You don't want to get mixed up in no street politics."

"You think it's really possible? I don't know how to get started walking the right path."

"Anything's possible."

"You don't even care I look like this, do you?"

"Why would I? You're alive. I'm your friend because I know who you are way down somewhere in there, not what you look like."

"You're the second guy who told me that."

"Looks aren't everything, Jalita. See what happens when you abuse them? Tomi had a commentary on what can be said for that."

"Wes told you the whole story, huh? That man can't hold water, I see."

"You didn't have to lie. We're supposed to be friends."

"Can we not talk about that? I'm not exactly proud of the part I played in that scene."

"But I warned you. I saw the possibility of something bad building up."

"I know I didn't listen. I look so ugly right now, I won't be in a position to turn a man's head anymore. Now I'll be forced to listen to morals being pushed on me."

"That's not true. Your hair and eyebrows will grow back, your bruised ribs and broken arm will heal, your black eyes will go away and your collapsed lung will be straight, too. The thing is you need to stop focusing on the part men see when you're put in the position to have to choose again."

"Don't pretend you don't see it. Shawn, I know about the four-inch gash on my face. I made the nurse bring me a mirror. The doctor said I might need plastic surgery if keloids start forming. Then what? I don't even have insurance to pay for my hospital stay. But I need my looks 'cause it's all I've got goin' for me, and I'm not college material. I'm fucked."

"Jalita, you can't give up, but you need to straighten up and stop chasing a star and be one. There's absolutely no reason why you can't get back on track. Did you know that Chris Rock was a busboy at Red Lobster, and Elise Neal of *The Hughleys* was a dancer with a Tennessee ballet company? You never know what the future has in store for you, ma, so why sell yourself short?"

"Good for them, but where did handling your business get you? A convenience store job. I'm not putting you down, but your story is more realistic. You and most Americans work your butt off and have nothing to show for trying to earn the unattainable American dream. I'm tired of hard times. I just had enough. I don't have the kind of patience it takes to be average anymore while other people like Wes walk around in high places. They have more than what they need, and half of those motherfuckers don't even deserve to be there. Now think about if hard work paid off for you, and see if you care about being late to ring up chips while people stop by your spot before they make that real paper. You ain't doin' a thing but making someone rich while you get next to nothing. I say as long as you follow certain rules and have a good reason for getting, go for what you can get on the down low. I need my looks back 'cause my money stays funny when I try to do right."

"Remember when I told you I was on probation?"

"Yeah?"

"I use to think just like you, until something showed me the long road is the safe road."

"If you don't want to tell me what happened, don't. I don't want to dig all up in your past."

"It's okay. I want to tell you."

"All right then, go ahead."

"Man, this is going to be hard, but here it goes. My pops, well he was a real man, not a man's man. He dropped me off at school in the mornings, taught me how to fix things, put alcohol and a Band-Aid on my knee the first time I fell off my bike. He played hoops with all the kids; he was just the father some kids in Baltimore dream of but never had. The yard stayed packed with boys wanting to get some time from him. He was the perfect father and husband."

"I wish I had a dad like that," I mumble.

"He told my mother she should have a comfortable life so he went to college and put his love of sports to use. He started a sports management firm and built it from the ground up. He got a client coming out of high school a huge contract. His twenty percent cut translated into big money. After the dude became a star in the NBA, business picked up. My pops told my mother he wanted her to raise me and my brother, Sammy, so that was her full-time job. Every Friday when he came home from work, he brought my mom freshly cut roses. She'd kiss him, then fill the same glass vase with water every time. Just the sight of the flowers made her smile. I miss her smiling face."

"Now that's what I'm talking about. That's a real man who takes care of his family, right," I say.

"He treated her like a lady, up until the day of the accident."

"Accident? What happened?"

"One day my dad's car broke down just outside of the B/W Parkway, on the outskirts of the city. Since it was probably nothing serious, and he was good at fixing things, he popped the hood to see if he could figure out the problem so he could try to get to Richmond on time to meet a client. While he was looking at things, a drunk driver came by, hit him, and dragged him a hundred feet down the highway."

"Oh, God, that's awful, Shawn."

"That's not the worst. He was D.O.A. when he was flown by medi-vac helicopter to shock trauma at University of Maryland Medical Center. The bastard who did it didn't even bother to get him help."

"If he ran, how did they know the person was drunk?"

"Witnesses saw him swerving for miles. The tag number was called in, and the person had a string of DWI offenses, but got off every time, including the time with my dad."

"It makes me feel like there is no justice in America for all, sometimes," I blurt out.

"The doctor said had he gotten help immediately for his internal injuries, my pops may have survived," Shawn says, then begins to cry again. I want to reach out and rub his back, but I can't move to get out of bed. Instead, I look at him, and he's becoming a big blur; my tears are distorting my vision.

"You don't have to tell me anymore. I don't want you to get upset, Shawn. I know this has got to be hard to repeat," I tell him.

"No, I want to tell you the whole story. I don't know why, I just want to get it all out. It's like therapy with a partner you trust or some shit," he says in a shaky voice.

"Finish when you're ready, then. I love you, Shawn. God, I feel so close to you. You're like the family I never had. You can trust me with your feelings," I tell him.

"I know what you mean. I feel close to you, too, Jalita. I don't know what it is, but it's like I'm being led to tell you this. I've never told anyone the whole story."

"Just let it out then. Maybe it's time."

"He was a good man, Jalita. I don't know why something like that happened to him. We were robbed. There was some confusion with the insurance policy, and his partner turned on my moms. Moms didn't get a dime to keep things going, so she had to take on two jobs, plus one under the table. She went to college, but she was a stay-at-home mom and didn't have much work experience, so she wasn't making hardly anything and had to put up with dick-head bosses. All of the stress from my pops death and lack of rest took a toll on her health. Our house was foreclosed, then she had a stroke. We straight up hit rock bottom, so I thought.

"Right after that, Wes's father left his mother hangin' because he was too busy acting single, chasing women, and then had the nerve to run off with a skinny White woman who didn't even have a high school diploma. When he got sick of Kate he moved to California. So then there were two families in trouble at the same time. Wes's moms worked as a toll collector on the Harbor tunnel full time and worked in a club downtown part time. She always wanted to be an actress, so she gravitated toward being around people in entertainment. Since both of them were strapped for funds, my moms and Aunt Vikki teamed up, and we all moved into a two-bedroom apartment on North Stricker Street. It was Wes and his twin brother, Malik, and my brother, Sammy, and myself. Things were getting better, and our mothers were focusing on getting out of their ruts, for a while. Since Mom couldn't work, she was able to get disability for a minute. While she was recuperating, she baby-sat and helped with homework, and Aunt Vikki worked," Shawn says, then pauses. He covers his eyes, drags his fingers down to the bottom of his jaws, then cracks his knuckles like he's nervous.

"Relax. You're doing great," I say gently to encourage him to stay calm.

"When everyone went to bed, Wes's mother would tip in blitzed out of her mind. She just did this 180. The next thing we knew, she said she was tired of not making any money, and Mom found out she was stripping. They constantly argued about what she was doing. Mom said bad ways would rub off on her, and she needed to stop shaking her ass in public. Instead, she ended up finding some loser who portrayed himself to be a manager and convinced her to run off with him, and leave my mom holding the bag with all of us. She came by on the weekends, only for a few minutes or to pack some fresh clothes. My moms got sick of it and told her to just go on about her business or step up to the plate and be a mother to Wes and Malik."

"Can I meet your mom, Shawn? I never had no real mother. She sounds so strong and real."

"You can't."

"Why? You don't trust me enough to take me around her or something?"

"If you shut your trap, I'll get to the part of why," he snaps.

"My bad. Damn, so you do have balls after all."

"Instead, she chose the man over her kids and ended up getting strung out on drugs and prostituting herself on the block. It wasn't pretty; I tell you that. The doctor told Mom she shouldn't be working yet, but she took the three jobs again because she had five hungry mouths to feed. I was the oldest, and I saw signs that her health would not hold up too long. I had to do something, so I took matters in my own hands. I was bitter after watching the good old boys building industrial parks and throwing up high-rise buildings all over the city, while all I felt I could do was keep the bills paid and a good dinner on the table every night by selling drugs. At night, I'd leave money on my mom's dresser. She didn't know who put it there, or how, until my guidance counselor called her and told her I was in danger of failing for missing so many days in school. She put two and two together and made me promise I'd stop and graduate high school. I graduated but I didn't stop because we all ended up sleeping on a park bench in Patterson Park and lived in a shelter for a week. I couldn't take it. I had to go back to the game.

"After three days of hustling, I put myself back on the map. We moved into another little place on Saratgota Street. Two years of dealing everything from acid to weed and coke led me to be able to stop hanging on the curb and work the VIPs in the nice neighborhoods and stars passing through staying in four-star hotels. They were willing to pay more for me keeping my mouth shut. More money started appearing on my mom's dresser again. This time she was okay with it because she couldn't work two jobs plus one under the table anymore; her health was just too bad. She told me I must stop as soon as she got better and could start working again. I got bitter that the people I was selling to had too much and families like us had too little, by no fault of our own, so I kept up what I was doing, against my mom's wishes. She didn't even know I was still doing it. I was saving up money to buy a little rehabbed house, so she could just be done with having to live in the worst places in the city. I couldn't bear for us to go back to the bottom. Then, one day I had to hide a stash in the house while I was waiting for this customer to page me back," Shawn explains. His eyes begin to water. He sighs hard, then adds, "It was a rule I had never to keep drugs in the house, but that one time, just that one time and— "

"What, Shawn? What happened?" I interrupt.

"Moms took Wes and Malik to the store. She asked me to watch Sammy. He was always special. Sammy was born with a developmental disability, but the funny thing was that he always had this sparkle in his eye. Everyone was just drawn to him. Not too many people understand how much work it is to make sure a kid like that is properly cared for. I spent every second I could with Sammy. I loved the little man so much. He was so strong and brave," Shawn says with a far-away look in his eyes.

"He does sound special, but what did you mean by was?"

"He always was sneaking snacks. Utz chips were his favorite. I told my mom I'd watch him, but instead, I stepped out to make a delivery while he was rocking back and forth, eating a bag I gave him so he'd stay quiet. Five minutes later, I got a call that someone from the neighborhood watch dropped a dime about what I'd been doing. My ten-year-old brother was shot during a raid on my mom's house. My mom told him never to open the door for a stranger, so he refused to open the door when I left. Things got out of hand, and the police shot at him, thinking it was me in there yelling back at them and screaming. They should have known better. They should have know the difference between the sound of a person with special needs and a high drug dealer. The bastards didn't give a fuck to use their search warrant the right way, that's all, " Shawn says angrily, then lowers his head. Tears are everywhere.

"I'm so sorry, Shawn. I had no idea you've been through so much hell," I tell him.

"Yeah, they found one little boy's body and no drugs. Sammy would be here right now if I would've done what my moms asked. I'll have to live with that shit for the rest of my life. I spent one year of my life locked away, talking myself into life still being worth something. My mom's blood pressure shot through the roof one day, and she had a fatal stroke. God rest her soul, she died at Mercy Hospital, and I didn't even get to say good-bye."

"This is a rough-ass story. Got damn," I mumble. Then I ask, "Well where in the hell were you?"

"I was doing my time for assaulting the officer who fired at my brother. We ended up wrestling, and the bullet just grazed his leg, but I still got time. I didn't want to go to my mother's grave in shackles. I just couldn't shame her like that."

"Where was Wes?"

"Wes took advantage of my dad getting him interested in sports, went to college on a basketball scholarship, and got drafted and signed right before all of this happened. That ungrateful motherfucker I was helping to feed forgot about me, and no one else headed my way except—"

I interrupt him, and finish his sentence by responding, "Jackie."

"You've got it. She's got her ways, but she warned me to stop dealing. That girl stuck by my hard head when everything went wrong. She bought me things, wrote letters, and accepted my collect calls anytime I could use the phone. That's the real reason I let her show off so much. I couldn't blame her for trying to move on with her life. When I got out and found out she had a man, she was torn between him and me. Now how could I blame her for that?"

"Damn, Shawn. I'm speechless."

"The night I did drugs in the bathroom, I just had a flashback and was so scared of losing her that I decided to try what I use to sell. That was the first and only time I've ever touched the stuff," Shawn says, then begins to sniff.

"Grab some Kleenex on that table over there," I tell him. He does. Then I say, "Now come give me a hug, but not too hard, and don't make it a habit 'cause I'm still no softie." Shawn embraces me lightly, smiles slightly, then sits back down in the chair.

"With this collapsed lung, breathing hurts and wears me out, Shawn. I'm so miserable right now, but at least I've got life. You just made me see that bad can always be worse."

"All you've got to do is worry about the inside as much as the outside, and you'll be straight by the time you get on your feet. You can rise up, I know it. With all the guilt I'm carrying, I'm still here walking around, and I'm rising up a few inches every few months."

"How'd you get to be so smart?"

"I'm not where I want to be yet, but I learned some things in jail and over the last few months myself. Plus, I had a few bad ass whippings myself back in the day, but don't go around broadcasting that."

"It's funny how I've cried more recently than in my whole life."

"Like they say, this too shall pass."

"Shawn, I need you to do me a big favor?"

"What?"

"Promise me you'll come back to see me. I don't want to be alone; you understand some things. Maybe one day I'll open up to you, too."

"I was going to be here tomorrow as soon as I get off work. You still don't understand how it feels for people to care about you, do you?"

"No, I don't. I let it pass me by once with someone, but I won't let it happen again."

"I'm not going to keep you talking, Jalita. You look like you need some rest."

"Yeah, I'm starting to get sleepy. But before you go, I'll tell you where I was staying. I want you to take this key and straighten some things out for me there and get my things. Oh, and I want you to check my P.O. box, too. When you get inside of the motel room, use the gold key on my key ring in the top dresser drawer to check box 2402 at the post office. Go to the Mitchellville Branch at Pointer Ridge Place in Bowie." I hand Shawn the key.

"I can do that as soon as I leave here."

"Okay. I appreciate it. Shawn?"

"What?"

"I hope one day Jackie realizes how far you've come," I say with heavy breaths.

"Me, too, Jalita. Me, too, 'cause I have. Life has been a bitch, I tell you, a straight-up hemorrhoid in the ass, but I've got to keep trying to redeem myself."

"I know the feelin', Shawn. All I can say is it wasn't your fault either. You didn't ask for those things to happen, they just did. You were just tryna feed your family, under all of those fucked-up circumstances. I never understood some things about the drug game, but now I do," I say. The loss of Shawn's brother's life proves that wheeling and dealing just aren't worth the chance it takes to dabble in the shit.

"Thanks for not judging me," Shawn says, then drops his head.

"Why should I? All you did was try to take care of those who needed to be taken care of. Things just got out of hand, that's all. We all make mistakes, for our own personal reasons," I tell him with sorrow in my voice. "And Shawn."

"What?"

"Hold your head up."

"I'll try," he says, wiping another tear from his eye.

"At least your mistakes were made for good reasons. You're one of the most compassionate men I've ever met. Your parents are proudly looking down on you with smiles and tears of joy."

30

AN APPARITION

The longer I stay in the hospital, the more I realize how blessed I am. After the nurse helps me to shower, I begin to feel slightly refreshed. I lay back down in bed, close my eyes, and imagine the joy it would bring me to look up at the sky on a clear day and watch thousands of butterflies passing by a flowering field. I crave the smell of fresh morning air and the appearance of daylight. I'm figuring out that the little things can turn out to be major things when I consider that I could've lost the right to cherish these things again.

Just as I'm engrossed in my solitary thoughts, I hear, "Everything's taken care of, baby girl, and your car is safe in my hands. I won't drive it all over town on you." Shawn bends down to kiss me on the forehead.

Instead of being startled, I simply reply, "Thanks, Shawn," and smile when I open my eyes.

"You look like you're feeling a little better today," Shawn says.

"Sort of," I tell him.

"Well sort of was better than a 'no, I'm not.'"

"If you say so. This is depressing, and I'm still worried about this damn scar."

"Being depressed won't get you far. Look forward and never backward, baby girl."

"So you do have balls after all," I say, then smile again. I want to appear tough and can't admit I've been feelin' and craving more peace in my heart.

"My balls are not up for discussion. You're always trying to talk about my balls. Stay out of my pants," he teases. Just as I'm about to muster up enough breath to say something smart, Shawn adds, "By the way, the manager at the motel sure was acting strange when I told her I'd be taking care of your business because you're in the hospital. What was that all about?"

The good feelings leave, and I feel a burning sensation in my stomach. I ask him, "Do me a favor?"

"What?" Shawn asks, looking me dead in my eyes.

"No questions. If you really like me for me, let it go."

"It's gone. Oh, you have one letter with no return address waiting on you."

"Nosy ass. I wasn't expecting any mail though. I'm surprised about that," I tell Shawn.

"I'm not nosy. I just pay attention to mail after getting the crazy letter Tomi sent."

"With my arm and all, I'd rather you open it and read it to me. Would you do the honors?" I ask, handing it back to him with my good arm.

"Whatever you need," Shawn says. He sits next to me in a padded green chair. I look in his direction, wondering who in the world wrote me a letter.

Shawn lets out a heavy sigh, silently mouths some words then wipes his face straight down with his left hand. He sighs several times, then says,

"I don't think you need to hear this right now. In fact, I'm sure of it."

"I asked you to read it. Don't leave me hanging, boy," I insist firmly.

"Jalita, you should wait until you're feeling better. Trust me on this one."

"Look, whatever is in that letter, I want to hear it right now. All you're doing is making me curious."

"I don't even feel right reading it. It's personal and deep," Shawn cautiously responds.

"You know I trust you now, Shawn. I don't have much more energy to argue with you. Please don't give me stress."

"Are you sure? It's not good news. This is my final warning."

"Don't you think I figured that out already? Just do it, please."

"Okay. Here it goes: Dear Jalita, You know they say there's two sides to every story, right? Well if there's really a good side and bad side, you're about to get the side that isn't so good. If you're reading this letter, I've probably already died. Shortly after your visit, I found out I was dying from terminal cancer. Serves me right for the rot I done, I guess. The doctor gives me a month or less to be around here. I'm not the sensitive type, but I'm making one exception for what I did to the daughter I publicly denied. I asked the hospice nurse to mail this the day I shut my eyes. Before I remain silent, there are some questions and problems that must be solved.

"Every day since you asked who's gonna love you, I beat up on myself inside. For you to do something like that, I musta ruined your life, and put you through a hell somethin' awful.

"No mother forgets everything there is to know about her baby's face, hands, eyes, and presence. See, I know I was acting like you were some crazy woman out to swindle us that day, but I did to recognize you on that step. I've just been running from my past and kept running until this diagnosis taught me to stop—at least in private. Now that I don't have a chance to talk to you ever again, I understand the negative impact I had and the ton of rot I did by the pounds. Talking about ashamed and scared, that's me. I don't know if I'm gonna see heaven or hell for abandoning you and leaving you with complete strangers.

"I'm not gonna write some fixed-up letter, and what I'm about to say might border on cruel, but you need to know the truth. I've lied to you enough. I was ashamed I had a Black kid. Now before you get me completely wrong, understand that you're one beautiful young woman. Your skin is the prettiest I've ever seen. It always was, even when you were born. You're gonna be a heartbreaker, if you're not careful to turn out just like your dad. It's just that I cheated on my husband, the man who came to the door, you know? Now he ain't no Clark Gable. Your dad was a Black one of those, but my husband was and always will be a hardworking family man who took care of his responsibilities, like a responsible man should.

"I don't know why I up and did it, but I made myself another life away from him for no good reason. I split my time in an apartment with your dad. That's why I use to tell you I was going to work and would leave you for days at a time locked up in that roach-infested hellhole when you could barely understand how to lock the door. It wasn't right that you didn't have much to eat. I knew all about you eating those sugar and butter sandwiches. You'd always spill the sugar when you tried to pour it onto the bread. It wasn't right you had to be scared when you were alone in there either. The neighborhood was full of crime and street life. Anything could have happened to you. Things fall apart when lies hold them together. Don't you think, Jalita? Have you noticed that in life?

"I'm in tears right now as this letter is being written. I wasn't woman enough to admit to the world and my husband that you existed. I'm still not no real woman neither. I also was scared of what he'd do to get back at me. See, back in West Virginia, I dropped out of high school and never even bothered to get my G.E.D. As you know, states like where I'm from often don't have much to offer, so I went to work in a sewing factory and got sick of it. How could a woman like me live without being taken care of by somebody? I mean, I ain't have nothin', so I turned to livin' on my looks. Then I was left to depend on what men gave me. When you were a little girl, part of me figured out you just might be better off if I abandoned you for life. I couldn't provide for you, and I wasn't prepared to raise no Black child I had when my husband was shipped overseas. Do you see my problem? I felt trapped and confused.

"The guilt ate me for years. I drank most of my liver away and chain-smoked like a freight train. The doctor said that's why I ended up with cancer. See, my own rot and runnin' from my past killed me way early. I also ate myself in a size you wouldn't believe. When you saw me I had started to lose weight. I was way bigger than that. No other man woulda taken care of a fat woman like me, just 'cause she use to be Ms. West Virginia back in her heyday. I don't agree with Forrest Gump. Life ain't just like a box of chocolates 'cause who can you run to when you make bad mistakes and still need love?

"I will tell you what I know about your father. I met him because he was the mailman. I know that sounds like a classic thing to happen, but it really did. I was all alone and pretty, and I thought he was all alone and one of the most handsome men I had seen—White, Black, Chinese, or whatever. He was one of them men who had six-pack abs and a thirty-two inch waist. I'm sure you know the type. I know he and his good looks moved to California, but that's it. See, your dad's name is Todd Lester Harrison. He was quite a ladies' man, so it turned out to be.

"After three months of knowing him, I got pregnant with you. I had a lot of complications during the pregnancy. I spent a great deal of time running back and forth to the doctor. The day you were born, your father told me I was having false labor pains. I made it out into the hallway of the apartment building and luckily a minister was leaving after visiting one of his church members. He gave me a ride to University of Maryland Hospital and called your father when I arrived. Todd showed up, but you were already born. I went through the whole birthing experience alone.

"I often wondered why we had no common ground, then I finally found out. Todd had another family in California and decided to return to them. I guess he got tired of me demanding decent conversations over things like paying the rent on time to the landlord and why he could never take a turn buying you shoes or a box of cereal. In no way could he be called responsible. Todd preferred to spend money on women instead of you. As you can see from this whole thing, looks aren't enough to keep a man, even if you got a whole lot of 'em. All it does is get you a whole lot of attention, but it doesn't mean you're gonna be taken seriously, just conquered in a small way. Do you see what I mean? Having sex and making love are two different issues. Your dad could only give me sex, but that's what I get for cheating on the man I married in the first place.

"You might try looking Todd up, if you don't hate what he done to you too much. I know he did really love you, it's just he was a ladies' man who couldn't get his priorities straight at the time. See what happens when people turn love into games? It starts to become one big, ugly circle that goes nowhere good.

"And oh, you've got you some brothers and a sister by me. Judy is three, Mike is seven, and Randy is thirteen tryin' to be about thirty-seven. Now, that Judy is strong-willed. Mike is a silent thinker, but nobody better not sleep on him because he's smart and will pin you down about something when you least expect it. Now Randy is rebellious and a royal pain in the ass (I do cuss). He's into the punk crowd. The first day he came home with all them earrings and something round his neck that looked like a dog collar, after announcing he was going upstairs to dye his hair green, I wanted to stuff him back in my womb. Maybe if you have kids someday you'll understand that feeling. Don't rush to have none though, because once you do it, it's done. Have kids by a man who enjoys making love to you, not just having sex. I guess you're thinking I have a nerve to give you any advice, but I feel that it's an important thing to say, and so is what's coming next.

"My husband is a good man in most ways, but he don't like Black people. What I mean is he can get along on the street or on his job, but he don't believe in race mixing or being friends with none. Now here comes another bumpy part. He's been a member of The Ayran nation for the last twenty years. Your stepfather says his beliefs have something to do with the way he was treated when he was growing up. Black kids use to beat him up, steal his lunch money, and make fun of the White boy. I reminded him kids are good for teasing, and they just did it because that's what kids do. He said he didn't care because Blacks are a lazy breed of thieves of pains. I know that sounds funny in this day and time, but there are some people who still can't accept we are mostly the same. Obviously, I never felt that way or I wouldn't have fallen for Todd.

"I did put my foot down about one thing though. I let him know that I didn't want my kids raised to join the Nation. I can guess what's going to happen after I close my eyes. I tried though, I really tried. There's no way he'd ever let you near those kids, talk to you nice, or even believe what's in this letter if you showed it to him yourself. Do yourself a favor. Don't go knocking on that door. All it's going to do is make you want to do it again and again 'til more rejection screws your head up worse and maybe for good.

"I convinced him you were lying, so I just made bad worse so he'd keep taking me to my chemo appointments and holding my hand through each update with the specialist. It was such a scary experience, Jalita. I don't even want to describe it. All I can tell you is I paid for what I did to you real bad. I'm going to physically suffer right up to the end, and all this morphine they give me don't do a thing. I've got stage four cancer, and the survival rate is only an eight percent chance. Right before they gave up on me, the doctor offered me to get into a clinical trial for some cancer research, but I'm tired of being examined and what seems like tortured. I cry most the time when I'm not sleeping because the pain is so bad. Serves me right, don't you think?

"I'm real weak from the chemo that I know didn't do nothing but kill the good cells. I lost all my pretty hair and even my eyebrows. I'm so bad off, the hospice nurse has been writing for me a little each day for a while, on days when I could remember where I left off because I stay so drugged up on medication. This lady is real nice to care enough to do this for me because she doesn't get paid to care like this, know what I mean? She's crying, too, and has been through a whole lot of tissue since we started. I asked her to promise to mail this off when my time comes to escape from misery, and I trust that she'll keep her word. The doctor said go home and die, so that's what I'm about to do, Jalita, close my eyes one last time, and just die.

"Now I'm about to say one of the saddest things of all times, but here it goes. I can't tell you sorry. I can't answer your question about who's gonna love you, neither. I can't say sorry because that would be a cheap thing to say, and you deserve way better than two words that mean nothing on paper. I can't tell you who's gonna love you because I wasn't no mother to you for real. I never did love you and never will because you stood to expose my rot to my White family, even my parents. In fact, I did everything I could, hoping I'd have a miscarriage, but you made it here anyway. Had I raised the money for an abortion, there would have been no Jalita, but Todd wouldn't give me the money to have things taken care of and swore to me he'd be by my side through the whole nine months and then afterward, too. That was the biggest lie ever told. Some people out there think when a Black man gets with a White woman, she gets treated so much better, but in the end, there's no color issue, just an issue of behavior. Behind closed doors, a man with bad intentions will still be a man with bad intentions. And Todd, well, he was a man with intentions of doing what he wanted. The man was a master at disregarding everyone else's feelings, Black or White. Now that I think of it, I did the same damn thing myself. Like they say, it does take two.

"Go ahead and hate me if you need to. If you do, you have every right to be angry and bitter. The truth sometimes hurts, doesn't it? Well knowing the truth is not always good because sometimes it isn't easy to deal with, and you end up wishing you never asked for it to find you.

"Just do one favor though, and this is for you, not for me. Don't grow up hurting people just because you can get away with it. Don't go round tipping with men just because you're pretty as a picture and they'll try to buy your time. Don't break up no home like me. Don't break no hearts, if somebody is being nice as they can and you know it. I mean, just look what I did to mess up our lives. Pretty bad, don't you think? One thing I learned: You can't repay people when you rob them of their dignity. Once you do it, it's just gone. There's no way to pay them the balance of what you stole. So please do yourself a favor, and don't start no battles when there's no need to fight a war. It could cost someone innocent everything. Too many people are hurting out here already, so don't pass on no legacy of doing the wrong things. It's never worth it, even if there's some short-term benefit involved.

"Maybe you can be the one to raise the bar for me and let me see you do a better job of living life like people aren't rag dolls and chess pawns you can play with. I hope you got a high school education because the world is hard enough as it is, and I'm a White woman telling a Black woman this. I don't even want to imagine what I hear about racism is true, but I know it's possible because of how my husband thinks. I hope you go farther than high school because you always were smarter and stronger than me.

"I've got to stop now because the nurse says I'm pushing myself too much. The pain is just so bad I can't put too many more words together. I think her fingers are tired of writing, too. See, I'm trying to think of others now. I hope you find out who's gonna love you because I messed my part all up. Again, I don't know who's gonna love you, but I hope this helps just a little. I don't hate you—I just hate the circumstances that brought you here. I guess I'm one of those mothers who chooses to take out the father's wrongs on the kid. I really thought Todd was going to do right by me, but he's such a smooth talker and gets over by using his looks. I wonder if he's still trying to live that way. If you ever meet him, let him know Kate died. Before she departed, she figured out what took him so long getting that carton of milk from the store the day you had that awful ear infection. Also let him know that I got his tailor-made suit out of the cleaners and gave it to my husband, after wrapping it up like it was new. I did it as spite for his racial prejudices. He wore it until it didn't fit anymore, so it was my own private joke. Oh, and also tell him I did pay the sixty-dollar parking ticket he made when he went to see the ugly woman across town.

"Anyway, I know writing this helped me to see some things I never thought about before. Now I can almost forget it ever happened and rest in peace. If there's a God in heaven, I hope He'll forgive me for my shortcomings because I've already experienced hell on earth, and now I want better. Death to gain a new life is what I'm hoping for, even though I don't deserve no mercy or nothing good. "P.S. It was nice to see you kept your locket Todd gave you on your fifth birthday. Oh yeah, I just remembered that Todd's social security number is 212-15-5988. Good luck in life, Mom."

By the time Shawn reached the words *Todd Lester Harrison,* his red eyes nearly bugged out of his head like a cartoon character. They stayed dilated until he reached the word *mom*. I stopped crying long enough to ask him what in the hell was his malfunction, but he could barely make his mouth move to blurt out something audible. He sent Wes a two-way message and told me he hoped he was wrong about something, but he didn't think he was. Now I know that no news is usually good news, but I want damn near every headline I can collect because shit ain't gonna get better by pretending it doesn't exist. As soon as I catch my breath and wipe my nose, I will suck up all of my current hurt and demand Shawn tell me what the fuck is goin' on, so I can just throw it in the mix with everything else.

31

KINDRED TIES

I feel the neurotic energy about to leap out of me and stand on its own. I return to my hyper self. I begin getting loud like I'm standing in the middle of the floor at a club, not pitifully reclined in a hospital bed.

I take one last breath of air, before I bellow, "Negro, what's wrong with you? Tell me what's goin' on! Why'd you stop halfway through the letter?" I ask Shawn, between crying.

"I can't say it, I can't say. Motherfuck. Motherfuck," he yells, sniffing.

"What? Do you think you can speak like the intelligent person you are, and clue me in so I can let out some motherfucks, too? Hey, you better let me know something, boy!" I say, then pound on my bed with my good arm until my breaths grow short again.

Just then, Wes walks in looking like he's just seen a ghost. Wes and Shawn disappear into the hallway. The door flies open, then Wes shouts, "*Jalita?*" He's dressed in a black tailor-made suit.

"I'm telling you . . . yes, she is," Shawn says, pointing at me like I've been accused of something evil.

At first, I think Wes is stunned by the ugliness I'm wearing after my beatdown, but I rule that out after I hear, "But, but, but, that's impossible, and we don't look alike either."

"Her mother is White," Shawn tells him, pointing at me again.

"White?"

"Yes, White."

Wes stutters and shakes his head then says, "So, so, so maybe that part's a coincidence. That doesn't prove a damn thing, Shawn."

"Wes, her mother is that Kate woman. What are the chances of the first, last, and middle name of your dad being the same, the time frame, location of everyone, plus the Kate woman with the G.E.D.? You tell me that. And look at her long fingers and eye color. Those are Harrison traits. Look at your hands and eyes, if you don't believe me," Shawn says, letting his arms smack down at his sides.

Without any explanation, Shawn and Wes see fit to do a verbal Q & A. The dance ends with Shawn ordering Wes to show the old picture of his dad that Wes brought along. When I saw Todd's smiling mug, it all comes back to me like it was yesterday. His face was etched in my mind for an eternity, and I didn't know what my birth father had to do with all of this drama, but I knew it wasn't good.

I look up at Shawn, then Wes, and don't say a word because I can't find a way to express what everyone was hoping I wouldn't say, "Yes, that's him." Wes runs to the mirror to look at his eyes, then inspects his hand, shakes his head again, and begins to back up away from me like I'm a leper, then belts out, "I've been fucking my own sister. How did this happen? We don't even look alike, besides the hands and eyes. Of all women to hook up with, I find my sister this way. This can't be real. This must be a nightmare. No, it can't be. This shit is insane," Wes mumbles.

I shoot up straight as an arrow in bed and scream, "What? Did he say sister!"

"Jalita, Todd Lester Harrison . . . is Wes's dad. And Wes, you definitely aren't having a nightmare. You're living one, man."

"When I get straight, I won't abuse my looks anymore, Shawn. I'm gonna get a dream and make something of myself as soon as I get out of this hospital. I was just fantasizing about watching birds in the sky and feelin' fresh air. No more gold digging, no more borrowing men without asking either, so stop joking around. I understand what life's about now. And Wes, you're a good actor your damn self. I get the point; y'all are something else I tell you!" I say, then laugh.

"I'm not playing, Jalita. Think about it. Why would Wes have your dad's picture at his house? I wish this was just a ploy to teach you a lesson. It's the real deal, sweetheart."

"I said knock it off, Shawn. I told you that I get the point. You expect me to believe this wild-ass story? Try again, brotha. It was a good laugh and tactic to convince me to do some soul searching though."

"This isn't a joke. Wes is your brother, and I'm your first cousin. Montgomery was his mother's maiden name. She had her, Wes, and Malik's last name changed back to hers because she was so mad at Todd before she left my moms holding the bag," Shawn tells me with a face of stone.

"No, this isn't happening. This is a living nightmare. Nooooooooo. Tomi's curse worked. Nooooooooo. Noooooooo. Nooooo," I scream until my throat is sore and nearly hoarse.

"What the fuck are we going to do?" Shawn says, then looks at Wes and me. I ignore him and say, "This is your fault, Wes. You never should have come on to me that night. You never should have licked your lips in your pool. If you would've kept your wandering eyeballs on Tomi's ass, this never would have happened to us. See what happens when a player plays too close to the edge," I belt out in a raspy voice.

"No, it's your fault. You knew I belonged to someone else, but you called anyway. You wanted to play my game; no one forced you to get with me. You were the damn gold digger who didn't need much convincing," Wes screams back. A nurse pushes my door open.

She says, "I don't know what's going on in here, but if you all don't keep the noise down, I'll have to call security. This is a hospital, in case I need to remind the three of you."

Wes turns toward her and responds, "Do you realize who you're talking to?"

Her facial expression changes from disdain to elation. She clenches her hands together while squealing a high-pitched, "Oh my Gooood, it's Wes Montgomery. My son would love to have your autograph. Would you please sign this?"

She shoves a patient's chart in Wes's direction but he ignores her and turns back around when Shawn says, "It's both of your faults! I told Jalita to leave you alone, and Wes you were just greedy. You've always been a cheap, greedy, skirt-chasing son of a bitch."

The nurse continues to invade our privacy and asks Wes, "Can I touch you? I just want to touch you so I can tell the other nurses. Would a hug be all right? Just a quick one?"

Wes growls, "You're getting on my last nerve. Can't you see I'm in the middle of something right now?" He grabs her chart, scribbles something fast, then pushes it back in her hands.

The nurse high-tails it out of the room saying, "I'm gone. Thank you, thank you, thank you. I can't believe this." Then she squeals one last time as she closes the door, making as much noise as we had in the first place.

When the door shuts, Wes says, "Now that's a perfect example. My fans respect me because I worked hard to get to the pros, not you. I also have a fetish for a fine sista. Are you an undercover fudge packer, b, or just hating on me 'cause you're jealous that I live large?"

"You said it right, 'cause you musta thought your own sister was fine. You fucked everyone else. It was bound to happen that you'd end up fucking a damn relative. You treated your own sister like a slut. It was okay when you were doing other people's sisters wrong, but now you got to feel as dumb as you look," Shawn screams. I'd never seen him so animated.

I chime in and say, "It's your fault, Shawn. You didn't have to deliver the note from Wes to me after the party. Why did you go and encourage a hookup, then tell me not to get involved with him?"

"Girl, please. The way you were so hard on me, I had no idea you'd go for Wes. You even kept telling me he wasn't your type, and I wasn't your keeper. I thought you had better taste than that."

Wes rises back up on his toes, and yells, "Call me dumb again, boy, and I'll knock your teeth down your throat and show you what I'm made of. Just 'cause your mom held shit down and my mom had a little addiction, you think you can insinuate things and judge people?"

"I wasn't insinuating anything about the past. You need to stop smokin' that shit that makes you a moody, crazy motherfucker, that's what you need to do. I smell it all in your clothes, and your ass has hickeys all over your damn neck, too. Since you want to bring the past up, you are acting like your mom right now," Shawn yells. The nurse and a man that has that reporter look are whispering at the edge of the door.

"Yeah, I had a little something something before I got here, so the fuck what? I ain't no addict like she was or nuthin'. Thank God you didn't get me hooked on the real shit, from you having it in the house in the first damn place, like you did my mom . . . and you know the rest of the story with what happened to your brother. Keep talking trash about my momma and see where it gets you." Wes shoves Shawn, and Shawn shoves back. A man edges into the room and whips out his paper and pen. His glasses seem to take up half of his face.

He says, "Miles Washington here, reporter for TV 12 news. I was visiting someone for a story and found out you were here. Could I interview you about the attempted murder that was made on you and your mistress's life. Is that her, Mr. Montgomery? Was she injured by Ms. Montague?"

Shawn looks up and Wes ignores the reporter, still arguing with Shawn. He says, "That's not true. You blame the hustler for your mom's problem, and as far as what I was doing, I was trying to keep food on the damn table. In case you've forgotten, you were one of the mouths that needed feeding. You wouldn't have been able to hoop it up in summer camp if I didn't pay for you to go, you asshole."

While Shawn and Wes are arguing at the top of their lungs and poking each other in the middle of the chest, I begin crying so hard I get hysterical, and my good lung is burning just like the bad one. When Wes admits he was fucking Jackie, Shawn went off, became hysterical, and ripped Wes's designer shirt.

Shawn says, "Why don't you give the reporter something hot off the press. Don't you have something to say about the point shaving, or would you rather tell him about your drug addiction?" When he says that, the reporter begins writing ferociously on his pad of paper.

Then he nervously pushes his glasses up on his face, and says, "Would you care to respond to that, Mr. Montgomery?" I can tell he's excited that he's getting what he feels is good dirt, which will make his boss happy.

Wes says, "No comment."

The reporter responds, "So you're admitting both claims?"

Wes walks up him, snatches his pad of paper out of his hand, and throws it on the floor. Then he says, "I never agreed to a damn interview. I'm tired of the media digging in our business after the buzzer ends. First y'all try to make NBA players say things against our teammates then you try to dig up trouble. Since you wanted to follow me in this hospital room and invade my damn privacy, I just want to say suck my big fat dick and that's a direct quote. As far as the trial proceedings, wait and see if the judge gives permission to turn his courtroom in to a circus in twelve months. Now get the fuck on out of my face, man, before I help you out of it myself."

The reporter looks fearful, yet excited Wes lost his cool. He pushes his big glasses up on his face then runs across the room to pick up his pad of paper. On his way out the door he moves quickly while scribbling more notes. My world goes blank while I'm considering that I've got to deal with my private pain and live with the worse scenario that came true. It's time to get a life of my own and work on mending myself. If I hadn't been gold digging and disrespecting what Tomi tried to convince me she almost had papers on, none of this incestuous shit would have gone down. I'll go to my grave, never fully coming to terms with the fact that the man who could get me to shed my thong because he could get me behind the velvet ropes was my own blood brother whom I had no idea existed.

32

RESOLVING THE UNRESOLVED

"Wake up, baby. You'll oversleep," Grandma Beverly says gently. I feel three pats on my left arm.

"Where am I? What time is it?" I ask groggily and squinty eyed. I look around and realize that I never was on the commotion-filled set of a gossip show called *E Live*, insisting that I wasn't a groupie out to trap Wes into marriage and knock Tomi off. I breathe a sigh of relief, looking at the silver-haired woman.

As my bare feet hit the carpet, I hear a mellow voice tell me, "Time for you to get up. That's all you need to know."

"Oh, now that you've polished off the order I snuck in from Levi's, you think you can get some bass in your voice," I say, stretching and yawning.

"It's not like you bought me what I *really* asked for. It was a waste of time putting my good teeth in for that meal."

I roll my eyes, and say, "Well it may not have been ham, chitlins, pig feet, or anything like, but I don't see not a crumb left. If you want to, be my guest and go back to rubber food and pudding or those canned sardines you keep on your shelf for Fridays. That can be easily arranged, you know."

"You take all of the fun out of eating, that's all. Don't take what I said as an official complaint. You better show back up with my goodie bag next Friday. I've got enough bad girl left in me to put you in check," the lazy, playful voice warns me.

"I hope so. Why do you think that I preach about eating right? So your ancient Chinese secret tail can live some more to raise hell and kick up some dirt as long as you can, that's why. I need you around a long time from now. What I do is for your own good. You know you've got to get your blood pressure down. You really need to be thanking me for being your personal healthy meal police person. When I met your butt, you were a walking medicine cabinet."

"Yeah, yeah. I love your big mouth, too. Now shoo, shoo. Go on, but straighten up the pillows first."

"You must have a date with that old man across the hall. Don't think I haven't noticed him checking you out," I reply, arranging burgundy chenille textured throw pillows.

"Don't you worry about it. You're just too fresh for your own good. Get to work. Now where's my hug, buttercup?"

"Bye, Grandma Beverly," I say.

"Bye, chile. You do me one more favor and have yourself a good day."

"I will, only because you're bossy, you're two centuries older than me, and you ordered me to. Don't forget to go power walking. I'll find out if you skip out on the group."

"Only if you don't forget my numbers."

"Deal," I tell her.

"Pay attention to the boxed ones. That can make or break my hit. If I hit and you don't play them, I'm holding you responsible for the value of what I was supposed to get. I can still count good, so don't try me."

"All right. You notified me at least three times. And I'm goin'. I'm goin'. You're worse than an alarm clock with no snooze button," I playfully complain.

I walk from the senior's home and hop in my Toyota. I smile, feelin' a warmness that is indescribable. If I had a dime for every time I asked myself my favorite question about who is gonna love me, I'd already be rich enough to hire servants, a chef, and sail around the world. But since I don't have it goin' on like that, and I now know that Wes really is my brother, I don't have to worry about being tempted to let Wes smack my phat butt and manipulate me into playing the game his way anymore. Like it or not, I was more than a piece of pussy to him by the time he made it to the hospital. The whole tragedy is so odd that we have a hard time holding a simple conversation. I didn't burn my bridge with him though. I guess he's tryna ease into brotherhood since it's a new kind of commitment. I figured a new and fresh start in a better environment could motivate me a little more, and it has. I accepted Wes's offer of his giving me an alma mater hookup but I'm sitting out this spring semester since school was already underway. Wes tried to twist someone's arm so that I could begin auditing some classes I'll be taking for credit this summer, while recovering from my injuries, but it was much too late to allow me to do so, although Wes is who he is. I'm learning quite a bit about myself while ringing up all sorts of goods in Wal-Mart full time.

Nevertheless, I've already begun setting up a pilot's program to help seniors and volunteering at the university. It all started when I saw them in need of assistance when many shopped alone at Giant. It made me wonder how many don't get regular visits from their family or may need someone to talk to or run an errand. Part of my journey to heal and improve is to help others. Life no longer revolves around me and my needs. I've integrated some balance, here and there, but I get something out of the deal, too. Who would have thought anyone would have claimed me as the granddaughter they never had? Grandma Beverly lets me crash at her place and feel the love of an adult I've never experienced before. Now I have an authentic mentor in my life. We cherish each other's presence, and I can't go one day without picking up the phone or stopping by her little crib on the third floor of Wingate Manor. At eighty-four, she's cool as shit, and she knows she can pull a man in his early sixties.

Grandma Beverly explains a lot about navigating through life and assures me that the rumors about my dealings with Wes will subside when Tomi's case on Court TV is over, but that's twelve months from now. I will have to testify, and I don't feel a hundred percent good about it, for obvious reasons. So far, the issue about Wes and me being relatives hasn't surfaced, and I hope it never does, but my heart is in my mouth concerning that one when I take my seat on the witness stand. In fact, it's one of my biggest fears. I'm not up to being dragged through the mud while Wes is portrayed as being the victim of two catty, greedy women. The media even forgave his public service announcement about sucking his dick because his publicist, Patty Bingham, did a good job of cleaning up the context of his comment. He's right, she is an authority on making him look good.

I can't tell Grandma Beverly about every rung of my sorrow and sadness, but I do crave the spirit of peace to move freer through my body. That's why I'm off to my fifth session of therapy, compliments of Dr. Brenda Brown, thanks to Seth's guidance. Like I said before, it's all about balance these days.

"Jalita, come in and have a seat."
I throw up my left hand and say, "Hey, Dr. B."

Dr. Brown crosses her legs, puts on a serious face, and asks, "How are you holding up? I know things got pretty ugly with the media. I've been following it."

"They follow me everywhere, trying to get me to give them a preview of the scoop. I have no idea why the judge agreed to the Court TV drama. I can't remember the last time I had a good night's sleep. I keep having nightmares that the media will manage to tear me to shreds in public. I'm still standing, though. I'm not knocked down flat on my face too easily. I guess I can't ask for much more than that. I'm determined to do whatever I can to straighten some things out upstairs. Had I not read *4:17 Vinegar Blues* from cover to cover, I never would have written you that thank-you for sharing your personal story, and I never would have trusted anyone else to understand my broken, healing heart. And right now it's in so many pieces, you just can't imagine."

"That's nice of you to say, Jalita, but I'm just doing my job."

"Don't be so modest. You're not even charging me because you know that I'm broke and struggling to pay my hospital bill since I'm uninsured. Just like Seth said, you're a really nice and caring person. You're one of few people who has ever cared about me and my well-being. Most have been downright nasty and trifling enough to star in a movie script."

Dr. Brown interlocks her fingers then lets her hands rest on her knee. I can tell she's choosing her words carefully.

Next she tells me, "If you trust me as you say, I'm hoping you'll one day feel comfortable enough to open up to me and reveal what's on your mind a little more. Doctor-patient confidentiality applies here, and there's no reason to fear the media getting a hold of anything you tell me. You can trust me, Jalita, and I'm truly concerned about you. What is not addressed will cause an explosion, so never put undue pressure on yourself by ignoring what you need to work out."

"I feel you on everything you said, but I don't want to be a repeat dummy who can't control feelings and words before using good judgment. I'm sort of in hiding, and that's why I've been a little ambiguous about certain specific locations of me and my family. Like I said, I still don't trust anyone with my eyes closed, outside of Shawn. It's not that I don't think you care though. Perhaps one day, the words will flow. I want them to, I just need to feel purely moved to do it."

"You've mentioned Shawn once, but I'd like to know more about why you trust him so much. Instead of thinking so hard, just speak. You will never have to defend yourself to me, I'll be a neutral party every time you walk through my office door."

I follow her advice and find that I suddenly have no control over my moving lips. I begin to explain, "Shawn is my . . ."

Just as I'm about to work my way up to recount the events that led up to hospital scene that led to me finding out that Wes is my brother, Dr. Brown says, "Hold that thought, Jalita. I have to take this emergency call." After a few mmm-hmms, and an "I'll squeeze you in at seven," I feel my heart pounding away like a rhythmic African drum. I want to continue, but I can't resume with clarity and focus.

"I'm sorry about that. Please pick up where you left off," Dr. Brown says.

I stall and fall back into my previous mode of censoring my words. Instead, I tell her, "I was just saying that—well, never mind. Kate was right about a lot of things that she wrote me in that letter. To think, Tomi's gonna birth a baby just 'cause love was misused. I know it's wrong for me to hope for Tomi to hop up on an abortion table, but she has no more business becoming someone's momma than Kate did. I don't wish the kind of childhood I had on my worst enemy's baby. It's never right to use a child as leverage or an ace for spite."

"Why are you so adamant about this point? Clue me in here."

"Well, there have been studies that concluded that a woman's habits during pregnancy affect the child's disposition. We don't need one more screwed-up kid in the world. And as for me, I really shouldn't have been going around hurting people just because I could deceive. It serves me right to have all of the nightmares I do. I yearn for one good night's sleep, and I can't find four straight hours worth."

"Well, let's flip this scenario over and turn it around. Every experience is a learning one. Did you learn anything from what has occurred?"

I sigh once, and reply, "I did figure out who's gonna love me."

Dr. Brown nods and says, "Tell me more about that, Jalita. That's a foundational point."

"I'm pleased to announce that, *ahhhem*, I am. If I don't love myself first, no one else can, so it really doesn't matter that I don't have a mother or father to pave the way. That's the whole reason I won't be looking up my dad. If he really loved me, Wes, or Malik, he could have done a little bit of the right thing and sent his baby mommas some money, or in most recent years, tried to hunt us down. He didn't, so I'm spent with him!"

"Excellent explanation. You also have a brother named Wes. Hmm. That's rather coincidental. Strange, in fact," Dr. Brown says, scrunching her nicely arched eyebrows.

My hear starts pounding again. I feel like I'm on the verge of hyperventilating, if I don't make it out into the fresh evening air. I mumble, "Extremely. By the looks of your clock, our fifty minutes are up, and I'm gonna get out of your face on time. Good-bye and thanks. See you in the same place, same time next week."

I nearly sprint out of Dr. Brown's office. I don't want her to look into my eyes, so she can read the windows of my soul to take her comment about Wes's name any farther down the road. In my flustered effort to escape, I bump into someone without looking.

I say, "I'm sorry. Excuse me," then look up quickly, only to discover my beloved Seth, and he's already wearing a wedding ring that's shining like it's meant to be a visually blinding piece of expensive bling-bling.

33

BROKEN HEART, HEALING HEART

I hop into my Toyota, only to find that it's struggling to start for the first time since I've had it. After I pump the gas pedal three times and the engine still doesn't turn over, my heart begins to pound and my eyes begin to tear up like I'm chopping onions. In frustration, I run to the trunk to rummage through it for a flashlight. I'm livid that my car has decided to act a fool the very time I need to jet out of dodge like a 747, and hope that I'll easily find the cause of the delay.

I hear, "Excuse me. Do you need help of some sort?" A dark brown-haired twenty-something White woman is dressed in a chinchilla mink coat and is sporting this huge wedding ring with much attitude. It is the kind of ring that a high-maintenance Tomi type would've bitched and hoped for. I survey my immediate surroundings and discover she hopped out of a showroom new, black 740 IL BMW.

As I piece two and two together, I growl at her like an angry dog, "No, I don't. Go away."

She replies, "Have I offended you in some way, miss?"

I grab my flashlight out of a dollar-store bag and rudely reply, "In fact, you have, but what's done is done now."

Seth comes running over then touches her on the right elbow. His wife still hasn't caught the trouble vibe. She points into my trunk and cheerfully adds, "Look, Seth, she's got a change jar and a copy of *Vinegar Blues* in her trunk just like you use to. Isn't that odd that you both shop at the dollar store and have stubborn old cars, too?"

I feel my nostrils flaring, throw down the flashlight, and say, "Seth was mine. He was supposed to be my husband, not yours. You were his second choice, not his first. Why did I have to run into you two of all people?" The woman's face cracks up with grief and confusion. She looks over at Seth like he should take my words back and shove them into my mouth, but he doesn't make the effort to convince her my words are untrue.

Instead, he gracefully attempts to diffuse the situation and tells his wife, "Honey, I'll explain this all to you later. Do me a favor and go sit in the car. I'll take things from here."

She mutters, "But who is she to you, Seth? She said I was your second choice. What's that all about?"

"Please, follow my lead, Daria. Show me that you trust in me," Seth insists then kisses Daria on the lips to erase her fears. I can tell Daria is not happy about removing her presence, but she does and leaves to sit her narrow ass down in the roomy BMW.

As soon as Daria closes the car door, I shout at Seth, "You deserve all the best, and so does your mom who never put you down when you were tryna get up on your feet and grab your dream. All the world may have pencils and pens, but not all the world can write and touch lives with the ease of a summer's breeze. I truly see that now, and I was a fool for the things I said. You should be kissing my lips, not hers, but I know I messed up."

"Are you actually apologizing to me?" Seth asks in astonishment.

"Yes, I am, but enough about you because I'm not hardly comfortable with Daria playing with your hair in bed, just yet. I'm gonna ask Dr. B if her husband can give me a jump so I can get out of here before it gets dark. This is absolutely humiliating, but I can't say I don't deserve this," I ramble.

As I'm about to cross the street, Seth says, "Why would *you* care if I married Daria? Aren't you and Wes Montgomery a hot item?"

I turn around and tell him, " Oh, hell no, it's not what you think. The only way he's gonna get it up in the near future is with the help of some Viagra and checking a woman's first, middle, and last name after he gets to know her as a person, first. If you only knew how awful things turned out, you'd understand. The trial mess is just the beginning. I came to Dr. Brown because you told me to start tryna work on the inside, and I've been taking your advice. My mother died of cancer and sent me a letter admitting she wished I was never born and I was also brutally assaulted. I only have two people in my corner in life. I'm scared to death; I've never felt so damn vulnerable. It's like someone hijacked my confidence, and I don't know what to do next." I wipe my tears with my coat sleeve.

Seth says, "Come here. I didn't know you'd been through all of that. I'm so sorry, Jalita." I walk toward him. Seth's warmth and love feel like the home I've never had.

I push myself out of his arms, look into his eyes, then he gently releases me from his grip. I tell him, "Why would you care about my feelings after the way I treated you?"

Seth returns the same gaze, and replies, "Because a real man would, and I'm a real man who values people. Gloating would give me no satisfaction. I'm too old for that sort of thing."

"But your handsome face is everywhere, and it seems like you're on damn near every talk show there is to be on. Why aren't you strutting around like a peacock yet?"

"I told you I'd always remain levelheaded. I wasn't just saying that. I may have some material things now, but so what? There's a lot of things money can't buy. I was blessed many times over, and I'll never take my success for granted. The Creator led me and gave me direction. Blessings flow from Him, so I can't take complete credit for anything. That would be foolish."

"I can't believe someone who I heard just signed a million-dollar book deal and will be writing a series of books for a major publishing house would say something humble like that. Hell, I'm the one putting the Coinstar change to use now. In some ways, we've switched places. I congratulate you on your success and marriage. The whole nine. If you're happy, then I'm happy for you and the Daria woman. Now that I've calmed down, I have no right to be jealous because it was my fault that I missed out on you. You tried to do your part."

Seth smiles, then tells me, "I can't believe I'm hearing this. You really are beginning to change. I'm proud of you for maturing. If I weren't a married man now—"

I interrupt Seth and explain, "You don't have to say it. I know you're faithful to Daria, and I no longer want to be a party to destroying the good in people's lives." I sigh heavily, then lower my head.

"You're right. I'd love to show you exactly how much I long to hear you out in detail, but I have to go home and live the life I've begun with my wife. Life is about doing our best to make good choices. Be strong, Jalita. There's always a dawn after darkness. Remember that, no matter what happens next. Keep trying to do right. It will pay off someday." I hear Daria blow the horn. We both turn in her direction. Seth throws up his index finger to notify his wife he'll be shoving off in a moment.

As he lowers his arm, I reply, "Daria's running out of patience, so you better go."

We face each other again, and Seth tells me, "This may be the last time I see you again. Please finish before I walk away."

"Okay, here it goes. Maybe I'll fully be able to be who I am after I dig way down deep and become that morning flower you told me you saw waiting to bloom. When I do, I'd love to go on that *Maury Povich* show and invite on one of those school bullies who almost was the cause of me dropping out of school. But before I face someone who use to pull my hair, shout out that I had no momma, and spit food in my face at the lunch table, I want to be completely whole. All things in due time though. Change is coming. You never lied to me before, and I know you're not lying now. I respect you for the way you handled all of this. Daria is one lucky woman. They don't make too many men like you anymore. Thanks for the closure. It's a sad thing, but I got it. I hate men like fifty percent, but that's a hell of an improvement, thanks to the few good guys I met along the way like you. I've kept you long enough, but I wanted to explain that I had my reasons for acting a fool. I was living with so much hurt that I became bitter from all of the issues." I wink at Seth, then sniff. Instinctively, we both know that the conversation is over, so we say our good-byes.

Just when Seth bends to give me one last hug, I peripherally catch a glimpse of the BMW charging toward Seth. I forcefully push him out of the way, then jump backward and fall into the bushes.

Daria speeds past like a rabid, possessed bat out of hell, obviously disappointed that she missed her male target.

She throws on the brakes, making them squeal, and screams, "Don't even think about it with her. You have a blatant disregard for anyone's feelings but your own. I refuse to put up with this disrespect. How dare you have the audacity to flirt and exchange numbers in my face. Get your ass in this car right now, Seth."

Seth is busy helping me out of the bushes, and obviously isn't in a rush to answer Daria's charges. I brush dirt and dry, brittle leaves off myself, confused as to what Daria is ranting and raving about.

Seth sternly replies, "The hell if I will. You know I don't do drama, and you just gave me way too much. I've only been talking for a few minutes, and I told you I'd explain when we got home. You tried to run me over and jeopardized everyone's safety in this community over me having an innocent conversation? If I were you, Daria, I'd leave right about now before someone calls the police, and it may turn out to be me."

"Oh, really?" Daria replies with a sour face that makes her look like she sucked on a fresh lemon.

"Yes, you heard me," Seth says with a stone face.

Daria hops out of the car, slams the door, snatches three of Seth's books from a bag and angrily begins ripping pages out of each one. Her cheeks puff and redden.

He says, "How could you? After all I told you I went through to get published, how could you destroy my words like they're trash?"

Daria ignores Seth's question, and replies, "Simple, and I'm *not* going to tell you again. Get you ass in this car, right now." She grips the remainder of one of the books and gets back into the car.

Seth and I begin picking up the ripped pages that begin flying all over the street like wind-blown leaves. Somehow we don't fear Daria attempting to run the both of us over. I feel Seth's pain, and I hurt for what he's discovered about Daria's shallow, ugly streak.

"Well, are you coming or not?" Daria asks, slowly driving alongside of Seth like she is sure he'll hop in next to her.

"I think if I were, I would have been sitting in the car by now. If you don't respect me, then what the hell are you doing here, Daria?"

"Don't get smart with me. You think you're something now that you have some money in your pocket and people stopping you on the street for autographs? Well I won't back down because of it. I'm from money, so you don't move mountains in my world, Seth."

"Are you finished now?" Seth asks.

"No, I'm not. You're married to me, and you will act like it," Daria screams, then throws a hardback book at Seth's head. The pointy edge of it hits Seth on the right temple. I bend down to pick it up, place the crumpled pages inside of the book, then look at Daria like she's a heartless murderer who deserves to be sitting on death row.

Seth rubs the side of his head, looks at Daria, and tells her, "Thank you for showing me you were my number two fan because of my book deal and not the artistry of my work." Seth's eyes begin to grow glossy as new marbles. Then he adds, "It took me ten years, ten whole years for my dream to come to fruition. When I graduated from Morgan State, the economy was good, and I still couldn't find a real, professional job. Not one human resources manager would take a chance on me, and that was a blow to my ego and my financial status. I worked in department stores, cut lawns, raked leaves, cleaned office files in law firms, worked at a gas station, and even walked dogs and waved a construction flag to make ends meet. Things got so bad, I had to file bankruptcy, but I bounced back. I asked God to have mercy upon me and show me that things would work out if I kept believing and decided what I really wanted to do with my life. That's when I decided to do something with my writing. The Creator brought me from barely being able to afford ink to print out my manuscript, to having more work than I can handle. Now look at things. It's no more Seth has his head up in the clouds. Seth is wasting his time. Seth is lazy. Seth needs a real job. *Seth made it.* There's no way that I'll allow you to reap the benefits of labor from the sweat of my brow with your mentality. You never cared about me. Since that's the case, I'll contact my mother's lawyer regarding an annulment. You blew it, Daria. I have nothing left to say, except our marriage is over, and I refuse to sleep one more night with the enemy. The rest is a matter of paperwork. There's no point in wasting any more words on you."

Dr. Brown runs outside to investigate what all the commotion is about, just as Daria shouts, "Who cares about all that? You got lucky after that first book distributor took a few cases of books off your hands a week before Oprah gave you some airtime at Harpo. Who in their right mind makes a reservation to sit in the audience to attend a taping and catches a red eye to Chicago just to leave a book they wrote on a chair with a letter begging Oprah to give it a read before leaving the after show segment?"

"Someone with faith, like me, Daria. That's who," Seth answers soberly.

Daria draws a long breath, then adds, "You just don't get it, you moron. Every since her people gave you a call back and invited you to be a featured author on one of Oprah's Book Club shows, you seem to think you have legitimate writing talent. Well I've got news for you: you don't, Seth. And you'll never sell enough copies, publishing deal or not, to make it on the *New York Times* Bestseller's List, so keep dreaming 'cause it ain't gonna happen in this lifetime. Your book is the dumbest thing I've read. It was all hype generated by a good marketing plan and a stroke of luck. I've been an avid reader all my life, and I can tell you this, your words are trash. You're right. I never loved you anyway. And just so you know, I'll fight for half of what's mine, so who cares if you don't come home tonight. It's not like your ass can't be easily replaced by a man from old money or even a lonely one on MillionareMatch.com who's willing to pay top dollar for this trophy pussy." Daria mashes on the gas and does about fifty miles per hour down the long residential street. The three of us watch her disappear around a curve.

Dr. Brown shakes her head, and says, "I take it the pages you two are holding were once in my autographed copy of *Faith Has Gathered Here*. What a shame. I was looking forward to reading it this evening."

Seth replies, "Yes, we are."

"What happened?" Dr. Brown asks in bewilderment.

"It's all quite simple, Dr. Brown. Faith has gathered here. That's why I'm willing to let something counterfeit go, retaining the faith that true love will find its way back to me. Life is too short for living in denial about the reality of what we see. I'm not big on pretending about anything, and I won't become a hypocrite now. Daria doesn't realize my book proceeds aren't community property, and when I say my financial house is in order, it is. She can't touch a thing, so Daria may as well be happy with the few material things I bought her out of love. What do you think about all of that, Jalita?"

I find myself feelin' like I'm in a trance as my lips being to move. I say, "Oh, shit. What was I doing? I use to be Daria. I became what I once hated in others. I've been shallow and manipulative, walking these streets, handing out thick, thick drama. I feel awful about what I've done to people."

"But you're not her now. That's what's most important. Tomorrow is a new day, and you will have the benefit of owning a new outlook," Seth explains.

"You know, Seth, I've learned a huge lesson from being a lady player: Just 'cause love don't love you doesn't mean you have the right to keep it from someone else who has committed to a love with someone that's not you. Just 'cause love don't love you, it doesn't mean you need to go around mocking the good in it by pretending it found you, at someone else's expense. Just 'cause love hasn't found you yet doesn't mean it doesn't exist and can't sprout. Just 'cause someone wasn't considerate enough to love you doesn't mean you've got to go around not lovin' people who come afterward. Some people will never apologize for the hurt they caused, so you can't expect them to. You just have to swallow that pill and keep living. Most importantly, love will always love you, if you love ace number one first."

"Are you trying to tell me you love yourself now?" Seth asks.

I answer, "I halfway love me, and that will suffice for the time being." Dr. Brown crosses her arms, raises her eyebrows, and smiles.

Seth says, "I'm in shock over the turn of events, right now, but I must admit that I've been waiting to hear you say something like that, for what seems like a half a century. You finally deciphered the message I was trying to send you when I gave you Dr. Brown's book. I told you I don't think I know everything, and I just proved it. Maybe after I get my annulment, I can get to know the real you, after all. If you open your heart, and the other party can finally see that it's in the right place, it makes room for the possibility for friendship and forgiveness. And whatever is meant to be, as a result of that forgiveness, will be. The first cut is the hardest to heal so I can't promise you anything with me, Jalita. Ill words don't have to be the last things standing between us though."

My heart feels as if it dropped out of my chest, and I stare at Seth like he's from outer space. More than anything, I want to explain that penalizing me after he's single would be like someone telling me that I'd only have twenty-four hours to live and to enjoy any wish that I wanted to come true. From my vantage point, Daria had it all, but I never did. I have a big heart, I just never had a chance to open it up. I was a parentless victim of inner-city struggles where loyalty, respect, and honor are the ideal, but can rarely be appreciated, if you're determined to survive. In my former world, living to see the next minute came with a price of developing bad habits, becoming the victim of abuse, and numbing me of a sense of accountability to the Creator, but I can't make the words leave my mouth so Seth can understand the big picture.

I turn my head away from Seth and begin to cry again. This time out of sheer joy and affirmation that I'm embarking upon a healing journey. What I must do next is recover from my ugly past without leaning on excuses for behaving poorly and being regarded as someone's enemy, when he hadn't even started a war on my turf. While spinning around, I look up into the mouth of the dark sky and say, "Kate, now I understand what you meant by raising the bar for you. I see the light of reconciliation so clearly now. For the first time in my life, I feel that I will get my love, the right way. I'll enjoy my future and make every day count the best way I can manage."

When I stop, I stand still. I tilt my head upward, and add, "I won't ever take the energy to turn my head to look back again. My past won't control my future, even if it's true that all this motherless child ever wanted was to feel loved by somebody. When I become that somebody and wrap my arm around myself, I'm gonna love me for good. And when I'm fortunate to find that strength, on that sweet day, I will I raise the bar for you and end the legacy you started, Mom, because Jalita La Shay Harrison won't be a motherless child ever again."

When I look down, I begin to walk toward Seth, feeling the hope of cherishing the day that I put that knife away for good and let all past ugliness and strange twists of fate go. This girl locked inside of a woman's body may have been abandoned and even slept in abandoned buildings, but the good news is that she can't abandon herself in my personal space, and Seth was trying to show me that all along.

I ask Seth if I could have the honor of having his autograph. He answers, "Sure, Jalita." He removes a pen from his shirt pocket and writes on one of the torn pieces of paper from his book, *Pray. Believe. Praise. Receive. Dare to chase your dream, and remember God's grace allowed you to prosper, when you get to where you're going. Best regards from Seth Culligan, your number one fan.*

After reading his message I look him dead in the eyes. I feel tears building up. My voice begins to shake as I say, "I'm depending on that day I get my peace and put some things behind me. Just like you said, Seth, we really all do need a living, breathing dream of our own. I'm gonna reach out and grab mine. Now I know that I've got to take the steps you did to get to somewhere I'll be proud of standing." I can't resist kissing him on the cheek but I know Seth is holding back. After I do it, all he does is say, "Handle your business, then. Just pick yourself up with faith, build a relationship with the Father, and handle your business."

Seth slowly walks away toward Dr. Brown's house with his hands buried inside of his jacket pockets like he's in a reflective mood. We both manage to turn around and look at each other at the same time. As a smile stretches across my face, a shooting star lights up the sky. This private clue confirms that I've begun taking the proper steps to resolve unresolved conflicts that have tormented me for my entire life. I'm relieved that the curse has been lifted. A true Christian with the love of God in His heart sparked a hope within me that I can be free. I will finally look forward to redeeming the hope of the best that life has to offer is yet to come, despite all of the shadows that have blocked my beautiful light. And if I forget about my journey over this past holiday all I have to do is run my fingers across the fading scar on my face. Keloids didn't form after all, but even so my looks won't make me the baddest bitch from coast to coast—becoming more of a woman than Kate will.

34

THE MEETING

Wes

"Wes, it's been a long time," my former girlfriend, Marquita, says.

I hold my breath, wondering if she's going to add something vindictive to her statement but she doesn't.

I reply, "You're looking well." As we share an awkward moment of conversation I'm thinking that Marquita still has sex appeal, spunk, and principle—the kind of woman that should have been living with me in Mitchellville, but it's too late for us now.

I hear my daughter, Dominique say, "Why is that man staring at me like that? He is sooo tall."

Marquita replies, "Because that's your biological daddy. Remember me telling you what biological means?"

"Yes, Mommy. I remember," Dominique says, rolling her eyes.

Marquita replies, "His name is Wes Montgomery. Go say hello to him. He's come here to meet you."

Dominque releases her grip from her mother's hand. We walk toward each other slowly and gingerly. She looks at me like the stranger that I am, like she's unsure if she wants to come closer.

When she stops at my feet, looking upward, she says, "Hi, I'm Dominique. My mommy says you're my biological daddy. Is that true? I don't know because I don't remember my real daddy coming to see me. Mommy told me all about how babies are made and the man that made me is missing. I wish Mr. Mike was my real daddy because he tells me he loves me every night when he reads me a bedtime story."

I begin to weep. Her words are sharp enough to cut through my heart. I remove my dark sunglasses and instinctually bend down, grab my daughter, and hold her in my arms like I'm trying to mend every broken thread with a single hug.

I answer, "Yes, and I'm sorry for leaving you."

She tilts her head and answers, "Why are you crying? Are you sad? I cry when I'm sad."

I reply, " No, I'm happy . . . very happy to see you." After I wipe away my tears with my left hand I play the tough guy role but it isn't an easy thing to do. I'm a nervous wreck. This is worse than the day I was drafted into the NBA. I feel so vulnerable just looking at Dominque, the six-year-old daughter I haven't been a father to. She's beautiful—she actually favors her mother and me. I feel more tears streaming down my face against my will because I can't hold back the pain, a player's pain. A pain I created from hopping in bed with too many women I didn't know anything about in city after city. I wouldn't even be here in Florida owning up to my known responsibility if Marquita hadn't announced on national TV that I had a child I wasn't taking care of and her lawyer hadn't sent me papers about owing an astronomical amount of back child support immediately following the trial to resolve the Tomi attempted murder mess. Marquita said she sent me a letter to the beach house warning me before she agreed to an interview on a national gossip show, but I honestly never received one word of it. Who am I fooling though? I wouldn't have paid her words any mind then.

I take one long sniff, then say, "Starting today, I'm going to be a part of your life. Would you like that, Dominique?"

She replies, "I have a daddy already but he's at work right now."

I answer, "I know that, and I don't want to take you away from him. Now you'll have two."

Dominique speaks over my shoulder to her mother and says, "Mommy, can I?"

Marquita replies, "It's 'may I.' You asked me to find your biological dad. There here is, so answer him."

"But would Mr. Mike have to leave our house? I'd miss him."

"Mr. Mike is going to take you all the places he usually does and do all the things he normally does with you. He's not going anywhere, Dominique. He's apart of our family," Marquita explains.

Dominique responds, "I guess that would be okay then, Dad. I lost me a tooth yesterday, see?" Dominique says, showing the gap in her mouth. Then she continues, "Mr. Mike slipped a dollar under my pillow and tried to tell me the Tooth Fairy put it there. I told him there's no such thing as the Tooth Fairy but thanks for the dollar, silly."

Marquita says, "That's enough, Dom Dom. Give your dad's ear a break. He just got in town."

Hearing Marquita's voice again brings back memories. She'll never know it but she was my soul mate, the woman I could've grown old with. I ran away from her because I wasn't ready to settle in to love with a woman worth the effort. When it comes down to it and the room clears all I'm left with is a big empty house with no one to love me if I woke up and decided never to put on my basketball uniform again. Not only did I lose her to another man but another man won over Dominique's heart, too. I'd be lying if I didn't admit that hearing about this responsible, loving brother is eating at me like acid because the three people in this room should've been a family living under the same roof but I bailed out so I could continue having my fun with drunken freaks and greedy hos with no character.

My daughter ignores her mother and continues to ramble. I lift her up in to my arms and learn to listen to a child's concerns. The law will force me to mature even if the NBA can't. After all, I'm still an egocentric asshole who still needs to grow up. Helping to raise a little girl while becoming a real man in the process will be a gargantuan challenge but all I can do is suck it up and try my best.

35

LOCKED DOWN

Tomi

Boy, do I miss eating quiche and clinking champagne flutes at functions. As the guard leads me past the row of cells, escorting me from isolation, my mind is invaded by thoughts of more rules, more back-breaking work and more hard looking women screaming unsolicited comments. Me, Tomi Montague, from Ivy League to holding pen at central booking. Last stop, living life behind bars until my court case comes up and I've got to divulge how and why I ended up here on Court TV to determine my fate.

I hear, "Can't speak today, Patches? You're a jailbird and violent offender now so you better stop wearing that cute little ass on yo back and acknowledge somebody. Keep having a hard head and see where it gets you around here... stuck up bitch." Due to my unsightly bald spots and thinning hair, two dikes nicknamed me Patches and it stuck. Thanks to stress, my bra-strap length hair won't stop falling out in massive chunks. I can forget an emergency treatment or a touch-up to slather on my new growth, which is now breaking off. My nails are jagged as a saw blade but use of a file is off limits. My skin feels like sand paper because I have no lotion. I don't look or feel like Tomi, but I am.

"The judge wouldn't allow you to post bail, huh, Patches? Even if he did you don't have the cash it takes to post it. Welcome to hell. You're looking at eleven years in jail to rot behind these ugly walls with women like us," the most experienced jailhouse lawyers tells me, half laughing, then throws feces on me through the bars of her cell. The excrement lands on my right arm. I continue looking straight ahead with a solemn gaze, concentrating on my steady footsteps. The guard doesn't reprimand her, and I'm now accustomed to tolerating ill deeds, listening to the unsettling chatter of bored minds and a cacophony of eerie noises.

The guard closes and locks my cell. I hear the clang of metal that cages me like a rabid animal. I smell the stale air and grab hold of the bars and begin shaking them, longing to stand on the other side the way I use to before things got out of hand. I repeatedly shout, "Will someone please let me out of this damn stinking place? Let me out of here. I want to go home. Let me out of heeeeere. I want to go home."

The guard walks back toward my cell, places her hand on her hips, barking at me, "Shut up, Montague. You are one hardheaded brat. Are you trying to tell me you want to go back to isolation?"

I shake my head no, quieting my noise. I fall to the concrete floor as tears blur my vision, making my surroundings become hazy, but the reality of my whereabouts remain.

When I begin sniffing, I hear, "I'm tired of this shit you pull every damn day. This time I'm gon' have to give you a word that's gon' hurt. Assault with a deadly weapon is a federal offense. How could an educated woman like you be so dumb? You had it all, Patches, but you blew it in life over bullshit. Men come and go but your freedom is another story. I'm sure a wanna-be upperclass ho like you use to look down on someone like me but now we be on the same level. You could've had anything you wanted if you spent time using your smarts, though. Wes is free on the other side of these walls, but where are you? Stuck with dirty bedding, scarce toilet paper, and rat droppings. How it feel to have to go through a rectal inspection to get ready to go to the isolation room? Not good, I'm sure. A concrete cell with no mattress, no heat, and handcuffs for twenty-four hours with only one hour of light ain't treatment for spoiled suburban girls, is it? Now this be your new life so get use to it, Patches. Rita will never pity a bitch like you who had every opportunity to keep yo' freedom. If anyone should be screaming to get out of this mother it should be me. I been in here six years for a robbery I ain't commit. Now kill all that noise so I can enjoy me my last cigarette in peace, and I dare you to complain about the motherfucking smoke. Why they put me wit' you, silly yellow heifer," Rita says.

My cell mate intentionally blows a cloud of smoke in my face to antagonize me. As I fan the stench of a cheap cigarette, I walk over to my bunk and sit the edge, slumped over, thinking that I should've focused on my own life. Daddy sent me what he said was his first and last letter explaining that I'm a disgrace to the Montague family and he's not wasting one penny on my representation—I'm stuck with an unskilled public defender. Now the dead silence from across the miles is deafening. No care packages, no phone calls, no visits, no more letters. Not a word from one friend in any part of the country. The day I had my miscarriage while working in the Inmate Laundry Unit, no one mourned for me but me.

My free ride, living easy, dressing in the latest fashions, and worrying about showing up other women is history. The two things I want back most are what I dream about when the lights go out and every inmate's footsteps are still: The freedom that I foolishly threw away and my baby's tender smile that I'll never see. That's enough to make me lie down and hope that I never wake up to live one more day in this hellhole.

36

YO, LISTEN UP!

It's Jalita here. If I can have just one more minute of your time, yo, listen up. I was cleared of any possible charges for shooting the goon without having to prove things to a grand jury. Me pulling the trigger twice was a clear, justified case of self-defense. Thanks to the bear in the bedroom at the beach house that recorded the whole fight scene and supported my story, paperwork hadn't been filed to put me on a witness stand for that issue before the tape in Tomi's spy toy was discovered. Although that's the case, the goon who threatened my life was put on life support and didn't pull through. That's the kind of thing I was trying to avoid. Now I've got to live with a whole lot of skeletons in my closet. Everywhere I go, people whisper about me behind my back. I'll remain silent about my personal life and won't say much more than Tomi's face isn't the only one pasted up on a website or two.

Something interesting happened to Wes. His game has been so terrible that he can barely make a basket. There's been talk of the possibility of trading him and the fans boo him every time he comes out on the tunnel. Miles Washington, the nosy reporter, put the dirty mouth out on Wes. The press has been down on him since they found out he flat out dissed Miles in the hospital room. There has been a buzz circulating regarding Wes's alleged drug use and the point shaving is up for issue. I'm glad I didn't get smart with that reporter dude with big glasses and he didn't come in the room when we were battling over our family secret. Something tells me it's 'cause he's struggling to be a father to Dominique, but doesn't quite know how now.

As for Shawn, good karma did pay off for him. The day after he bid Jackie farewell, he was discovered by a talent scout who had been hunting and hunting for a short Black man with an exotic look. Now Shawn's mug has been casted on a national commercial, and things are starting to look up for him, thanks to something called residuals. Go, Shawn!

Before I shut the gate, I want to holler at my girls of all ethnicities. Some of you may be gold-digging playettes on the down low; maybe no one's peeped your game just yet. Some of you out there may be blatant with it, chasing limos and tour buses, researching when and where the ballers will be staying in your neck of the woods, and doing X-rated things in exchange for a payback. Some of you also may be telling yourself nothing strange like this could ever happen to you, so you'll keep playing and digging for money, gifts, favors, or whatever floats your boat. I've neglected to say that married women can be gold diggers, too, in case I need to address some Darias out there. Those of you in that category need to listen up good.

I hope I made y'all stop and think about how cheap some of us make ourselves look to everyday men, ballers and shot callers, and that schemin' ain't all peaches and cream. If you're feeling what I'm saying about walking the long road, accept the fact that you're a queen, not a prostitute. Think up a dream and own it. Don't depend on a man to pay your bills; get that paper for yourself so you can have your own fat bank roll. If he knocks you off his pedestal 'cause he's ready for someone else to sit up there, you won't have to panic 'cause you're prepared to take care of yourself. I know shit can be hard, but if you have any doubts about being on someone else's personal payroll, I advise you to consider making a plan and taking that first step toward independence. I'm going to get you started, then I've got to head on out to my j-o-b. If I'm late, that's money out of the kid's pocket.

Here's a twelve-step plan for a recovering gold digger who wants to move toward the bounds of reason. Even if this isn't you, share it with a sista who may have issues. Leave the book open to this page on her coffee table or something. We aren't hard to find, that's for sure. Here are the twelve crucial steps to getting your own life:

1. Love yourself. I don't care if you're a tattooed sista from the hood or a diva from the suburbs, if you don't love who you are and what makes you who you are, all bets are off. Give yourself an emotional makeover. If you can get all fly to hit the club or get all cute to go out on a date to try and impress someone with a penis, you can take the time to work on the inside. If you're not hip to the mind, body, spirit principle, learn all about it. Each segment connects to the other. If you work on each thing, you will smooth some corners down you didn't even realize were sticking up. Results won't happen overnight, but if you work on them little by little, chances are you'll get there, even if no one's loving you at all. The lamp of the wicked always grows dim, so if you want mercy to stay in your house, put your shovel down and concentrate on building your own world instead of digging up profits from someone else's toil. If you need help to get off the ground, look within and be true to yourself: Good karma will make a way for compassion to find you.

2. Quit playing and own a dream. It's the kind of risk worth taking, if you acknowledge a dream's presence in the proper fashion. You can't just say it and make it so. You must stop spinning your wheels and make a plan. Do your homework and find out what it takes to do what you crave to do. If you don't own a dream, you best figure out what fires you up. When you figure out what you're really put on this Earth to do, you must unite thought with action. Don't talk about it, be about it. If you're lazy, you're perpetrating. Perpetrators don't deserve shit in my book and a whole lot of other people's. If you try hard enough, at some point the possibility of making your dream real will hit you. Why should a man who has it going on be genuinely interested in you if you aren't acting like you're responsible for your own destiny. Sexing him only goes so far; the value of getting off will run out. If you want to be taken seriously, act like it. And just to clarify things, acting like it doesn't include using a man as a stepping stone. Success won't count if he gave you all the ends to go for yours. Find your own resources or limit his financial involvement in your venture. If he puts up some ends, you must be fair and cut him in on future profits you rake in or pay him back in full.

3. Find a role model or mentor. Turn to someone who can serve as a good example for you. I'm not talking about a sista on the screen scene or shaking what her momma gave her in the latest video. Good for them and all, but I mean an everyday person who's got it going on. If you don't know that woman personally, that's okay, too. Think of what she did and how she did it when you need a glimmer of hope that whatever you're trying to do can be done. If this means tearing out an article in a magazine and taping it up in a place where you can see it every day, go there. If you've got hang-ups about feeling goofy by motivating yourself by any means necessary, lose them. If you're really trying to transform yourself, you've got to stay deep into the get-ahead guide. This isn't the time to act cute. When you've officially got it going on, then you can do that.

4. Stay focused. You're going to have enough stress hustling to get things done. You don't have energy and time to waste, so be committed to the cause. There's always going to be someone or something that has the potential to sidetrack you. Stay away from gossipers and drama kings and queens. You are worthy to succeed, and you've got to run your program like you believe it. If you become distracted, correct the problem and get back on track. This is your world, and no one's going to do a thing for you to operate for you, but you. You may as well get started today. What are you waiting for if you're not afraid of some hard work?

5. Be realistic and patient. You're not going to see results and get paid right off the bat. If you want to eat shrimp and lobster daily instead of hot dogs and beans, it's going to take some time to earn that privilege. When you're earning yours, there are no shortcuts. Don't get a defeatist attitude when you hit some bumps in the road. Do what people told me: Keep trying until things come together, but visualize a positive result. In other words, don't give up or give in. It will be harder to get what you want when you earn it, but everything you do will make a difference. Your efforts will be worth it.

6. Ignore the haters. Don't get too personal with all the people who take up space and use oxygen. Keep your mouth shut, and don't spread around your plans, making the long-distance carrier real happy. If you run your mouth too much, someone out there is going to tell you how you should be running your life, why your plan won't work, or hating on you in private, hoping you won't make it. Some haters are that way because they don't like what you stand for. They can't understand why you're taking a risk to get what you really want out of your life. They can't accept that they don't have the heart and diligence to be like you, so they will criticize you to try to throw a wrench in your program. For these reasons, confide in a select few. Keep your phone bill down, and forget the rest.

7. Fake it until you make it. If you can't afford the snakeskin boots, you have no business even thinking about putting one foot up in them. Don't get tempted to hint around to a man that you've just got to have some. When your time comes, you'll be able to make up for having to pass on whatever turned your head. Remember, you're going for long-term benefit, not a short-term solution. Until you get to where you're going, work on saving that paper. If there's a way to get a discount, you better go for it without shame. I'm talking about thrift shopping, hitting dollar stores, bargain hunting at yard sales and flea markets, using prepaid long-distance calling cards, and not getting your hair and nails done on the regular. Learn to do what you can for yourself or stretch out your salon visits. And if you're rolling your eyes at me, I know plenty of wealthy people who do just what I told you to do. The ones with sense don't give their money away by being flashy. The ones who weren't use to anything in the first place are the ones caught up showing off with the bling-bling lifestyle.

8. Surround yourself with positive people. Disregard negative perceptions. Your friends are either for you or against you; there's no in between. I call them self-esteem helpers. If they're handling their business the right way, take notice. Observe and learn from those who know more than you do who are farther down the road than you are. As for family members, there are some who may need to be cut back. You know the type I'm talking about. If birds of a feather really do flock together, you need to make sure you're keeping the right company. Don't spend too much time taking advice from people who are so caught up in pretending, they appear to have it going on. These types rent furniture at ridiculous interest rates, but will tell you it costs too much to buy a book or start a small business.

9. Get connected. Don't play like you don't know how to be aggressive. If you could tell a man what he wants to hear to get him all tangled up with your old ways, you can use those same skills to network. Who knows whom? Find out. Who knows what? If it means getting an internship to get started, sniff one. If it means joining a group where others in your profession meet, investigate. Most major cities and towns hold networking functions. If where you live is dead, find out what's happening nearby. Do what you have to do to get in the know.

10. Pay what you owe. Don't let any man do too much for you, unless you don't mind dealing with a control freak who owns you. If you don't want to have to submit, pay what you owe and handle your business. If he didn't help make the bill, he shouldn't be paying it. Men aren't stupid. Once they find out where you're coming from, they're going to break you down, cut you off, or make you pay them back in some other way. Accept small gifts and favors, when it's appropriate, but don't let a man you're not married to furnish your apartment. Most likely, if you go there, you will live to regret it. Also, if you are willing to stick your hand out and receive, it's a must do to give a little something thoughtful to keep things even. I'm referring to helpful things you could do that are worth something. If you're selfish, this will be a tough job, but you can do it, if you try hard enough. This is called treating someone the way you prefer to be treated.

Remember, rely on what's in your bank account, not someone else's. Have your own shit. If he wants to marry you and has more than you, make it clear that you like him for who he is, not what he can provide. The thing is, a smart man will expect you to prove it. If your heart is in the right place, you will make sure you're working on your dream or are currently living it. Both parties should have positive and productive elements to bring to the table. Don't mistake this as just being financial. Soul food has to be in the mix, too. This is an emotional, spiritual, wholesome, loving, mutual energy that is an integral part of bonding in a long-term, monogamous way. It's not just "what do I need?" anymore, it's "what do we need?" If you can't think like that, you may still be stuck in the gold-digging mode, so shame on you. You aren't ready for the real deal, baby girl.

11. When you make it, watch out. Success is hot. When everyone sees that you've made it and are achieving a little something something, you're going to attract triple the attention you use to. Watch out for the male gold diggers, fake friends, and what-can-you-do-for-me folks. In other words, watch out for people who are like the old you. Make sure people like you for who you are, not what you have become. Keep around the people who supported you from jump and would still be there for you if you went broke all over again or something devastating went wrong. As fast as you go up, you can come down, so always remain humble if you end up walking on some red carpet. Don't trip and treat people as if they're beneath you just because someone tightened the screws on your butt when you were down and out. Keep it real and be an ethical, grounded person. Never lose all that you've learned. Without respecting your past, you can't dare to value your improved future.

12. Trust in progress. There will be times when you roll past a house and see shopping bags set out by the trash cans or a man paying for his woman's clothes while she tells the cashier what a good man she has. There may even be times when you have to visit a change-to-dollar

Coinstar machine and risk everyone in the store turning around to see who it is making the thing work so hard. These are nothing but growing pains, and they do hurt, but I've got something to say about that, too. Protect your dream with hope that you can meet your challenge. That confidence should serve as a reminder of why you shouldn't revert to your old ways. Money is nice to have, but it isn't the only thing to have. Keep everything balanced and in perspective by keeping your self-respect. The potential consequences of being a gold-digging playette should be enough to sentence you to a lifetime of probation of keeping your standards high.

Unless we want men to think they're the only ones who can be large and in charge, we've got to show them that we, too, can meet the challenge of getting paid in full. If they call us "bitches," let it count for something: a **B**oo **I**n **T**otal **C**ontrol of **H**ers. Now the next time you have a chance to gold-dig, pass on up with a damn smile. Keep your head up and run your own show. If you really want a life, don't chase a star, be a star, baby girl. You can and will run your ship, if you make self-love stick . . . and throw your damn shovel down.

ABOUT THE AUTHOR

Andrea Blackstone was born in Long Island, New York, and moved to Annapolis, Maryland, at the age of two. She majored in English and minored in Spanish at Morgan State University. While attending Morgan, she received many recommendations to consider a career in writing and was the recipient of The Zora Neale Hurston Scholarship Award.

After a two-year stint in law school, she later changed her career path. While recovering from an illness, she earned an M.A. from St. John's College in Annapolis, Maryland, ahead of schedule and with honors. Afterward, Andrea became frustrated with her inability to find an entry-level job in her field and considered returning to law school.

Andrea found that she was happiest when she was using her writing and research skills. Jotting down notes on restaurant napkins and scraps of paper became a habit she couldn't shake. One day she pondered over her predicament and emptied the contents of a box. In it she found an old photograph of she and the late Alex Haley looking over her writing, taken during the eighties when Andrea was a shy high school student. She was reminded that her uncle complimented her work and offered encouraging words that Andrea should continue writing. Andrea felt that finding the keepsake was a sign that she should make an effort to do what her heart was telling her would bring her contentment. In 2003, she created Dream Weaver Press in an attempt to realize her dream. Andrea's long-term goal is to use the written word to entertain while encouraging others to reach their maximum potential by overcoming obstacles to live a balanced, blissful life.

Dear Readers,

Thank you for your support. I truly hope you enjoyed the book. I'd like to remind you that much of how we behave depends upon how we choose to treat others and live ourselves. Despite our pasts or circumstances, we are capable of confronting our dreams to invite reality. It's an individual responsibility to become inspired to release our disappointments and continue pressing forward, despite them.

Regardless of who we are, where we reside, and the title that we may or may not have, dysfunction can be generated or perpetuated if we don't opt to treat one another with respect, as most of us would our family or loved ones. While no one is perfect, I feel that we should strive to do our best to live up to our legacy as kings and queens. If more of us make a legitimate effort to do this, we may have less social ills to contend with and more time and energy to live a balanced, calm life. This is why I feel children should look to their parents, relatives, mentors, and teachers as role models instead of celebrities who may not prove to serve as the best example. Lastly, money surely can't buy happiness, so it does little good to chase someone with money thinking they can provide happiness through their wallet.

I'd love to hear your comments and questions. You may visit me online at *www.dreamweaverpress.net* for contest information, updates, readers' companion questions for book clubs, or to order copies. You may also write to me at *dreamweaverpress@aol.com* or at the address listed below. If you wish to order books by mail, you will find a form following this page.

Dream Weaver Press
P.O. Box 3402
Annapolis, MD 21403

Thanks again,
Andrea Blackstone

ORDER FORM

You may order books at www.dreamweaverpress.net or use the form below.

Please mail money orders to :
Andrea Blackstone
P.O. Box 3402
Annapolis, MD 21403

Please send me _____ copies of *Schemin': Confessions of a Gold Digger* @ $15.00 each. (Please add $2.50 for shipping and handling. No cash, checks, or C.O.D. s.) Maryland residents, please add $.75 to allow for state sales tax.

Recipient's address:
Name _____
Address _____
City _____ State _____ Zip _____
Phone _____